Shirtless Men Drink Free

Shirtless Men Drink Free

A Novel

DWAINE RIEVES

Leapfolio

A joint-venture partner of Tupelo Press
North Adams, Massachusetts

Library of Congress Cataloging-in-Publication Data

Names: Rieves, Dwaine, author.

Title: Shirtless men drink free : a novel / Dwaine Rieves.

Description: First edition. | North Adams, Massachusetts : Leapfolio, a
joint-venture partner of Tupelo Press, 2019.

Identifiers: LCCN 2018028542 | ISBN 9781946507044 (alk. paper)

Classification: LCC PS3618.I3927 S55 2019 | DDC 813/.6--dc23

LC record available at https://lccn.loc.gov/2018028542

ISBN: 978-1-946507-04-4

Cover photo by Dwaine Rieves
Book & cover design Margery Cantor

First edition: January 2019.

Leapfolio, a joint-venture partner of Tupelo Press
P.O. Box 1767, North Adams, Massachusetts 01247
(413) 664–9611 / info@leapfolio.net / www.leapfolio.net

For Joy
in
Another Mississippi

Contents

The night was dark, no father was there
The child was wet with dew
The mire was deep, & the child did weep
And away the vapour flew

—William Blake

Shirtless Men Drink Free

A Fact

IF PRESSED, SHE JUST MIGHT SOMEDAY describe the experience as a *vision,* but that word alone would be insufficient, if not false, for what she had seen above the bed was more than apparition, more than a visual thing. There, sitting beside her dying mother, she'd sensed another presence, a new being, energy membrane-bound, translucent and hovering, alive in the air. The sense was volatility, the struggling with a decision, a choice—most definitely a choice—more why than when, more God than science. There, fibrillating above the bed was a soul. It was her mother's soul, the very soul of her mother deliberating its only options: whether to stay or depart, this world or another. And in the instant before it abandoned its literal form, whatever her mother's soul accepted or denied had to have been better than the body below, the face still puffy from chemotherapy, that halo of resurrected hair.

Something else must have mattered in this world, some undone task or rethought decision, something noble in the making, for her soul clearly wanted to stay. But it couldn't. It simply couldn't.

Perhaps *revelation* would eventually prove a more credible label. Or *insight.* Regardless of what she might ultimately call it, she wanted to believe the whole episode was a lesson for the scientist within her, a gift for the daughter who had to make sense of the inexplicable she'd seen. No. No one would ever believe she had witnessed such agony above the bed, the struggle between what the body demands and the soul needs.

Such thoughts she knew she must keep to herself, that *vision* or *revelation* or *insight* from a few months back, the soul of her mother wrestling with the air.

Tonight, Doctor Jane Beekman is alone. She sits on the back porch at home, a rocking chair helping to hold her there. The sky is closing in yellow, the world that was almost gone. She is motherless now, the backyard calm in disbelief. In the wake of her mother's final breath, in the air that struggle— why? The question will never disappear and the more she stares, the more the world before her eyes darkens any possible answer.

The air is unsteady, too uncertain. It trembles as if still above the bed, as Jane saw it and forever will. That odorless instant when decision turned gunmetal thin, she will smell it always. The distance between struggle and release, its clamor breathed clean. That morning her husband held her mother's hand, but never did Price waver, never did his eyes leave the body. Her mother's soul had battled the air and Jane, she alone was the witness.

Her body demands a reason. Her soul needs more gin.

Leap

NEVER HAD SHE GIVEN MUCH THOUGHT to politics, never had she pictured what a brief speech might come to. But to understand that trajectory as she ultimately came to follow it, you must first step back a few months, take a determined breath, and stand with Jane before a plateau of silvery eyes. The titans have gathered, gawkers shoulder to shoulder, a certificate framed on a tripod far stage right. The words have power, authority—2004 *Chamber of Commerce Business of the Year.* Lights are low, God and the crowd focused. The podium is all Jane's, the first slide at her back. On the canvas, a ladder of DNA coils ten feet high in Christmas colors. Five-carbon sugars twinkle for emphasis. Base pairs stiffen then jitter like ill-tempered brothers. Finger the laser pointer's bump and the hot red dot jumps. Control goes with accomplishment. Smile.

Jane is on the stage because she and her husband Price accomplish great things. She is proud of this. Atlanta is proud, no doubt all Georgia. But this award is not about her or Price, she tells the crowd. It's about their baby, CellSure. It's about the company's birth and maturation, teamwork in translational science. She uses that word *translational* and thinks *transcendent.* They know what she means. "People, CellSure is a company that can take less than a nanogram of genetic material and in a matter of hours match the specimen to a criminal, a fraud, a father."

More than once Jane says "genetic material" and each time she sharpens the syllables. "Yes," she proclaims, "with less than a snippet of tissue CellSure can even diagnose—" She pauses for air, for the air to settle. "Yes, we can even diagnose cancer." Applause comes. The great polynucleotide pulses. People stand. They point. Jane has become one with her company. She can even diagnose cancer.

"And with more CellSure innovation, I have little doubt that the same tissue indicating a cancer will also identify a treatment. Yes, my friends. The CellSure technology that pairs a precise diagnosis with a precise therapy will make most cancers curable and the few incurable ones truly treatable conditions." She thrusts a decisive finger into the air. She is transcendent. "Mark my words—as CellSure pairs ingenuity with our city's fine medical research institutions, Atlanta will become the nation's go-to hub for hope, a city where the word *impossible* never crosses a lip."

People whoop and stomp their feet. They slap shoulders. Strangers hug. The air vibrates, every face catching the glow of the great iridescent molecule, the image secured by the clicker Jane controls with a single finger.

❧ ◉ ❧

To stand before a crowd and be comfortable with the attention, you must be prepared. You must have done your homework, aligned your priorities. Otherwise, you can't take the faces. Let the record show that Jane did her homework, that the faces approved. Remember it as a standing ovation. Now, step from that stage and listen for the sound that lingers after the crowd is gone. It is not the silence of a job well done. It is the silence that follows months of regret after a triumphant speech, the hush following futile therapies and no more options. It is the evidence of misplaced priorities, the error within an empty chair. It is the reason Jane now sits before a desk, her eyes fixed on the chair behind the desk, that empty chair.

Jane is in the office of her mother's beauty shop, here to cross off the last item on her mother's list. Once the attorney arrives and the papers are signed, the shop's new owner will be Lily Blehart, her mother's best friend.

This morning Lily sits beside Jane. They are alone in the office, Lily and Jane are, each staring at that empty chair. Breathing is the only sound. Jane's mother called it a process. The process was meant to be efficient for Jane, to simplify the disposal of a beauty shop that—in her mother's words—was never meant to be a ball and chain. *Honey, I want you back at work right away. Y'all working, moving on.* Jane needed to remember those words. She needed to remember that work would keep her too preoccupied to look back. Work would keep her doing the important things her mother wanted her to do. Yet that chair—she can't ignore the fact of it, the mother who isn't there.

The empty chair testifies to another fact, one speaking only to Jane. And she hears it, completely. The fact says she lied. She cannot diagnose cancer. She can't even say the first signs were subtle. She can only stare at an empty chair and listen for the voice that isn't there.

It is the last day of February, the leap year's leap day, and the shop is closed for cleaning. God took Jane's mother in a leap year. Say "leap" so many times you consider it an order. Say it like Jane keeps saying it to herself—*Leap!* Then call that order a mistake, another one. Say you're months away from CellSure, admit the chemo and weeks of radiotherapy changed nothing for your mother. Say you can do this last thing that must be done. Say life has no bottom and the bottom, no life. Say the voices inside your head are sick from all the leaping. Grab the arms of your chair and hold on until God gives the next order. *Leap!*

Lily is restless. She reaches into her satchel, pulls up the beauty shop's most recent ledger and plops it on the desk. Jane winces, her thoughts dismissed by Lily's quick-moving hands, the reality within an old-fashioned, leather-backed ledger. The process has begun. "Baby, your momma sure was the keeper."

Jane reaches for the arm of Lily's chair. She needs something to hold on to. "You know, we really don't have to go through with this."

"Good Lord, your momma and me, we had a deal."

Jane hears an order from her mother, a hush-up order, so she hushes up. Lily must understand that the order's come, for she stares at the ledger. It is a solemn stare, one that seems just fine with a decade of declining revenue.

Lily and Jane's mother had a history. "The pepper to my salt," Jane's mother said more than once from her hospital bed. "Lily and me, we're the Spice Girls of North Atlanta." Jane's mother would then laugh and reach for Lily, the hug vicious and lippy. Nurses were awed by the sight, a white and black woman going cheek to cheek like sisters. Visitors smiled like polite witnesses. Smiles piled up like reporters. Laughter turned to coughing, coughing to blood. Kleenex never left the table. Doors were always closing.

The attorney is late—ten now after the hour according to Jane's watch. Lily seems oblivious to the lateness. She is quiet, determined, her face prepared for the worst. It's the face of a woman who forty years back would move not a muscle as white boys dumped mustard and pepper sauce, anything handy, atop her head. A sit-in, the newspapers called it, black college kids at a table, two guys and a girl. Lily was the girl. Rich's Department Store, the Magnolia Room—the front-page picture capturing all the faces—Lily with ketchup in her hair, Jane's mother, cigarette in hand, watching from another table. White tablecloths and unlit candles. Later, it would be Jane's mother who made sure Lily knew all girls, white or black, deserved a good shampoo and set, especially after something nasty as this. Jane can never forget Lily's face in the picture. It's always frightened her.

Lily is an accomplished accountant, probably the wealthiest woman ever to frequent the shop. She retired early, went to working in politics, first balancing the books for city council candidates, then salvaging the iffy finances of Atlanta's last mayor. So back in 2000, when Jane's brother-in-law Jackson was running for attorney general, Lily was the one he turned to for some butt-saving number crunching. This was the gist of the sermon Jane's mother preached time and again to the ladies in wash chairs. "Lily's a Cracker Jack, I tell you, Cracker Jack. Best bookkeeper in town." And so it's gone, Lily now the Cracker Jack accountant in the campaign that should make Jackson Beekman the next governor.

Beekman04—maybe the campaign money numbers are looking so good, Lily's actually up to keeping the shop going. "Are you sure you're okay with this?"

Lily turns to the empty chair, the corners of her lips climbing. "Yes, ma'am," she says. "We'll make sure this shop's around for a whole new generation." Her eyes go to Jane. "We will, won't we?"

Jane nods. To ensure the beauty shop's survival is not what she needs. She needs to get back to CellSure. It was what her mother wanted for her. It's what she needs. She says, "But the campaign, Lily. It must be too much."

"We'll make it, Baby. We will."

Lily bends forward to the ledger, pulling out a *Beekman04* bumper sticker. She studies the glossy letters a moment before returning the strip to the spine. "Your momma knew I'd keep the place on autopilot until after the election." Lily shakes her head at whatever she must see in that empty chair. "Yep. Autopilot. For now."

A syrupy silence follows Lily's voice. Yet inside Jane, the process is speeding up. No lawyer should be this late. Early this afternoon, the healing needs to begin; the process must continue as her mother wanted it to. It must.

Lily seems to sense Jane's worries hovering in the space between them, for her hand goes to slapping those unsettled thoughts to the floor. "Oh, he'll be here. We need a little time to visit."

"To visit?" Jane's voice is sharp, impulsive. It is proof she needs to visit with Lily. It is proof of what she'll always believe—had the diagnosis been made earlier, her mother would be sitting in that chair. A chest x-ray even three months earlier could have made the difference. The chair is a rollabout, the seat cushioned in orange velour, the frame an aluminum spine. It wasn't made for stares.

"Yep. You and me, Baby. Wanted a little time for us girls to visit."

The absence in that chair will never disappear. Jane's lip quivers. She tries to steady it with a finger. She is edgy. The walls of her heart strain.

Questions cake the valves. She leans back, crosses her legs and calls visiting a good thing.

Lily turns her face to make her eyes line up with Jane's. "Baby, I think they want to get rid of me."

"They what?"

Lily takes a massive breath and shifts her shoulders to free Jane's hand. "Last meeting, two of the district captains pretty much called me baggage."

Lily's voice is teetering. It is the voice of someone who needs to visit.

"But I'm taking a stand, I tell you. No more name-calling now." Lily tells more of last Monday's tough meeting and, as she speaks, the heft grows in her voice, the determination. "Yep, a stand." She plants her eyes on the chair behind the desk.

➤ ◉ ➤

OUT FRONT, BEYOND THE CRACKED OFFICE DOOR, a woman yelps. A bucket hits the floor and soon the air's filled with the odor of Pine-Sol. Then, a racket of quick Spanish words, the kind of laughing that seems to draw the entranced Lily back to herself. She grips the arm of her chair, directing a defiant look at Jane. "That Jackson. No way is that boy gonna back out of his promises. No, ma'am! He keeps every commitment *and* me. We're not about to let them run me off. We're not now, are we?"

Jane takes Lily's hand and squeezes. "I can't imagine. It's the last thing—"

Lily lunges toward her satchel, pulls up a folded newspaper and thrusts it before Jane. "No New Taxes" goes the small headline at the bottom of the page. It's a feature on Pete McGee, the main competition in the primary.

"When McGee pulled a cheap one," Lily says, "it sent Jackson's loud-talkers to backtracking. So, I spoke up. Sure did. Reminded the whole bunch that the only thing that got him elected four years ago was that tobacco settlement, which included—in case they'd all forgotten—a commitment to raising cigarette taxes. Yes, ma'am. Slapped the facts right before their faces and that's when they did it, the trash talk. Pretty much called me baggage, me and tobacco a nineties thing." Lily jostles her head at those smart-ass captains she must still hear. "Can you believe that? A nineties thing? Like no one smokes anymore?"

Lily draws the newspaper article close, starts reciting bits and pieces in a God-almighty, heaven-have-mercy voice. "No new taxes, McGee claims. Not even the promised Beekman increases . . ." Lily pauses, glances to Jane to make sure she caught the name, this same Beekman name that Jane shares. "Yep, the *Beekman* increase in cigarette taxes."

Lily uprights herself then reaches for the old bronze ashtray on the desktop. She picks it up, studies the metal bed where the lighted tips were crushed. She tilts the tarnished bronze toward Jane.

"Cigarettes, Baby, can you believe it? They're back—after all this."

Jane shudders. She looks down. Lily has brought it all back, the obvious. Jane's mother simply couldn't quit smoking. Her mother was a setup for cancer and Jane knew it. The gum and later the patch simply turned her mother into a backyard smoker. Never again would Jane mention cigarettes. And she hadn't, not even when the coughing got so bad her mother began to carry a handkerchief. Yet the throb within the silence never completely dulled, for only days after the convention was over the telephone call came from the waiting room of a radiology suite, the facts now speaking for themselves. Jane had missed the most important diagnosis she might ever make. Doctor Jane Beekman had failed her own mother.

Lily returns the ashtray to its original spot on the desktop. She shuts the ledger, settles back in her chair and says it won't be long before the lawyer's here. "A doctor. It's what the lung association wants—a medical headliner who knows firsthand what tobacco can do, how it's still a big deal." Lily seems pleased with her now verbalized thoughts, pleased with the sharing. She fingers her chin, once more studying Jane.

"Lily, are you asking me?"

"Tobacco, Baby!" Lily throws up her hands. "It's what your momma wanted!"

"My mother? She never mentioned—"

"Girl, last year that speech you gave sent shivers down my spine. Shivers, I tell you." Lily crosses her legs, starts rocking a foot, her rhythm steady, confident. The pace slows none when a two-pinged chime comes from the front of the building. The front door slams and a man's voice fills the air. He's soon laughing with the cleaning ladies.

"Next Monday, Baby. Let's meet at the new headquarters downtown— perfect talking place." Lily pulls a business card from her satchel, passes it fast to Jane. "Can't miss it. On Pike, near the Deposit Guaranty Building."

"But Mondays we always start early—"

"Well, drop by when you can. Like your momma always said . . ." Lily hesitates, raises her once-rocking foot to show Jane the stubby tip of her pump. "Yes, indeed. Like your momma always said: No hill for a stepper." Lily jiggles the stylish shoe, appraising it as if it too might create a legacy for a new generation. "Good God, when I think about all the high steps your momma took!" Lily hums, glancing to the family picture on the wall, the shot from the night of Jackson's attorney general victory. "No, ma'am. I'm not about to let that boy undo himself."

Undo himself? A strange nerve fires in the upper reaches of Jane's spine. Her shoulders stiffen and her head draws back from Lily. Jackson's about to undo himself over tobacco? Jane wants to ask the question out loud, but before the words come, a knuckle raps at the office door.

"Well, well," says Lily, hopping to her feet. "Look who's here."

Price Beekman, 2004

ON THE MORNING OF FEBRUARY's last day, Doctor Price Beekman was comparing himself to the man who sat beside him at his desk. Alex was a regulatory affairs contractor, a blubbery guy of about Price's age whose raspy voice and flushed complexion, let alone his edginess, almost surely meant too many cigarettes and too many deadlines. Price had last used the guy a decade back, Alex then a long, fiddle-faced man who said "gotcha" way too much. To look at him now, Alex seemed top-heavy, his chest too full of those "gotcha" jobs.

Surely the years hadn't been that rough on Price, at least not his body. Fact was, except for more wrinkles, he was pretty much still his lanky self. High metabolism was a blessing. Of course, he didn't smoke, nor did he say "gotcha" to people regardless of how ludicrous the request. Never would. CellSure was all about the truth, painful as it was. For a biotech business that processed samples to solve questions of paternity and crime, not to mention ID the diagnoses that might otherwise be missed, "gotcha" was a word no one liked to hear.

Alex flipped the slides on a laptop as Price watched the screen. They were alone in Price's office, a third-floor suite where one wall held certificates and family pictures, windows lining the three other walls. Below them, CellSure technicians were busy extracting the truth from blood, saliva, and semen, making matches and diagnosing diseases. These people were providing answers, and to Price Beekman nothing was more important than answers. Answers brought you peace. A compendium of federal bureaucrats must have thought so also, for a contract was in the making, one that could take CellSure nationwide, perhaps global. All contingent, in large part, upon Alex making another deadline.

"Gotcha, chief."

The contractor punched up a new slide, sputtering, "Formatted to meet Homeland Security CTD specifications." He inched the laptop closer to Price. Click. A crucible of arrows appeared.

"Five modules with hyperlinked references to archived master files." Click. Up came stick figures, light blue balloons billowing from their mouths, each filled with mathematical formulas. What Price saw was a crew of rakish creatures, empty heads belching strange Greek letters and tussling numbers.

"Statistical methods will be conducive to data dissection."

Price leaned forward, dropped his elbows to the desktop. Statistics were too much. Not now, not this morning. "So, can we meet the deadline?"

Alex slurped up the juice in his lower lip, answering the question by talking faster. "And here we have the clearance pipeline."

A solar system appeared, *CellSure* stamped across the face of a pulsing sun. The yellow globe grinned while about it, planets twinkled out government acronyms: *DOD, OES, HHS,* on and on as new planets appeared. Alex blabbered. Price watched. He could hear Jane next week accusing Alex of being too lost in the trees to see the forest, a strategic mistake. Eyes rolling, fingers drumming. But they needed regulatory expertise, he would remind her, and if anyone had the bureaucracy under his belt, that would be Alex Havelchej. Bureaucracy and deadlines, Jane—no wonder the guy looked a mess. Click.

Alex coughed, showering the computer screen with tiny specks of spit. He dabbed away the drivel at his mouth with the back of his wrist. "And when it comes to the timeline, this slide shows a logistic regression analysis, bootstrapped of course . . ."

Price wanted to care, to be compassionate. He took a look and kept listening as his thoughts drifted to the immediacy of things that would remain on his desk once the laptop was gone. He tilted his head. His outbox was empty and as usual, his inbox too full. He eyed it closer, that bulging box.

Among the flyers and letters, there it sat—a fat yellow packing envelope, a delivery that should have arrived on Monday. Alex charged in so early this morning, Price had no time to go through his mail.

Alex kept blabbing and when his attention sank on a slide, Price pulled the plump envelope from the stack. This was it, the letter from his father, the answer.

Alex pointed to the laptop screen, saying something about limitations. "Hmm," responded Price, grimacing at the screen to show he too was concerned. He placed the yellow packing envelope on the desk, address-side down. He reappraised Alex, making circling motions with a finger, grunting to reinforce the need for speed.

"Gotcha."

All week, ever since the telephone call, Price had been thinking of a packing envelope from Egypt, Georgia. Inside was a letter that had been hidden away for half a lifetime, unopened and ignored, waiting. The existence of that letter was revealed only once Gerald Dalton died and his grown kids decided it was time to empty their daddy's old trunk. Last week came the telephone call. "We opened the letter," said the oldest Dalton son, "but not the eyeglass case. They were taped together." And when the postmark date was quoted, Price knew this must have been his father's last letter, some final message not to be shared with the family, but with the man who lived on the other side of town—Gerald Dalton. Yet this man simply stuck the letter away, maybe kept it for a time when, of these men—Lucius Beekman and Gerald Dalton—something better might be said.

Price inched his hand closer to the packing envelope. And once he touched its distended edges, his heart flipped sides and simply lay inside him, that great salvation organ too limp to push up the blood.

"Doctor Beekman, you okay?"

Price reached for his neck and started rubbing. "Let's close off, Alex. Finish up next week."

"Just a handful of slides left, not much longer."

"Alex, we're done."

Alex started to say something, but Price reached over and snapped shut the laptop. "Next week, Alex. It'll be good. Jane will be back."

The contractor sat agape, eyebrows scrunched, his keyboard-diving finger weaving in the air above the laptop. It took a strong arm to haul him away.

Price closed the door behind Alex, returned to his desk, and once more weighed the voice of Gerald Dalton's oldest son. "Doctor Beekman, I think you should have it."

Price had asked no questions. He simply supplied an address and an offer to cover the shipping charges. Gerald Dalton died only a month ago, but Price's father had been dead for more than forty years. Lucius Beekman was a picture on the wall, little more. At least until the telephone call came, and suddenly the dead face in a frame belonged to a man who had yet to quit waiting.

On the wall, Lucius Beekman had held a smile for years in an army uniform, that churlish lippy coil of a soldier at risk for more than military misdeeds. Price had long imagined his father content in that frame, up there, isolated from his wife and boys. Of course, what Price imagined was wrong, for the family his father knew consisted only of a wife and one boy, not two. So when Lucius Beekman drew the barrel of a gun to his chest, he had no idea that he was leaving a pregnant wife behind, a baby even then hiding within her belly like another waylaid letter.

Price ran a hand over a raw spot on his neck. He reached for the yellow package but stopped. Blood coated a finger. He stood, moved to the bathroom off the back of the office, touching nothing. In the mirror, he examined the slit his razor made this morning, the scab. He dabbed at the bleeding point with toilet paper, kept dabbing until he recognized once more his father's brow and even more clearly those Beekman cheekbones. The way his mother spoke of the Beekman cheekbones, it sometimes felt a curse.

In fact, the way his mother often talked, some might think she'd never married a Beekman man. Any question about the man in the picture on the mantle was quickly hushed. And to mention the name Gerald Dalton was a complete prohibition for the Beekman brothers, a firm promise to their mother. How that promise came about, Price couldn't remember so well, but it followed some boyish ruckus. That much Price could recall. Odds were, Jackson started it, Price the boy at fault. Price was always the boy at fault. It was the kind of fault that followed a boy who could only guess at the meanings within the night's loud voices. Sometimes Price thought his mother knew he'd heard those voices. Maybe that was why Jackson was so special to her. Jackson had no voices to figure out, no deep-voiced cry to remember.

Of course, the boys kept their promise. Never again did Jackson or Price speak the name Gerald Dalton around their mother. Odd, but that promise never crossed Price's mind as he and Jackson watched their mother's casket enter the earth, Gerald Dalton's oldest son directing the service. *Dalton Funeral Home* read the words on the tent above their heads. *Dalton Funeral Home* read the nametags of the men with shovels. The gravelly dirt of the Egypt Cemetery fell loudly upon the casket's steel vault. The void within that sound returned even louder last Tuesday when Price spoke Gerald Dalton's name over the office telephone. All the while, his father held smug in his frame, the grin unwavering.

The bleeding staunched, Price flushed the stained tissue paper down the toilet, returned to his desk and drew a slim white envelope from the yellow packing cover. Next, he pulled out an aged green eyeglass case, the kind that might hold spectacles. As far as he knew, his father never wore glasses, but Gerald Dalton did. Price had seen a picture. Gold-rimmed spectacles could never hide those cocklebur Dalton eyes.

The flap on the white envelope had been slit, so when Price bowed the sides, a folded note appeared. He pressed the note flat and read.

Gerald, I'd sure appreciate it if you could pass this along to Price when he's old enough to really understand things. Tell him I meant it for the new baby. Maybe Price can someday explain it all. He's a smart boy. Thank you, Lucius

Within Price, the blood stopped. Every valve shut. He reexamined the handwriting. He reread the words that said, in cold black ink on a white slip of paper, she lied. For most of her life, his mother lied.

As she'd told it in the church parlor and over the telephone, only during the funeral did she first feel the stirrings in her belly. Time after time, her tone implied a miracle. Quickening was a common word. Heads shook at his mother's revelation. If only he'd known, more than one person said.

The letter now proved it. He'd known. Yes. His father knew a baby was on the way. And the fact that his father knew and his mother only pretended to know now made all the capillaries fully dilate within Price, the blood cells loosen and freely flow. The heat was bizarre, but good. He could handle it. And more important, just as his father wanted, Price could explain it all.

The first Beekman family, he might tell Jackson, had to be bisected to thrive. And while their father had started that cut, their mother completed it. Not intentionally of course, just what she had to do. This was the lesson Price wanted to remember when he explained the letter and his mother's lie to Jackson, everyone simply doing their best to survive. After all these years, to think otherwise was pointless. Blame was a sixties thing.

Price wanted to rub his neck, but he knew better. The skin needed to heal. Even now, he felt the wound closing. The letter proved that the time for healing was here. And to that thought, his father grinned as he'd done for years.

Price opened the eyeglass case. Inside, as if laid with adoration in a tiny casket, was a money clip attached to a clump of twenty-dollar bills. Price lifted the bills, examining the silver clip that held them tight. He had a duplicate at home, still with one hundred dollars wadded up inside it. And now it's clear—his father had intended the same gift for Jackson, the new baby. Price had been correct all along. His father was a good man.

Clamping the lid on the eyeglass case, Price fingered the curious medallion that crowned the money clip. He pulled the bills to his nose and sniffed the winter of 1961. In his mind, the voices from that year were now saying things that made perfect sense.

In the newest picture on the wall, the grownup Price and Jackson were hugging each other, their smiles so lavish and similar, so hopeful. The photograph had been taken at the victory celebration barely three years ago, Jackson almost beside himself over the lopsided vote that made him the state's top lawyer. "Attorney General Jackson Beekman," he recalled his mother—or maybe it was Jane's mother—shouting as the camera flashed. The fatherless boys had succeeded. They'd kept their promise. The Beekman family had done what it took to survive.

Price set aside the money clip and reached for the note. In the process, he toppled his coffee mug. He jumped to his feet, jerking all the papers on his desk away from the spilt coffee. He was rattled but quick. A clump of paper towels quenched the pool.

Price cleaned up the mess, tossing the stained felt pad in the trash and swabbing the underlying glass. The reflection was dark, but as Price rubbed the brown paper towels over the shiny surface, he could see himself as he was in Jackson's room nearly half a lifetime back—playing a father even then, stroking the green diamonds of a Navajo blanket that covered his little brother, who lay crying in bed. That night he'd rubbed Jackson's back until his sobs dissolved in a silence that proved Price loved his brother, even if Jackson had started the squabble. "Piss-ant perverts," the gap-toothed Jackson had called the two men in a picture Price found in the attic. How Jackson picked up such words was always a mystery to Price. But the good part was that neither he nor Jackson that night spoke Gerald Dalton's name.

Hours could have passed once Price reclaimed a seat at his desk, as he thought of miracles that never occurred nor were actually needed. Hours it seemed, but he knew it hadn't been so long at all when the telephone rang and Jackson asked, "What's new?"

Price Beekman, 1961

Y OUR DADDY CALLS YOU THE PRICE of his life. "At least the asking Price," he tells the man who laughs like a monster before he reaches down to shake your hand. You do not shake hands, never have and, until this moment, have never imagined that your daddy could talk so much like a preacher. So, is he selling you or his life? This is your first memory of your daddy talking to a strange man, you and your daddy on the sidewalk outside the barbershop, the strange man someone important because your daddy holds you by the shoulders, so it is impossible for you not to shake hands with this black-suited stranger who wears a hat like old men do in yellowy pictures.

Yellow is the color of Egypt, the whole town awash in the kind of sandy shade God probably knew some things best be pictured in.

The yellow is mainly a reflection from the walls of your house, a kind of washed-out yellow that your daddy calls the natural look of Santa Fe stucco. You watch your house a lot this year, not only as you walk home from school, but sometimes during the day when you poke your head above the high windows in your classroom to find your stucco house look- ing back at you from halfway down the street, its big picture window fixed like a radar dish on where you are, the house doing its best to figure out what you're learning in school. It's different from other houses, a peculiar sort of difference that you're not sure is good or bad. Your daddy works at the bank, your mother too, so you hope people understand your house has to be modern and different because of the money things they do.

"Price, say hacienda for Miss Hattie," your mother said not so long ago. You spouted it out through some missing teeth, and then your mother repeated it. "Ha-chee-enya—isn't that cute?" Miss Hattie, who lives next door in a house with a roof shaped like a pyramid and a porch that runs all the way around it, laughed but your daddy didn't. He pulled at his collar and looked at your mother in a way that Miss Hattie noticed. "Peggy, don't tease him," he said before he walked away to do something important. He's very proud that you're a boy.

It is early December, another afternoon after school when you're stretched out on the new couch. You're watching television and eating marshmallow treats, which your mother made. She gets off early on Wednesdays, so she's already collected clothes from the line and will soon start ironing, but until then, she's catching up with Miss Hattie on the telephone. Today is different, you can tell it from the way the marshmallow drips really slow when you hold a treat above your mouth. You can also tell it from the way your mother slammed the ironing board on the Santa Fe tile, the way it screeched when she spread the steel legs. It's different because there may be ice soon outside. That's what she said when she first called Miss Hattie. They've gone on from there, moved on to serious things.

"Hattie, I've had it with him," she says and you think *me,* she's had it with *me.* You're the *him* she's telling Miss Hattie about, something the house picked up on radar, something she'll later tell your daddy once you're in bed and watching for the lights to go out.

"Absolutely right—you were, Miss Hattie. At the bank yesterday, someone left the newspaper unfolded on my desk, that picture face-up. No . . . no telling what people think."

You hold the rice crispy treat in the air, watch the white goo leak out. It's not about you. It's about the newspaper, the one that's unfolded on the coffee table where they left it last night. You heard them talking through the walls.

"Oh, he said exactly what you'd told me he'd say—just an advertisement for Gerald's flower shop, that open house next week. Said Gerald's funeral home was doing better than his flower business. But both of them, there in that picture, two years in a row?"

The sound of her voice is like the white goo, too cold to be runny. Pull a treat apart and it sticks in the air. Gerald is just a friend. She ought to know that by now. Friends act funny sometimes, even when they don't mean to.

"As if they're proud of it, the two of them propped like bookends before that church door—people can't help but think things."

On the television screen, the duck has drawn a gun on an old prospector. They've gone at it before. The duck wins.

"No, from what I understand, Gerald stays in a motel . . . Well, maybe. I know Lucius has a room somewhere on the campus. Apparently the chapel has a few rooms they rent out to men."

Your daddy called it a goddamn room, a goddamn room in a goddamn cathedral. You didn't understand what goddamn was and the way your mother shouted, she didn't either. Just as you didn't understand why he went where he did that weekend, except that it was some kind of pageant, some ceremony called Hanging of the Green, which, when he first said it, made you think of a bad dream where your daddy and Gerald Dalton chased down the Martians and then hung them from the tree limbs, all those skinny green bodies whipping about in the breeze. Only it has to do with Christmas, your daddy said, church decorations. Your mother sometimes helps decorate the church for Christmas. You don't understand what's wrong with him doing such a thing up where he went to college. That's why you need to go to college, to learn about Hanging of the Green.

"Oh, he says their days as roommates are long over. Says they drive up to Sewanee just for that pageant. A tradition they call it. God knows what they really do up there."

Your daddy's got a diploma that's framed and on the wall behind his desk at work. When your mother started work at the bank she just picked the money stuff up, so she's taking some classes on Tuesday nights. You heard her tell Miss Hattie that she's keeping an eye on him. She doesn't seem to like where she sits at the bank.

"Well, he did . . . Sometimes during the summer, usually on Thursday nights, right after supper. Business talk, he'd say . . . What, Miss Hattie? Sure did, a little after midnight. So yes, I knew. But you better believe I put an end to those escapades."

You believe in a great many things, but you don't believe your daddy was in an escapade. Escapades are like capers, like they have in old cartoons. Your daddy doesn't watch cartoons and your mother doesn't either. Maybe they both should. Anything can happen in a cartoon. The duck's old-fashioned, fat in the behind like Miss Hattie.

"I told him point blank last night . . . I sure did. Lucius, I said, you go with that man next year, don't come back thinking things will be the same."

Static sometimes just means the cartoon's old. It's trying to be the same, but it's not. You poke out your tongue and lick the hanging goo. You take it in a way that lets it sit in your mouth, nothing chewed. The prospector's back. He didn't die. You thought your daddy kissed your mother last night. You thought that was good, but then they cried.

"Well, he got the message. I think he's learned a lesson. Sure do . . . There really wasn't much to it, but even if there was . . . You're right. It's over, history."

History reminds you of George Washington, but your daddy doesn't look anything like George Washington. He's tall and brown-eyed, always seems to be looking up, even when you know he's not. At night, when he bends over you, he smells like the ocean when the battle ships go down. Your mother's nice looking also although she seems to look down a great deal. She can't help it since her nose is Lebanese and heavy. She told Miss Hattie her blood's Lebanese. You pray for her most every night.

"I don't know what I would have done without you, Miss Hattie. Between Lucius and Price, work and school, I sometimes just feel like I can't go on."

Your mother does have a lot on her. You wish you could iron. Sometimes you pick up the dirty things. You wear socks. Socks keep your toes from going between the tweed and making holes in the couch cushions. There's already a hole in one of the cushions, the one right below your feet. Your daddy said it looked like a rat gnawed on it, but it was really your toe. He laughed when he said it, but your mother didn't. She flipped the cushion, so the upside went down.

"Then I'll say to myself, just look at Miss Hattie, if she can raise six boys, I can raise at least one, give him a decent start."

Decent is a word that, if it has a color, must look a little like Santa Fe stucco, with ridges coming out where the ice cream was pushed about until all the milk evaporated and the cream turned to concrete and then stayed like that, stuck. You've scraped off some parts that pooch out. It's chalky, nothing like real ice cream.

"He's a good man. He said he wanted a baby. But I tell you, I don't know. For sure—he doesn't have to waddle around with a watermelon in his belly."

You didn't know he wanted a baby, never heard him say that. Maybe that's what they were talking about last night. Maybe you're not enough. But a baby, inside a watermelon?

"I'm praying too, Miss Hattie. When Kennedy's sworn in, I'll bet the Pope will be sitting in the front row. At least we elected a man who knows war."

At school, the teachers talk about war. You hear them out in the halls, at the corner where they smoke cigarettes. The war will start with Sputnik missiles, may come right over your school, but Kennedy's going to fight to keep the Russians out, even if he talks a lot to the Pope. You want to fight like Kennedy someday and go to college but you'll never go to Hanging of the Green. Egypt's got plenty of pageants, good churches that let you in even if you don't go to college. That's really what it's all about, why your daddy won't take your momma to Hanging of the Green. He can't. They won't let him because she didn't go to college. Only he can't say that. You'd think all those college people would know better. Hanging of the Green— you'll fight if your daddy tries to take you up there.

➶   ◉   ➶

IT IS DAYLIGHT NOW, CHRISTMAS COME and gone. A new year starts tomorrow. Your mother is putting on her earrings while looking out the kitchen window where, you already know, the red birds are sitting on the steel cable that runs to a power pole. It's frosty out there and when you first looked, you thought it was snow, but it never snows in Georgia so the red birds make do. Your daddy says the frost freezes the bugs, holds them still so the birds can eat them, but once the sun heats up the grass, the birds disappear because the bugs have thawed out and gone down their holes. Your mother's going to work today because they need banking people to work on the last day of the year, which must be important because they've sent your daddy to a really big meeting in Atlanta, which is why he was up so early. The birds must have been surprised.

Before he left, your daddy gave you a present, a secret present. "It's a money clip," he said. He'd come into your room while it was still dark outside. He leaned over you, pulled the pillow off your head and kissed you there, where the hair begins. "Price, I've put some money inside, but you save it now, maybe buy a motorcycle when you get old enough to drive." His face felt rough even though you knew he had shaved. You smelled the Navy cologne your mother gave him for Father's Day last year. You could almost taste it, that stucco kind of taste. Your fingers almost fit inside the metal pinching part.

"Son, I want you to keep this with you, fill it up with more money, but save some space for me." He was nuzzling close when he said that.

"Okay," you said and, "Yes, I will," after he told you to be a good boy. "I love you, now," he said, then pulled the blanket up about your neck, leaving that money clip next to your nose on the pillow where you kept smelling him in the money and metal, you again dreaming of the battleships where

Kennedy keeps the radar antennas aimed toward Russia while the men in their white sailor suits cheer.

A money clip is a silver metal thing that's folded over on itself like a paper clip, so it squeezes down and holds your money safe. It has an emblem on one side, a fancy decoration that looks a little like a coin but instead of George Washington's head, there are two letters—U and S—each one spaced apart and lying special on a bright purple background. It's cold to the touch and valuable, so once you smell the sausage and biscuits your mother has cooked for breakfast, you place it in the bottom of a drawer. You won't tell her about it. Your daddy wanted to keep it a secret between him and you. Us—that's what the U and S means, you can tell it. There's a lot you can read.

Today you're to stay with Miss Hattie and watch television or go through her attic where she keeps the uniforms her dead husband used to wear. Your mother has the whole day arranged and, once she drops you off at Miss Hattie's place, it is to pass just as she said it would, except the day stays cold and your daddy stays in Atlanta.

❧ ☸ ❧

IT IS SUPPER TIME ALREADY AND YOUR mother has cooked macaroni and cheese, mixed in some chips of Spam that, when washed off with the milk you spill into the bowl, look just like the tiny bricks a tornado tossed about when it came through. When milk meets cheese, it looks like stucco. But it's good and your daddy would enjoy it also if he'd been on time only he's not, and your mother has called Miss Hattie. She's worried. You can tell it from the nervous way she squeezes the telephone receiver between her head and shoulder so she can pull back the curtains and look out the kitchen window to see where your daddy's car is not parked.

"Miss Hattie, have you heard of bad weather up north?"

She writes her words in the air, points to the north, which is in the direction of Miss Hattie's house, only way beyond it and the school. The red birds probably head up there once the sun burns frost off the grass.

"Makes me wonder about car trouble."

Your mother is good about holding the telephone receiver, so her hands can move like the preacher's do when he tells a story, like when he described how Jesus saved the sinful woman that the Pharisees wanted to stone. Russians are like the Pharisees. They'd be better people if they had Spam in Russia.

"I'm sure you're right. He's bound to call if the car needs towing."

Your mother hangs up the telephone, and you both finish the macaroni and cheese and move to the living room where you stretch out on the sofa and watch Jackie Gleason while she sits at your feet. She runs her fingers down a page of one of those open-book tests they give all the women who want to sit at new places in a bank. Sometimes she looks to the picture window and gives herself time to think. It's a college class, she's said, so it has to be decent and anything decent is also hard. That's how a college teaches people to think.

People who think all the time still need to feel things, so you are not surprised when your mother puts her hand on the sofa and looks up from her book and all that thinking. She likes to feel your feet, but soon she's up.

Your mother paces before the picture window, looks out the glass and you join her there, the two of you looking out to where the porch light has covered the front yard in a cold macaroni color that almost runs to the empty space on the concrete where your daddy's car should sit. Atlanta is a dangerous city. You've heard her tell Miss Hattie that, and she must remember it because she pulls a fingernail to her mouth and bites at the polish. She holds her finger there while Lawrence Welk polkas so loud on his television show it seems to upset her. She looks at you, says nothing and runs to the kitchen telephone. You follow her, sticking your head around the doorway and watching even though you are not a spy. You just worry about her a lot.

She has barely finished the dial when she tells Miss Hattie, "I'm calling the sheriff." She braces her right hand on the kitchen counter as a bunch of words come and go, and you can't follow them all because they're quick and spinning so fast they almost make you sick.

"I'll give you a buzz when I hear something."

When your mother gives Miss Hattie time to speak, you know what she says. It's always what Miss Hattie says, something about keeping everybody in her prayers. She says it even when you first pick up the telephone and then hand it right over. "Price," Miss Hattie says, "I'm keeping y'all in my prayers." You always feel a little sick when she says that because it sounds like she knows something's about to happen, something that's never good.

Once your mother hangs up the telephone, she holds her lips together tight then tells you everything is just fine, that Miss Hattie thinks there may be some sleet up toward Atlanta and your daddy is so smart he's probably driving real slow, especially over the bridges. She tells you to go back to the couch and you do. Next thing you know, she's waking you up and the flag's flying on the screen while the television preacher prays.

"Price, let's go to bed," she says as you wipe the crust from your eyes. "I'm sure your daddy will be home any minute now." She turns off the television, walks you down the hall, kisses you good night and tells you she will leave the porch light on, so your daddy can find his way home.

Your mother doesn't know about the money clip your daddy gave you this morning. She doesn't know that he's probably working a little longer so he can bring home more money, maybe enough to fill up the money clip. It's an important thing to know, and if your mother knew it, she'd probably feel better. But your daddy meant it to be a secret. Otherwise, he wouldn't have talked about that motorcycle.

Sometimes it's important to keep a secret even though people might not worry so much if they know what you know. Maybe that's why Miss Hattie always says she's praying for people. She knows people just need to keep some secrets, even if it means they'll be late and their kinfolks worried. Miss Hattie's had a lot of kids. She ought to know.

❧ �--- ❧

THIS IS NOT A DREAM AND IF you've been dreaming, then the dream is over because the doorbell is ringing. Dreams are meant to end by themselves, and if they don't, there's a problem. Like when somebody's cow gets out. You grab your pillow, hold it to your chest just in case. A pillow could block a sword if it had to, or at least slow a bullet. It is a shield, a good one. You hold it like a Roman. "Price," your daddy would say if he was here, "be brave."

The doorbell is ringing again and there's a shadow—it can't be a burglar because it smells too much like your mother—moving down the hall. She walks like a cat when she's not sure of things. But that's during the day and this is night, so your daddy should be going to the door. He would already be there if he was here. But tonight, he's not here. You can tell it—your mother walks like a cat. Something bad has happened, just like Miss Hattie always knew it would.

Maybe your daddy is the man behind the door. Maybe he forgot his key and when your mother went to bed, she locked him out. She must think so because she's moving faster now. You can hear her stepping over the living room rug, moving to the door like it's important. A cat would be hiding behind the couch. She flips the switch on the front porch light. More yellow comes, the kind that bugs don't like. Then the lock, it's your mother unlocking the door. There's got to be a man out there, so she cracks the door just enough to look. You know how she likes to do things. But right away she screams, and she's not supposed to do that. She screams again, so you jump from the bed and go.

You inch into the hall, the pillow before you for protection. Nothing is right. You're wrong. Your daddy never made it home last night. There is a war. You just feel it, there's too much breathing in the air. The army's been called up, troops surrounding your school, the new president coming through the door. He's serious. Maybe the Pope's been called. You lean against the wall, drop the pillow, move your hands along the wall and follow where they lead.

You bend low and peek, so your mother won't see you. But you can see her, your mother as you've never seen her before, shaking and pulling at the man in the doorway. He's trying to stay back from her, trying to keep her hands off his arms.

"Oh, Officer," she says, "don't tell me. Please don't tell me."

He will tell her. That's his job and the world better get ready for it. The officers are behind him. They're all here in the middle of a war, a really bad one. Your daddy is a casualty, a hero. You always knew he would be one. "The final sacrifice," the president will say and then put his hand over his heart. You'll salute like a soldier. Or maybe he survived, your daddy out in the car with the other officers, your daddy waiting for a surprise appearance. Your daddy saved the nation, the man in the suit will say, a heroic effort for a noble cause. The news, though, is probably bad. It is news about your daddy, news that your mother probably can't handle, but you can. You'll accept the medal on his behalf.

You listen as your mother steps back, so the official and his soldiers can come inside. You hold the corner, and when you look again, a soldier is hugging your mother, she on the couch rocking back and forth in his hands. He's a fat man in a caramel-colored uniform with black boots that reach his knees. There are others. Stars glow on their collars like little satellites, souvenirs from important launches.

"I'm mighty sorry, Missus Beekman," the officer says. He says "mighty sorry" again and again, as if he is actually telling her about a secret tunnel they've had to build, this tunnel she and you will need to run through before the Russians come. When another uniformed man takes a seat in your daddy's chair, you bend forward so you can hear their secret plan.

"We got a telephone call at headquarters shortly after midnight. The police, the patrol up in Tennessee said they found a body at the University of the South, a man shot dead on the chapel steps up there. They had his wallet, ran the ID."

You shake. The bad words belong on the television, but they're not there. They're here, coming from a soldier who sounds like he's saying what a general told him to say. "Mighty sorry, Missus Beekman, just mighty sorry."

Just is the wrong word. *Mighty* is even worse. That officer's got it wrong, the general's confused. The guy shot dead is always the loser. Your daddy is no loser. Your daddy is big in Atlanta. He makes that kind of money. Your mother knows that, but she can't say so because they are soldiers who simply take orders. The orders have taken over. There is no plan. You are wrong. You close your eyes and check the wall.

"From the way they found the gun, it seems he shot himself . . ."

Something falls, hits the floor as your mother screams, a hard wet scream that spills loud then drags her down there with it. It does. It's wet and it drags her down.

You're scared, but you do it anyway. You run into the room and see her there. You see your mother looking up at you, your mother on the floor, raising a hand. You reach for her, you scream also, and she takes you into her hands. You both are alone, so alone down here on the floor. There is no tunnel, no secret plan. She pulls you to her chest and together you rock, just the two of you at the knee of the man who wears boots that reach his knees.

◆ ◉ ◆

THE FUNERAL HOME IS A PLACE WHERE people don't belong. The rugs on the floor are thick and fancy. The shapes in the wool look like the colors swirled to the point where they got stuck. Red is darker than blood, blue something lint will always stick to. Miss Hattie's front parlor is kind of like the Dalton Funeral Home. It's supposed to be used only for special occasions, like when the preacher comes or something needs to be signed. The funeral home is like a museum. Nothing can be touched, so you stand back and hold your mother's hand as she hugs people who must like the smell of carnations.

Your daddy would not like this place. He wouldn't like the faces some of these people are making. He'd call them fake, tell people to lighten up. He'd tell them to get back to work. He'd be like Jesus, drive the money-changers from the temple. This place is full of moneychangers. They're in disguise though, because people write checks now and try not to talk about it. Women poke at the flowers and whisper. Men pretend to listen. Your daddy would tell you to watch out for spies.

You walk with your mother to the back room. She holds your grand-mother's arm, and with her free hand, she tugs you. You know where you're going—deep inside the heart of the temple where they keep the bodies. But you follow because she needs help, the reinforcement of family. "Price, you're my family now," she said, "my reinforcement." She knew you'd like that word. You don't need to remember *reinforcement* now. You just need to remember there's a spy in this crowd. Your mother knows it. She knows who to look out for.

The casket is metal, long like an altar. But this is no church and these people no worshipers. They are here to watch, like moneychangers. You stand with your mother before the casket. People cry behind you, move closer to your mother's back. They think she might collapse, but you know she won't. She is a strong woman. She knows what must be done, and you're prepared to follow her orders. You'll need to start thinking like your daddy did.

Your mother's black dress crinkles at the elbows as she picks you up so you can see. She wears gloves, each finger black and stiff. She moves like a machine. She lifts you high, so you can see the body. She moves closer, and then bends you forward, so you look him directly in the face. "Price Sweetie, just look. It's your daddy."

Your daddy lies below you, the top half of his casket open, the inner lid covered in puffy silk that's the color of milk but also seems to glimmer at times a little pink. The lamps at each end of the casket are tall, the fat white globes painted with red roses that coil among green vines and golden ribbons. Your mother holds you in this lamplight, but you twist around, so you can look back to where your grandparents stand together and watch. They mean well. They stand back some distance. Your mother has given them orders.

"Kiss him," your mother says.

She turns you within her arms, so now you see his face again. His skin is wrong, too dry and powdery. You look at this man who should be your daddy but is not, so you want to tell them all what you know, that this man is not who they say he is, that they've got it all wrong.

"Go ahead, Sweetie. Kiss him."

You turn away from the head, push at her arms.

"Price, you need to kiss your daddy. Go ahead, kiss him goodbye."

This is wrong—you can never kiss your daddy goodbye. This cold strange thing is not your daddy. She is wrong. They are all wrong. You look at her, all these people. They are nodding. They are all watching. Your mother pushes your head down with her black fingers. You start to cry. Lilies reach up, Easter lilies that smell sweet and confused, the odor wrong as the body of Jesus was when they left him in the tomb. You need Jesus.

"Go ahead," your mother says. You fight her hand. "Kiss him."

You sniffle some before you lean on into the casket. You try not to breathe, but you can't help but smell the casket air, this fake smell of starch and money. It smells nothing like your daddy. It's too full of the Holy Ghost, too white and cold. You close your eyes and kiss the face of this imposter. You kiss the cold stucco.

Your mother pulls you back to her black, crinkly chest. She holds you tight while everyone looks, while you pray for Jesus and his stucco taste to leave your lips. She lowers you to the floor, stretches her neck and looks up to heaven. She cries quiet and you cover your eyes. You can't help it, and she knows it—you can never kiss your daddy good-bye.

When you look up, a hand passes over your head, a hand in a black suit sleeve that gives where a stiff white cuff pokes through. A metal cufflink shines only inches from your face, a round, coin-like medal that strikes you as odd, so you look closer. Two great letters say U and S, each on a bright purple bed, the letters that you have hidden at home now here in this bad place. The hand reaches over you, the smell of salt on steel following it, the Navy breath your daddy carried back to your bed where he kissed you, that odor again over your head. Us, it says.

The great hand reaches inside the casket and rearranges something before it withdraws. You look up and recognize Gerald Dalton, the undertaker your daddy was supposed to stay away from. Mister Dalton owns the funeral home. Your daddy never said he was a spy. Mister Dalton pulls a gardenia flower from somewhere within the casket and hands it to your mother.

Your mother goes hard as Mister Dalton holds the flower before her. She pulls you tight against her legs and holds you with one open hand while she looks at the flower. He pushes it closer to her, but she's hard. She won't take it.

People are watching behind you. You can tell it because they're shuffling about, breathing loud. The people are moving as though something needs to be done. But your mother is giving the orders now, and they can only watch and listen.

"Sir, you've done enough," she tells Mister Dalton without looking to him at all. She turns her head around, looks to your grandparents, and once she grabs your hand, she pulls you back quick to where they stand.

You watch the casket. Mister Dalton has stepped behind some flowers in the corner of the parlor. He must know he needs to hide. You can't be a good spy if you don't know how to hide. There's no question about it now—Mister Dalton is the spy. Even though he is some distance away, you can smell him, that stuff an undertaker probably must wear because bodies can't help but smell bad.

Your mother couldn't help but drop the flower. Your daddy couldn't help what he did either. You know that, you and all these people do. What they do not know is that they were wrong about that body in the casket, that you did not really kiss your daddy. You will never kiss your daddy good-bye.

Nested

THE PARKING LOT WAS PACKED, cars astraddle the driveway curb, CellSure people parking like Europeans or team leaders late for a meeting. Maybe new hires. Maybe so many last-minute, end-of-the day conversations were now in place a surprise visit would go completely unnoticed. Maybe a blessing, Jane thought. A check-in with Price, then two hours with no interruptions: the office organized, emails sorted. Could prove an omen of how a routine might return next week, how easily she could pick up where she left off. Indeed, the entire day was proceeding much as her mother would have wanted—the beauty shop signed over, lunch with Lily, the shared memories. But Lily's request, her plea—was that also what her mother would have wanted? Jane felt her head shaking in disbelief, her mind puzzled by Lily and why so many CellSure employees were parking like Europeans.

A blue Volvo was parked in her spot. She stopped, inspected the tag, then inched her car forward to circle back. Again, she steered to the spot where only she was supposed to park. Maybe maintenance had changed the signs.

Once more, the blue Volvo. Maintenance had not changed the signs. All that was left to do was park in the front lot spots reserved for visitors. So Jane parked and made her way back to the building like a visitor.

The main entrance would have been too much, the receptionist too gushy for a day that might prove a harbinger for the week. Her return had to be quiet, her reappearance natural, so she walked to the back of the building and faced the dull green door that she'd long taken for granted. She swiped her security card before the square gray box. She waited. She grew nervous. The little red dot blinked fast before it slowed. And just as it seemed the light was gone for good, the lock clicked. She shouldn't have been so anxious. Of course, the building remembered. A building would never forget a woman who'd sat with it far longer than she had her own mother.

As usual, it took some muscle to break the back door's air seal. The building was negatively ventilated, air sucked in from the ground level and exhausted even faster through filtered vents in the attic. The system controlled the flow of any carcinogenic fumes from the laboratories. The system also sealed every entrance and Jane welcomed the pull, the muscles it still took to get inside the door.

The stairwell was empty. Three stories straight up, every door was closed, each secured with a lock that required the card key and a code. Again, each little light sputtered before Jane's card until, like a machine programmed to simply create anxiety, the lock gave. Never before had she noticed how barren and indifferent the third-floor walls were, how the aging hall lights made the air a little yellow. The celestial white hall she remembered had been yellowing for years and not once had she noticed it or the process.

She wanted to disturb no one as she moved down the hallway, to interrupt no deep thoughts inside an office and certainly not the critical steps in an assay. She did her best to keep her heels from clicking.

As she neared her office, red shadows flashed in the door's high window. Moving closer, she stopped and looked through the glass. Inside were boxes, three small white boxes stacked atop her desk. A black logo ran over the sides of the boxes—*VitaTell*—*the best in nested primers*. They were kits, the mass-manufactured kind she would never order.

Jane unlocked the door, stepped inside and flipped on her desk lamp. The red light was coming from her printer, the lid open, cartridge missing.

A couple of gnawed-up pencils lay scattered about the telephone. Never had Price mentioned someone sitting at her desk. Or maybe he had. Maybe she'd been too distracted with her mother to notice what he was saying, too outside herself. And now that she was doing her best to reenter her life, someone had repurposed her desk, her place, literally.

Maybe a surprise visit was not such a good idea, some disarray inevitable when people were covering for her. Made sense, maximized space. She recited the sense in it as she left for Price's office. At this end of the hall, clicking heels didn't matter.

The door to her husband's office was open, Price seated at his desk, poring over a document. She tapped on the wall. "Remember me?"

Price jerked up his head, a startled pale going red. "Jane . . . well looka' here . . . it's you." He rose from his seat, rounded the desk and hugged her as if he feared every technician in the building might be watching, his movements censored, not quite sincere. "Something come up at the shop, a problem?"

"Not at all." She was tightening her lips about the words that wanted to declare every day of the past six months a problem. "Just me," she added, rushing a smile to indicate maybe she was a fixable problem, one that would need his help. "I'm back."

Price scoffed, grinned hard and pulled her closer, the hug so consumptive she could only shrink within its clutch. Once his secretary stuck her head in the doorway, smiled and waggled her fingers like a woman who enjoyed other people's problems, the hug broke. Price seemed to enjoy the secretary's interruption, the brief audience that proved he knew someone would be watching. Standing proud before his desk, hands on her arms, he studied Jane's face. "So Lily didn't back out?"

"Not at all. But I might. Lily wants me to—"

"See what we're doing." He tugged on her hand, dragging a guest chair behind the desk so she could sit alongside him. "Just got a project from the Birmingham Police Department, a five-year retainer, if you can believe that." He flipped the contract pages, his shoulders high, face ignited. He looked a full decade younger.

Smile, her body said. Listen. Let him talk. And because she did feel a little like a visitor, she smiled and listened as Price went on like a much younger man.

"Every day," he said, "is a surprise." He paused, anchoring his eyes on the Birmingham contract's tiny black words before catching a breath and going on from there.

Jane's eyes followed the text, but they veered when the little black letters blurred and something curiously quiet sneaked into her field of vision. There, on her side of the desk was CellSure's ticket to the future, the official document up-front, unavoidable. Price had been obsessing over the letter from Homeland Security for weeks, the short timeline for a response, the money. She'd grown tired of hearing about it, but now that she saw the imprint of a notary's seal, the governmental expectations seemed even more daunting than Price had implied. She pulled up the letter, pressed it flat before him. The Chief Operations Officer was back, the fixing process started. "We really need an extension on this, don't we?" A coffee stain had smeared the blue eagle.

"Not anymore, Doctor Beekman." He took the letter from her hand. "Alex is ahead of schedule. You remember Alex, don't you?"

Oh, she remembered. She remembered the gnawed pencils and jammed printers. No doubt Alex had been sitting at her desk. "Gotcha," she said. "And I take it Alex has also been parking in my—"

"Temporary," Price snapped. He patted her shoulder the way you would a kindhearted but forgetful little girl. "Remember?"

"No. You told me?"

"Sure did, back in the hospital waiting room one night. Remember?"

Jane lowered her eyes to the floor. Price was undoubtedly correct. Too much had happened. It was silly to think she could simply pick up where she'd left off. It was her error, another one.

Firsthand, Lily had said, a talker who knows firsthand what tobacco can do. The campaign work was a choice now, hers. No need for another diagnosis, no point in any more questions. Maybe something good could come from all this after all.

Price stood, a car dealer's smile strapped across his face. He went to reorganizing all the papers on his desk, yanking at things that didn't need to be yanked at. Within him, something had to be hiding, something else she'd probably overlooked.

"Nested primer kits—I guess Alex left them on my desk?"

Price thrust back in his chair, smartly, as if confirming the matter was rickety but settled. "Alex thinks it'll make PCR nothing more than a dipstick."

Her heart jarred. "Alex . . . he's changing the assays?"

Price considered the question and after some thought, brought his face closer to hers. "Trust me. Assays don't change without the okay from Doctor Jane." The voltage inside him was steady now, the mechanical parts engaged. This was not the man who'd trudged out of the house this morning, deadlines shackled about his ankles.

"And what else has changed?"

"My father."

Price pulled a white slip of paper and eyeglass case from a desk drawer. He placed both items on the desktop, centering the case as if to form a tiny monument, the letter before it a placard. "It came today."

The letter—she knew what it was. From the time Price got the call last week, he'd been edgy. Mumbled when he talked about it.

"Know what this means?" He gestured to the letter.

Jane examined the handwriting, focusing on the part that called the boy Price smart. "It's not the least bit nasty. Looks like you guessed wrong."

"Not at all." His smile angled, one corner skewed high. "She lied."

Jane recoiled. He came closer.

"She did. She lied." The lights inside the pupils of her husband's eyes were victorious, the intensity almost dangerous. "My father knew a baby was on the way. And my mother most certainly did." He fingered his chin, moved his eyes to a picture on the wall. "My father was something else, wasn't he?"

Within Price a harp string had been plucked, a reverberation that came from decades back. Jane knew the sound, the dissonance of old thoughts connected to the here and now by a tune only he could recognize, the music only he could share. So she said nothing, just listened for Price and his other sounds.

He opened the eyeglass case, pulled out the money clip. He freed the twenty-dollar bills and lifted the silver clip to the ceiling light, moving it before her eyes. "See. It glimmers."

In the center of the medallion, the letters *U* and *S* were raised, each resting on a bed of purple. Jane knew those letters—University of the South. Price had his father's diploma somewhere at home, the certificate framed, probably up in the attic with his father's other things. She took the money clip from his hands. Without the folding money, the clip seemed an elegant but dangerous device, some instrument a surgeon might use when bisecting an aorta.

Price drummed a finger on the desktop, counting. "It's just like the one he gave me. Think I was six then." His eyes were empty, his focus steady on the spot he tapped.

"Surely your mother didn't lie."

"No, seven. I had to have been seven."

Jane lowered the money clip, entombing it and the twenties once more in the eyeglass case. "Think about it," she said, snapping the lid. "You were just a boy."

"Trust me. I remember." Price pulled the eyeglass case to his nose and sniffed. His lips leveled and his chin rose just as they did when the first assays of a specimen gave the answer he was expecting. The pronouncement. "Jackson used to tell people God was his father, him and Jesus the world's only miracle babies." Price pointed the eyeglass case at her like a fired-up professor. "Jackson was most definitely no miracle baby."

"Maybe he was in your mother's eyes."

"Well, if he was, the miracle was her creation." He lowered the eyeglass case back to the desk, patting the cloth-covered lid, pressing the loose fibers into place. "Tomorrow, I'll put the case right before his face, literally."

"Don't say she lied."

"First thing tomorrow. He called me this morning."

Price paused, letting the importance of his words sink in, the one high syllable of *me* almost squealing as it rose into a memorable nothingness— Jackson called *me* this morning.

Price and Jackson rarely talked. And when they did, most always Price did the calling. He could leave so many messages on his brother's machine, it often seemed a routine, like bills at the end of the month.

"Doing breakfast tomorrow," he said in a smart stride. "First time we'd spoken since your mother's funeral." He paused to exaggerate a sigh, twisting in his chair. In the process, he jostled the mouse to his computer, which sent the darkened screen bright. At the sight, he flipped about, moving fast to try to change the picture. He was too late. On the screen, an engineering diagram lay blood red on a bright yellow background, lines tracing the dimensions of a motorcycle. He swallowed noticeably.

Jane peered closer. It was a detailed drawing. She reached for the computer mouse, but he beat her to it. He clicked and up came a multicolor view of a motorcycle cresting a sun-drenched hill.

She gripped his chair. "A motorcycle? You?"

"Just a thought."

Price stretched his neck, turning his attention back to the eyeglass case. "My father's doing. Save up, he said. Maybe someday buy a motorcycle." Price shifted his gaze, scrutinizing her face, the pent-up energy inside him finally dissipating, the voltage flowing. "Sure did. Something else wasn't he?"

Never in her wildest dreams had Jane imagined her husband on a motorcycle. Yet there it was, some guy cresting a hill. "But Price, you? To ride?"

"Jackson thought it was crazy too."

"So all this, he knows about it?" Jane motioned her eyes to the eyeglass case and letter. "You told him?"

Price cuddled the case in his hands. "I told him I had a package from Gerald Dalton's son."

"And?"

"Hung up." Price shrugged, returning the case to the desk. "What can I say? He was rushed."

"Jackson hung up on you?"

Price kept his lips tight, his attention going everywhere but to her. "Tomorrow—it'll be good, good for us to start over with our father, a good way to spiff up the memory. Really good, don't you think?"

"Don't say she lied."

"Why not? She did."

"Jackson can't possibly follow—"

"Of course, he can. He's almost as smart as I am."

Price huffed in delight out his nose, the sound overly boyish but quickly erased by an all-too-mature silence as he stood and walked to the bank of windows that overlooked the parking lot. He gazed outside, keeping his back to her. Soon, he was talking of his father's troubles at the bank, how his mother always said those problems were to blame for his father's suicide. "Crazy," Price said, glancing to her, his eyes still on some distant place. "Jackson's never even asked me why."

Price returned to watching the world beyond the windows, shifting his weight from foot to foot as he often did when he was thinking. This was the Price Beekman shuffle, the correction of a pelvic imbalance that came from a short leg not fully corrected by a thicker sole in his right shoe. "Born hobbling," he'd often said. Jane hadn't noticed the defect back when Price stood lecturing before the Vanderbilt pathology residents, but when he pointed it out (first date, their own bodies explored to the point of pathology) she had little idea that the quirk would prove useful months later when the Tennessee two-step came so much easier for him than her. He was nearly thirty then, a pensive man who could explain disease and human suffering in a way that more often than not led to sex. Yet from the way he was rocking now something other than anatomy was off-kilter inside Price. And whatever it was, to him it wasn't obvious.

Jane wanted to stabilize her husband, to make him once again the man playing a game with business contracts. She pulled the Homeland Security letter from his desk. She stepped to his side, started talking about crazy timelines. "I can't believe they expect a response by the first of July."

"Alex," he said. "Total control." He took the letter from her hand, folded it twice and slipped it into his shirt pocket. "Leaves plenty of time for you to help Lily."

"Lily? Who told you about—"

"Jackson—that's why he called. Wanted to make sure I knew the idea was Lily's, not his." Price thumbed his chin. "Hope you said yes."

❧ ◉ ❧

MONDAY MORNING, JANE STOOD WITH PRICE IN the garage, the wide door open, the frigid world rushing in. Frost flocked the lawn and despite the sun's shrill dazzle, the air was biting. Price circled the motorcycle. It was a BMW cruiser, a special weekend delivery. In Jane's mind it was a consolation prize, or maybe a diversion from what Jackson shouldn't have done but did. He canceled, all but stood Price up at the last moment— no brotherly breakfast, no money clip or father's blessing. The voice mail message had left Price more sunken than perturbed. The motorcycle had to help. Jane couldn't say no. Yet even as she acquiesced at the breakfast table, she tapped her chair's wooden underside three times to make sure God knew the rules: Nothing bad was to come from a revved-up cruiser.

She took a sip of coffee, pinched her lips before moving to the motor-cycle's front wheel. Instead of tag-teaming Price today in a drive to CellSure, she would soon head for work in the opposite direction. CellSure might not need her but Lily did. And she needed Lily. Lily would help her rebalance the scale that might otherwise be forever weighed down by a misdiagnosis. In fact, Doctor Jane Beekman was lucky. She had a second chance. To prove it, she took another sip of coffee and looked to the stretched-out woman in the chrome fender.

"Amazing technology," Price said, licking a finger to rub a blemish from the leather seat. He steadied the cup of coffee in his other hand, reaching over to inspect the dashboard's many little dials.

Jane liked seeing him like this—fascinated with details, fingering a whatnot, second-guessing an arrow—in his way, pleased with the world, fitting into it. For when Price let go a mighty worry, he became handsome in a rebuilt sort of way. He'd work his hands like a magician, move with the deliberation of a pathologist in the midst of a complicated dissection. And he'd invariably smile, his long face making his engagement weighty and genuine, almost a burden given his ever-apologetic eyes. Unlike his brother, Price's hair was receding and the little left on top was fine and limp, fully reconciled with the future, beat down actually. Time had done this to him and to her also, time and failed dreams.

Ten years it had been since those failures brought them home to Atlanta, to this business of CellSure that began largely as a desperate act. Everything (and she meant everything) had until then failed—the research years at Hopkins, his unfunded grant, her ever-elusive tenure. And then the day when her body simply gave up—the hormones and shots, the baby that would never come. Price could handle it, but she couldn't. That day, that sickening day when life in Baltimore became a plan that couldn't continue, it was her mother who raced from the beauty shop for the first flight out, her mother who held her close as she rocked and wept on the sofa. "You kids need to remember Atlanta is always home." On that awful day, Price did what he could, but Jane would never forget how she rocked in the arms of her mother. That night, once no more tears could come, she and Price understood too well there were some things that even God could never fix. Failures simply had to be accepted, like her body, like Georgia. God had at least cleared a path. He was moving them back home. On that last day in Baltimore, it must have been God who made sure Price was up to driving the truck. Just as it will be God who made sure no bad things came to her husband from this barbaric cruiser.

Jane just couldn't see it as he did, this deep blue arthropod stretched between two fat wheels. Shiny black tassels hung from the tips of the fist grips. And between them, a tremendous plastic shield rose high and papal, the whole leather-saddled contraption reminiscent of a throne. She moved a few steps, so the woman in the fender might relax her face.

"Made for two," Price said, patting the front crotch-cupping seat and then the rump behind it. He paused, his hand on the empty seat. She crinkled an objection with her nose.

"Someday?"

Jane bent low, tried to see the two-wheeled creature another way.

"Price, I will never ride a motorcycle."

He thumped the leather seat, waved a hand over it like a salesman. "Think about it—Miss Lily could wheel this baby all over the state. All you'd have to do is hold on." He raised his cup to her. "*Beekman04*—biker babes with a mission."

Jane didn't want to play this game, but she did. She volleyed a contemptuous sound out her nose, a harrumphing dismissive sound that went fast above the leather seat to hit his face. The sound tripped the locks on a pop-up look of utter exultation. Still, he sipped his coffee, watching her ponder this game that, as much as she didn't want to admit, she was maybe good at playing.

Jane moved a few more steps to the side of the great six-cylinder bug. She wanted to see it in another way. It glowered all the same. It was smug and daring. Failures, it seemed to say, must be accepted. Jane, you can't run away or hide in the old routine. CellSure has grown up. Face it. You need to let it go. You need to watch your husband finger the tires of something dangerous a conscientious God will never let him ride.

"Hill-start control," Price declared, pointing to the dashboard. And once Jane crouched over to see what he meant, the shiny bug flashed its gas tank lid in her face like an orifice.

Price was focusing now on the glossy-ribbed engine, a suspicious glint in his eye. "Wonder what Jackson would think about my father and me on a motorcycle? Imagine his face."

Jane rocked her head in agreement, trying to ignore Price's hold on his father, his possession—*my* father—as if that father belonged to him alone.

After a brief lock-eyed moment, Price turned his head to gaze out the garage door, where the earth's deep silence was still rolling in. Soon it had surrounded them, the two of them encased in a heavy hush that was settling cold on the concrete floor. Price turned to her, and when he spoke, a visible mist preceded his voice.

"I was so much older, sometimes I actually did feel like Jackson's father."

"No doubt."

His eyes didn't move. "When Jackson was a boy, he could get going so hard sometimes I had to put him in time out." Price shifted his attention to the motorcycle. "Maybe five or six then—Jackson would be running wild through the house, and I'd yank him up, lock him so tight in my arms." Price halted, as if to let the recollection mature before his eyes. "Yeah, I'd lock him up with my arms *and* legs. I'd yell 'Got you!' and Jackson'd yell back at me. 'No, you don't! You ain't never got me!' But I did have him, completely. Immobilized—the only way I could make him behave."

Never had she heard this before. Price focused on the motorcycle, his voice falling directly on the engine.

"Oh, he'd strain and kick, those skinny arms flying." Price stopped, drew a quick breath. "And then he'd whimper and after a while, he'd wilt." Price turned to her, his eyes calm, all light steady. Jane tried to look away but couldn't. Those eyes, they had her.

"Wilted," Price repeated. "Just hanging in my arms—nothing at all. Hanging, like a rag." The air seemed raw, the world's mouth open, its cavernous breath exposed. Price paused only a moment before he said, "Killed me when he did that." He looked directly to her, tilting his head as if to cap a point. "And guess what?"

She didn't answer.

"Sometimes I want to do it again."

Jane looked away. From the corner of her eye, she watched her husband raise the coffee cup to his lips and sip. Price stood there, saying nothing more as she tapped at the two torpedoing exhaust pipes, those chrome grasshopper legs. Are all motorcycles male? She touched the front handgrip, tried to make a joke. "So no rubber on Peachtree Boulevard, right?"

"Not unless you're the chick on the rump."

"Price, I may need to put *you* in time out."

He cut his eyes to her. Time out. The comment was cruel, souring the instant it met the air. This little joke that blossomed in her mouth had withered so quickly she'd simply spit it out. A thoughtless thing she'd said.

Price snickered with pleasure and skirted the motorcycle. He finished his coffee, positioning the empty cup like a memorial on the bike's driver seat. He folded his arms, striking that confident pose he brought to the amphitheater stage back when it came time for the chief pathologist to speak at Vanderbilt. "Lily's a smart woman. If she didn't need you, she wouldn't have—"

"But the contract," Jane implored.

"Alex. Remember? He's got it under control." Price aimed his attention to the bike once more. "Bet old Alex could tame this thing."

Price throttled his fists in a gear-shifting style before stepping to her side. He kissed her on the brow, told her the day would be fine, just fine. And when he told her that Alex might have a full first draft of the contract proposal this morning, she felt the motorcycle gloat.

"It will be fine," he said once more as he straightened the collar on her blouse. "Maybe you can work a miracle with my brother's schedule." It was such a quick and easy comment, it seemed inconsequential even as, from the way he dropped his eyes from her, she could tell it wasn't. She tensed her lips, responding only by crisping the tails of his red bowtie. He pulled his coffee cup from the motorcycle seat, passed it to her and, after another kiss, he moved to his car. She waved as he drove off.

In her hands, his cup contained a shallow ring of coffee. She tilted the cup, raised it to her lips and swallowed the leftover drops.

Ammunition

T O JACKSON, ANY EXPECTATION OF uninterrupted thinking time was a fool's assumption, so as he settled into a respectfully quiet campaign office he counted himself far more blessed than any other fool running for governor. He'd gotten downtown before daybreak, and if that's what it took for a few minutes of solitude, he was going to make it a habit. He was sitting at his desk, the door open and ready for Monday morning's usual rush of the pumped-up and whiners. Yet the God who had given him a restless night had also graced him with silence and the blessings of a three-page report that proved Pete McGee wasn't even a member of the NAACP, that the NAACP had never received a cent from McGee, and that—for what it was worth, which was a solid forty percent of the populace—Pete McGee's support for a mandatory minimum in all criminal sentencing fixed his black face in the very cross hairs of the Georgia NAACP Judicial Committee.

This report was good news. It was worth every dime of a generous donation. This was heavy duty, down-the-road ammunition. It was one of many reasons Jackson counted his blessings not only for some solitude but also for Daisy. Any girlfriend who could get her hands on an insider-only briefing document was a girlfriend to keep. And any girlfriend whose daddy was also a platinum donor to the Georgia NAACP was a girlfriend to nurture. There was an organic texture within that word *nurture,* the grit in the sound of its second half—the *chur* that he admired. He said it out loud, "nur-chur." The sound almost had an odor to it, a horse barn odor, rank but sweet. The odor fit his sensibility, for he was a nurturing guy, a stallion who thrived on the rank but sweet. He was made for this race. Shoulders strong, legs agile, motivation just. He could picture the banner across his chest— *Super Stud*. A landslide was a no-brainer, so Jackson took a pen and inked a happy face next to the paragraph on mandatory sentencing.

He drew three Mexican stars—the cross hair type with intersecting lines—next to the concluding paragraph that said Jackson Beekman had a consistent record on diversity in the hiring arena. An underline scored the section that mentioned how Jackson Beekman joined the NAACP when he was in college and has maintained full membership. A fat circle highlighted the word *associates* in a title: "Associates of Jackson Beekman Are Regular Donors." This was radioactive stuff, true facts lying fissile before potentially explosive eyes. God had made his choice. Jackson Beekman was the lucky Democrat. Not only did he have God and the NAACP on his side, but he also had the beginnings of a trap-door solution for McGee. Cite this paper, and the old Sambo would fall into such a deep minority hole the light of public visibility might never again meet his eyes. The nuclear option, some captains might call it; a scud barrage he'd insist on if McGee's retreat wasn't fast enough or fully complete.

Jackson closed the plastic cover over the report, studied the ghostly red letters marking it confidential. This was ludicrous. No way could he come across blacker than McGee. A trap-door was just that—a trap for whoever plays the race card first. Call CNN, get the helicopters circling and burly men to hauling big black cameras on their shoulders. Then send the entire crew packing. Say "Guys, sorry 'bout that. We almost had you a scoop." Yes, sir. This kind of report was best kept quiet in a file cabinet's bottom drawer, locked away until some nuclear need arrived on what Lily would invariably call their Hallelujah Day.

Jackson leaned back in his chair. He did it with stallion-worthy muscles, so the spring's great squeal might sound decisive to any reporter who just might be listening on a bug. His heart laughed at the thought of espionage. It laughed like the power organ of a privileged insider when the going's good. He dragged out the bottom drawer of his desk and propped his feet on solid wood.

Jackson held the report in his hand, let its meaning grow more mature as the more lawful angle of lamplight allowed a better perspective. Diversity was just one of his strengths, but if McGee pulled the race card, the NAACP report on diversity, which some reporter will have proudly uncovered, would be staring the geezer in the face. Women, Jews, green carders, even the guys with records—the Beekman packaging was stamped. At least one high yellow on every hall, here as well as in the AG suite. God knows, the billboard version of diversity was usually sitting in an office one door away. *Not only black, Mister McGee, but also like you—a little on up in the years.* And no token geriatric at that. No way was Lily a token. If McGee had seen her last week, he'd seen what it took to almost break a stallion. Of course, it would take more than Lily's temper to break a super stud.

Jackson stared to the open door where the real world might appear any minute now. He fixed on the void where he could picture Lily bleeding her heart out to his sister-in-law, perhaps on the telephone even now. What on earth was she thinking last week? It was a crazy question. Lily was thinking what everyone else was thinking, like how to lubricate the great rusty machine otherwise known as the Georgia Lung Association. Not that old-school politics was an outdated investment: Plug a medical person on the team and out comes the endorsement. You get what you pay for. Yet here comes Lily with her revival sermon on—of all people—Jane. "Why not?" Lily says. "Her mother just died of lung cancer. You people shouldn't overthink the obvious." The Queen of Diversity had spoken. No disagreement could undo the obvious. It was not an easy moment for a super stud.

In fact, he probably was over-thinking too many things, like how a plan to revitalize the state's public school system and retrain multitudes in the tech-heavy ways of the twenty-first century should ensure a Beekman victory thanks to the younger vote. Like how the nobility of that plan should trump any attack on the last century's tobacco deal. And that's over-thinking? Lily needed to cut the power stepper some slack—at least he knew what the state really needed. And at least he'd remembered to call Price with a heads up. Yes. Jackson Beekman could be a nurturing statesman *and* a brother.

Nurturing—sometimes he felt like a father to these people. Last week, after the captains ganged up on Lily, he'd planned some major nurturing. Great job, topnotch financial reports, on-the-nose advice. *So Lily, any talk about you being replaced was totally bogus.* He wanted to tell Miss Lily all these things, but the Diversity Queen clammed up after the tobacco talk, raced to her office and made sure everyone knew who shut the door. And when Lily's in holy hibernation, you just let her be. That's the accountant juice in her blood, opinions summed up on a line meant for the entire staff to see. And team, you better not cross that line because the rest of the world may overlook things, but Miss Lily wouldn't miss a stray move. Lily was always watching. And that was a good thing, always. Take it from the father.

Think about it. With an NAACP endorsement, folks just might someday look back and remember Jackson Beekman as the first black governor of Georgia. Of course, most Georgians won't see a diverse administration as much of an accomplishment. What will hold their eyes are all the great things only a daring stallion could do, all adult bodies employed at good jobs and making good pay. It's the reason a few members of the NAACP might someday go to sleep at night thanking God for the role they played on Hallelujah Day.

White Paper

THE FIRST THOUGHT THAT ENTERED Jane's mind was radiation. She was used to showstopper foyers, but the Deposit Guaranty Building's anteroom was excessive, cold-room cavernous and antiseptic in a style suggesting more than decorative purposes. The light falling from the ceiling seemed overly filtered, ethereal but purposeful. It made her fear looking up, even as she knew that fear was irrational. Such silly thoughts were quickly erased because standing in the center of this otherwise unpeopled first chamber was Lily. A brief hug and soon an elevator with art deco bronze doors—each embossed with Madonna and child motifs—was carrying them one floor down, the descent secured by Lily's key card and the black gadget eyes of two security cameras in the high front corners.

As the elevator crept down, Jane's sense of holding on was replaced by one of letting go, of having the world take her down as far as it cared to and once there, just dealing with it. Failures must be buried. Much as she had planned on returning to the world she'd known, where she belonged now was below it, deep down among the mistakes, bodies, and bones. And now that she was here, there was light, an unbelievable amount of it.

"Here we have it," said Lily, one hand swaying about a great circular room in the building's basement. "Our brand new digs—the *Beekman04* Think Tank!"

Gone was the ache in Lily's eyes, the uncertainty. In its place was a brilliance that rivaled the whiteness of the basement space. "It's so . . . oh . . . so, new," Jane said, slipping her satchel over her shoulder and rummaging for words, ". . . so light."

The great space-age cubiculum was awash in white fluorescence, the austerity broken only by the projection of CNN on two giant roll-about television screens. Gleaming ivory-marbled walls rose up to meet the flat skinny light of dormer windows, all views of the outside world confined to feet on the sidewalk, tires on the street.

"Secluded," Lily said. "Perfect for focus." She motioned like a salesman before a lot full of exotic imports.

"Amazing light," repeated Jane. "Windows . . . interesting."

Lily went on, maneuvering Jane about the room. "Yep. Here we hunker down, huddle, build teams. And here's the telephone team!" She pointed to the island in the center of the room where three young women bobbed up and down behind tall futuristic bank teller–like desks. Earplugs and hand gestures indicated serious telephone conversations were this very moment taking place.

"Jackson's motivational project," Lily explained, "gets everyone going." She thumbed-up the tele-talker dangling her torso over a Plexiglass counter. The girl wore a red tank top and candy-stripe hot pants and, in response to Lily's wave, kissed the air, a smooch that Lily promptly slapped away. The other girls, also dressed in Yankee Doodle get-ups, were too frenzied to notice anyone. "Braves cheerleaders," Lily said as she escorted Jane past the buxom crew. "Yep. Tomahawk Teamers—backups, cheap."

"Cheerleaders, answering the telephones?"

"Sure do. Realtor's package deal—that Jackson's got the gumption, ain't he?" Lily tugged on Jane's arm, pulling her close. "He's a fool for deals. You'll see." It seemed a motherly opinion, more acceptance than approval.

The campaign finance chairwoman seemed to take Jane's silence as awe, escorting her like a dutiful parent to a wide hallway. Thick yellow cords snaked along the baseboards. "Fiber optic cables, too tough for a butcher knife," Lily said, not missing a step. "With McGee's bunch, you just never know." To Lily's hint of sabotage, Jane hummed an acknowledgement that, in all this high-tech light, made no sense at all.

At the far end of the hallway a large banner swagged from the top of one wall to another—*Beekman04*. Beneath the plunging cloth, two double doors were open and inside was Jackson. The candidate was seated behind his desk, head lowered as if contemplating the budget for another deal. Dark shiny hair swirled. His shirt was military crisp, wide white stripes falling vertical on a bed of deep blue. In a chair before his desk sat a woman taking notes on a yellow legal pad, her plump legs crossed, one foot jiggling. The red pump looked new.

"Something, ain't it?" Lily said, hurrying Jane along with an instructive finger. "I'm here," she said, pointing to a doorway just off Jackson's office. "And inside my place, I've set up a spot for you." Lily stopped, latched her fingers together like an apologetic realtor. "Tight space arrangements. But, hey. Can't get any closer to Jackson's office." There was an emphasis inside Lily's eyes, a point more urgent than anything she'd yet to say.

To Lily's puzzling gaze, Jane felt her head nod. She couldn't say no. She had failed her mother and, instead of eternal damnation, she has been cast into an underground heaven, cheerleaders the angels, television screens displaying the dark world above while orders went out on knife-proof cables. God had cleared the path by bringing her down. From the basement of the rest of her life, she could only look up.

Inside Lily's office was a battered old oak desk, a green-globed desk lamp glowing over a pile of papers and books. There was another door inside Lily's office, one that suggested a closet, but the doorway was open and, given the sleek big-wheeled office chair before the white Formica slab of a desktop, Jane figured that improvised spot had to be hers.

"Yep. Even got your computer going."

But what if I'd said no, Jane thought for a moment, but the boundaries of that moment left no time for second guessing, for Lily was already strutting through the doorway to Jackson's office. "Great day in the morning!" she exclaimed, bending over Jackson's desk to look him in the face. Jane lingered in the doorway, but she could see enough of the woman in the chair to recognize her as Alice, the hefty, frizzy-haired campaign manager perched on the edge of her seat. Alice had hugged Jane in her mother's viewing line. It was a disorienting embrace because Jane had trouble remembering who Alice actually was. This morning Alice had a notepad on her lap and the butt of a ballpoint pen in her mouth. When she peeked back to Jane, she looked aghast. Still, Jane forced a smile, waving as if she didn't know better.

"Got me the help I'd been talking about," Lily declared to Jackson. "Topnotch help just like we needed—no need to get rid of me *or* tobacco." She hoisted a hand. "Come on in, Baby. You know this dude far better than I do."

Jackson's desk was almost a duplicate of Lily's, heavy wood that looked direly out of place given the newness of almost everything else. Behind it, a taped-up Georgia state road map covered much of the wall.

Alice stood, smiled to Jane before honing in on Jackson with her focus. He was hopping up from his chair. "To be clear, jail overcrowding," Alice said, "now's not the time to address it. Right?"

Jackson was stepping around his desk, Lily bird-dogging him with her voice. "I can probably get Jane lined up to meet with Hank Cowley right away. First time ever—a Lung Association endorsement! Can you imagine that?"

"Never mind these gals," Jackson said as he approached Jane. All ten of his fingertips were aligned to form a kind of cage, the tips bouncing back and forth. "They're tamer than they sound." He practically glowed as Lily clasped Jane like a trophy.

"Who," Jane asked, "is Hank Cowley?"

"President of the Georgia Lung Association," clucked Alice. She was looking to the doorway, her feet in motion but going nowhere.

"Big man," added Lily. "Cowley's a smart one. You'll see."

"Well, Doctor Jane," Jackson said as he moved to her side, arms raised in a gesture that suggested a hug or a handshake, the choice apparently hers. "Sure is mighty kind of you to come all the way down here."

Jane went politely into the arms of her brother-in-law, the hug loose and formal but deep in the scent of chewing gum, then the stronger odor of newly printed money. It came from his shirt, maybe some chemicals from the dry cleaner, all that starch. She withdrew, telling him, "People may be tired of hearing about tobacco." Her voice was full of a nervousness that she wasn't planning to hear. "But after my mother's lung—" "A saint," he said, chopping her off before any painful words were said. "A true saint."

Eyes went blank and all breathing hushed, the silence prevailing until Jackson offered a consecrating sigh and resumed talking. "We're all concerned about tobacco, aren't we ladies?" Lily nodded. Alice bit her lips. Jackson ignored them, going on before Jane as if to set an example for the women. "Having medical expertise on the tobacco team really matters. Listen. We really do value your time."

"Glad to be here," Jane replied in a brisk professional manner, her tone sharp mainly because Lily's eyes were clamped on her, the finance chief no doubt watching to see how her recruit might perform in this underworld circus.

"The final press release is due by noon," Alice said, working her way to the door. "And we can't talk about race disparity in prisons. Not now."

Jackson paid no attention to her. Instead, he returned to his desk and told the women that he wanted to talk to Jane a moment, alone. He stepped behind his chair and stood there, rolled up his shirtsleeves, pushing the cuffs above his elbows. Such a power lift of the sleeves was a pattern Price also followed, almost always before he put someone on a performance improvement plan.

"Later," Alice told her boss with a point of her pen.

"Always open," Jackson said, his attention moving between the departing Alice and Jane. "Always open," he repeated. He rocked on his heels, batting looks between Jane and Lily. "Know who said that?"

Jane started to offer up an answer, but Lily broke in, wagging a finger before Jackson. "And later I also need a word with you."

"Yes, ma'am." Jackson gripped the back of his big chair, leaning forward like a judge.

"Baby, come back to my office once he's talked you out. I'll give you the low down and get an ID card hung around your neck."

"Always open," boomed Jackson. His face drifted upward. "God said it. Sure did. Revelations 3." He hesitated as if humbled by the sanctity of the citation, and once the proper respect had been paid, he stood fully erect, cast a gaze heavenward and back, his face glowing as if he'd just been blessed. "Behold, I have set before you an open door, which no one is able to shut." He held fervent and grave for another respectful moment that barely passed before he cracked, a joking voice now directed to Lily, who was headed for the door. "No one," he told her, "is able to shut it."

Lily flapped her hand at him. "King James here better watch who he's quoting."

"No one," Jackson shouted to Lily's exiting backside. Jackson rounded the desk, motioned Jane to one of the guest chairs then sat down beside her. He let out a long audible breath and proceeded to cross his legs like a man pleased with his performance. His face was suddenly more solemn. He rested his eyes on the empty chair behind the desk, slumped as if he were a guest before his own authority.

The old leather-backed chair behind his desk loomed empty before them and Jane tried not to notice it, but it had that same worn look her husband favored in personal things. She wondered how many other similarities between Price and Jackson she might notice here—battered chairs and rolled-up shirtsleeves, pilfered quotes in a performance for employees, maybe more. She'd known Jackson for over twenty years, but he'd always been preoccupied with school or work, and the more she thought about it, the more she realized she'd never really known him as anything other than "Price's brother," a smiling but otherwise nondescript presence over a holiday table, a routine face at funerals and graduations. All in all, neglected.

They were now alone, the doors open, hallways quiet. Jackson was quiet also, thinking it seemed. Jane sensed some fatigue, a humility that she had never before noticed. Apart from Price, he seemed a far more complex man.

Jackson swallowed, crimped his chin. He hesitated a second as if reconsidering his thoughts. "Well, I never intended for us to impose on you like this. But Lily—she was so rattled by your mother's passing. Rattled, weeks on end."

"They were close."

He looked at his hands. "I'd told Lily I didn't think this was such a good idea, that you were probably still grieving and too tired—"

Jane touched his arm. "Listen. Lily knows I have to do something to help people like my mother."

"She also knows how hard you work, the connections." Jackson pushed up on the arms of his chair, lifting his shoulders, giving her his full attention. "That Lily—went into high gear back when McGee said he'd undo the cigarette tax plan. Well, next thing we know, she's gone to Hank Cowley looking for an endorsement." Jackson was pointing now, his index finger dabbing in the air with the rhythm of his words, his attention shifting between Jane and the empty chair behind the desk. "And low and behold, the lung folks agreed, if . . . " He paused, dramatizing the importance of the qualifier. "If and only if we recruit a medical professional to help explain the science that justified the tax in the first place."

"But the science—it's so simple."

He rocked his head in agreement, lowering his voice to a level that suggested he was familiar with grief. "Alice thought they didn't trust us."

The effort struck her then. In this conversation, Jackson was even more uncomfortable than she was, embarrassed in fact. He mentioned talking points, the technicalities in science, messaging. She said, "Maybe less political and more substance."

"Substance—exactly. That's when Lily started singing your praises." He grinned, dipping his head to her. "Not to suggest that Lily was exaggerating."

Jackson sounded like the man Jane's mother always said he was. "Fine boy," she'd said back when Jackson announced his run for attorney general. "I don't care if he is an ambulance chaser. Somebody's gotta pick up the pieces."

Jackson moved his face closer to her. "Listen. We definitely don't want this work to be a ball and chain. Part-time's more like it. We were thinking you could meet up with Hank and maybe some lung association board members, maybe help me understand what they really want. You know . . . medical schmoozing."

Jane had to pick up the pieces. She had an opportunity, a calling that would not correct a misdiagnosis but place it in a better perspective. A public health project was a selfless endeavor, a better reason to pick up the pieces of herself.

Jackson pushed back in his chair. He was looking about the room, pleased it seemed at the appearance of all his things in the office, but also puzzled by them. "Crazy, ain't it?" He ran a hand through his hair, mopping up the mousse then frowning at the sheen on his open palm as if he didn't know how it got there. He gestured comically and like that, he was back on the stage and working every inch of it. "You know, a week ago almost every staffer called any mention of the tobacco deal taboo."

Jane pulled a notebook from her satchel and started writing. She put two words in her notes, *deal* and *taboo,* not describing how the candidate's affect could quickly flip between apologetic and pagan.

"Everyone knows tobacco is my baby." He said it with momentous propriety, more owner than parent. "And next year, the settlement brings in one-point-five billion dollars to this state." His face visibly hardened. "Know who's responsible for how that money's spent?"

She didn't want to answer, but did. "I can guess."

"Every single penny of it. And if that governor is my ignominious opponent, then the whole freakin' pot goes to general expenses." His demeanor rose, eyes drifting down to an imaginary audience that must have been sitting spellbound before him. "Mark my words, not a penny will follow the settlement agreement, not a freakin' cent."

Jane wanted to repeat out loud that word *freakin'* and lift her voice as she said it, but Jackson seemed well beyond the need of any encouraging words.

"'Cross the board freeze on taxes,'" he stormed, "opposition to 'No Child Left Behind.' McGee's against much more than he's for." His fingers were coiled, the imperceptible edge of a podium gripped.

Jane moved closer to look him in the face. "But cigarette taxes?"

"Listen. On taxes, my goal is dollar-a-pack." His delivery was commanding. "Makes Georgia one of the highest tobacco-taxing states in the nation. The future—we target the future by keeping our commitments."

"Lily called it integrity."

"Integrity. Good word." The candidate studied her. He pulled a stick of gum from his shirt pocket and, looking only to her, peeled the gum from the wrapper, popped it in his mouth, and started chewing as he talked.

"You know—I've never had you guys up in the AG suite." He scanned his office, shaking his head. "Makes this place look like a Georgia Tech dorm room. But uptown, it's a whole different story—penthouse view and a rug on the floor that I swear must be larger than the one in the governor's office." He chewed his gum mightily, gazing at the ceiling in a pleasurable moment before the weight of that pleasure seemed ripe for sharing with her. "Before I leave that place, I've gotta have a picture made up there with you guys—you, Price, and me, the three of us standing in front of the desk, flags on both sides. How 'bout it?"

He didn't give her time to respond, turning about and mumbling some facts about tobacco as he pulled a document from his desk. "Got a white paper here. Lung Association's manifesto." He handed over a thick spiral-bound document that looked as if it hadn't been opened. He said, "Old Hank Cowley's group must've known I'd need help. Here. See what you think." He passed the document to Jane, telling her that he's used to groups making a few key points on a slide set, not clobbering him with a manifesto. He dropped his hands to the edge of the desk and, like a preacher after the pulpit invitation, waited for a response.

Jane thumbed the pages. "Lots of numbers," she said. "Probably impressive data." She slipped the document into her satchel. "I do have friends in the public health world."

"McGee couldn't care less about public health." He jabbed a thumbs-up in the air, shifted his attention to the open door, his gaze fixed on the hallway. He called connections the essence of politics, like deals and gum.

"Like gum?"

"Sure. You chew up what the world gives you, rework it, then spit out the nub when no one is looking." He raised an eyebrow to her as though he'd just revealed an intimate strategy. As if to cap off that revelation, he pulled a pack of gum from his shirt pocket and began to shake it, slinging it hard to liberate a stick. "Big Red," he said while fiddling with the pack. "The campaign favorite. You need to give it a go. It helps."

"With What?"

"Control."

"Of what?"

"Deals. Gum's disarming, relatable."

Jane took a stick of gum, unwrapped it, and started to chew. The taste was tart, the sensation suddenly reminding her of another reason she was here this morning. "You know Price really wanted to talk with you this weekend. He was hurt when you—"

"Sorry 'bout that. But I'd forgotten my calendar and bless Pat, wouldn't you know it? They had me booked." Jackson's brow was pinched even as the rest of his face seemed mellow. Overloaded, she imagined.

"It won't take long at all," she said. "Price is expecting you to call."

Jackson remained mute as if thinking of options or maybe trying to recall a blank spot on his calendar. He chewed his gum and moved his eyes from side to side like someone searching for a reminder on a shelf, a sticky note taped to a picture, some trigger to help reposition the upcoming week's workload. He finally fixed on her. "Sure," he said. "I'll give him a buzz. It's a deal." He tongued the gum to the front of his mouth and pooched his lips to spit the knotty gray nub into the palm of his open hand.

Jackson Beekman, 1969

TOMMY CARPENTER COULD SPEND HIS whole life tinkering with tiny men. "Jackson," he says, "the official colors are army green and bazooka blue." Tommy knows the rules. The army green is muddy and dark, so the soldiers can hide in the rice paddies where buffalo bones sometimes poke through their bellies and split their guts. The blue men look a little smarter even though they jump into ditches and dunk their heads beneath the water when the Viet Cong walk by.

"Look at all those turtles," the Viet Cong colonel says. "Amazing, Sir," his soldiers tell him, and they all keep walking. Vietnam, Tommy Carpenter says, is full of dead buffalos, blue turtles, and American soldiers who are trying to blend in. "Just to survive," says Tommy, "the Viet Cong!" He springs to his feet, karate chops the air, and yells like a general at Shiloh.

Tommy Carpenter wants you to like all his plastic men just as much as he does, wants you to line them up, so you can shoot them dead with a machine gun that kills row after row with a lawn mower approach, to scatter platoons then grenade them one by one, or maybe blow up a brigade with a bomb whistling Dixie down from a B52 that no one saw coming. But you don't like war, and you know you never will see men as Tommy Carpenter sees them, at least not these silly plastic soldiers he calls Marine tough. So when he drags them out and starts preparing for another war, you pretend to play for a while, but before the last man falls you stretch out on your back and watch the big white clouds practice for the second coming.

When the clouds fluff up before turning on each other to create a breakthrough place, the wild blue-eyed white horses will leap down toward earth, the white chariot following behind, the Lord God Almighty on board, He too magnificent to behold by any army of men. Tommy will be warring away the whole time, shouting orders and screaming with pain and sometimes talking like Walter Cronkite, using big words that actually are useful to someone who just might grow up and tell what he once saw in the clouds, words like *deploy* and *destiny*. *Deploy* is what soldiers are ordered to do. *Destiny* is different. "*Destiny* is a choice," your mother said when you asked her what the words meant on a fancy picture down at the bank. The picture showed an eagle soaring Colorado high, the big word running between it and the mountains. She went serious after she said it, and you could follow the choice part, but *destiny? Destiny* means the future, she explained, and somehow it did seem like a word God would use when he's talking about the future of eagles. What the picture is trying to teach people is important because the second coming has to do with both destiny and choice. People who make the right choices will rise up from their graves, while everyone else will be left dead in the ditches, their skulls stinky as the turtles in Vietnam.

You are already chosen, and you know it. Like Jesus, your father was in heaven when you were born. It's a kind of miracle birth even if Price says a true miracle birth means the baby never, ever had an earthly father, not even one before he was born. "We have the very same earthly father," Price says. "He just happened to die before you were born." If your earthly father just happened to die before you were born then you should have been born dead also, so everyone could say it all just happened, as it should. That is how destiny works. But you were not born dead. So there, there is the miracle. Price may go to camp all by himself, but he hasn't seen the clouds do all the things you have seen. "My big trooper Price and my little miracle Jackson," your mother says to the people who stop her on the sidewalk. At the second coming, the father Price says he remembers will rise up amazed at what he must behold.

You are surrounded by clouds and chariots and miracles floating in milk, the tiny round life preservers you behold in your bowl, the little Cheerio circles that float on the surface like the life preservers the lucky people in Mississippi may have floated on after the hurricane hit the Gulf Coast. It's gonna be another hot day. The cannas are already droopy outside the kitchen window, every flower blood-faced and ready to rise up like some of the dead will someday do, those lucky ones stunned at the good choices they never realized they had made. Sometimes miracles just happen. Just look at the survivors in Mississippi.

It is Saturday morning. Your mother is packing a snack of peanut butter and crackers, maybe some potato chips because she may need to work longer than half a day at the bank. "It depends on the business," she says. "Some people wait until the last minute to do anything." These people don't matter to you because you want to go to the bank with her anyway, you want to see how many people come to borrow money from her, what they think of these new banking hours. It is a safe place in case the Mississippi hurricane comes this way. The vault is made of metal and covered in concrete. Its door has spokes on the great wheel. Your mother can turn it with her bare hands.

"Goodness, at the choices some people make," she says when the radio announcer says some college kids threw a hurricane party when the warnings came. She and you and her boss and whoever happens to be in the bank will all run into the vault and close the door if the hurricane heads this way. Georgia should be safe, the radio announcer says. And you want to believe it will be safe because people here make good choices, but your mother says, "Goodness, we're mighty lucky this time." You will let her believe in luck because she was born the year a tornado came, a bad year that she calls "just my luck." Some day she will understand how God and luck are really the same thing. It all depends on the choices you make.

Destiny is up there on the wall, the fancy bald eagle rising high above the clouds, his eyes on God and all the miracles that may come to people who choose to put their money in the bank. A picture of ducks flying out of a lake is also on the wall, the ducks crazy mad and flapping hard because someone must have fired a gun. This kind of picture seems odd to be in a bank where people know money is kept and guns shouldn't be fired. The ducks are frightened. Maybe it is a reminder to your mother that she needs to press the special button beneath her desk whenever someone suspicious walks in, someone who just might have a gun. Back here, every desk is closed in by glass walls that would break into a million pieces if a gunshot came through them. You probably should worry about her, but she's a strong woman and she really looks it today, her hair done up just right and her orange paisley pantsuit fresh as ever because it's made of miracle polyester that will last forever. She is a powerful woman. She knows how important choices are.

You sit at the glassed-in cubicle back behind her cubicle, at the desk of a woman named Janelle who is off today and who left a large clean spot where you can glue together all the parts of a Bonnie and Clyde car. Too, you have Price's old Boy Scout handbook, the World Book volume *P,* a bottle of Coke, enough things to do, and still you keep watching who comes to her glass cubicle door. One of these people just might have a gun.

She keeps the door to her cubicle open, so you can hear what they say in there, especially when they first come in and the folks are nervous and loud. One lady is from church. She hands your mother a peach and a paper sack full of peaches and tells her, "Peggy, when I think of peaches, I think of you." They hug and talk a little. Your mother wants her to leave. You can tell it from the way she keeps looking to the lobby where a man in a suit sits in a chair. Finally, the lady does leave, and your mother goes out to meet the man in the suit, an important man for sure because she is smiling like a real banker when she leads him back to her desk. They talk serious stuff and give you ample time to plug the engine parts beneath the car's front hood, to attach the tail pipe that runs under the bottom. Your mother is smiling even though the man looks worried. When she pats the sleeve of his coat, you can hear her telling him, "Goodness now, it wasn't that tough was it?"

He thinks about it and finally nods. They both stand to shake hands before he leaves. Your mother shakes hands just like a man.

She sometimes comes back to check on you, but you're doing just fine, and she seems to know it because her eyes sparkle the way the fancy jewels must sparkle back there in the vault. The bank is the best place to work in Egypt, and you're counting your blessings when Mister Gilmore comes to your mother's door. Mister Gilmore is the bank president, a man who only comes around when something really important must be done. He really looks like a dead man, white skinned and stiff, the kind of look that probably comes from spending too much time in the vault. Your mother pushes back from her desk, stands a little like a soldier, and together they talk important stuff. You slip into another chair at the side of Janelle's desk so you can hear them better, maybe hide. Maybe Mister Gilmore doesn't allow his ladies to bring their kids to work.

Your mother is using her hands, whispering loud. The paisley creatures look ready to do something if they could. She looks directly at him. She says, "A loan for what?"

Mister Gilmore is definitely not looking back at you. He's completely tied up with your mother. He says something about a new funeral home building, and more loudly, "a new one in Athens, out near the new mall." Everyone is talking about the mall in Athens, the huge new Sears store that will be packed with bicycles and all the kitchen appliances anyone could ever need. The mall is important. Doesn't she realize that?

She nods her head as though she probably does remember how important the mall is to everyone. "I'm not sure I can talk to him," she tells Mister Gilmore, who frowns.

"Peggy, it's business. That's all it is."

"We have a history. You know that."

You grip the arm of your chair, look up to see your mother chopping at the air just like Tommy Carpenter chopped up the air when you told him his little soldiers were silly, the whole bunch only good for starting a fire. That kind of plastic is good for a fire. It drips. History means a long time ago, back when there were dinosaurs. They don't matter anymore. But your mother—she has a history? They, your mother and Mister Gilmore, keep looking toward the front of the bank where another man in a suit is sitting, another nervous customer who probably needs a loan. But this man must have more problems than the other guy, too many for your mother to handle, so she's doing her best to explain it all to Mister Gilmore. They keep at it until Mister Gilmore seems to settle things, both of them saying one after the other, "strictly business." If Tommy Carpenter were here, he'd call it a peace treaty.

Mister Gilmore goes to the front of the bank, then returns looking like a dead man, only come back to life and smiling. He's followed by the man who has problems yet still must need a loan. "Miss Beekman, Mister Dalton here is interested in a business loan." Mister Gilmore turns and shakes hands with the man before he looks at your mother to make sure she takes him in. "Mister Dalton's fine funeral home was just given an A rating by the state mortuary board. He needs to open a branch in Athens, and I'm sure we can help."

Your mother's face looks plastic, the new make-up she put on this morning suddenly way too caked-up for her, so she works to make her words seem natural when she speaks. She must realize you're watching because she turns her back to you so you can't see her face. Her voice is also hard to follow when she says something about the bank doing the best it can, given the business history. Mister Gilmore must need to count some money, so he leaves. Your mother sits very proper at her desk, and the funeral home man looks all about her office. Just before he sits down in the chair that the beggars take, he turns. He sees you.

You duck into the volume P, turn to the *View of Toledo*. In the painting, the sky is gobbed-up with dangerous clouds that will part at the first sign of the second coming. Price says the town is Toledo, so the painter called the picture *View of Toledo*. A man named El Greco painted it. El Greco is the kind of name that needs a karate chop after it. El Greco! You like how El Greco painted the clouds over Toledo. Toledo could just as easily have been Egypt, Georgia.

You keep the World Book volume *P* up over your face and, after you hear all the bank talk questions that come with answers from the man and your mother typing fast on her Selectra, the pings and hum explode with a snap of the paper that the typewriter spits out so fast it makes your mother shout at him. "We need you to sign here." She doesn't call him Mister Dalton, just "you." She means business. You lower the book to get a good look at the man. He runs a funeral home, a really important job. He may have to bury some of the soldiers coming back from Vietnam, even Mister Gilmore once his heart gives out. He looks like a man who could do that awful job, like a man who might also paint an El Greco kind of picture, a slow-moving man who touches his chin like a painter must do when the choice is between the red of a fire engine or a crusty scab. In fact, Mister Dalton just might have a painting in the World Book volume *P*. Surely she knows all this. He looks at you again. This time you do not hide. Instead you stare right back at him, and if Tommy ever asks you what he looked like, you'd have to say he looked like a man who could take care of a body once it came back from Vietnam.

They stand, Mister Dalton taking a large folder full of the homework your mother gave him. He seems happy with the work because they shake hands. They are talking like bank people usually talk when he raises a hand toward you, one finger stuck out like the barrel of a gun. He aims it carefully then winks. Shots are fired, or your mother must think they are because she suddenly steps toward him, her arm flying high as though she will slap his cheek. "You keep away from my boy!" People hear her. You do also, and you hunker down, raise the World Book volume *P* over your head as she growls at him like a Viet Cong colonel. "Business, Mister Dalton. You mail your papers in, okay?"

There's a shuffle of feet, what must be Mister Dalton heading down the hall to the front of the bank where he will have to pass all the people who will look at him. And after the people see him and his homework, they'll look at your mother. You lower the World Book volume *P*, and by the time it's down, you see people up front looking in their places.

"Sweetie," she tells you, "if that man ever tries to talk to you, you just ignore him, hear? He's a mighty sick man."

"What's wrong with him?"

"He's not right. Pitiful, you hear?"

She's running a finger through your hair, redoing the part that she must have thought got messed up when Mister Dalton fired his gun. You want to tell her that he's probably just worried about having to stuff the cheeks of so many dead people and painting their faces to look fresh, but she knows an awful lot about people who come into a bank, the choices they make when it comes to money. Painters know nothing about money. And they certainly should not be playing with guns, even if they are only make-believe.

❧ ◉ ❧

Tommy Carpenter has gone looking for bears in the Smokies. Tommy, his folks, and his two sisters all loaded up the station wagon yesterday—probably left before daylight, long before your mother went to work. "Jackson," he'd said, "next year maybe we can take you." Knowing Tommy, he'd forget it next year. And knowing his daddy, there's no way Tommy can bring back a bear. Tommy's daddy drinks tons of beer. Bears love beer, and Tommy's daddy is not about to share his beer with a bear. In fact, if the bears get hold of that beer, they may chase the whole family out of the Smokies, beer cans scattered all along the road back to Egypt. No one in town would be surprised. So you ride your bicycle by their house to see if they're back early, to look for beer cans on the road, maybe claw prints on the car.

You hurry. It looks like rain. The clouds are dark as they'll probably be on Judgment Day when Tommy's daddy will finally have to answer for all that beer. The thunder snarls like a drunken old bear probably did to Tommy, but you pretend you don't hear it because your mother said you could ride no further than the parsonage, and that's enough. Rain on a bicycle will make the chain rust.

Tommy lives next to the parsonage, so you'd think his daddy would know better than to drink beer. But he does and no, they're not back. No sign of a bear cage either. No beer cans on the road. You walk to the back of the house. And no, no bear tracks or beer cans, no signs of a bear. But Tommy did leave some of his tiny men outside beneath the big pecan tree, so you gather them up, leave them heaped in a pile on the front porch of his house. Tommy will probably think the men got lonely and marched through a swamp of sticky pecan tree drippings, right up the steps, and decided to camp out on the porch until he got home. Tommy believes these little men do that kind of stuff.

You beat the rain, get back in time for the Superman rerun then the Porter Wagoner Show, which your mother watches with you until the horn goes off and the announcer cuts in to say everyone should watch out for storms, maybe a tornado. Your mother is a tornado baby, born the year the whole town blew away, so she takes the warning seriously. You eat supper early and get ready to spend the night in Miss Hattie's storm cellar. Miss Hattie lives alone. Her oldest boy built the storm cellar in a fancy way that lets her spend the night down there. Otherwise, she could be blown away in the middle of the night, and no one would ever know it until the mailman found her dead in a ditch.

Miss Hattie's storm cellar is built in the side of a gulley that runs way back on her place. Concrete steps drop down to a full-sized door that, once you open it, leads into a little room that seems nice until you look close and see that the floor, ceiling, and walls are all concrete creepy, sort of like a bank vault. Miss Hattie has a cot and a rocking chair in there, along with a small table that holds an old-fashioned lamp, an oil-burning one that she says she bought back before the war. Once she lights it with a match, the lamp makes everyone's face peaceful and golden, what folks must have looked like back before the war, faces just like the picture of Jesus in the church social hall. Makes him look real, so it probably took a famous man to paint it. Funny it's not in the World Book volume *P*. Guess they forgot about it. Sometimes the storm cellar is not such a bad place at all.

The rain falls like a thousand drops of kryptonite. It's hard, hitting the tin overhang outside the storm cellar door. Thunder rocks the earth, but in here everyone is safe, the faces of your mother and Miss Hattie soft and glowing, just as the face of Jesus glowed when he calmed the oceans and commanded the demons to jump out of a crazy man's body. You stretch out on the cot, your feet in your mother's lap, and you watch her and Miss Hattie talk until you start thinking of Tommy up north in the Smokies, the mad wet bears crawling around their tent and Tommy's daddy still drinking all that beer. Sometimes you are glad you don't have a daddy. You keep dreaming of bears and bad daddies until you awaken to hear your mother and Miss Hattie talking real soft, like Jesus probably did long before Miss Hattie's war. It feels good to just lie here and listen, to pretend you're not really here at all.

Your mother is shaking her head, her voice shaking also because she is upset and can't help it. "I tell you, it was all I could do not to walk out on him."

Him? Was she walking out on you? Thanks to your superhuman powers, you keep your eyes closed, but you really don't. You hold still, weak as Superman in a kryptonite chamber.

"No. When that Gerald Dalton stepped up to the door, I thought about walking out of the bank for good. Didn't think I had it in me to face him like that."

"Hard," Miss Hattie says, "what you folks have to put up with."

"They made me. I couldn't look him in the eye at all. If I did, I knew I'd walk out right then and there. Gerald Dalton is responsible for Lucius. He's the very one who made my husband do what he did."

"Soul wrenching. I'm sure it was," says Miss Hattie while rocking in her chair. You want to say Mister Dalton is just sick like she once said he was. Didn't she remember?

"You know, I haven't been to that funeral home since Lucius passed on. Doubt I ever will go again. God's truth. The only way I'll ever face Gerald Dalton is when they make me. In a way, I think he killed my Lucius."

Mister Dalton killed her Lucius? She said it was an accident, a problem with his gun. She told Price to say so when people asked. An accident—that's all it was—doesn't she remember these things? She is crying. You want to reach up and hold her, tell her it's all going to be okay. You want her to know it's okay if you really did have a daddy because you're not a baby anymore. You know he had an accident, that's all it was. The war is over. Jesus is here. He knows she's not lying. She would never lie to you. Jesus knows the truth. Miss Hattie does too. The light of truth is in her lantern.

"He could have pulled the trigger," your mother says. "In some ways, he did."

"Tough, I know it is," Miss Hattie says.

"Well, it'll all come out on Judgment Day."

You are limp, all your powers gone. The storm is so bad, your mother talking so wrong. Maybe you are dreaming this up, you and that crazy Tommy Carpenter dreaming together beneath the pecan tree, your dreams all mixed up. If you had a daddy, then he had an accident. Mister Dalton would never kill you. Your mother gave him the loan. The wind won't stop. It sounds like there's a bear at the door. He's wet and mad, full of beer.

❧ ☉ ❧

THE TREE FELL ON YOUR BEDROOM. YOUR mother stands proud before it, here in the morning after a storm that everyone thank God survived. She says, "That it didn't do any more damage is just a miracle. Why, Jackson would have been crushed if he'd been asleep in his bed!" She glows like she's seen God. "A miracle indeed." If Price had been here, he could have been a witness. He sure didn't see a miracle like this at Boy Scout camp. Teaches him. Boiling water on a fire and tying a square knot in sixty seconds is nothing like a death-defying miracle. If your momma forgets to call it that, you'll remind her. "I could be dead," you'll say and that'll do it. She can't handle the idea of you being dead. You know how she thinks.

She and you are standing with the preacher and some other men in the front yard. One man says he doubts any structural damage. Another says the stucco must go. The preacher knows a good Christian contractor, so the guy must be fair, probably have the tree off the place by tomorrow afternoon.

Your mother is in control, talking like she does at the bank. No wonder they are making her a vice president. She does what needs to be done, talks to men who need to be talked to. She says, "We have insurance. The agent's to be out here by dinner." All the men around her look amazed. She is a powerful woman, and you are a boy miracle. The tree proves it, just like she said it did.

Days pass like troops on patrol. Price comes home from Boy Scout camp with three merit badges. Tommy comes back with a picture postcard of a momma bear and her cub. The troopers wouldn't let him near the bears. But he did get an Indian spear and a rabbit's foot, some magic ink that disappears when you rub it on your hands. His daddy still drinks beer. And at your house, the tree comes off, a tarpaulin goes on, and then the new wood that smells like what your mother calls the smell of progress. She bakes a cake to thank Miss Hattie for her help. You sleep in Price's room and he doesn't complain even though he knows you can swim a whole lot better than he can, and if he doesn't learn to swim, he'll never make first class. He is afraid of the water, so he's probably gone as far as he can go. But you never tell him that. There's always the possibility of a miracle. You remind him one night when you're both supposed to be asleep because school starts tomorrow. Yet the streetlight's strong through the window, and there's too much progress in the air. When Price rolls over onto his left side like the soldiers probably do in their bunks, you say, "Do you believe in miracles?"

"Sometimes."

That is an odd thing to say. Either you believe or you don't. You say, "It's a miracle that I'm alive."

"Maybe."

"You know what I heard?"

"What?"

"Momma said Mister Dalton could have pulled the trigger." The streetlight holds calm and when Price says nothing more, you make sure he understands what you said. You say, "She said Gerald Dalton killed our daddy."

"It was an accident. His gun went off."

"Then why did she say that?"

"It's complicated. She never liked Gerald Dalton."

"Why?"

"She thinks he's sick."

"Is he really?"

"He likes men."

"How do you know that?"

"That's what they say."

"He likes men?"

"That's what they say."

"That's sick."

The streetlight glows like Miss Hattie's lamp, and if Jesus was here his face would be peaceful, even when he has to hear about Gerald Dalton. Maybe Jesus can someday cure Mister Dalton, work a miracle, drive out a demon, make everything smell like progress. Maybe he can also teach Price how to swim. He really wants to be an eagle, but he's gone as far as the Boy Scouts will let him go unless he can swim. You know that, and maybe he does also. What's important is progress, the modern look of red brick instead of stucco. Progress is what the picture of ducks means in the bank. When someone shoots a gun, you flap your way out of the pond water and never look back. Price doesn't know this yet, but he'll learn. So, you say nothing more because only a miracle can change things for him.

Closet

SHE HAD HOPED TO START WORK well before anyone else arrived this morning, construct a better sense of this new working home and, more importantly, focus on creating a public health movement that, in the afterlife, would make her mother's eyes dazzle because—"Honey, you done good!" She would start small, reworking the Lung Association white paper into a coherent pitch, an impassioned presentation. She would simplify, turn numbers into bodies, cigarettes into guns. No distractions, no interruptions. Yet when she turned the corner to her office, Jackson was the first sight to meet her eyes. The candidate was fully illuminated, kicked back in the chair behind his desk, eyes cresting the top half of a newspaper. He waved. Jane reciprocated with three teetering fingers and a smile that probably concealed little of her disappointment. No surprise, she figured. A good candidate must also prefer an early start, the peace of darkened hallways, the midweek sneakiness. A Beekman thing.

On first entering Lily's office, she'd touched neither the lamp nor the light switch, allowing instead the hallway's angling amber to guide her path. In the shadowy basement silence, she'd made her way past Lily's desk to the workplace prepared for her alone, this small walk-in herniation of a redone closet, its sliding door stuck open. She slipped into her spot, plugged in the overhead lamp, and fired up her computer. Five minutes later, the wall started talking.

She heard Jackson say, "Senator Lambert, you awake yet?" His tone was brisk, the wall muffling only the edges of his words. Six-o-five AM winked the tiny digits at the bottom of her computer screen. She heard Jackson pace about his desk, his voice grow thin and tentative. She pushed back from the screen's blue light, leaning a little closer to the sound. "Down the road from Rome—now, just how far out old 29 is that?" She pictured the candidate inspecting the map on his office wall, maybe circling a town with a pen, underlining a faint county road. She heard him laughing. On her computer screen, the first slide was blank, the cursor blinking.

Overhead, the bracket for a pole pooched out from the wall, a blatant, whitewashed error. The sight illustrated how suddenly her life had changed, how you have to ignore the leftover parts of an impromptu office, the scab where the pole used to go. She leaned back in her chair, slowly, gravity calling her to a new position, a more observant stance. So much whiteness, drywall little more than hardened plastic. Made her have second thoughts about her assigned place in this faux-techno cellar, this lesion-pocked closet. Enough of this bellyaching. Second chances were supposed to be tough, filled with sacrifice. A computer in a reworked closet was all she needed. Perhaps even more than she deserved. The wall resonated with a metallic creak, a stuck thing's release in a leathery squeal. Jackson had to be shifting positions. Feet on the desk, the lip of a warped drawer. "Senator, say your boy headed for Mercer?"

Tomorrow she would bring in a small radio. Maybe a white noise machine. But for now she'd do her best to focus. Two days of orientation had left her hungry for real work. And finally, her focus lay on the untilled row of this morning's assignment, the Lung Association white paper open beside her computer, the page turned to epidemiology data. Jackson said, "Senator, you heard about the new honor system at Georgia Tech?" She bent closer to the wall. Couldn't help it. Dangerous political leaks probably sprouted this way, and by good people too.

Jackson raised his voice. "Oh, you haven't? Well, it's a mighty simple honor system to my mind. Goes something like this: Yes, your honor. No, your honor." A howl or boisterous cackle was supposed to follow, this Jane was prepared for, but instead there was silence—the space occupied no doubt by the senator's laughter. Which seemed to prompt an impish voice from Jackson, his legislative points all that more powerful thanks to the disarming frame of the Georgia Tech honor system. The conversation's strategy needed little analysis. Nor did some take-home point that Jackson sealed when he told Senator Lambert that a good Mercer man would never get caught with his pants down. "You take care now." A quick thud followed, what had to be the receiver on its cradle, the conversation closed, of course, on Jackson's last word. Finally, silence.

Jane could focus. She was fired up. Last night she talked for over an hour with Nancy Currier, one of her classmates from medical school. Thanks to that conversation, Jane now had an on-the-road, catch'em-while-you-can idea. Actually, it was Nancy's idea—Jane just made it better. It was the reason she wanted to get a jump on the day, get this white paper summarized and out of the way. A daybreak start. Like the early days at CellSure, she was needed.

She was needed because the Georgia Lung Association had dire trouble communicating its message. No wonder the legislature ignored their briefs. The best points were riddled with statistical mumbo jumbo. Any doubts? Ask Jane, the new lady. The proof was wide open on her desk, pages three and four—too many p-values and confidence intervals, too much medical jargon. Here was the reason they insisted Jackson hook up with the right kind of medical person, a translator, a talker. Hopefully—she told herself—he did.

Analytical work did come easy to her. But it needed to come doubly easy now because she was working with not one but two Beekman men. Comparisons, she quickly reminded herself, were not part of the job. The next slide was a simple copy-and-paste from last night's notes. See, three whole pages summarized in one bullet. And yes, she's also successfully tuned out Jackson. She's condensed ten long tables into three simple slides. The realization of some success, or maybe it was the new tone in Jackson's voice, made her stop and once more absorb the message from her loud neighbor. "Judge, you heard about the Bulldogs' new honor system?"

Out of nowhere, the lights went bright in Lily's office. A hefty sack plopped on the floor. "Baby, that you in there?"

"Back here." Jane hit the save key, sliding around in her roll-about chair to welcome Lily. Daylight was loud in the window. Only two bullets occupied her newest slide. She sat in the closet doorway, legs crossed, a determined grin directed to Lily. "Wanted to get a jump on this mess of a white paper. Takes a medical degree just to figure out what they're *trying* to say."

"Girl, you got the heebie-jeebies?" Lily was bracing her backside against her desk, sizing up Jane. She motioned her head toward Jackson's office. "Thought only a jittery politician would ever hole up so early down here."

Lily's face was vibrant, fresh. Red lipstick, golden hoop earrings, and close-cropped silver hair—no doubt last trimmed at the Delta Salon she now owned. Jane wanted to memorize this moment, her mother's best friend arriving for work and her mother's daughter working right beside this majestic lady. She said, "The Lung Association is a complete messaging mess."

"Hank Cowley," Lily answered. She turned, flipped on the desk lamp. "Always heard Hank was a micromanager. And penny pincher to boot. Probably wouldn't hire good people." Lily was now stepping toward Jane, peeking over her shoulder and craning to inspect her computer screen. "That old Dell working okay? Thought you'd only use it for email." Lily's eyes went from the screen to Jane, her brow worried, creasing as she backed away to create some talking space in the closet doorway. "And here you're already making slides. Baby, has that boss man given you a deadline?"

"This boss gives everyone a deadline," Jackson bellowed. Lily twisted about, freeing up more floor so Jane could roll her chair forward and catch the sight of her brother-in-law standing in the doorway of Lily's office, coffee cup in hand. "No slacking off even for kinfolk," he quipped. He was rocking on his heels, watching for a reaction.

"Good God," Lily jeered. "The last thing we need is a boss prowling about like some swamp monster."

"Deadlines," Jackson spouted back at her, "they're the only monsters in this swamp." He steadied his feet, steered his eyes to Jane. "Early starts are a Beekman family tradition. Right?" Before Jane could answer, he cut her off, grunting as if he'd just remembered something she needed to know. "And speaking of early starts—got a date with Doctor Price this Saturday. Hope to claim the first hot biscuits at the Cracker Barrel on Dalton Road." He grinned with great pleasure before drawing a sip of coffee, swallowing as he redirected his voice. "When the Beekman campaign promises, it delivers. Right, Miss Lily?"

The campaign finance chief stiffened, raised a finger to his face. "Listen. You better not run out on me today. You hear that? I'll be right in there. You hear?"

"Give me ten." Jackson eyed the clock on the wall. "One more phone call. Got to make sure a few senators are on board—" He stopped, speeded his attention to Jane as if he'd just remembered another critical family matter. "Such a coincidence," he said. "Last night I was at a meeting where one of the guys talked about making medicine from tobacco. Repurposing tobacco, he called it—ring any bells with the CellSure folks?"

Jane brightened. The technology had been talked about for years. "Recombinant genetics," she answered. "Serious science. Two of my Hopkins buddies started a company using the technology. They manipulate DNA in the tobacco seed, so as the plants grow they make mutant proteins in their leaves. Grind up the leaves and, if you're lucky, out come vaccines and drugs."

Jackson may have been listening, but his attention was moving to Lily, a bluster on his face and a rascally voice erupting. "Think we hit the Lung Association jackpot with our Doctor Jane here. Not just any expert, but an expert with genetic connections." He gave a pleasurable, throaty moan as if some delicious taste had leaked from his words. Yet Lily frowned and to her rejecting face, he seemed to suddenly remember the time she wanted with him. "And speaking of connections," he said, "I've got a conference room of folks expecting me at nine uptown. You ladies should count yourselves lucky—no ruckus from the neighbor this morning."

"Ten minutes," blared Lily, a hand raised. "And you better still be in there."

"Ten minutes, max," he said, turning to the hallway. "Just one more lawmaker to wake up." He sprinted away, his circling words sinking slowly in the doorway as the sound of his steps trailed him back to his office.

Lily flapped a finger to Jane. "That young man got away without talking to me yesterday. At least this morning I have a witness." She stepped deeper into Jane's closet. "Now, what's this rush all about?"

"Needed to get it out of the way because I've got something I want—"

"Baby, you better not burn out on me." Lily was shaking her head, her voice directed to the computer screen. "This tobacco thing's just a sideline. You just tell me whenever you've got to get back to that business." She was hovering over Jane, talking and positioning her body as if to block any escape.

"Actually, Price has a new contractor working—"

Lily shook her head. "I just didn't have time to lay out things for you like I should have yesterday." She rose from her crouch, grimaced in the direction of Jackson's office. "That boy, he had my brain too rattled. Anyway . . ." She pointed her eyes to the paper on Jane's desk. "Baby, this little job is not about to eat you alive. A few talking points from that monstrosity there and then helping us figure out what Hank Cowley really wants—that's all we need. Sideline only. Reminds me. I got to get you out to Hank's place right away." She stepped back from Jane, crossed her arms. "That Hank—no telling what the old miser might say."

"I think he'll be pleased," Jane said. "The health department's starting a new smoking prevention program. Heard all about it last night. And . . ." Jane paused, shifting her voice to the low secret register of backup plans. "I know how we can be a part of that program." Lily's eyebrows pitched lower, doubt hard on the sinking part of her face.

Jane kept talking, but she was nervous. She felt the nerves in her throat doing their best to contain what she feared would come out—some pointless remark about how she was more than the bounty for Hank Cowley's endorsement. Such a thing didn't need to be said. So she explained how

Nancy Currier thought it would be grand to have a pathologist as a speaker in the new program. "Nancy and I go way back," Jane said. "We were lab partners at Emory." Jane nested her hands in her lap just as she usually did when explaining a new genomic assay to Price. "Turns out, Nancy's office has spent the last six months planning a community outreach program. *Fresh Breath Science*—it's geared to teenagers."

"Baby, sounds like a breath mint, something to chew up and cover the odor." Lily twisted about, dragged one of her office chairs to the closet doorway and sat down before Jane. The squawk of a pained spring came from Jackson's office, followed by a regretful whine in his voice. "Senator, did I catch you on the run?"

"Good science *and* visibility," Jane insisted. "Beekman visibility. Sort of backdoor campaigning."

"Backdoor," Lily repeated.

"Solid," Jane said. "It's mainly a junior high school–level tutorial on the health effects of smoking. But . . . " She touched Lily's arm, draping her fingers in that same sisterly way Lily touched her last week. "The program includes a symposium series for the public—as in the motivated, *voting* public."

Lily did another sinking thing with her eyebrows. "They pay you?"

"Totally volunteer. Mainly show slides of what emphysema and lung cancer really look like, explain what smoking does to the body." Jane launched the uppity eyes of an expert. "I'm good at showing dirty pictures."

"Baby, sure hope that Hank doesn't expect too much from us." Lily stood, slid her chair back to its proper place before her desk. "You know," she said. "I do . . . I do have to catch that boy." Her hands were moving quickly among the folders on her desk when, as if stung by a thought, she stilled, pulled up an orange folder and waved it before Jane. "Baby, you just make yourself at home in here, now. Sit back, absorb this place." Lily stepped about her desk and, like a hoodoo priestess on a conversion mission, headed for Jackson's office.

Alone now, it wasn't long before both the walls and hallway resounded with the noise of her neighbor. Jane was trying to focus on the assumption methodology underpinning cost estimates for smoking-related illnesses. But Lily's voice was mixed with Jackson's protestations, his volume even louder now, tone more animated. Words hit the wall like buckets and wrenches—almost all of them Lily's. "Compilation thresholds," she said, which was followed by "first quarterly sign-off." "Brackets" was repeated. Lily was persistent, Jackson defensive.

It was impossible to concentrate. Too, there was too much stuff in this shared working place to absorb—Lily's many family pictures on her bookshelf, the cluttered desk. Not snoop, of course, just absorb. She and Lily—they were, after all, practically roommates.

The console behind Lily's desk caught Jane's attention, the mementos on the top of it: the miniature cannons, the toy monkey with cymbals in its hands, the stack of books on the corner. Jane crossed her legs and stared harder. At the top of the stack was probably a dictionary, a couple of text-books below it and finally the bottom one, a red leather-backed bible. The bottom book *was* a bible, wasn't it?

She stepped into Lily's office and examined the books on the console. The bottom one was indeed a bible, edges frayed, the cover engravings faded. Maybe the bible of Lily's father. He had been a preacher just as Jane's father had been—both men dying young. Strange, but Jane couldn't recall whether her father was a smoker. Closet smoker maybe—the worst kind. Despite their age differences, she and Lily had a great deal in common. Two talkers stepped fast past the doorway, and when Jane glanced up they were already gone.

On Lily's desk—Jane couldn't stop herself—was a bright blue folder. The tab carried her mother's handwriting—*Salon Plans*. It touched her. Lily touched her. This wasn't prying. It was Lily's heart that had called her out here.

The voices were coming louder from Jackson's office. They were draw-ing Jane back to her tiny space. Lily was angry. A chair screeched across the floor. Jane froze.

Lily's desktop was a mess of newspaper clippings and slips of paper, what a busy mother might leave when she's called away from scrapbooking.

Or maybe a grandmother, Jane was thinking when her eyes paused at the name beneath one of the clipped photographs. The picture was carefully taped to a white piece of paper. Preserved it seemed, for some important purpose. Plyer Hoots, someone—probably Lily—had written in sharp jagged letters below the shot.

Jane knew the name. Probably most Atlanta did. Plyer Hoots might someday be family—Jackson's father-in-law. No doubt Lily knew that potential. Indeed, maybe Lily had the inside story. Jane and Price certainly didn't. Never had Jackson offered more than a hint. Of course, Jackson wasn't around enough to offer much more, so all she and Price could do was speculate. "Marrying into money," Price would boast, the pride in his voice hemmed with suspicion and doubt. Or, was it envy? Regardless, Price was usually mystified, motioning his head in pity every time he spoke the name Plyer Hoots. As Price put it more than once, the problem wasn't Plyer's money, per se—it was the hype he spent it on, those do-gooder profiles in newspapers and magazines, the exposure. Price saw Plyer as a tabloid tycoon, less business and more showman. Jane had to agree. Some people, she'd learned over the years, craved acknowledgement—their version of fame—the public to console, to validate their existence, and yes—to make up for misdeeds. The depth of Plyer's hunger for it, though, was excessive. Even to someone who once gloried in the spotlight of a plenary address, Plyer Hoots had a ravenous ego.

Plyer was an electronics guru whose company—as the *Journal-Constitution* sports pages made prominent two years ago—fully funded the Braves scoreboard. In the half-page picture, the StarSat Electronics name flashed its bright yellow letters at the base of the Jumbotron. More substantive, the company donations—mainly to colleges and high schools—were always part of the graduation season news. Plyer and his daughter would pose with one scholarship recipient after another. Neighborhood news usually, yet Plyer's face always suggested he craved the publicity anyway he could get it.

Lily had taped other newspaper clippings to white printer paper. On one page Jackson was hugging Plyer's daughter Daisy. Nice girl, but a little standoffish, maybe because she went to Cornell Law School. "Ithaca," she always called it. It was a kind of New York aloofness that, in Jane's mind, operated on the level where limos picked you up and the drivers were quiet and intense because what you read in *People* magazine mattered and Mother Teresa was, after all, a virtual saint—God bless her. That was Jane's take on Daisy—the hyped-up do-gooder detachment of a hifalutin' lawyer eager to be something she's not. To Jane, both Plyer and Daisy looked as though they had something to hide. "Maybe so," Price would say, shaking his head and snickering as he added, "Ithaca."

The sounds were coming loud but choppier from Jackson's office. Seemed as if Lily might storm out any minute. Lily's cluttered desk—so much was there. On one piece of paper, at the top of the page, Lily had circled the name Plyer Hoots. An ink line fell from Plyer's name to two offspring circles, one labeled Atlanta, the other Newark. DAISY, the name all capital letters, occupied a side circle at the bottom of the page, a hashed line connecting her to her father Plyer.

"Hoots," Jane was now hearing from Jackson's office. Lily was saying something about Plyer Hoots walking the halls. It felt a bizarre coincidence, a set up. Had Lily intentionally left these things face up on her desk? Jane hurried back to her makeshift cubicle, stared into her computer screen, and listened as the voices went at each other.

Of course, she hadn't been snooping. Not at all. It was Lily's generous heart or maybe God who had called her to Lily's desk. She had simply been stretching her legs, which was true, and what was also true was that the privileged information she'd found on Lily's desk and heard through the walls was secure in her mind, just as the ethics section of the computer tutorial said yesterday: "Privileged communication must not be taken outside its context, nor disclosed without clearance from the communications staff." Everything Jane saw and heard would not be taken out of context and, if asked, she wasn't sure of the existence of any of it, which was completely true. A bizarre coincidence, and that's the truth.

The sound of pacing—Jackson no doubt, Lily on his heels. Wheels squealed and from the walloping of springs, odds were that Jackson had taken to his chair.

"You told me," Lily said, her voice so dramatic she clearly wanted it heard by more than one person. "Last week, you told me you'd put an end to this."

Something thumped. A book, thought Jane, a book on his desk.

"No more," Lily continued. "I'm not waiting one minute more. Sent each and every one of those checks back to Plyer Hoots just like I told you I would."

"Listen," Jackson insisted, laughter on his breath, "probably a simple mistake. You know Plyer."

"Bundling," Lily said, almost growling.

Bundling was a political word, so Jane scratched the word *bundling* on a notepad in haphazard letters because it sounded like something a staffer should write in a way that no one would recognize.

"Out-of-state, Jackson. You hear me? Not only bundled, every one of those checks came with an out-of-state address."

"The guy's connected—what can I say?" Jackson sounded like he had much more to say, just not to Lily.

"Well, I tell you this—no way am I about to let them say I put up with bundling, especially when it's—"

"Like I said," Jackson snapped, "a simple mistake. That's all it was."

Another thump, another creak of springs. Lily's voice came on the rove. "Out . . . of . . . state, Jackson. Reporters. Reporters would stab these checks with a steak knife and then they'd eat us alive. You hear me?"

Jane felt stuck, manipulated. She was sitting in a closet and absorbing, just as Lily wanted, as Lily maybe planned. Lily repeated the question, this time even louder. "Out . . . of . . . state, you hear me?"

Yes, Jane wanted to yell to the wall. Yes, Lily. I hear you. But Jane stopped, for she was listening to questions not directed to her. She was eavesdropping. So, no was the answer. No, Lily. I don't hear you at all. No,

I never did. The word on her notepad was indecipherable. She was glad it was.

"Trust me," boomed Jackson from a mouth that had to be smiling, "Momentum doesn't stop at the state line."

"It by God does," answered Lily, "when I've warned you before about Plyer's money."

"And by that same God," Jackson said, his voice light but falling, "consider it fixed, done."

Feet stomped. A drawer thundered shut. Jane imagined Lily closed it, but then it could have been Jackson, maybe God. But it most definitely wasn't God who soon rushed past the doorway to Lily's office while mumbling something about a judicial briefing. Of that, Jane had no doubt. For once she rolled her chair to where she could see the door to the hallway, she saw no one, but smelled the odor of chewing gum and the suspicious edge of newly printed money.

Perhaps it was that odor that kept Lily's attention because her head was still fixed in the direction of Jackson's exit when she entered the doorway. But she quickly turned, pronging her shoulders high at the sight of Jane. Music tinkled from the telephone station in the great room, soft ridiculous beach blanket music. Within the air of that sick low sound, the eyes of Jane and Lily met, the connection demanding silence, respect for what Lily had wanted Jane to hear. That Jane had heard it didn't need to be said. She had not only heard it, she had pictured the kind of faces that went with the names.

"Baby, I had to lay it on the line."

"Bundling seems serious."

"Going too deep in Plyer Hoots' business dealings is the real problem. What Jackson doesn't understand is that in a shallow world like ours, looks matter an awful lot." Lily stepped into her office, lifted the folder that contained the plans for the Delta Salon from her desk. She opened the folder, inspected a page, then stilled as her eyes went blank. "Your momma knew more about looks than any person I've ever known." Lily stood within the thought's comfort before shifting her focus to Jane. "That's what a beauty shop teaches you—the importance of looks. And that lesson may seem silly, but this old woman's had enough crap dumped on her head to know that looks can change the world. Your momma—she sure healed mine." Lily stepped around her desk, sank into her chair, and sighed like a much older woman. "Nothing illegal about bundling, but it sure as hell looks bad."

"And Hoots?"

"Plyer Hoots knows exactly what he's doing." Lily diverted her eyes to the clump of papers scattered over her desk as if she couldn't explain much more while looking at Jane. "Business," Lily said. "We gotta' make sure these business arrangements don't pull us under." She fiddled with the newspaper clippings, slipping all of them into a single folder. "And that Jackson—we gotta' watch him too. We do." Lily didn't wait for a response, just turned and clicked on her computer, then yelled like a woman finally beginning a much better day. "Baby, that health department program sounds like a winner to me. Go for it."

✦ ◉ ✦

A COUPLE OF NIGHTS LATER, A THUNDERSTORM LASTED throughout the meal of Thai takeout. Jane welcomed the storm, the rattling windows and waves of rain, she and Price safe and talking at home, a bad winter departing with one thunderous send-off, a new season in its wake. Tulips from carrots and roses from radishes—they ate it all and talked of her first few days in the campaign and the beautifully sliced peppers that were too hot to eat. The wine was white and dry, the curry sauce more lime than lemongrass green. The week was leaving with exotic tastes and small victories that proved even a missed diagnosis just might have been a part within God's great plan.

Now upstairs in bed, they were into late-night reading, thunder gone but the rain relentless, a breeze sometimes whipping fat raindrops against the windows. On Jane's side of the bed, the light from a distant streetlight bejeweled the windowpane. The world was ready for a new season, so she repositioned her head and focused on a new section of the tobacco white paper called, "Political Ramifications."

Once again, more text than tables, important numbers embedded among trivial legislative bill enumerations. When everything is important, nothing is important. But Jane did like the lengthy history, the call to action within the word *you*. She repeated some facts and figures in her brain, imagined how she might spit out so many numbers before a crowd, *you* would know what *you* had to do on Election Day. She imagined telling Hank Cowley all about the science of backdoor campaigning.

"I've heard more from Jackson in the last few days than I've heard in years," she told Price, who lay supine at her side. Her husband hummed an acknowledgment, shifted the papers in his hands to better catch the bedside lamplight.

Jane lifted her head from the pillow, squinted to see the names of the Georgia counties where tobacco farming was still important, thirty-five of them, a two-hundred-million-dollar crop in 2002. "Price, you wouldn't believe how often your brother can tell the same joke over and over. And that laugh, it never changes." She paused, considered the other things she'd heard, including Lily's admonition. What she couldn't recall for sure were Lily's exact words, the ones that came at a point when she was preoccupied with the mess on her desk. "We need to watch that boy"—those were the concluding words Jane heard. She was sure of it. And whether Lily said them with her voice or with her eyes, Jane couldn't recollect for sure, but the directive had come, and it seemed like something that shouldn't be repeated. So she said, "And he can have quite the temper on the telephone."

When her husband said nothing, Jane rolled over on her side to face him directly. Price smiled to her, sank his head lower on the pillow and returned to staring at the details of what the government expected in a contract. The Homeland Security specifications had arrived this morning. Caught everyone off guard, sent people home with a mandate to digest the details.

For days, Price had said nothing of the eyeglass case or the motorcycle. Untouched, they sat in the places where he'd left them, the little case turning holy on the bedroom dresser, the motorcycle leaning like a drunk in the garage. Outside the breakfast room window, every morning the Bradford pear bloomed.

Price braced the document on his bare chest. To her preoccupied husband Jane said, "Should be quieter next week. Jackson introduces me to the group on Monday, then he's out a few days."

Price rattled a page, tightened his grip. "They want an eight-hour turnaround once a sample arrives. Damn," he moaned. "Incredible."

Jane touched his shoulder. "Are you sure you're fine with me spending so much time downtown?"

"Why wouldn't I be? Alex is ahead of schedule." He jostled the document before her face. "Think you can give this thing a look?"

"Sure. Take far less than eight hours, promise."

"You campaign folks must be scheduling the be-Jesus out of Jackson. He called today, wants to get together even earlier next Saturday, about six."

"On a Saturday?"

"Said Alice turned the day upside down, called it a big fucking deal."

"Price, he didn't?"

"Caught me off guard." He paused, moved his eyes back to the contract document and snorted. "Made me think something was different." His voice suggested disbelief, some uncertainty directed at Jackson or maybe the contract offer. One or the other, Jane couldn't tell.

"Saturday is the big day," she told him. "Rollout for the education program. They're all nervous."

Price looked her in the eye as if to learn more about what he might expect on Saturday, whether Jackson might be stressed or moody, the conversation pointless, what might be different. Actually, there wasn't much more she could say about Jackson's mood or the education proposals or the rollout plan for Saturday. She'd been too busy with tobacco. But she had learned a few quirky facts from the education chatter behind the walls. "Did you know," she asked him, "that only a little more than half of the kids who start public schools graduate from high school?"

"Yes." He turned flat of his back once more, the contract document again receiving his full attention.

She also turned to lay supine, dropped the tobacco report on her stomach and practiced her facts. "Well, when it comes to cigarette taxes, did you know that Georgia's are so low, we're forty-eighth in the nation?"

"No."

Jane roused up on her pillow, flapped the tobacco report before his face. "Want to read it?"

"No."

Price rolled to his left side, away from her, and mumbled something about eight hours. She examined more of the tobacco report, the many annotations in the appendix, the smaller print.

"Price, this would turn your stomach."

"What would?"

She began to quote a footnote, word for word. "Over the past twenty years, the Georgia Tobacco Growers Association has successfully fought every cigarette tax proposal brought before the legislature. In 2003, the association tamped down a new tax bill by conflating its purpose with the state flag controversy." She paused, launched a voracious shiver, and called the whole thing a stomach-turner.

"What turns my stomach," he said, "is an eight-hour turnaround."

Jane resumed her quote from the tobacco report, this time louder. "Floyd Devereaux, the president of the Georgia Tobacco Growers Association, called the newly approved state flag 'nothing but a spit-rag' when he announced the group's support for reinstating the 1956 version, which contained the controversial Confederate battle banner." She made a gagging sound, exaggerating her affectation. She wanted her husband to share in the disdain, to signal his support.

Price grumbled something that sounded like an agreement, some guttural rumble that seemed in sync with the rain and his opinion of the contract specifications. It was a feeble response but enough, for she was tired. She sank her shoulders deeper on the pillow and tried to hear more of the rain. She gazed at the ceiling fan, the air turning above her. Never had she asked Price, never had she planned to do so. Yet he'd been there, kneeling at the bedside, her mother's left hand in his hand. He'd called the ambulance, helped the men move her body to the gurney. He was quiet tonight, caught up in too many new numbers to worry about old moments.

"Price, back when my mother was taking her last breaths, do you think she knew we were there?"

"Sure." His shoulder blades were in her face.

"And do you think our being there made it harder for her?"

"Harder?

"You know, harder to leave?"

Jane swallowed many complex words as she waited for an answer. To not sound silly or superstitious had been her goal and it seemed to have worked, at least to her ears. Her husband didn't answer, the silence occupied only by the drumming of raindrops on the front porch overhang. "Harder to die?" she asked, her eyes closing at the sound of those words. Those words, the mention of death, the idea of it, didn't belong in this bed, nor this air. The words belonged to the air that condensed into a translucent being above her mother's body, the air that held her mother's soul in its awful struggle. Jane could see it still above the bed, the incomplete work, the unbelievable in this world alive, there.

"I think we did the best we could do." He was speaking to a government document.

"And when she took her last breath, did you notice it?"

"I saw the breath, I think. The last one."

His answer carried a weighty tone and also a hint of fear, as though he couldn't speak of something he might never explain. He was tense and when Jane said nothing more and the rain came louder, the wall of her husband's shoulders jostled a little but held as he flipped more pages.

She turned away from Price to that window where raindrops were collecting on the pane, the amber from the streetlamp and garden lights illuminating the glass in prismatic waves that solidified into golden curtains that glistened before they parted. And from those shimmering drapes, her mother stepped out. Her mother for sure, alive and almost posing, one eye on the verge of a wink. Her hair, that frosted wedge, was tussled in spots just as she'd worn it at the inaugural ball three years ago. And the dress, what her mother had proudly called a loud-ass white-and-crimson swirl, the long slinky dress that Jane had actually dared her to wear—there that dress was and her mother was in it, grinning again.

Jane held motionless, her focus fixed as her mother tipped her head and pulled a cigarette from the air. She drew the delicious thing to her puckered lips, sucked hard then exhaled. And as the smoke ascended to the point where the windowpane stopped, she began to inspect the cigarette's orange tip. It was a contemptuous look, a sour smile. Soon the smoke was gone, and the woman whose soul almost never left this earth stood solemn. She raised her head, dropped the cigarette, and winked to her daughter as if she knew what Jane was doing, as if a missed diagnosis really didn't matter now, as if it never really had. The motion was a confirmation, an assurance, a sight that Jane wanted to believe was real. She chilled as a breeze whipped more rain against the window, her mother dissolving among the wet patina that clung to the glass once most of the running drops were gone.

Uncle

THE NAMES CAME FAST. ONE AFTER ANOTHER—introductions just for her, first from all the people sitting at the conference room table, then from all those clumped like steerage shipments in chairs that lined the walls. The voices were tart, staffers all but strapped in place, backs straight, feet braced. Indeed, on a quick look, the boardroom could have passed for an overpopulated aircraft cabin, the buckled-up crew in the midst of an immense lift-off.

Jackson sat at the head of the table, the candidate white-shirted and snappish, his head nodding in curt approval as each face announced its name. Silky blue stripes raced through his tie, the knot loose in a way that suggested he knew rules were simply guidelines. To Jackson's right sat Alice, the campaign manager scribbling fast in her notepad. Lily, just to Jackson's left, kept her attention on a laptop screen. This was the trio piloting the great airship—Jackson, Alice, and Lily—the proudly vocalized name of each steerage passenger lifting the jet ever higher.

Jane was sitting in a chair against the wall and wishing, much to her amazement, she was closer to the table. Matching the many names to faces was, of course, the new-girl challenge, one Jackson made clear when he joked to her at the end of the roll call, "The test is coming."

"So cheat!"

The yell came from a wiener-lipped man who, having shared his opinion, gaveled a fat fist to the table.

"Or gamble," squealed an unidentifiable voice.

"Okay, enough!" Jackson said, waving the team down with his hands. He stood, moved to the white drawing board behind the head of the table and set the Senior Leadership Team meeting fully aloft in the agenda. "The SLIT team meeting," Lily had called the weekly gathering, adding, "The *I* is for *idiot*, meaning Roland. You'll see." Little doubt Roland was the guy with the wiener lips.

TOBACCO, Jackson wrote on the board, his left hand dabbing out the letters in fierce strokes before he turned back to the crowd, anything but a smile in his voice. "Like I told you last week, Jane has important insights on tobacco and the healthcare business community, so when she comes to talk, listen up. Thanks to her, we've secured a key group." His features softened as the sound of success wafted through the air, his demeanor almost magically transformed by an erupting core of what everyone could tell was boyishness, the vigor of boyishness. "She's also my sister-in-law, so be gentle—and that's an order."

"A wake-up order!" whooped the wiener-lipped man. The crowd turned to him. Lily grimaced. Roland for sure, Jane guessed, the SLIT team's pointless *I*.

Jackson ignored it all, sketched the word *REPURPOSE* on the board. With a deliberate, almost sadistic hand, he dragged an arrow from *REPURPOSE* to *TOBACCO,* nodding with pride to the connection. He spun about. "Loraine, I want you to meet with Doctor Jane right after this meeting. You need to learn what *REPURPOSE* might mean for our tobacco farmers." Jackson's eyes were fixed on a thin weathered woman in a sleeveless navy turtleneck, who robotically grabbed at her larynx, first with the right then the left hand. She had a religious look about her, long dark hair drawn down her back in a kind of Holy Roller ponytail. "Loraine here," Jackson explained, "is in charge of outreach to the farmers." He switched looks between Loraine and Jane. "Loraine, repurposing tobacco belongs in our rural technology improvement plan." He raised his eyes as if to address the crowd's higher thoughts. "That's right. Someday technology might even salvage our tobacco farms."

Alice was shaking her head in complete disbelief.

"Oh, we've been talking," Loraine said as she motioned to Jane, the statement somewhat true because she and Jane had exchanged one-word greetings in the hallway last week.

"But like I've also said," Jackson instructed, "our focus is far, far from tobacco." He turned back to the board and slashed a long streak through TOBACCO. A glow came to Alice's face.

"Amen," shouted Roland.

Jackson rotated to the happy Alice and stared. The stare was a powerful one, one Jane first took to mean the campaign manager had to do something about Roland, but it actually proved a cue for Alice to speak because she jumped to her feet and began to cluck. "Folks, I want you district captains to make sure an education push-package is hand-delivered to every newspaper, radio, and television station by noon next Thursday. Hand-delivered, Roland." She hesitated, scanning the faces. "And what's the main pitch?"

Alice hawk-eyed the group, her fists resting on her substantial hips as every captain at the table took a hasty breath and shouted in unison, "Community college no more than one county away." Alice churned her head in approval. "Alright now. And remember to email me a copy of your signed-off checklist by Thursday, close of business. Got that?"

Alice didn't want an answer, given that she quickly slashed a big X-mark in the air and motioned with her head to the slashed-out TOBACCO word. "Now that we're putting this nasty threat to sleep, we build some real publicity."

Lily huffed, defiantly. "To sleep? Since when?"

"Later," Alice said, grinning to everyone but Lily as she returned to her seat.

While Lily and Alice battled each other with eyes and snarls and Jackson moved on to other agenda matters, Jane seethed. Tobacco was no sleeper issue. Tobacco was the leading cause of death in this state. Alice was clueless. Alice was the enemy. She was a thing to be worked around, an obstacle to be jumped. And Alice was the head of this team, this SLIT she'd just entered?

Jackson was talking of his education plan, but Jane couldn't follow him. Her eyes kept going to Alice, her thoughts doing their best to stay on an even keel, where every experienced part of her brain was arguing that Alice meant well. Alice was no obstacle. She was simply a banty hen, the jumpiest bird in the coop, the one whose neck was most vulnerable to being wrung or pinched apart by an eagle's claw. This was the most logical reason for Alice's jumpiness, Jane assured herself, probably the reason Alice kept pulling at the collar of her blouse.

More subjects followed education, including a brief dialogue on privatization of the state's prison management, which would require legislation but could be tied into an omnibus bill that better funded a statewide four-lane highway plan. On the tail of that discussion came Roland. "I've been told," he said with good-ole-boy bluster, "that the long-distance truckers' union might soon endorse McGee."

Roland's lips hung damp and drippy as his last word—*McGee*—levitated for a moment before it sank to the middle of the table and pooled there like an environmental hazard. From that ominous muck of an idea back to Roland, rancid looks came.

"No way," the wiener-lipped staffer boomed, lunging forward to wave down the faces. "I'll talk to those guys, get this fire put out." Roland fixed his arms about a plump imaginary hose and started to douse the circle of flaming faces before wedging his bulky shoulders back between his neighbors.

Jackson, now seated at the table, pulled a stick of gum from his shirt pocket and started chewing, shaking his head at the bumbling Roland and sometimes eyeing Alice. Soon Jackson was tapping the tabletop with a central trio of jumpy fingers that accelerated to a frenzy then abruptly stopped.

"Folks, following the Lung Association example, I want you to think of any and all groups that can be added to our endorsement portfolio." A profound silence fell. One staffer closed her eyes, paling impressively as if she knew something important was coming. The candidate placed both hands on the table, palms down. It was a curiously somber act, one that commanded attention perhaps not because of what might follow the gesture but rather, as Jane could so clearly see, because of his total commitment to it. The time for thinking had come. Endorsements were critical. Heads bowed as Jackson's eyes patrolled the subdued group. He chewed his gum and, at the conclusion of the inspection, he also lowered his gaze to the table as if in prayer. A kind of prayer circle, Jane guessed, some quaint team ritual. Jackson's mother would have liked this managerial ceremony, his spiritual style.

Hushed seconds passed until, on the tail of the low ticking cortege, Roland sighed. The solemn Jackson drew his hands back to his sides, a gesture prompting heads to rise. In the room's slow reanimation, a great flurry of doves suddenly skittered up from the center of the table and even though only Jane could see them, the whole crowd seemed to know that they had arisen, these miraculous vote makers ready to swoop all over the state and return with ribbons of endorsements in their beaks.

The inspired speakers began, staffers fully tanked, a kind of verbal scrimmaging erupting with hums and seconding cheers at tossed-out ideas and names. Jackson refereed the pile-up of potential support groups by scribbling acronyms for unions and associations one by one on the board. Clearly, endorsements were a big fucking deal. Jackson didn't say that, but Jane imagined he could have.

Jane also imagined a better use for the Lung Association's white paper, its objective redirected to focus squarely on the target that mattered, the Georgia Tobacco Growers Association. She had an idea. She had an idea that Loraine Delery could help make a reality. After all, Loraine was not only the agricultural outreach captain but also the daughter of a one-time Colquitt County Tobacco Festival queen. It was a gossipy fact Jane picked up on another phone call with the health department's Nancy Currier. Seemed Loraine's family—the Delerys—once had vigorous tobacco-growing roots in southwest Georgia, a legend of influential connections. If Jane could bring a first-ever endorsement from the Lung Association, what was to keep her from accomplishing the same unbelievable feat with the old boys who called themselves the Georgia Tobacco Growers Association?

◆ ⊙ ◆

THE DOOR WAS CLOSED. TWO TAPED-UP POSTERS of row crops occupied a wall, one corn the other soybeans, bright yellow identifiers and logos for seed companies in the bottom corners where weed-free dirt blurred to a mahogany smear.

Loraine Delery sat behind her desk, a threatened look in her eyes. "Tobacco farming has been tanking for years in this state," Loraine said, gliding her face forward as she spoke. Jane scooted her chair closer to the desk, aligning herself for a full face-off. It was easy to picture the dour Loraine at the high wheel of a cotton picker or soybean combine, those eyes undaunted by the many acres yet to be covered. Loraine's left hand rested on her throat while the other one held ready to record every word Jane spoke on a long yellow notepad. Loraine was a piece of equipment, reluctant but engaged, her row crop wheels turning and her processing belts spinning, so Jane started.

"Any idea why the Tobacco Growers Association became so active in state politics?"

"Old bunch," Loraine answered, vacillating a second. "In the news, you mean?"

"The flag fiasco, don't you remember?"

"No."

"Little over a year ago."

"Must have been during the drought." Loraine focused on the words she'd written, circling some and marking through one.

Jane sensed success, the offense. She crouched down to ladle up Loraine's eyes. "The Georgia Tobacco Growers Association waylaid the new cigarette tax by tying it to the flag controversy. Remember?"

"Old money," said Loraine. "I think the group has an endowment."

"You think?"

"Yes, I . . . uh, think they do."

Loraine wrote more fiercely, her attention shifting between the page and Jane. "No," said the agriculture outreach captain. "I know they do. Floyd Devereaux's been the president for years. Big man in Moultrie." Loraine greened, scribbling circles with her ballpoint pen. "But what," she whined, "about this repurposing business?"

"Re-engineering tobacco," said Jane, who saw her words turning into perky shorthand on the page. "Bioengineering will take years. But an endorsement might take—" She reached over and yanked the pen from Loraine's fingers. Jane couldn't believe what she was doing, but her body was in an automatic mode, her muscles eager. She couldn't stop the impulse. So she went with her instinct, placing the pen on the desktop, insistently. Within Loraine, it seemed every John Deere wheel and cylinder had stopped. Green soon meshed with yellow, crank with cog, and once some power seemed to stall inside her field-worn body, Loraine began to creak.

"Off the record," said Jane. "How about us just talking as girls. You know, girl to girl?"

Loraine batted her eyes.

Jane took it as agreement, so she rested her elbows on the desk, steepled her hands to support her chin. "Moultrie's home, isn't it?"

Loraine nodded, a tiny dip.

"And you probably know Floyd Devereaux. Right?"

Once more, a confirmatory nod. Something unsaid was expanding in the air, something so big and quick the office walls seemed ready to give. As if alarmed by the danger and the need for some motion that might deflate the pressure, Loraine undid the ribbon that bound her brunette strands to the nape of her neck. She shook her head, flopped a hand through the liberated hair. "Uncle Floyd," she said. "Jackson doesn't know."

Jane wanted to write that relationship down, but she remembered they were talking as girls, everything in the air and nowhere else. "So Floyd Devereaux, the man who called the new state flag a spit-rag, is your uncle?"

"Great uncle, actually." Loraine unhitched her shoulders with a good shake, almost wiggling as she spoke. "In girl talk, though, that's not really kin, now is it?"

"Of course not. Think Uncle Floyd and his boys might endorse a really fine candidate for governor? Say, Jackson Beekman?"

"Doctor . . ." Loraine was teased but almost euphoric.

"Call me Jane."

Loraine picked up her ballpoint pen, held it close like a precious toy. "Jane," she said, "the Georgia Tobacco Growers Association has less than a thousand members." She tilted her head, as if in apology. "It's tiny."

"But a big name can carry a tiny thing far. Look at Bush."

"Wicked," Loraine howled. She reached over and slapped Jane's shoulder. "Girl, we can't let the old devil get the best of us!" Down went the pen to the desk.

"So, have you asked him yet?"

Loraine wilted. "Tobacco is no headline," she said. "Didn't you hear Alice?" The agriculture outreach captain looked at the words she wasn't making on her notepad and to the absence, she blinked several times before returning to Jane. "Why in the world would a tobacco grower support a man who raises cigarette taxes?"

"Credibility," Jane said, now confident that Loraine was on her side. "Tobacco growers have lost the battle and they know it. So they're turning to the public battles they can win—the flag, for one."

"But Jackson?"

"Like I said—credibility. A Beekman endorsement gives them credibility, makes them relevant for the future, maybe a comeback. When it comes to repurposing, tobacco growers can't be all that crazy."

"Well, Uncle Floyd . . . he is, you know, a little . . . " Loraine raised her head, circled a finger about her ear. "Well, let's just say Uncle Floyd is sometimes . . . not quite right."

Of course he's not right, and that's a good thing, went the fast thought inside Jane. This was a thought that no shortage of outreach captains would likely call insane, but also one that might accomplish far more than repurposing tobacco ever could. An endorsement by the Georgia Tobacco Growers Association might do far more than put any tobacco issues to rest, it might sway more good ole Georgia boys than Roland ever could. And given the elbowing power of all the good ole boys in this state, that bloc alone might tip the election.

❖ ◉ ❖

JANE AND LILY STOOD CHATTING IN THE doorway of Lily's office, both talking fast because Lily had a one-on-one shortly with the boss. They stared down the hallway. As always, the door to Jackson's office was open, shadows and bodies, hurried motions and voices. He was pacing about his desk, Alice at his back.

Jane dove to the point. "So you think the Georgia Tobacco Growers Association—Floyd Devereaux's group—might endorse Jackson?" As soon as she said it, she wished she could take back the tone, rework the question to end it in a more uplifting lilt, one that could only be answered in the affirmative—*Of course, he would.* Lily kept looking down the hall, swatting at her chin with a rolled-up piece of paper. Was she even listening? Jane repeated her question, this time louder and with the appropriate lilt.

"An endorsement from the Georgia Tobacco Growers Association would be a headliner, don't you think?" Jane locked her attention tighter on the preoccupied finance chairwoman. "A major headline. Right?"

Lily jerked. As if some jack beneath her body just slipped, some awareness just pained. She placed the paper beneath her arm, reached out and grabbed Jane by the cheeks, giving each jowl a wiggly pinch. "Now, that's audacity in action, your momma's audacity!"

Lily's scent was strong with the burnt orange odor of *Caesar's Woman*, the cologne a favorite, the all-time favorite of Jane's mother. Her mother used to order *Caesar's Woman* by the six-pack from the Las Vegas casino shop, the scent from the boxes bedewing the gifts beneath the salon's old pink-frocked Christmas tree in an exotic—what the labels called alluring—mystery. Jane's gaze went blank at the recollection, for the odor was a sign, an omen. It was, of course, a silly thought. But she had to believe it was a signal that she was on the right path, an assurance from God, or more importantly, her mother.

"Not saying it's impossible," Lily asserted, her eyes turned once more down the hallway. Alice was marching from Jackson's office, her heels making sharp, confident noises. Lily rotated back to Jane. "Baby, ask old Hank Cowley about Floyd. They've been going at each other for years."

The finance chief smoothed the lapels on Jane's blouse, admiring the stitches before she turned again to Jackson's office. Far down the hall, the candidate stood in the open doorway of his suite, one finger pointed to Lily, the tip of it wiggling like a worm.

Shamu

COME TWILIGHT, THE FAR SHORE of the Chattahoochee River was lost among the cypress overgrowth, a smudge of thickets on the horizon, the approaching night like workings within a bad cloud. At the bistro on the river's higher bank, Jackson was ensconced in an alcove with Daisy Hoots, their table surrounded on the dining room side by ceiling-to-floor burgundy curtains, all velvet and tightly drawn. Riverside, the alcove was walled completely in glass, the dining spot virtually suspended over the water. One level below them, spotlights illuminated the part of the river that lapped gently beneath a dock. Deep mucky green, then silver, then dull green all over again. From the dock, a young girl tossed crumbs to the water. Jackson could see the girl, and in a way he could hear her laughter, muffled as it was by the fish that bobbed up for the crumbs and soon started chomping. He could also hear Daisy talking, but he couldn't tell what she was saying because the fish were too loud, too busy masticating the handouts that hit the water. Pointless circles they were making, all that bobbing and rowdy chomping. These fish were the superficial kind of politicians who changed nothing, the kind he was not. A few surface crumbs may need to be swallowed to win an election, but once you've won it, you don't need to keep biting at the surface; you dive deep, create undercurrents that reshape the shore, and in the process, the geography of a great state. Real power, as any successful politician knows, operates far below the surface of what people see.

Jackson Beekman was a deep politician. He had deep plans. And any crumbs that he must snap up to win an election would be dragged to the world's deeper parts and digested in silence until every calorie within that energy went to the good of all. Bobbing at the surface time and again changed nothing. That he could see clearly. In time, everyone would.

Daisy kicked his ankle and raised her voice. "Enhanced, Jackson." And again but even louder, "*Enhanced* enterprise zones, E-E-Zs." He turned to her, the fish still smacking their loud fishy lips, still chomping inside his head. "We need to talk more E-E-Zs," she admonished.

"*We* need to talk?"

"Yes, *we*." She picked up the knife, coaching him with it. "*We* need the eminent domain authority, so we need to start at least mentioning E-E-Zs. Otherwise, the warehouses are impossible. Don't tell me you've forgotten what Daddy said."

"But so soon?"

"The demand, Jackson. We balk, and the center tanks. In a speech or two, just start dropping the letters. E-E-Z—it and it only gives us the authority." She smeared a crusty piece of bread with herb-speckled butter.

"Well, sometimes I think *we* already have all the authority *we* need." He said nothing more, his attention meandering back to the window.

Daisy couldn't hear the fish chewing, but he could. And she knew it. Daisy knew he could hear sounds coming from this world's murky parts, that he knew those sounds were saying something provocative, if not good, so of course she turned to gaze out the window to see what she was missing.

Daisy's hair was blond, long, and limp, her face devoid of those tiny wrinkles about the eyes that, by their mid-thirties, most women have pretty much accepted as impossible to hide. She was tall and lean, did yoga by kudzu-scented candlelight, sometimes in the nude with a private instructor and a couple of her long-legged girlfriends, and sometimes him. In her penthouse twenty stories up, there he stood and stretched—Jackson in gym shorts despite Daisy's insistence that he needed to commune raw with the spirit. Designer suits in beige linen fit her well, slacks when she was working on contracts for her father, long modest business skirts for charity event evenings with Jackson downtown. Tonight, it was a sleek ivory cocktail dress, a necklace of aqua-tinted sea glass. Sea glass was a favorite of hers, and his also, what he encouraged her to wear. To be seen with a woman adorned in sea glass let the world know the kind of couple they truly were. The stones illustrated what time and persistence could do to an otherwise undesirable thing. That's the kind of couple they were. They were in this world to make it better; they were together for the beauty in things that endure because they change.

Daisy was, in one word, clean. She understood how beauty—nobility even—might come from a power moving far below the dirty surface of things. Drive, persistence, and, above all, no fear of getting dirty—these were the guiding principles of the Hoots family business. To Daisy, her daddy's deep business model was more than legitimate; it was critical, given the flatlining of the printed circuit board industry and the ever-growing number of small tech companies about to go under. Which meant, when it came to subsurface product diversity, Plyer Hoots was the East Coast king. High-quality products, like miniaturized computer hard drives and just about anything that could be shipped in boxes designed for Walkmans or cellphones, all clean and convenient, thanks to subterranean enterprising. Politicians could learn quite the lessons from watching Plyer Hoots. Jackson had. The Hoots business model was one of the main reasons Jackson was attracted to Daisy. She knew how a sinking soul could, despite all, rise up clean. She knew how the process worked, while Jackson knew why. Together, they had to thrive.

Daisy smiled at him even though she obviously couldn't see or hear the river's deep green justice like he did. Still, she appreciated his ability to perceive such sights and sounds. She valued it—that's what the flicker in her eyes said. She valued his ability to see things way below the muddy surface, to hear the core sounds, so she fixed her attention on him once more, sliding her tongue over her lips to lick away any hint of doubt. It looked so pleasurable, the way her tongue went before him. He felt his eyebrows rise and an urge take over, for he was ready to climb back up to her surface. This was the other reason he found her attractive: Daisy regarded most of his urges as laughable matters. So, without a second thought, he lifted his chin and said, "Not only do we need a new international terminal at Hartsfield, we need a perimeter of enhanced enterprise zones—E-E-Zs." He opened his mouth to her, fishlike.

Daisy struck a demure but serious pose as she tore a plug of bread from the small loaf on the linen-draped board. She rolled the bread between her palms to form a ball. Jackson opened wider. She aimed and tossed. Ka-ching! Jackson chomped and suddenly about him dark river waves erupted, the great tumbling surface soon catching Daisy, the passing tide leaving her head bobbing in fantastic disbelief.

"Oh, please," she implored, eyes rolling.

He waved his hands like flippers. "Woman, you doubt my sincerity?"

"Yes, Shamu. I doubt you." She twisted a playful finger against her cheek as if to tighten something within her jaw that must be screwed back into place. And once the problem was secured, she offered up a fixed business face. She told him, "I need you to make sure our tech platform includes small business enterprise zones, enhanced ones, okay?"

"Okay."

A doubtful pout appeared. "So what kind of enterprise zones are featured in our tech plan?"

"Enhanced." Again, his mouth was a perfect fish hole. She palmed a plug of bread and once more aimed the ball at his open maw.

"Make the announcement," she commanded, "like you mean it."

He cleared his throat, coarsened his voice, keeping the words sincere as they left his lips. "Enhanced enterprise zones are a key feature of our small business advancement plan."

"Perfect." She tossed the bread ball in a flawless arc.

Again, he caught it with his tongue. And again, he paddled his happy flipper hands. At the sight of what he'd taken from her and where he was bound to go with it, Daisy offered a fabulous sneer. In this little game, the muddy world between them was perfectly content with its less than ideal condition, its deep parts receptive to change. He liked it this way and so did she, so he shook away his fins, added salt to the olive oil there in the fake mollusk shell, and together they dipped and chewed until the waiter, whose nametag said "Larry," stepped in to gaze mindlessly out the window while they pondered the Saint Patrick's Day menu.

Her foot was tinkling. Like chimes, as Jackson heard it, her foot swinging back and forth beneath the table. Her head rocked to the rhythm, whatever she was contemplating seeming to move with it. She was good at self-amusement, so good it sometimes made him feel paternalistic toward her, his role to keep her out of spiritual as well as earthly trouble. He dropped his menu to the table. Outside, the crumbs had ceased, the river surface stilled. He rested his brow on the window to see if the little girl was gone. She was and in her absence, only tattered green shadows occupied the dock. Daisy kicked him again.

"Urban blight, Jackson. I said many businesses—not just StarSat—are eager to create warehouses in blighted areas."

"But Hapeville's not blighted."

She swept the words from the air with her hand, reached over and tapped the tip of his nose. "That's where the E-E-Z comes in. With enhancement, everything's blighted." She exaggerated a happy face, smiling like a squeeze doll with protuberant eyes and projectile ears. "Speaking of blight," she said, "is that ink on your cheek or a zit?" Before he could answer, she licked her fingertip and worked the blemish from his skin. "There, fixed you." He preened his freshly cleaned face before her, one proud cheek then the other. He liked to be fixed by her hands.

The waiter, who had been waiting like a stump, cleared his throat and mentioned how the pasta special was green for the day, homemade with Georgia spinach. He spoke with a sincerity that, as Jackson quickly realized, belied his festive and formal attire: brilliant green cummerbund, matching silk bowtie, a tiny green jewel attached like an asterisk to the last letter on his nametag. Larry suggested the fish instead. Daisy went bubbly at the thought (she was great at going bubbly whenever someone was watching), calling fish perfect, considering. She waved Larry away, the waiter turning as she commanded, his right fist riding tight about his taunt backside as he exited through a part in the curtains. "Larry looks familiar," Jackson said.

"He's new."

"Your foot tinkles."

"Ankle bracelet, Airbus 330s."

"Airbus?"

"Cargo jets—gold charms came with the contract. Can you believe it—just for me?"

"The contract?" Last week Daisy said her father was not going to make any commitments until the election was decided. And now, a contract for Airbus 330s?

Daisy reached over the table, grasped his fingers in her palm and steadied them. He hadn't noticed they were twiddling until then. "Yes, my dear. Daddy wanted me to lock in the fuel prices. With this Iraq mess, you just never know." She lifted her hand to admire her glossy fingernails in the burnt yellow glow of the pendant lamp that hung between them. From his side of the table, the aqua nails were almost phosphorescent, five glittery little creatures that would never hesitate to dive deep. "With you, Governor Beekman, daddy's committed now."

Her foot was moving up his shin, the tinkling gone. Outside, the dock lights had changed colors, the river now more militaristic, camo-dirty. "With the European expansion next month, I'm thinking of throwing a party in Paris," she said, "maybe the Pompidou Center, top floor—George's." She practiced the restaurant's name, dragging out very nasal two-syllable versions of the letters J and Z—"Jhor-jezz. Jhor-jezz."

"Remember July," he said, admonishing her with a dive of his head. "Primary's July the ninth, remember?"

"How could I forget? I'm helping with our high-tech plan, remember?" She kicked his shin, the tinkling Airbus 330s coming faint but prickly clear to his ear. It was a sound he could adjust to, its rhythm the result of a forward-thinking contract, the give and take of deep-water things. Plyer believed in him, completely. This was good news—the money would flow, the election was his, all inevitable because only the deep parts mattered.

The good sounds from Daisy seemed providential because Larry the waiter returned and took the order. He refilled the wine glasses before solidifying his gaze on the river.

"You look familiar," Jackson told him. "Mighty familiar." Larry stepped closer, the waiter assuming a sultry face, one that Jackson had seen plastered to a billboard. Somewhere, definitely had. As Jackson deliberated the location, the waiter's bow tie flared loose and his white shirt melted away leaving strange leathery odors in the air that no doubt Daisy could smell, for her tinkling was growing faster. "You dance?" he asked the waiter.

Larry held steady, his clothes intact. "Sometimes."

"That's it," Jackson declared, "on Boulevard Drive, the billboard. Didn't recognize you with your shirt on."

Larry raised a pleased jaw, one corner of his lips coiling up like that of a man with a price, a nonnegotiable one. "My other job," Larry said, a hint of invitation in his voice.

"Dancing," exclaimed Daisy, jumping to her feet. "We love to dance." She slipped behind Jackson, ran her hands through his hair with profound familiarity. And once the tousling was complete, she arched over to plant a kiss on his lips. A long moan of tasty enchantment arose from her throat, one that Jackson joined, so together the kiss closed with a duet of gleeful moaning agreement. "I'm a good dancer," Daisy told the waiter, "but he's a klutz, especially with his shirt off." She ran a disrupting hand again through Jackson's hair, rustling it like a coy lover before leaning down to kiss the top of his head.

The waiter, who had stiffened and draped a wine towel over his arm, mentioned the halibut.

"Make it two," said Daisy, hands resting on Jackson's shoulders. "Blackened, but rare inside. We both prefer flesh a little raw."

"Of course," the waiter answered, his attention once more solely on the river. "Raw," he repeated and, like that, the billboard star was gone.

"You're so cruel," Daisy chided in baby talk, flattening Jackson's hair with her hands. She returned to her seat, scowled into the leathery scent Larry's presence had left over the table. The noisy little airplanes on her ankle were louder than ever. "The next governor shouldn't tease like that. It's . . ." She studied the options for words, and once she found the right one, looked Jackson firmly in the eye. "Unwise. It's definitely unwise."

To his jet-jiggling, photogenic sea-glass girlfriend, Jackson raised his wineglass, took a sip and told her she was right. These were unwise times. "Lily caught the checks," he said.

The tinkling stopped. "But I told Daddy's guys to do it just like you said. Individual checks, hand signed."

"But with out-of-state addresses? What were they thinking?"

Her face sagged. He hated it when she sagged. He told her, "Lily's sharp. Caught it right away . . ." He tilted his head in disdain. ". . . and as usual, Lily's right. Looks bad."

The sagging Daisy stared at the seedy nub of bread, biting her lips as if she too couldn't believe what those guys had done. Beneath the table, Jackson slipped a foot against her heel, toying with her ankle. He wanted the tinkling back. "Listen, it's easy," he said. "Just tell the guys to use Georgia addresses, in-state only."

She pressed the sea glass rocks to her chest. "Anything else?"

"One check to an envelope."

"Done, my dear governor. The more envelopes the merrier." She pulled at the slim lapel on her dress. "You know Daddy's at it again—more hints about marriage." She looked to the curtain to make sure Larry wasn't working a crack. The drapery was thick and sealed, yet she lowered her voice to a whisper. "He thinks marriage might soften your image. Says all your legal talk makes you come across as just another lawyer." She secured her stylishly hollow temples with her hands. "Daddy gets so worked up about this campaign stuff, sometimes I think he's losing it."

Jackson squeezed her musically charmed foot between his ankles. "Let's do it," he said.

"Do what?"

"Get married."

"Listen, this girl has her limits, remember?" She gave him a defiant jaw. She had the jaws for defiance.

"Careful," he insisted, mocking her by shifting his eyes about in search of that ever-lurking spy. And, of course, she looked also. So majestic, he thought, how she followed his lead. Low about her neck, the glass stones lay clear as the tide on a lazy Caribbean beach. He wanted to dive inside that tide, the water to take her with him, the two of them paddling deep to the spot in the ocean's floor where they might devolve into a tectonic power. They would change the world, and once the world adjusted they would return to the surface, clean and unblemished.

He told her, "You can tell your daddy airport expansion is a given." There was a belittling tone in his voice, and he regretted it because worry was essential to the Hoots business model. Worry kept the clients secure, the money coming. Besides, an international terminal at the airport was important for StarSat Electronics as well as the state's general economy. The plan was a deep-river thing.

Jackson studied her. He could see her trying to explain things to her father, the old man blabbering about simpler days, and, as always, that sermon about NAFTA and the death of American manufacturing, what trade deals have done to his printed circuit board companies. "No wonder people need so much help now," Plyer would insist (to Jackson's ears, the bellyaching never changed). "People need relief any way they can get it." Jackson's eyes fell to the crumbs on the tablecloth. He said, "I'm beginning to think only fools make good fathers."

"Daddy's no fool. And you know it." She feigned a pout. He wasn't looking at her but he could feel the heat of an inflamed pout.

"If you're lucky like me," he said, "your father checks out once the sperm's donated. Self-elimination, the most expeditious thing for the fool to do."

"So, is that why you'll never be a daddy?"

"It's the reason God made people who know better than to procreate."

"Jackson, don't tell me you're now blaming God."

"Trust me. God had nothing to do with me. I made me."

She chuckled in a way that suggested she wasn't sure why she had to, but she had to chuckle. He was glad for her need to do things she didn't understand. It amused him. It seemed an instinct, probably the same kind of fizzy-headed instinct that led to most sperm donations.

Daisy talked more of her daddy's jumpy ways. "Of course he's nervous, Jackson. You know the Mexicans will walk away—Atlanta or nothing." Her cheeks were pink and radiant as the flared gills of a goldfish.

"E-E-Z," he said. "It's the hot new thing in Georgia."

She reached across the table, touching his shoulder as if to declare him the tagged "it" in her special version of the game. She recoiled in outlandish pain. "Whew, you are so hot."

"Hope you think I'm still hot after Saturday night. Lukewarm never does well on Radio Dusty."

"Hmm . . . maybe I'll call in, heat things up!" The words trickled like tiny bubbles out her mouth. "I'll ask about enterprise zones, the kind that matters! Remember the kind?"

"Enhanced."

"Good boy—no spanking for you."

He sighed in great joking disappointment and she did also, for they were professionals when it came to mocking themselves. It was the truth within the logic of people born to go deep, and once that truth was acknowledged with the swap of mutually content looks, Jackson shifted his attention to the river. He leaned closer to the window. When Daisy asked what he saw, he let his voice explode like a hothead on the radio. "Yes siree, folks," he said to the river and all those fish hiding hungry little faces beneath its lapping dirtiness, "It's time to *Caaall Dusty.*"

"Let me, let me!" she shrieked. He turned to her, watching her hands flap like the flippers of a naïve young seal, its mouth agape as though soon above it a fish might dangle.

Slingshot

L ILY SAID HANK COWLEY HAD A new-money kind of mansion— three-story tacky white pillars out front, concrete lions at the gate. But the view from the back porch, she assured Jane, was well worth the drive. On the telephone, Hank sounded like a gravel-voiced curmudgeon who might enjoy some backyard politicking. "Filthy old coots," he'd called the Tobacco Growers Association when Jane mentioned their name. "Never had any use for them. Bunch of fools, no good at all."

She had yet to press the doorbell, but already sharp-toothed growls and scratching were coming from inside the house. She double-checked the time, thought about returning to her car and calling Hank on her cellphone. But just as she turned away, the door cracked and a voice barreled out.

"Slingshot, down!" The dog kept pawing at the base of the door. "Down, you beast! Down!" The doorway widened until a bearish snout appeared, and soon the dog's full wall-eyed head. "You better behave!" The dog whimpered but quieted when the door swung completely back. Suddenly, out lurched a jumpy storm of charcoal-and-white fur, the dog rushing about her legs, its snout breathy and probing, one eye brown, the other blue.

A short egg-shaped man appeared in the doorway, his attention directed to the dog. "Much more of that," he said, "and I'll shoot ya. You hear?" The dog seemed to laugh. The man gestured a pistol and aimed it to the dog, yelling, "Pow!" The dog looked thrilled.

"Mister Cowley?"

"Why Doctor Beekman, sorry 'bout this. Old Slingshot goes wild when he smells a woman." The apologetic man took her hand and steered her inside as the dog circled her legs, sniffing.

Hank Cowley was no smug southern grandfather in a white linen suit. More Delray Beach, Jane thought, the cup-holding-recliner type with a big house on the seventh hole. His shirt was a golfer's tangerine knit, his high-riding trousers tennis-club white. A yellow baseball cap gave him the flare of a cupcake candle. "Call me Hank," he said. "Dahling, the wife's out back, and mighty, just mighty eager to meet you."

The faux Floridian, Humpty Dumpty head of the Georgia Lung Association walked Jane through the great hall, talking the whole way of money, saying things like, "Gulf Coast casinos, hot dodo," and "Sold them all, made 'em pay big." He flung his arms about to dismiss one gold-filigreed mirror after another. "Take a lesson from me," he said. "When it comes to casinos—don't. Someone's bound to be lucky, and odds are it's an old fart like me." At this he touched her arm and pointed to Slingshot, the dog dripping saliva as it laughed at his joke.

The back porch stretched the width of the colossal house. A central sweep of pristine white wooden steps opened to an enormous lawn that glistened green, thanks to what had to have been a recent sprinkle from a concealed system. Weeping willows lined the lawn's perimeter, the leafed-out tendrils forming alcoves for more concrete lions, each chalky casino white. The willows and lions, a pseudo-Greek glamor, seemed perfect company for tobacco talk, a perfect setting for the pitch.

Hank was obsessed with a concoction he called magic tea. He kept talking of its beguiling simplicity as he and Jane settled into high-backed wicker chairs, a table between them holding glasses and a pitcher of his magical mix. Jane pulled a notebook from her satchel and dated a page. Just beyond the base of the steps, Slingshot played a sphinx on the lawn, his goal clearly one of making sure Hank never strayed.

"Revved it up with little more than a touch of vodka." Hank was filling the glasses. "Here, taste it." He watched her sip and swallow.

"Peachy," she said.

"Good. A few more slugs of the stuff and you'll find the world's not the hellhole it looks like. Right, Slingshot?" The dog flopped out its long tongue in a yawn as Hank took a gulp from his glass. "Whew-wee!" he exclaimed once the tea went down. "Dahling, I was tickled pink when Lily told me you'd joined the team." He began to bud and blossom in his chair, both cheeks erupting in a bouquet of fuchsia splotches and cascading venules.

"Science," Jane said. "I'm comfortable with the medical science, but politics is a totally different ballgame."

"A game we're gonna win." Hank lifted his glass of tea in her honor, proceeding to leisurely sip as if convinced of his prophecy. She followed his lead with the tea, careful to barely wet her tongue, for this meeting was meant to accomplish things, not party.

Time was adjusting to Hank's schedule, so together, they sat and watched the lawn and its substantial wall of lions and willows, the bowers where sunlight whiled away. There was a light wind, an occasional gasp from the panting dog, a bristly wheeze from Hank. Neither rumble nor creak came from the house as Jane pictured a petite wife upstairs applying eyeliner and last-minute rouge. Lily had said he liked to show her off. Indeed, Hank Cowley seemed the kind of man who needed the company of a woman who enjoyed looking good when he told her what he wanted her to hear.

Hank crossed his legs and examined his guest. Soon, he stooped forward and again raised his glass to Jane. "Doctor, on behalf of the Georgia Lung Association, I salute you." He took a swig of the tea and swallowed. The dog raised its head. "Mighty good," he boasted. "Drink up now." Jane swallowed more from her glass and both the dog and Hank seem pleased. He positioned his glass on the table and gave one long noisy sigh, which left him practically deflated in his chair. He fixed on the dog. "I want you to meet my wife Alberta. She's heard nothing but good stuff about you."

Jane waited as Hank continued to address the dog. "Alberta," he said, "this fine lady is Doctor Jane Beekman, the new tobacco advisor."

Jane looked around. Alberta was neither at her side nor behind her.

Hank kept going as if Alberta was directly before him. "The doctor's the smart one from the fancy speech last year. Remember?" Hank's face was placid as he spoke to the empty air. He strained his eyes to examine something in the distance. He postured a moment then licked his lips. Jane thought petit mal with oral fixation, so she reached into her satchel for the cellphone in case he came to the need for 911. The threat of a seizure vanished, though, when Hank swiped a hand over his lips and gestured to the dog with his head. "Buried her out there," he said, "beneath Slingshot." At the sound of its name, the dog placed its head on its paws as though humbled by a compliment. "Dug the hole myself," he added, "six foot down and completely legal. Slingshot guards her like a T-bone." He paused to catch his breath. "Good dog!" he yelled.

Lily didn't say Alberta was dead. Surely she would have said something if Hank had mental problems. Jane released her satchel to the floor and tried not to inspect Hank Cowley so closely as he talked and sometimes wheezed. "Died of lung cancer three months ago. Someday, I'm gonna have my body chunked down right there beside her." He pointed to the dog again, his hand once more a gun. "Me right there, Alberta on one side and Slingshot the other." He aimed for the dog. "Pow!"

The dog perked up its ears.

"I'm so sorry," said Jane.

Hank dismissed the sympathy by coughing hard and swallowing the phlegm, which allowed a low, authoritative voice to tell her that note taking made him nervous. She closed the cover to her notepad, and in the process her cortical worries about Hank Cowley seemed to tingle, no doubt a consequence of the tea. She put her glass on the table and shifted in her chair to better examine an old man who didn't seem to mind being examined at all, so long as no notes were taken.

"Oh, I know what you're thinking. Casinos—all that smoking. And you're right, I learned the hard way." He pointed a finger again to Alberta's plot. "In her, I won big."

"She sounds like a very special woman."

"I'm a lifelong Democrat," he said, "a Democrat who's gonna back Beekman, and I'll tell you why. The tobacco settlement—he and that Mississippi lawyer worked out the best public health deal this nation's ever seen. Dahling, you see our white paper?"

"Yes, sir. I did."

"Hank. The name's Hank."

"Sure . . . Hank. White paper, good reading, ample numbers."

"And Dahling, I want you to talk it up to the team." He pitched forward, aimed a knotty finger to her face. "When I heard you speak last year . . . Great . . . God . . . A-mighty, I told Alberta . . . that girl knows what she's talking about." Hank slumped in his chair and stared at his hands as if they were two regrettable but necessary instruments. "Lily probably told you I stutter when I get nervous."

"No, not at all. Said you were a pretty persuasive fellow."

Hank Cowley roared back and slapped his knee, telling her he was glad Lily Blehart finally had some real talent on the team.

"Most people see tobacco as old hat," she told him. And Hank agreed, telling her that he feared Jackson Beekman would be called a one-trick pony because of the tobacco deal. He said something else that made her think Hank and Lily Blehart were regular powwow buddies, but she missed the details as he swept out his words, his voice gnarly and low, as if fighting back a stutter. He was soon hunkering over the pitcher to pour more magic tea into the glasses, mumbling as he reconsidered the Beekman options. After blessing the tea with a prayerful regard, he offered her a full glass. She took it.

"Lily tell you why I'm here?"

"Dahling, you're here because I wanted to meet the talker who's gonna say things to the Beekman team that old Hank Cowley can't." He lifted his glass and this time toasted Slingshot. The dog's eyes were half-closed, its snout to the ground, the bottom portion of each pupil tracking Hank's spirited hands.

"Just talk to the team?" Jane asked. "That's all you wanted?"

Hank juddered forward, dipping his head to her as if to scoop up whatever skeptical thoughts she might be thinking. "And to win, Dahling. That's what we need you to help us do. You inspire people, that I know. And . . . you're a winner. And winning's the whole point ain't it?"

"Entirely." Within Jane, the machinery of a great collaboration was now whirring. "So tell me what you know about the Georgia Tobacco Growers Association."

Hank drew his left hand to his chest, where his fingers curled as small, trembling muscles moved beneath the skin. "Have to say—just hearing the name of those bastards brings a misery to my heart." He scrunched into the deeper part of his chair, all the time watching the dog play dead.

"Lily said you were familiar with the president, Floyd Deveraux."

"Great misery is a'squeezin'," groaned Hank, "the very name of that bastard narrows my coronaries." He swiveled his head to face her. "That bunch is enemy number one." He held his face before her, the burgundy cheeks and jokester eyes. And what she saw was a mealy-eyed man made for complicity, which was probably how the old guy got so rich in the first place. And once she explained how an endorsement from Floyd Devereaux's group might prove so astounding it would most likely seal the fate of any threats to the cigarette tax commitment, Hank took to slurping his tea and salivating in a manner reminiscent of his dog.

"But Dahling, just how would one pull off that miraculous achievement? Old Floyd's not known for his political benevolence."

"Suspect he's no fool either—probably glad to do almost anything to try to pull the reputation of the Tobacco Growers from the gutter."

Hank was looking into his tea glass, jostling the ice cubes, watching them bob. "Nah. I just don't know. Old Floyd's a sorta dense bastard."

"He sure can't be all that dense considering the Tobacco Growers hid the cigarette tax bill beneath the flag fiasco last year."

"Floyd did do time in Korea." Hank began stumbling over his words, stuttering and trying to hide it. "Had to sit . . . there. Sit there . . . and watch thuhhh . . . VFW pin . . . ah metal on him." He halted, took a raspy but ample breath and stretched his mouth in a way that suggested he'd learned an oral maneuver to fix his stutter. "Yep, tore my heart out to see that bastard get ah ah cert-if-if-a-ca-cate and met-tal."

"Tells me Floyd Deveraux's probably up to doing something mighty noble for his group of growers. Tells me he might readily entertain the higher calling of endorsing a candidate who's determined to make good on the state's agreement. Especially when McGee's already promised to torch the commitment. Pretty un-American to elect a liar-in-the-making, don't you think?"

Hank placed his glass on the table, lifted his face to reveal fresh strawberry dimples on the high extremes of his lips. He assumed a royal stance in his chair, adjusting his cap like an ill-fitting crown. "Dahling, Floyd's a sick man and to see him again makes me a little sick myself." The tone hinted of vulnerability, a frail spine. He daubed at his nose with two jerky fingers. "Good Lord, you got my snot flowing."

Jane circled Floyd's name on her notepad, boxed in the word *sick* next to it. Out on the lawn, the grass had dried and dulled to a more realistic green. "So what's wrong with Floyd?"

"On oxygen. Heard the emphysema's pretty much got 'im." Hank licked the rim of his tea glass, keeping his eyes on her. "Used to smoke like a fiend. Bet the old fart lost a lifetime of breaths and at least a couple of crops at the blackjack table." Hank crossed his legs and set his gape on the whitewashed lions as he seemed to think out loud. "Maybe there is some justice in this hellhole of a world."

Jane veered closer. "You talk to Floyd?"

"Pitiful guy from what I hear."

"Well, do you? You two talk?"

"Doc, why in this world would I be talking to Floyd Deveraux? Like I said, I've washed my hands of the casino business."

Hank shifted his eyes to her, gestured to the ground near Slingshot. "My Alberta taught me what really matters in this world. Redemption."

"Redemption," Jane said. "Maybe Floyd Deveraux deserves it too."

Hank Cowley stiffened. He blinked and raised his eyes to her, both eyeballs substantially larger. "Doc, don't you go squishy on me now."

"Redemption might prove the only real treatment for a man dying of emphysema."

Hank massaged his neck. "Dahling, that tea's doing a number on you."

A deal was in the making and Jane needed more than idle talk to seal it. She needed details, and no shortage of details followed Hank's musings on mercy for gamblers, so many details, in fact, it seemed he might have been long dreaming of such a plan. Hank was to offer the gift of redemption to Floyd Deveraux, the opportunity for him and the Georgia Tobacco Growers Association to fully redeem their reputations by endorsing Jackson Beekman, the announcement to come once the education hype died down. And if the sound of redemption didn't sit so well with Floyd at first, then Hank just might host one last blackjack party at his house. Maybe send a limo for Floyd, loosen him up with a win or two while drinking a few glasses of magic tea. Maybe Jane could join the partying hubbub, talk Floyd up more, maybe have Floyd spend some time out here with Alberta. Hank's face was almost purple with possibilities.

"God needs dealmakers like you," she told him.

"What if I stutter?"

"Before God?"

"Yes, ma'am."

"You always have the gun." She made a pistol with her hand, aimed it to God in his high heaven. "Pow!"

HANK CLOSED OUT THE VISIT BY REINVIGORATING Jane with two strong cups of coffee and a promise to make this wacky thing happen. These were the reasons Jane found herself singing with the Supremes on her drive back to town, the radio tuned for the first time in months from news radio or NPR. With such a prize endorsement, the prayer circle's work in this endorsement phase was probably done. Jane had not only developed a deal, she'd sealed it. No simple tit-for-tat arrangement, no back-row player for Doctor Beekman in this game. Alice could quit her squawking about the publicity bleep of tobacco. Tobacco was a political asset and the entire team would now have to admit it. The Beekman commitment to raise cigarette taxes could actually make McGee look like a blabbering fool, any debate or argument only digging his hole deeper. The preservation process for the tobacco settlement was set. Jane would be glad to sit beside Lily and watch this process play out, this tobacco vulnerability maybe the only true reason they'd ever needed to watch Jackson in the first place. To make sure, Jane lifted her pointing finger and three times—no more, no less—tapped the steering wheel. Her mother would have been proud.

Cracker Barrel

"HEY PRICE . . . MAN, YOU GOT here so early. Was the place even open?" Jackson was tieless, his khaki pants and white shirt impressive with their stiffness, the unbuttoned shirt collar making him look polished yet human, approachable as a guy in a cologne commercial.

"First customer," Price answered, slipping out from the dining room booth and hugging his brother in a way that might preserve the crispness. Even that seemed too much for Jackson because he abruptly pushed back, giving a punchy tap to Price's shoulder. "Guess my big brother deserves a head start."

The waitress, a middle-aged woman with a vigorous, grapefruit bosom and momentous head of artistically teased hair, was standing beside the men. Jackson turned to her, examined the lady's nametag and tossed out his hand, which seemed to take her aback. Jackson persevered, reaching to shake her hand as she blushed. Her name was Betty. She held a coffeepot in her other hand. "Why Betty, my name is Jackson Beekman and this fine young man here is Price, my brother."

"We've met," Price said. "She unlocked the door for me." Betty shifted hips, scanning every inch of Jackson as he slipped into his seat. Price claimed the seat across from his brother and watched as Betty poured Jackson's coffee, the waitress talking to him about the early bird crowd and omelet specials, glancing a time or two at Price. She took their orders and gave Jackson a knock-me-over look when he told her he'd be honored to have her vote for governor.

"So, that's who you are." Betty's smile hung like a welcoming banner across her face, her fascination directed entirely to Jackson. She told him the eggs were fresh, the Plantation Platter a wise choice, and before she marched away she swept her voice past Price. "The yogurt and granola's not bad either."

Alone now, Price was pleased with what he saw in his ebullient brother, even as the vigor made him feel soft and old, a weight maybe on Jackson's day. And given that potential, Price felt compelled to talk and to talk quickly because his brother was poised on the edge of his seat and waiting, it seemed, for the first chance to sprint. So Price talked of how much Jane enjoyed working with Lily, the challenge of a new work experience, so many people and teams, her excitement over the upcoming endorsements.

"Miracle worker," Jackson said. "Absolute miracle worker and a complete dynamo with Lily. I owe those two."

"We all do."

"Yes. We do."

Jackson's voice was tentative, the vibrancy strong but restrained as it had been years back in the campaign commercial that some claimed sealed his first election. In the thirty-second clip, a front porch swing dominated the scene, their mother clutching Jackson's waist as she talked of a boy with big dreams and hometown values. The scene had humanized Jackson, told people the tough lawyer was at heart just another momma-loving Georgia boy. Now, their mother was gone and Jackson was apparently doing his best to once again give the appearance of just another crisp momma-loving Georgia boy. Working hard at it, keeping his clothes extra clean.

Price said, "Jane thinks the endorsements will put an end to any cigarette tax problems."

"No doubt they will."

Price felt a distance, so he leaned forward and tried to mellow his eyes. He said, "That education program—on the radio this morning, the guy called it unprecedented, called it bold." He paused, pumped more amazement into his voice. "Audacious, in fact. Daring."

Jackson sat expressionless, hands before his coffee cup, a small but definite wall that held Price at a distance, a barrier that seemed impenetrable until Betty reappeared with their order.

"Fresh country eggs," she told Jackson, who moved his hands to make room for the plate.

"Betty, you're a wonder woman."

"I try." She batted her eyelids at the candidate before disappearing within the clatter of pots and workday voices coming from the kitchen. The clamor made Jackson's stilted demeanor all the more obvious.

Price mentioned the motorcycle, called it an impulse purchase. "Yeah, when Gerald Dalton's son called and told me he had a letter from our father, that last morning came back like it was yesterday. Save up, he said before he left. Keep saving and someday you just might have enough to buy a motorcycle." Price heard a dreaminess in his voice, so he stopped to let the recollected words mature in the absence of his own voice, to give Jackson time and space to imagine the moment, to picture it real and him within it also, two sons with their father. Price said, "After all these years, I can still hear him." Price rested his eyes on the black coffee in his cup. "Old Spice. I swear I can still smell it."

Jackson remained mute. He shifted his attention to the immense stone wall at the back of the restaurant, gave it a dismissive look as if he thought, as had Price when he stepped into this place, the big fireplace was a joke, the heap of clay logs a sad fake. As if this entire conversation was also a fake. Within Jackson's mind, the ratchet wheels of deeper thoughts appeared to be grinding about something other than the appraisal of the fireplace or an all too one-sided conversation. Price wanted to believe that Jackson's impenetrable thoughts had nothing at all to do with their father—the campaign maybe, the hour's next appointment.

Price said, "Promised Jane I wouldn't ride it, but hey—a promise sometimes needs a little fine-tuning, some parts adjusted." He waited for a response, but nothing came. "Like a motorcycle," he added.

The Plantation Platter sat untouched before Jackson, steam rising from the eggs. He seemed oblivious to the food, his stare focused on the back wall, his expression stiff as his unblemished shirt. It was the stare of a crisp Georgia boy who had heard something indecent, something he might have to report to his momma. Price was embarrassed by what he'd said, his silly motorcycle analogy, his secrets. He circled a finger about the rim of his coffee cup and secured the trapdoors in his brain that had allowed his private thoughts to escape. The possibility of riding the motorcycle, the mention of, it had never been in this morning's plan.

Outside the front windows, daybreak was lightening. A car had entered the driveway. A Cadillac, a long old-fashioned sedan. Price was glad to soon have company in the dining room, so he sipped his coffee, focused on his brother and kept talking. "You know, if Momma were alive, she'd be having such a good time. She so loved this campaigning."

Price pulled a check from his shirt pocket and placed it on the table, nudging it with pride toward his brother. "And I want you to have this, a gift to you personally—not the campaign—so no donation records, no reporting." Price swallowed. He was hoping he wouldn't need to swallow. "A gift . . . from the family." He was pleased with the handwriting on the check. *Personal gift*—he'd written on the subject line. The check was for a considerable amount of money, but not too much money. Too much money would have come across as patronizing. Price was not a patronizing brother.

Jackson lowered his eyes to the check, his focus slow and contemptuous. His eyes were calling the check an untouchable thing, a sad desperate act by a burdensome brother. Many seconds came and went in silence, Price second-guessing the appropriateness of the gift until Jackson spoke. "You know you don't have to do this." His voice was directed to the check. "Go ahead," Price responded. "Just consider it a gift from our folks."

No aspect of Jackson's face softened. And in the stillness of inflexible flesh, the hush turned viscous, weighty over the table. Price lifted his head above that muffling stickiness, but he couldn't look at his brother. He just couldn't take any more of those ill-fitting features on Jackson's face. He wanted to believe the underside of that face was now loosening with appreciation, Jackson's silence simply a struggle for words. So Price looked away and listened, for he had to believe these tight-lipped seconds would eventually give way to at least a courteous sound.

"I was supposed to explain this," Price said, pulling their father's note from his shirt pocket and placing it on the table. He pulled out the money clip and the folded twenties inside it. He placed it all on the table, looked down and smoothed the note, reciting the words his father had written, keeping the cursive directed to Jackson, so he could see it clearly and maybe follow along. But Jackson avoided the sight. Price could tell it without looking at his brother, the motionless indifference, the chill. And when Price did look up, sure enough, Jackson's attention was fixed on the fireplace at the back of the restaurant. His jaw was secure, the cleft in his chin deep.

"For whatever . . . reason," Price said, his words stumbling, "and I've been thinking about this . . . for whatever reason, like you know . . . he was attracted to Gerald Dalton. Whether they were just buddies or . . . "

Price tried to steady his voice by pointing a finger to the written words from their father, the confirmation as he saw it. "Whether they were just good buddies or lovers . . . I'm not certain of it, but what I am certain of, what I'm convinced of . . . is that our daddy did the best he could."

Jackson sat mannequin-white, his gaze anguished. Music came, a cacophony of twanging banjoes from the ceiling speakers. The sound was wrong, a mockery of this moment. It hurt Price to hear it, hurt him to see Jackson's diverted eyes, the glassiness and compacted pain. Price knew his explanation was incomplete, but no more could be said. More of Gerald Dalton would have been unbearable for both of them. Price Beekman was perceptive. After all these years, he was still a smart boy.

Price picked up the folded twenties, angled them so Jackson might— if he looked—see the medallion on the money clip, the shiny purple bed. He said, "It's just like the one he gave me that morning." Price tapped the butt of the money clip on the table as the overhead music came kinder, less plucky. Within the comfort of the inconsequential tune, he spoke. "Something, ain't it? What he wanted us to remember. The U and S, Jackson. The 'us' he left for us."

As Price heard himself speak, his explanation sounded silly and child-ish, and as he ran his finger over the clip's embossed letters and thought of all the effort he'd put into trying to explain what his father had done—all but writing it down—he felt stupid for making so much of the old situation. So what if his father had a lover? God knows, fathers commit adultery every day. Price lifted the money clip and snickered at it, so Jackson might, if he cared to, also laugh at what his nervous brother had made of it.

"Price, she didn't lie."

Jackson's words sounded dangerous, a warning. They hung before Price, like Day-Glo letters on a *No Trespassing* sign. No way would those words disappear and Price knew it, so he lowered the money clip to the table. His brother might at least acknowledge its existence. But Jackson's eyes were acknowledging nothing. In fact, he seemed ready to bolt from the booth, only his anger anchoring him here. Price focused on the money clip, calling it something special once more. He pushed the gift toward Jackson's coffee cup. "Here, it's yours."

Price didn't wait for a response. He picked up a spoon and tasted the granola, swallowing and humming in appreciation for the taste of good things in this world. Eating grounded him, the thoughtless effort in it helped put everything in a Cracker Barrel context. He called the yogurt fresh, lifting his voice to a conversational tone because the morning sky was vibrant, the day in gear. Jackson remained immobile, hands on the table, a wall once more before his coffee cup. And as Price fingered the money clip so the folded bills brushed Jackson's knuckles, he said, "Maybe bring good luck for the campaign." Price accelerated his words. "Crazy, I know. But hey, here it is—what Daddy wanted me to give you. Here, it's yours."

Jackson gripped the edge of the table, hands tightening as if he might flip it. "Listen. What your daddy wanted is yours, Price. All yours." He shut-tled his face forward, spitting his words directly into Price's eyes. "Unlike you, I don't adjust my promises."

Price couldn't move. The spoon was locked in his hand, his whole arm immobilized by words he not only heard but was also breathing, bad words, dirty ones. He couldn't swallow.

Jackson said, "Momma, Price. The promise we both made her—you do remember, don't you? Or are you still too drunk on the odor of Old Spice?"

Price lowered his spoon to the table, dropping his eyes to the granola. Jackson seemed ready to toss coffee in his face. And if he did, Price would take that too. He would take it all and call Jackson's response—like their father's suicide itself—an impulse-driven mistake. Something to be expected, something Price had to take. Something he had to endure until possibly, just possibly, his endurance led to something better. And he could do it. He was his father's son, a smart boy.

"But in case you don't remember, Price, I do. Momma made us promise that we'd never mention that man again. That was her plan and we both agreed to it. You did. I heard it like—as you say—like it was yesterday." Jackson was shaking, his eyes lying bitter on their father's note. "Price, that whole mess—I thought we'd moved beyond it. What were you thinking? Tell me. What on earth were you thinking?"

Price could not answer because his thoughts, all of them, were sweaty and choked. His brain wasn't working. Making something better out of Jackson's words was out of the question.

"And I keep my promises, Price. I do." Jackson cut into a sausage patty, took a bite and as he chewed, the opinions within his eyes came more firm, his points more definitive. It was a clarity of perspective and stance that all but declared him the far more intelligent Beekman boy.

Price pushed the money clip and its folded bills again toward Jackson, all the while keeping his eyes on the medallion, the beautiful purple bed, the letters spelling the word that he once thought would always matter— the U and S, the "us" inscribed in metal.

Jackson's eyes were stalking his brother. "So Price, are you adjusting the promise you made to our mother, that one also?"

This was it, Price told himself, the end. If Jackson didn't take the money clip, then he'd keep it himself. In time, Jackson would want it, maybe even more of the story. Price tried to convince himself that the face he saw before him belonged to a man who was scowling because of pain, not anger. Pain only, and Price understood that. He, too, had felt the pain. But Jackson was running wild with his pain, and Price could do nothing about it. Decades back, a solid time-out clasp would have quenched that pain, subjugated its power. But now, Jackson virtually gloried in it.

From the ceiling speakers, harsh metal strings were being struck, the reverberation soon sending the whole ceiling of another decade to the floor. The tiles and girders of those bad years fell soundlessly about Price and his brother as they sat and pretended to be interested in the food that, as Price saw it now and maybe Jackson also, best not be eaten. The yogurt was sour, the granola a collection of gravel.

"Don't you get it, Price? That money and hokey clip, that note—it's all yours. What you want to remember is all yours to keep, but to me the whole mess stinks."

People from the Cadillac were making their way through the front door. Jackson was twisting about to look at them over his shoulder, to examine the source of the foot stomping and on-going conversation. The noise was building as Jackson hurried his voice. "You know this is exactly what we promised to stay away from." He yanked up the money clip, pulled the bills from the silver struts and hurled the emptied clip to the fireplace at the rear of the room. Back there, some distance above the fake logs, the clip smacked the back stones, plunking to the fire pit floor with a hollowing thud.

Price blanched. The sound of the money clip impaling the stone had shattered the most empowering part of his heart. And from the shambles of that wrecked device, a beautiful but confused lion was pawing out. The escaping beast was frantic. Yet he couldn't get away, for the loss lay within the limits of a stunned but still-beating heart. The lion soon stilled like a dazed child before proceeding to die a horrendous death, its life dismembering from the inside out. But another part of Price was still working well enough to redirect his head, to send his eyes back to the spot where the money clip hit the fireplace wall. He had done what he could. He just wasn't as smart as he once was. He wasn't that smart at all.

Jackson sat seething. The man Price saw now wasn't the brother who had hugged him only a few minutes ago. Nor was this a simple, clean, down-home man running for governor. This was a brother whose complex inner corridors were possessed by a boy running wild with his pain. Only this time, the long controlling arms that might help the boy could come only from time itself.

Jane was right. Jackson had no interest in their father. Too many years, too many bad times to remember. Price folded the handwritten message and slipped it back inside his shirt pocket.

Jackson twisted forward in his seat, speeding his voice, keeping it low. "Your daddy, Price, that man who made our mother work nearly a decade to pay off his debt, that man who made sure his life insurance would pay nothing, that man who made sure you'd poke your head up the embalmed butt of his bastard lover—that man, Price—that man may be your daddy, but he's not mine." He drew a swift breath and when he exhaled its full volume, Jackson looked like a man who had conquered the world and regretted not the battle but the conquest, for there was nothing left to destroy. He stiffened his lips and jutted his head forward as though to rush a benediction.

"Each vote I get is a poker up the butt of your daddy's boyfriend, Price. A poker I'll twist, each and every time."

"That's sick."

Up front, the entering men were huddled close, joking louder. The jovial commotion rattled Jackson, seemed to make him want to spit. "Yeah," he said. "It's sick alright, almost as sick as your daddy was." He turned to the front of the restaurant and, meeting the attention of one of the men, tossed a high hand. The fattest man waved back. Jackson shielded his voice with a raised palm, telling Price, "It's Dale Vandiver." He volleyed looks between Price and the arriving men. "Yeah, Dale Vandiver—writes the 'Dale's Day' column in the paper. Bet the crew's been working all night."

"I'm going," Price said.

Jackson motioned to the clump of twenty-dollar bills in the middle of the table. "The money's for Betty, the tip for cleaning up this mess you dragged in here this morning." Jackson grabbed the check Price had written—the gift from his family—and ripped it apart, crumpling the pieces over the granola. "Don't need it, Big Brother." He grinned at the sight, lifted a hand to his shirt pocket and pulled up a stick of gum. He unwrapped the gum, popped it in his mouth and told Price that he understood the intention was good, that he probably meant well and that oh, some other time there would be better things to talk about and yeah, these days were tough, tough on everyone.

When Price started to say something back at his brother, Jackson turned completely away, for the three men at the front of the restaurant were now party-time jolly with their surroundings, each man shuffling on into the dining room.

"God in heaven," shouted the portly man leading the group, "look who's here!" The man clomped forward, one hand batting the way with a rolled-up newspaper. The other men tagged behind him as Betty, with the oversized plastic-coated menus in her hands, tried to steer the trio to a table.

Price did not want to meet these people. He whispered quickly to let Jackson know that he was ready to talk some other time, that he was one telephone call away. Jackson acknowledged the offer with a forceful thump on his brother's shoulder, a pressured smile erupting as they arose from the booth. Jackson turned to greet the big man lumbering toward him, and at the quick dismissal Price headed for the back door.

Jackson was way overloaded, thought Price, who looked back to see his brother stand tall and lax, almost giddy as he greeted the newspaperman named Dale. Overloaded goes with a job in politics, Price counseled the part of his brain that needed therapy quick if it was to heal. His father had been wrong. This world had things in it no smart boy could ever explain. That fact was undeniable now, this truth of his own insufficiency, his inability to make something better from what his father wanted. It was the kind of insight that Price wasn't expecting, the kind that just might make a man ride out the rest of his life on a motorcycle going nowhere at all, just going.

❧   ◉   ❧

To JACKSON, THE TIMING COULDN'T HAVE BEEN better. A solid "Dale's Day" feature on the Beekman agenda could seal metro Atlanta. Make copy, as they say, presses rolling.

The ceiling music had a swing in it as Dale roared into Jackson, the man's enormous arms waving his buddies close as the candidate stood in the midst of the encasing huddle. "Glory be done," Dale chortled. "No laying up in bed for this guy!" Dale slipped the newspaper beneath his arm, shook hands and lightly shoulder-bumped the trapped laughing candidate. Jackson weaved spry-faced before the men, his mind focused on what might be the day's first run, the feature on last evening's press release, the bold vision of an education czar. Czar was a good newspaper word.

Dale introduced his proof editor and assistant, all three guys blowing forth locker-room style and slapping at each other's body and sometimes Jackson, who finally pointed to the newspaper. "You caught me," he said. "So maybe I can give you guys even more eye-openers."

Dale cartooned a face to his buddies, mimed his hand into a microphone that prompted a probing of the candidate with a wide-mouthed horsy voice. "Mister Beekman, here's your chance. Your perspective, Sir. How about it, something on the record?"

Jackson played along, manipulating the magic in his hands toward the invisible microphone. He said, "Guys, if you can't get anything else correct, just let the words go forth—college tuition tax breaks, an expanded community college network, modified *No Child Left Behind* policies to truly meet the needs of Georgia children, wider pre-school education programs—and if you can't follow all that, just go to our Internet webpage and you'll see it word for word. Guys, with my ERP there's no stopping the future for our great state. That's my quote, what you can call my record in the making." He glanced to the baby-faced guy who should have been scribbling notes. The boy looked lost.

"And on Turner, Mister Beekman, you ready to make a statement?"

"Turner?"

Dale stepped back from the bunch, assessing Jackson like a perplexed yet fascinated purveyor. The circle widened. Dale cast a quizzical look to his confederates and when he saw that they too were confused, he rubbed his belly as if something pleasantly tart had just exploded inside his gut. He waved his crew tighter about Jackson. "Mister AG, haven't you heard?" Dale swayed, smug in the blissful tone of his question. And when no answer came, he flung the newspaper to the table, where it opened front page face up.

Jackson quaked, his mind racing to prepare a sidestepping perspective about some comment a spokesperson from the communications office had failed to circulate. He arced a look to the newspaper. *Augusta Sentinel*—the headline running the width of the page—"Turner Mardi Gras Escapade."

"So what you think about the picture, Mister Beekman?" Dale pointed to the off-center, tabloid-style photograph of two shirtless men with pitchforks in their hands and horns on their heads, both in leathery underwear. Dale dropped a finger. "That's Turner, in the thong."

Jackson looked up to find Dale of "Dale's Day" thumbing the luxurious layers of his chin. "Yep," Dale drawled, "turns out our quiet devil of a treasurer's had a horny little boyfriend down in Lucy Land for years." He chuckled, jiggling his measurable breasts. "Pride of the Tinkerbelle Krewe, we might call it. Boyfriend's the king and, sure enough, Boss Man, guess who the queen is." The newspapermen belly laughed, group flopping their pendulous fat within the circle they formed about Jackson. Dale veered closer to get a good look at the candidate's face. He said, "So General Beekman, seems our state treasurer has officially been outed by the *Augusta Sentinel*. Any statement?"

Jackson scanned the full length of the fat, salivating Dale Vandiver. He thought. He studied the headline and also the variegated facial features of Dale and his appendicular flunkies. He refolded the newspaper, rolling it into a tight log, which he poked into Dale's belly. "Looks like you guys screwed up big—got scooped by the *Sentinel*."

Dale drew back, snarled happily as though he'd practiced his response. "Mister AG, the story's not over yet. Our analysis comes out tomorrow."

The assistant craned closer. "Stay tuned."

"Oh, I will."

Dale shuffled forward. "So how about it, Mister Beekman? Think we need an investigation of Turner?"

Jackson motioned to the table where Betty was pouring coffee into cups for the new guests. "You guys would reprint the phone numbers in a toilet stall if you thought it would sell a newspaper." Jackson yanked the notebook and pen from the assistant's hand and wrote one word on the blank page. He underlined it with harsh strokes and returned both notebook and pen to the guy, saying, "Education—spelled it out for you."

Dale persisted. "So I take it you're *not* surprised?"

"I'm surprised you guys are not interested in what matters to most Georgians. Education—that's my statement for the morning."

Crimson waves of intense pleasure pulsed through Dale, his hands moving to a sequence of places on his body—first, his pockets, then his chest, and finally the proud nest of squiggling fingers that he presented to Jackson. Within that fleshy cage of fingers, it seemed a magical bird might any moment break forth and chirp. "Oh, Mister Beekman, we're gonna cover your education plan, alright. Watch tomorrow's paper." Dale flung his squiggly fingers into the air, the magical bird beneath his knuckles a complete joke, which sent all three newspapermen into gut-holding laughter. And as the comedy played out and Dale's belly began to steady, he pondered Jackson. "Education," said the newsman. "Yeah, we've got a new gal working the story."

"It's not a story," Jackson corrected. "It's a plan."

"I know," Dale said, drumming all ten fingers on his inflated belly, "a plan."

Call Dusty

I T's THAT TIME AGAIN! WE'RE LIVE in the all-seeing, all-telling glass-enclosed nerve center deep within the gut-grinding studios of WROL and tonight, all you truth-seeking Georgians—just turn up the volume, reach for the receiver and let go with all those questions that demand answers—and yes, I say, *demand*—your answers. Tonight, we've got us a mighty special guest, so everyone out there in radio land stay tuned for a Saturday night free-for-all! All here, all live tonight on . . . *Caaall Dusty!*

Valdosta, you're leading the line. So Caller, let 'er rip.

Dusty, this is Ed. I got two points. First, I want you to know how much I enjoy that new opening music. It's the original, ain't it?

Well, Ed, your ear hole's not about to be fooled. Yes siree, folks. That's the original Miss Del Wood cranking out an old Georgia favorite—"Down Yonder." Hey Ed, know the year?

Dusty, I know my year—1959. That honky-tonk piano set our whole roller rink to circling crazy leg forward and back.

Well, Ed, now that I've got your legs a-shakin', what's that second point you kicking at me?

Dusty, I want to know just who footed the bill to have that Ten Commandments monument hauled off the grounds of the Alabama capitol building. The guy who put it there lost his case, so don't you think he should've paid up to have the stone hauled off?

Ed, you've got Ole Dusty on that one. I have no idea who paid to have the tablets moved out. But Ed, son, you know what? The way the world works these days, I'm pretty sure the taxpayers bellied up one way or another. You hear me, Ed?

Dusty, Man, well, regardless of the final bill, we're in a heck of a shape when there's no place for God near a state capitol building. I'm just glad nothing like this has come up over here in Georgia.

Hey Ed, if it's any consolation, I happen to know that we've already got a copy of the Ten Commandments in our state house, lined up in the basement right alongside a copy of the U.S. constitution.

Amen, Brother. Amen to that!

Speaking of laws, Ed, tonight I've got our state's top law authority here sitting with me. I want everyone to move closer to the speaker now because tonight we're starting Dusty's one-on-ones with the candidates in the upcoming primaries and folks, kicking off this Jubilation-T-Cornpone of a parade is our number-one legal eagle in the hot seat, the real man himself, Mister Jackson Beekman. That's right—our state's one and only attorney general. Yes siree, the Beek-Man's here to take your calls. And folks, I'm sure you're all aware of the new education proposals he let loose this weekend. So Mister AG, tell us what might soon be shakin' over at the schoolhouse.

Dusty, as always, I'm honored to be your first guest as we move into this all-important election season. I'm also proud to present my vision for our great state as the home of the best-educated, most highly trained workforce in the nation. As my team made clear this weekend, my education program will ensure that Georgians lead the way into this high-tech twenty-first century. So what I want to also emphasize tonight is the role of small business in our future, the international trade hub we must create right here in Georgia.

No argument there, at least not from Ole Dusty's take on the concepts. But those education details I saw on the Internet got my old head to spinning just a little. Boss Man, want to elaborate some? Say, explain why a Democrat might be ringing the school bell over a Republican manifesto called *No Child Left Behind*, which I guess means we stick our kids out front to get run over by the bureaucratic mess this thing is. Catch my drift, Mister AG?

Well, Dusty, I'm thrilled you brought up that law because what we've got on www.Beekman04.com illustrates the Beekman vision of cooperation, reaching across the aisle and finding the good in good intentions. Dusty, the new law brings money into the state—big money—and it takes big money to do big things. And one of those big things we must do is to ready ourselves for the international trade that accompanies an educated and highly trained workforce. Dusty, I want to announce it first here on your show: yes, a new international terminal over at Hartsfield is one of those big things we must do. That terminal will build on the Beekman small business grant program as well as a new redevelopment program that creates enhanced enterprise zones, or what we call E-E-Zs. Dusty, with an E-E-Z program in place, we can create economic development corporations, or E-D-Cs, that will work with HUD and our GDCA to make sure that any above average de facto—

Stop the horses, stop the horses! Let's all unsaddle our brains in this Great Valley of No Fancy Pants Facts! Sir, I want you look me in the eye. Good. Now, do you see a guy who's above average? Nooo . . . nooo waaay. Folks, that's Ole Dusty's version of truth in action. And the other action we need tonight is to get our telephone lines humming with down-to-earth questions for Mister B. Enough of this international wacko-lamola. So while we're waiting on our next caller, Mister B, let's follow up on Ed's question. How 'bout it? What you say to that fiasco over in Alabama?

> *Dusty, I know Georgians value their God-given right to free speech and their ability to worship whenever and wherever they please. And, as you point out, our state capitol building has honored our biblical tradition for years. So, I don't see the Alabama situation as relevant to us. We've moved beyond it. Education, Dusty, business and trade expansion—these are the programs that will teach us all how to express ourselves and respect any differences of opinion. But Dusty, on this E-E-Z matter, I want—*

Whoooa . . . now! Let the word go out, Mister B's just twisted his first big one. Mister Beekman, our listeners want an answer out front, clear up and unspun. Are you saying you'd support a Ten Commandments monument right here on the Georgia state capitol grounds?

> *Dusty, I'm saying we could work something out.*

Well, count your eggs while the hens are sleeping 'cause Ole Dusty's going to take that egg of an answer as a "yes." That's what education does to you, folks, it helps you figure out what just might hatch from some political egg. Go ahead, Miss Calhoun talker. Little Lady, you're on the air!

> **Dusty, I've got just one question for Mister Beekman, and that is: If he's governor, how is he going to limit these free trade agreements the U.S. Congress seems to be ratifying right and left? Up here in the Calhoun-Dalton area, we've got mill after mill shutting down because carpet can be made cheaper in Mexico or God knows where. It's a shameful situation. So Mister Beekman, just what are you going to do to fix it? This is Eunice, up in Calhoun.**

Mister AG, Ole Dusty wants to hear that answer also since we all know what NAFTA's done to us here in the South—factories boarded up, Main Street empty, jobs gone to Mexico and banana nations. Speak some truth to power now, especially to the worried little ladies up at the mill.

Dusty, I appreciate what you and Eunice have observed because I see it also, every day. Day after day, I feel the emptiness, the despair in seeing our hometown stores go belly-up. That's why I think the E-E-Z program is so critical to the future of free enterprise in Georgia. Dusty, with a new international terminal at Hartsfield and the E-E-Z program, our state will be on a world-class path to prosperity.

Now, Mister AG, sounds a bit like you're saying we just ignore that great sucking sound coming from Mexico. You remember Ole Ross from Texas, don't you? That great sucking sound? Well, Eunice says it's louder than ever up in Calhoun.

Dusty, like I said. I hear it day in and day out. You and the listeners, y'all can rest assured a Beekman administration will keep manufacturing jobs here in Georgia. Dusty, we're not only going to keep them here, we're going to make them better paying.

And Mister B, just how might that happen if Governor Beekman can't get his E-E-Z program worked through the legislature?

Glad you asked that. As you know, I have a solid track record of working with our state leaders to accomplish great things. And I have no doubts about my business enterprise program, just as I have no doubts about the value of education and a new international terminal out at Hartsfield. Dusty, I've got an entire team working right now on a collection of tax incentives geared directly at manufacturing and small business development. Eunice, you folks up there in the Calhoun-Dalton area, get ready. A Beekman administration's going to turn things around.

Folks, you hear that? To Ole Dusty, sounds like you've got some sort of think tank working on projects. Any of those think-tankers out of state, say from Massachusetts?

Dusty, the Beekman teams are all solid Georgians. We're hometown folks just like Eunice up in Calhoun. Y'all can rest assured the Beekman administration will be entirely homegrown.

Folks, you know what I'm getting at don't you? Just today—the news from those liberals up in Massachusetts—gays getting hitched up there like regular folks, and for all we know, recruiting kids in schools to profligate their radical agenda. Now Mister B, don't you think these Massachusetts shenanigans are really all about the homosexual agenda? Before you answer that—Macon man, you're on the air!

Dusty, this is Ross down on Main Street in Macon. I'm glad you brought up this homosexual thing. I run a Holiday Inn with a bar down here and I want to know just what Mister Beekman really thinks about this war of morals that we're in. And Dusty, that's what it is—a war of morals, a war on the family. That's right Dusty. They're flaunting it, right here in downtown Macon.

Ole Dusty hears you, Ross! Odds are, there's a caravan of gay marriage agitators rolling down I-95 this very moment. So tell us, Mister Beekman, just where do you stand on these so-called *special* rights for homosexuals?

Dusty, I think Ross has some opinions that are worth talking about. Protecting the rights of our Georgia citizens is, without a doubt, a top priority for the Beekman administration. As y'all all probably know, no other candidate in this primary can match my legal experience. So Ross, you rest assured Jackson Beekman knows where you're coming from when it comes to legal matters. What I want to emphasize though is the growth of business through enterprise zone programs. I have three points I want to make—

Whoa horsey! Now call me hard of hearing or *special* with respect to my questions, but to Ole Dusty, that doesn't sound like much of an answer. Just where *do* you stand, Mister AG, on the homosexual agenda? Ross down in Macon has some important worries—we let *special* rights for homosexuals take over and we might as well go the way of old Rome. And folks, Ole Dusty's not talking about Rome, Georgia. Mister AG, you got any opinion—special or not—on this homosexual threat?

Dusty, I'm an optimist and my optimism tells me Georgia has room for all types of folks. That's our tradition, our Southern nature. At the end of the day, what really matters are the opportunities—

Now pardon me for interrupting, but Mister AG, am I hearing you right? Should Ole Dusty take it that you support these radical gay rights?

Dusty, I want to make it clear that I support the right of every Georgian to life, liberty, and the pursuit of happiness. As my legal practice record makes very clear, my leadership style is not built on excluding good people from our government or our society.

Hear that folks? Sounds like some buzzwords in there, doesn't it? So Chief, can you simplify it for all those simple-minded Georgians like me? *Do* you support this radical social agenda? Folks, get those lines a-buzzing!

Dusty, I support the Beekman agenda, which is all about progress, hard work, and accomplishment. Working with all the good people in this state, we can make Georgia the nation's leader in education, employment opportunity, and most importantly our way of life. Above all, I believe in the people of this state!

Well, paint my pony with stripes and call it a zebra. Ole Dusty wants to know what you folks think about this Beekman agenda. Which, best I can tell, is all about—now, how do those Yankees say it? Oh yeah, "inclusiveness." Inclusiveness, and we all know what that means! Yes siree, folks—inclusiveness to the point of socializing the unsociable, if you catch my drift.

> *Hold on there. Dusty, I repeat myself. I offer the best plan for the people of Georgia! Education and entrepreneurial empowerment, small business expansion—that's my plan. And what I want our listeners to remember is the importance of thinking big, of doing great things that reflect the welcoming spirit of our good Georgians. Manufacturing, service industries, communications and high-tech innovation—in a Beekman administration, the Georgia can-do attitude will fully blossom. E-E-Z—Dusty, remember those letters—E-E-Z.*

Holy alphabetical gobbledygook, Mister B! What we all want to hear tonight is what Ole Dusty calls E-Z. Yep, Mister B, let's stick with the subject at hand—which is all about certain *lifestyle* choices. Listen. You probably know like Ole Dusty knows, one of our great newspapers has just published a picture of our state treasurer—a Democrat, mind you—cavorting in the semi-nude down in New Orleans with his boyfriend. Any comment, Sir?

> *Dusty, I'm not going to comment on a picture, especially when the facts of the situation have yet to be made public. I'm hoping Mister Turner can shed some light on this. What's important is what I want to highlight tonight and that's the need for industrial redevelopment. As I was saying, there are three points—*

Whew-wee, folks hear that? Sounds like the front-page news is not a front-page matter in the top dog legal arena. Mister B, you think state funds paid for any of those shameful shenanigans?

> *Now Dusty, I said I'm hoping Mister Turner will shed some light on this. I expect him to, and I'm sure you and our listeners do also.*

Tylertown, does it sit right with you? Phil, you're on the line.

Dusty, sounds like Mister Beekman's supporting an expansion of the Hartsfield Airport so we can take in a whole bunch of foreigners. Well, what that means to us folks in Tylertown is that we better get set for even more camel jockeys coming down Main Street. God knows how many terrorists will be in the thick of it. You know, some nights when I have the windows up, I swear I can already smell 'um. Rag heads— we already got a couple of 'em in Tylertown. Tell me, Dusty—that stink made your place yet?

Publicity

LILY'S FACE WAS SINGED WITH GREEN, her eyes luminous as they narrowed on the computer screen. She was totally focused, as if the screen might soon reveal some secret behind its iridescent energy. Her office door was ajar, a commotion building in the hallway. It was Monday morning, only minutes before the SLIT meeting. "Right there," she said, fingering a splashy cyber bulletin called *New Jersey Update*. She motioned. "See. Right there. They're passing up on Newark."

Before Jane's eyes were two sentences that said Plyer Hoots was looking to relocate his company's shipping facilities to another airport. "Atlanta," Lily said. "Old Plyer and Daisy behind it all—that new terminal at Hartsfield their idea, completely." She was practically sputtering. "Crazy. The airport's city property. McGee's gonna fire that bullet so fast Jackson won't stand a chance." She confronted the offensive screen directly. "And a new terminal? Hell, all the governor can do is talk."

"But he sounded so confident."

Lily threw up her hands. "And that shillyshally nonsense about enterprise zones—where on God's green earth did that come from? And, to go from education to enterprise zones? Good God, what's next? Jackson and Plyer teamed up in infomercials?" Spittle laced the lower half of the computer screen, tiny droplets that caught Lily's attention and prompted even more frowning. She pulled up a Kleenex, wiped the wet blebs away and clicked up the StarSat homepage, a watery smear distorting the bottom half of the screen. She pointed. "Mark my words. Plyer's trolling for an airport bargain." She shook her head, shifting her attention to a pop-up box that begged for contemplation. "That boy's just too good a listener, Baby. And don't get me wrong—listening is an asset—but listening to Plyer Hoots, dealing with him, this mess will only get his little ass kicked. And I've told him that—told him, time and again."

Outside Lily's doorway, the staffers were growing louder in the conference room, voices sour, words gnarly and all too predictable: "Creamed us," and "Yeah, sounded weak." Someone grunted. Hell was mentioned. No good sounds were audible.

Jane examined the press release that said Plyer's Juarez plant would expand to better accommodate the European demand for printed circuit boards. She thought geography, Atlanta a better, more efficient route to Europe. She remembered the bureaucratic hurdles in renovating the old schoolhouse to accommodate CellSure, the arms she and Price had to twist to get an exception to a zoning law, the sometimes murky give-and-take, the silly promises. She told Lily that sometimes you just have to hold your nose.

"Baby, these donations—I don't know. They're not out-of-state anymore, but they're almost all from Cobb County. Hell, some of the addresses match up with Plyer's building."

"But they're legal. They are, aren't they?"

"Good God, at this rate, we'll have Plyer's name flashing from the capitol dome."

Jane wanted to remind Lily that even she once said the campaign's only real priority was to win. Win the election and the tobacco tax was secure, maybe even higher taxes over the next four years. The give-and-take, Lily—remember?

The finance chief moved to the doorway to size up the crowd gathering in the conference room. She groaned under her breath, biting her lips and shaking her head even harder to the in-coming crew. "Strategy. We need us a strategy. Maybe I can handle the Hoots nonsense, but this radio rabble's real trouble. Just you wait—Alice and the captains are gonna skewer him over that *Dusty* gobbledygook. Cook him alive for not saying more about that Turner mess. And bet you ninety to nothing, he'll listen."

Jane would never admit it, but at one point over the weekend she wanted to skewer Jackson, make him regret everything he said to Price. Still—even as he moped around the house—Price kept taking up for Jackson, kept calling him stressed, over caffeinated, ornery. Jane never bought it. She wanted action and, thanks to Ole Dusty, she got it. The talk in the hallway confirmed it. On his statewide radio debut, Jackson got skewered.

Lily returned to her desk chair, twisting about. "Listen, Baby. The one *good* thing that boy did the other night was to steer clear of Turner. Dusty kept baiting, but Jackson didn't bite one bit. That bunch out there—" Lily stopped, gestured her eyes to the conference room. "That bunch will be ruthless, worse than Dusty. What we'll need to do, what we must do is make sure the boss keeps his mouth shut."

If only, Jane thought. If only he'd kept his mouth shut with Price last Saturday.

"Offense," Lily said. "When they start baiting, we'll go on the offense with your Tobacco Grower news. And when Alice starts shouting out for publicity—and trust me, she will—we'll be ready. And . . . "

Lily pulled a slip of paper from her desk and held it before Jane. It was an email, Hank Cowley's name in the upper corner. "Yep," Lily said. "The Lung Association's not only endorsing him, they're calling him a hero. Look." Lily danced the email printout before Jane's face, reciting the subject line word for word. "Healthcare Hero of the Century. Popped the email to Jackson last night. Made sure he knew we needed to talk."

"But Lily, Turner *is* the news. What if McGee says something?"

Lily returned the email to her desk, snorting to some unbelievable thought before raising both palms to Jane, all traffic hers to stop. "High road," she said. "Jackson's gonna lean toward the high road on Turner, and that's where we best keep him headed. But when it comes to business, now that's a tee-totally different . . . " Lily swiveled her head in a spaced-out wacky lady way. "Yes, ma'am. Deals just seem to run in that boy's blood."

She walked again to the doorway to inspect the gathering staffers, the fingers of her right hand balling up as the talk came louder.

❖ ◉ ❖

THE DOORS OF THE CONFERENCE ROOM HAD just closed, yet the atmosphere was already stale and weighty. "First time we've ever shut the doors," said the scarlet-cheeked staffer seated next to Jane. At the table, the captains sat stilt-shouldered and edgy as Jackson, who was studying his notes in the chief power seat, lifted his chin. Gone was the swagger of a veteran airline pilot, the stolid expressions of a man in charge. Instead, Jackson's face was a collection of padlocked emotions, as if the restrained tempers within him were teetering on open rebellion. In his hands, he twiddled one of those black government-issued ballpoint pens that he seemed to always keep handy, working it as if the motion itself was therapeutic. Soon, he steadied his hands and let his words fly like those of a man determined to complete an unwanted but essential process.

"Okay, folks. We did a fine job in rolling out the ERP and even building it up with some business matters, but what I sense this morning—" He suddenly stopped, pausing long enough to sniff the room's staleness. "What I sense is some concern about our performance." He moved his eyes to the pile of newspapers in the center of the table, resting his gaze a moment as though to meditate on the evidence. He then locked eyes with Lily, and after apparently seeing what he expected, he looked to the male staffer at Lily's side and then the staffer at that guy's side, on and on down the line, one inspection after another. Jane saw pain in the effort, an injured spirit hobbling about just as Price had said—Jackson in pain.

Once the survey was complete, Jackson lifted his chin and resumed talking like a businessman with a weekly report that never changed. Only a slight quaver humbled his voice as he told Alice to outline the agenda, so little hesitation and so much equanimity within the order you had to believe his spirit could handle even more pain. Endurance, true endurance—Mis'ess Beekman did just fine by her boys.

"Folks, we tanked," Alice said, lifting the front page of the *Journal-Constitution*. The photograph of Brad Turner in a leather thong was centered between her knuckles. "What do you people see here?"

The crowd stayed silent. After a few painful seconds, Roland coughed, shifting his walrus flanks in his chair. "I see trouble in the land of Oz."

"Wrong!"

Alice glared so hard it seemed she could peck him apart. "No! This is what opportunity looks like." She tossed the newspaper to the center of the table. "To me, the response is simple. To regain the front-page momentum, we drop a statement on Turner. This afternoon—something modest, but eventful." She returned to her seat, her eyes patrolling everyone but Jackson. The candidate, who was leaning on the arm of his chair for support, asked the district captains to speak up. "I know you folks have an opinion. So, go ahead. Don't be selfish, now." Many eyes were lowered, most lips tight. Jackson's directive occupied the air like the exhaust from a bad engine, a backup generator blowing toxic below the conference room table. In such a dense cloud, voices seemed dangerous, silence the only antidote. Everyone waited.

Roland Creaser broke the stalemate. He called Alice correct. "Anybody else think Turner's boyfriend looks a little like Yanni?"

Edith Johnson said Turner had to go, a statement essential.

Brad Renshaw seconded Edith.

"Now or never," Carl Hadoway said.

"Pass," Naomi Gueli said in her Naomi whine.

"Press release, pronto," Rita Moreland said.

"Here, here," seconded Virgie Correli.

Loraine Delery said she didn't know.

"Better beat McGee to the punch." Howard Elam was, as always, cautious.

The domino roll continued until the majority opinion fell clearly into Alice's camp, a result that seemed to thrust the regular engines inside Jackson's face into overdrive. He pushed back from the table, surveyed the victorious Alice. "Tell me what Turner's done wrong." To Jackson's directive, Lily raised an eyebrow, cast a cunning look to Jane.

Alice stood, folded her arms across her chest. "People, the *Wall Street Journal* poll starts this week. Hear me? A statement is essential to keep our name in the news, our stance relevant. Ladies and gentlemen, the absence of an opinion from the state's next governor suggests we're tuned out, or worse—actually supporting the guy. We should, at least, express concern about Turner's lack of respect for his office."

Lily raised both hands in that all-traffic-stop gesture she'd practiced on Jane. "Why should we say anything? Can an empty-headed press release really help?"

"Pub-li-ci-ty," Alice answered, parsing the syllables and plunging a dollop of frustration atop each one. "People, how many more times do I have to say it? Pub-li-ci-ty is what gets voters riled up enough to actually vote. Pub-li-ci-ty is what will get us elected."

Lily wouldn't have it. "And I'm here to tell you that winning a debate trumps any publicity stunt."

"Stunt? Speaking the truth is a stunt?"

"Okay, ladies," said Jackson, who shot to his feet and spoke in such a suddenly authoritative tone it seemed to spook the flappy Alice. With her big eyes stuck, she weaved a moment before returning to her chair. The emotions within Jackson's face were now unlocked but incredibly docile, any leadership uncertainty, any fear of it banished. "Folks, I think we've got other publicity options. For one, Dusty's invited us back for a follow-up." He turned to the white drawing board behind him, lifting the black marker like a youthful professor at the height of his powers. POLARIZING, he wrote, all letters capitalized. "We don't go there." He brought his eyes back to the crowd, where they roamed for an instant before anchoring on Lily. The noxious air had thinned. It was almost as if the power of Lily's will alone was working.

Never before had Jane seen Jackson so heroic in his stance. Resurrection, she thought. We have all witnessed a resurrection. The reanimated Jackson made Alice look petty, the captains inexperienced. No one stirred, and no one dared to look away from the boss as he reminded the team that, as attorney general, he must maintain an impartial stance on incidents with legal ramifications. He squeezed his hands together like an angst-ridden faith healer before opening them noticeably, each palm rocking on an invisible scale. "As I've said before, it's a balancing act," he said, "publicity here, substance there." He seesawed his hands, planting a word in each open palm. "Publicity." Down went one hand. "Substance." Up went the other.

The staff sat awed. Jackson Beekman could control a difficult conversation and, more importantly, measure the weight of common sense with his hands.

"Yes, indeed," Lily chimed.

"A statement on Turner is polarizing," Jackson instructed. "Polarization helps no one." He told the crowd that no statement on Turner would come. "At least not until the legal implications have been fully vetted. But we *are* creating more publicity." He anointed Lily with a head-bowing gesture that indicated it was time to make the good news public. His face was liberated, glazed with insight as he sat down and smartly subjugated himself to Lily. This was the professional Jackson, Jane thought, the public persona that indeed would get great things done in this state. It's the other Jackson, the off-the-record haughty one, who could benefit from process improvement, starting with how he related to his brother. Jane was beginning to see Jackson as a vulnerable but noble man, a fully human leader. She was beginning to see what the endless demands on a politician could do to a noble man.

Lily stood. "Just a few weeks from now," she said, pausing to fully inflate her voice, "the Georgia Tobacco Growers Association will endorse Jackson Beekman for governor. Never before ... " She halted, lifting a God-As-My-Witness hand much like Jane's preacher father had done whenever the spirit descended over the pulpit. "Never before has the group endorsed a candidate, but thanks to Doctor Jane back there, history will soon be made." She scanned all the witnessing faces. "People, the association is endorsing our Jackson because of his leadership skills, his commitment to public health, and ... " Once more she paused, this time her hand sweeping the crowd until it rested an aim on the candidate. "His ability, above all, to do the right thing."

"Yes, indeed," Jane said, jumping to her feet. "Which includes talking cigarette taxes at the debate."

"Amen," Loraine yelped.

The elegant features—leadership features—on Jackson's face turned monumental. He lifted his shoulders and, as Jane and Lily returned to their seats, a smile adorned his lips. He began clapping in a salute to Lily and Jane, which proved contagious, every staffer soon clapping with him, even the scowling Alice.

"Folks, this is a good deal," Lily howled. "It means double billing—first, the Lung Association and right after that bunch, the Tobacco Growers." Lily funneled her hands about her mouth and launched her next words to Alice. "Yep, get lots of pub-li-ci-ty!" Jackson piped up, waving down the two women with talk of "another time" and calling a truce in such a commanding tone, the static of the murmuring crowd stopped. Soon, he was calling for ideas on the debate, especially the opening statement.

"But the poll," groaned Alice. "The endorsements might not make the poll in time."

"Hell, girl," Lily stormed. "Don't you get it? Two endorsements—each unprecedented, each timed perfectly. Fact is, Doctor Jane here has made tobacco a nonissue, wiped it completely off the stage. And, as you probably know, or should know better than any of us, it's the debate that matters." Lily looked to Jane, and together the two women went celebratory when they raised their right hands and smacked the refreshing air.

❦   ☉   ❦

THE TEAM MEETING COMPLETE, JANE STOOD IN the doorway of Jackson's office not because she wanted to be there, but because justice demanded it. Her hand was on the doorknob, her foot on the concrete block that doubled as a doorstop. "I need to close the door," she told him.

He lifted his eyes from the document on his desk. "Oh, my door is always open. Remember?"

"Is it? Is it always open to Price?" Jane kept her voice breathy and low so it wouldn't travel down the hallway. "Last Saturday," she said, "you slammed the door in Price's face." She pushed the concrete block aside with her foot and closed the door.

She claimed a seat before Jackson's desk, watching as his once heroic countenance withered, his chair squeaking as he leaned back in what could pass for a painful retreat. He was biting a fingernail, doing his best to not look at her. Price had been hurt and Jackson knew it. She waited. If need be, she would wait forever. This too, he had to know.

"I had a bad feeling," he finally told her. "Saturday morning was not a good time to talk."

"You hurt him."

"I'm sorry." His lips barely moved.

"And that check, the money was from your mother. Price would have explained that, if you'd not snapped at him."

Jackson pushed up from his chair like a man who knew something was going wrong inside his body, some problem that could only get better if he shifted positions. He paced. Sometimes he looked at her, sometimes he didn't. He moved to the closed door, stood facing the flat panel of the door's upper half, his back to her.

"So will you take the check?"

He gave no answer.

"So will you at least apologize, if not take the check?"

Jackson perceptibly inhaled, stretching his neck as if maneuvering the muscles about some bony burr on his cervical spine. And just when it looked as though he might walk away from her, he spun around. "Of course, I will. Tell Price he should have told me it was a check from our mother." He propped the door open with the concrete block. And as he moved back to his desk, he pulled a stick of gum from his shirt pocket, plopped in his chair and tapped the edge of the unwrapped piece on the desktop.

"I'll take the check," he said. "But I'm not going back. I keep my promises." He pulled the wrapper from the gum, popped the powdery stick in his mouth and started chewing. He placed a stare on Jane's face, the wounded but determined stare of a man with a forcibly contained fury. This was how a man stared when reprimanded for his core impulses, when he knew damn well he would make a good governor, impulses included. This she could follow, what she expected. Even without a commitment to an apology, Jane was victorious. Before her now the altar rail surrounding Jackson's full attention was waiting. The time for all-out testifying had come.

"I heard about the bundling," she said.

"Lily told you?" He didn't seem surprised.

"No, you did." She gestured with her eyes to the walls, called them loud when his voice was operating at even half throttle. He rubbed the palms of his hands together in great pleasure, overjoyed it seemed at the power of his voice.

"And did those walls tell you every donation is legal?"

"Plyer Hoots has Lily worried."

Jackson's lips levered a little before evolving into a smile that hung from one ear to the other, its riggings clearly incapable of collapse. "Plyer Hoots is a success story, an entrepreneur." He chewed, worked the gum forward to the bow of his sealed lips before tonguing it back.

"That boy," Lily had said weeks back, "I'm not about to let him undo himself."

Jackson kept talking. "Every cent Plyer's donated to this campaign has been legal. So why would the donations worry her so much?"

"The obvious. The way the checks stopped when she complained to you."

"My, my—what less worrisome things these walls do not say." The ache of a laugh's nervous spring was in his voice, a strained resilience that was also making the light in his eyes flicker.

Jane felt unstoppable. She said, "And that airport terminal. Lily calls it a back-scratching deal. Plyer itches, you scratch. Plyer donates, you deliver." She illustrated her words with a seesawing of her hands, mocking him with what she hoped was an affable rightness on her face. "He donates, you deliver. You deliver, he donates."

Jackson ran a hand through his hair, dragging whatever balm it might offer on down his face, allowing his fingers to rest on his jaw as if to lubricate some dry pain in the great bone. "Miss Lily, Miss Lily," he said. "How she worries about so many things, even things that the team's talked through. As you can tell—Alice and Miss Lily do not see eye to eye on a number of matters."

"Lily worries that you're using Plyer Hoots like a spigot. You simply turn him on and off." She paused, watched Jackson work the gum forward and backward in his mouth in confident, proud motions. "Lily worries that Plyer will do the same to you."

Jackson missed not a lick on his gum. "Completely legal," he said. "Every cent. Plyer only wants what's best for the great people of Georgia. Jobs, education, opportunity." He leaned forward, fixing on her, completely. "Less smoking . . . far less smoking, remember? Can't blame a person for wanting the best for his people, now can we?"

Seeds

I F ANY OTHER SPEAKER SAID "tobacco-access control" and "second-hand smoke" in as many outreach speeches as Jane did, the dedicated spokesperson would feel her mind losing access and her thoughts all but second-hand, most smoking. It was the reason Jane wanted to be working in the CellSure building when the big news broke. The crowds had left her feeling like a commodity, her mind an archive of boilerplate answers. The big Beekman news was the capstone of her statewide tour, the validation of her effort, the redemption in it. The big news was to break at nine AM on Friday, May 14, 2004, a time when her mind had to be weighing the risks of less volatile things, things that had nothing to do with smoking. Chilling out with a CellSure challenge, Jane told Lily, the rebalancing of smoke- free priorities.

The big news was to break in less than an hour, the very moment when Jane and her husband were supposed to be discussing a risky government work commitment with Alex. For this reason, Price sat at his desk studying a draft document prepared by the contractor. If a committee of Homeland Security experts accepted the company's response, CellSure revenue would more than double. But revenue was not on Jane's mind. What she was contemplating, as she stood looking out a window in her husband's office, was Alex. He was late and also standing three stories below her, Alex and the backpack that he'd dropped on the parking lot asphalt. He was toying with

Price's motorcycle, swinging a leg over the seat as if he had a key and was ready to jazz the engine and ride. And this was the guy, the distracted and tardy guy, who had taken her place at CellSure?

"Price, your motorcycle is doing a number on Alex."

"Again?" He seemed more amused than surprised, standing to join her at the window. "Yesterday, I thought he might snatch a spark plug."

Alex climbed off the motorcycle seat, stepped back, and lit a cigarette. He drew a few puffs before tossing the cigarette to the asphalt. He toed the glowing tip, smearing the crushed butt before leaving it in a spot where no one could miss it. Didn't give it a second thought, just as he probably didn't give a second thought to trashing her office or ordering a case of worthless *VitaTell* primers. She said, "Think the draft response interests Alex as much as your motorcycle does?" The words were abrasive and she flinched as they left her mouth, this snide eruption from the woman within her who had yet to shed the remnants of a crusty CellSure mindset, the obsession that had led to an overlooked cancer. Jane was no longer that woman. Her life was larger now, the people in it far less consumed by science and its technicalities. She and her life were more than a company. She had a husband who wore a biker's leather jacket as he rode to work on his motorcycle. She had a brother-in-law daring enough to run for governor, a leader who would probably take better care of this state than she had her own mother. She was glad for all the changes, the opportunity for a second chance, glad also to know the hyper-focused Alex was actually distractible. She said, "I think Alex is making some serious motorcycle plans."

"Odd," Price answered. "He's never asked about it. Nothing at all."

The contractor was reclaiming his backpack, his attention turning repeatedly to the motorcycle. Finally, he glanced to his wristwatch and bolted up stiff as if he had only just then realized his lateness. He spit twice on the asphalt before sprinting to the building's back door.

When Alex made it to the office, he was breathless. "Time sneaked up me," he said, panting. Red faced, he claimed a seat alongside Jane, the two of them positioning themselves before Price's desk. It was the typical setting, the prep position for a line-by-line discussion of the draft proposal—Alex speaking, Jane and Price critiquing. "Thought the stairs . . . " said Alex, working to catch his breath, "thought . . . they might be quicker."

The contractor sponged the wetness from his mouth with the back of a wrist. He passed out a timeline and a revised draft of the contract proposal, fanning his face with his copy, telling them, "Submit by the tenth, and I'll bet we have a response . . . " Abruptly, he ceased, pulling up the papers to hide his mouth as he worked to reclaim his breath. He said, "So, if we submit at least by the Fourth of July . . . " He stopped once more to breathe. But this time a cough erupted, a wet bronchus-sweeping cough. The rising phlegm caused him to lock his lips, to yank a crumpled paper towel from his pants pocket. He captured his spit, blushing with embarrassment. "No doubt," he said in a stronger voice. "No doubt we'd beat their summer staffing problems."

Price hummed, his tone abrupt, a ripsaw. "Don't you leave in mid-July?"

"Gotcha. But this baby'll be done . . . well before I'm out of here." Alex began to chuckle, but the effort ended with a cough. Once again, he was spitting into his paper towel. But this time Alex was pale. He glided forward in his seat and spread his knees. His belly bulged lower, which seemed to help his composure. He lifted his copy of the draft response document, sank his full attention on the paper. "Which means . . . we need to start on . . . " Short scratchy breaths interrupted his words. He intensified his gaze, all but hiding his face in the document.

Jane touched the arm of his chair. She wanted to believe Alex was simply nervous even as she knew he probably needed a few puffs from his inhaler. Surely, he had one. She said, "You know, we could review this after lunch." She kept her voice light to help lessen his embarrassment. She said, "It is a lengthy—"

"No!" Alex snapped, waving her back. "No. We need . . . to . . . finish it." He gasped between his words. "This morning . . . " His voice stopped and his face went red, his brow damp, sweat beading. "This morning . . . we need to . . . if we can."

"But we have ample time. Here, let me get you some water." Jane rose, glancing to Price to find he too had doubts about Alex. The contractor raised a hand to his forehead, keeping it there as if to curtain his face. His eyes darted about. Sweat trickled down his cheeks. "Page three," he said. "We need . . . page . . . ahh . . . three . . . to keep . . . "

"Enough," Price declared, tossing his pages to the desk. "We'll do this later." He arose, and before he had cleared his seat, Alex began to tremble. Price moved steadily, but speeded his words. "Jane, why don't you call for some help?"

Alex fought to keep the proposal steady in his hands. "No," he huffed. His face bleached ghostly gray, sweat surging. "Page three," he screeched. "It is . . . uh . . . where—" He stopped. His head sank to his chest as his shoulders lunged forward.

Jane jumped to the front of Alex, catching his head in her hands, bracing his shoulders up on hers. His weight was on her now, all of it moving forward. "Carla!" Price shouted to the open doorway, his secretary only steps away. "We need help in here!"

Price moved behind Alex and tugged on his shoulders, securing him in the chair while yelling again for Carla. Alex's skin was hot, soggy, and congested. Profuse mucus dripped from his lips to Jane's knees, but she held him. She held him completely as Price pried the chair away, as together they eased Alex to the floor.

"Call 911!" Price shouted to Carla, who was already heading for the desk telephone. "911!"

Price and Jane sank to their knees beside the contractor, who lay face up, now ashen and lifeless on the floor. Carla—Jane lifted her eyes and saw her saying things fast into the receiver. She had the address correct. Jane was sure of it. Carla had the building number correct, the third floor.

And Jane was doing the right thing also. Crouched over Alex's head, she was sensing his signs. "No breath!" she shouted, slipping her hands along Alex's big neck. "And no . . . no pulse . . . I can't feel it!"

Price had ripped the contractor's belt loose and was groping for his femoral artery, his eyes racing over Alex the whole time.

"Price, you pump!" Jane applied her hands about Alex's head to fix his airway in that sniffing position she'd practiced so many times before on plastic stand-ins. She blew into Alex's mouth, but no air moved. She tried again, repositioning his head, pinching his nose and coupling her mouth completely with his—two hard breaths going thank God deep enough this time to expand his chest, to make it go big just like they taught in the basement classes. Price followed her success, his hands springing up and down on Alex's chest as he counted out loud. "One and, two and, three and . . . "

They were a team, Price calling loud numbers as he churned his hands and Jane blowing tough when her turn came. Fifteen to two. Now, blow. And those returning breaths, Jane awaited them each time, keeping her own mouth near as the air erupted from Alex's heavy lungs, that cigarette odor coming back at her moist and reeking of blood. White laced the blue in Alex's skin, ethereal doilies soon slithering, wet and all of it suddenly chilly. Price kept counting, his hands one atop the other, palms down and plunging. The process was in place. Time was running steady. Time was running backward.

At what point does the soul abandon the body? Had it already left Alex, his spirit above them now watching as they worked to thrust life back into his body? Was Alex okay with this? The questions rumbled among the numbers Price was repeating and before any answers could come, Jane was blowing twice and Price nearing another pinnacle of his countdown. Her only job was to breathe for Alex, to share her lungs with him, to ignore all those questions she knew God would never answer.

A crowd from the laboratories gathered about them, medics circling low, chest pads secured, a button pushed. The voltage was delivered, a moment then passing with the small green screen recording a smooth yellow line. Shortly, out of nowhere, it broke. The line shot up, a discharge that sliced the room's silence with the blip of a beat. And then, another one. "A pulse," a man with a tattooed Jesus on a big biceps and jingly scissors on his belt called out. Price held Jane, and as the seconds gained forward traction the patchy blue on Alex's face faded. Pink came, a wet dainty pink. He moved a hand. He breathed.

The resuscitated Alex was lifted onto a gurney, and once the straps were buckled, his eyes rushed to and fro as if he couldn't believe this world he'd come back to, the faces of people above and at his sides, the strangeness in a world that was carrying him away. "Buddy, we gotcha," Price said while squeezing Alex's arm. It was a sick joke, but Alex nodded as if that was all he really needed.

Price was to ride in the ambulance, Jane take care of things here. It was a little after nine and a large part of the working day remained undone. The Tobacco Growers and Lung Association should have issued their press releases, the publicity spiraling to front pages and news reports all across the state. But to Jane, the timeline and the unimaginable endorsements mattered far less than they did so many minutes ago because outside the windows the clouds had thinned, and on the mimosa trees no longer did the leaves shake.

◆   ◉   ◆

SWEAT PURLING BLUE, A BREATH OF VAPOROUS tobacco, sirens closer than ever, those scissors. The resuscitation of Alex was rewinding its most vivid moments in Jane's mind, one stilled frame leapfrogging another as her brain extracted the essence of sensations she could never forget. There was a purpose in those intensities, the engravings and discolorations in her thoughts, if not her soul. There was also a purpose in making the next day a Saturday, time slowed for reprocessing the musty sweetness of the death she'd sucked from Alex's lungs. This morning was full of a massive sun, a solid sign of the world's inevitable healing.

Below this tangible proof of a merciful divinity, Jane was gardening. She was turning the dirt in a backyard flowerbed, using an Irish spade to mix horse manure into a small strip of broken earth just outside the kitchen window. It was a tradition for a Saturday in mid-May, her tradition. Every year, she's had the gardener leave this one patch bare for sunflowers. And today was a fine morning for renewing the tradition, a morning when the name Jackson Beekman was making headlines all across the state thanks to her work with the Georgia Tobacco Growers Association, Jackson's upcoming election the one good thing to come from her mother's suffering. Alongside this promising news, Jane's thoughts kept returning to Alex. He was doing better. She needed to remember this. Next to Alex, the political clamor seemed a little trashy.

Yet among the trash, the Beekman name was pervasive. Take Atlanta—lower half of the morning newspaper's front page—"Georgia Tobacco Growers Endorse Beekman." AP carried a feature nationwide. "Special Report" went the subtitle to a "Dale's Day" column that opened with a question—"Say what?"

The word from Alex was coming even faster than the headlines. Yesterday afternoon, a cath and stent. This morning, he spoke to Price over the telephone, weak but talking. "Sore?" Price asked. "It's Alex," he shouted. "He's better."

Jane was better. Her family experience with tobacco carried a new vigor, an easier testimonial. When the next speech comes, she will talk of the resurrection of Alex. Any mention or thoughts of her mother she now could keep to herself—as it should be. Maybe her mother actually sent Alex as a gift, an accolade. For Jane, the reward of a safer talking point—all thanks to the woman who must have been playing God like a puppet. Jane pictured her mother—hand on hip, that wink. Thanks to the Tobacco Growers, the impossible was only beginning. "Honey, you done good!"

Cigarettes taxed at a dollar-a-pack—Jane repeated the words to herself as she turned the manure and dirt.

She leveled the bed with a garden rake. The dirt—Georgia's dark, soft and rich dirt—smelled of a benevolent earth, the sweet aroma of life before it begins, of death after it's passed. *Cigarettes taxed at a dollar-a-pack*. The words belonged in a limerick, a plow song, a new tradition to be blessed. Jane chanted the line, and was on her knees with the seeds in her hands when Price called her inside to the telephone. "Lily," he said.

"Baby, flip on your television. WATL. McGee's supporting Brad Turner. They're together, side by side, live."

A dirty hand went to the remote. The picture appeared on the screen, a banner, a breaking report. A gear slipped within Jane's heart. Something rusty was struck, and once the endocardial locks caught with a thud, the next pumped-up wave was a massive one. It traveled all the way through Jane's body and engulfed her soul. The heat proceeded to swallow her whole. The taste, briefly, was rust.

"Baby, you watching?"

The news wasn't theirs. McGee was doing the impossible. The new world was falling from the hands of a clumsy God. And in that descent, McGee smiled, hugging Turner like a son. A dark-skinned priest stood to McGee's right side, a light-skinned nun on the other. Microphones aimed for McGee's mouth. And he was welcoming each and every one. It seemed there had been a contest, and McGee was ready to tell every listener who'd suddenly won. Even God.

"Baby, are you there?"

Trumped Again

JANE CLAIMED HER USUAL CHAIR IN THE conference room, placed a notebook across her lap and braced herself for nothing short of a spook house ride. She was expecting it—voices sharp, faces inflamed, the hysteria anyone would expect following a publicity slam-down. *Ass whooped . . . cakewalk . . . left field.* More than one captain seemed dazed. Many were disgusted, most all alarmed. Quick looks came to Jane, but the eyes kept returning to Lily, the ferocity ramping up, glares loaded with metallic crosshairs.

Turner, if you'd only let us make a statement on Turner.

Lily had been wrong. Anyone doubt the evidence? Just look. There, the newspapers, every front page. McGee had pulled the very stunt Lily predicted would completely backfire if he did it. Yet the stunt had worked, no backfiring at all. She did it, her there. See. Sitting right there. Still, within the room's ruckus of looks and repulsive pheromones, Lily appeared resolute, her face turning not one iota from her laptop computer screen.

Jane was impressed. She was with Lily on this one. She and Lily could weather this gang of second-guessers, their knee-jerk hysteria and fickle opinions, their belief in the healing power of blame, some justice in it. To them, the long-term strategy no longer mattered. Only now. The showdown had come.

Who among you could have predicted McGee would embrace Turner? Who had any suspicion that the poll would show Jackson's lead narrowing? If that person was sitting among us, then he must stand up and confess his silence. This Jane was prepared to tell any staffer who even hinted that Lily was to blame for the McGee stunt. Or worse, declare tobacco a sleeper problem. This staffer, Jane was prepared to say—this staffer was the only one who needed his ass whooped.

The chattering thickened into a low rumble as Jackson entered the conference room, his shoulders high and his disposition placid. His bearing suggested a mind preoccupied with complex thoughts, his affect subdued as if important backup plans inside his brain were still brewing. He walked to the head of the table, all the while making curt welcoming waves to the seated staffers, winking to some and chewing his gum. Alice tagged along behind him, the manager jabbering at his back. She appeared to be appealing a point from some earlier conversation, some argument she apparently didn't win and was not likely to win given Jackson's current interest in any face but hers. Alice shortly went quiet, roosting in a chair to the right of her boss, who spit his gum into a doughnut napkin and called the meeting to order.

"Folks, as I'm sure everyone knows, the poll showed us with a slim lead, which may not be real given the margin of error. That said, what the poll did not reflect was the impact of the endorsements or McGee's statement on Brad Turner. These items, these key items, shift the sentiment to our favor."

Jackson's voice was curiously muscular, more vigor in it than Jane was expecting. Price was like that. When dire news came, Price invariably turned resolute and serious, some primal neurons kicking in to overrun his emotions, each neurotransmitter flaring with a backup possibility. It blessed him with a contagious serenity, which was a must-have for a leader. This morning Jane could tell from the way Jackson addressed the staff—he's got that auxiliary control also, that unflappable Beekman voice.

"Folks, what I really need to hear is your opinion on what we should say—if anything—about Mister Turner in the debate. Alice, it's all yours."

Alice was wearing a bright blue skirt and blouse, the ensemble webbed in a long yellow vest of loose cotton cord that gave her the look of an enormous duck. Yet she was poised like an experienced manager, unsmiling as she stood, hands commanding everyone's attention. "People, I believe this weekend's events have given us an opportunity—perhaps obligation—to make the statement that we considered last week and McGee has now dared us to make."

Alice stopped to make sure everyone was catching her points. She was no banty hen this morning. She was the lead duck in search of a flock of followers.

"People, our opponent has drawn a line, and I say to erase that line we must first cross it. I say we make a statement in *advance* of the debate, a statement denouncing McGee's support for a candidate who's brought disrespect to his office, a candidate whose personal behavior is unbecoming of a leader." She gave Jackson a cauterizing look, the whole time rocking her head before the crowd as if to acknowledge a fixable problem. "People, I can see how Turner's gay lifestyle is a polarizing issue, but an election is inherently polarizing. A choice *must* be made, and better we make it now before it's too late."

"Here, here," said Roland, his balled-up fist pounding the table. Alice ignored the outburst, mouthing a *Thank-you* to no one in particular before taking her seat.

"Amen," Rita Moreland said.

Jackson asked for other opinions on the matter. Silent moments crept about the room like invisible beggars until a few voices began making desultory peekaboo observations that seemed to reveal the same question until it was all too obvious—should a statement come now or later? The candidate gazed to the ceiling an instant before lowering his eyes to the staff, some supervisory insight suddenly dazzling his face. "Folks, I still think we need to stay away from name-calling. To me, McGee's setting a trap. He wants voters to know we're focusing on a trivial consideration when far more important problems face our state. And, you know what? If we take his cue, he'd be right. Folks, what I'm saying is that I don't really see a reason to change directions. I see no reason at all to abandon a winning strategy."

The candidate called for a show of hands. "Guys at the table first, then the full room." The choice was, in his words, between name-calling or not. His eyes were ignited, both diodes glowing. He looked from one side of the table to the other. Alice sat like an avian specimen, her lips retracted in what Price would call a shit-eating grin, a smile that indicated—regardless of the vote—she would ultimately prevail.

The nays predominated, and at the tally, Jackson's eyes flared rapturously before lowering to more functional flames. "Okay, folks. Any name-calling is sidelined for now."

"Yes, indeed," exclaimed Lily, wiggling ten red fingernails in the air.

Jackson ignored Lily's accolade, rubbing his palms together and spreading his shoulders like a professor who needed to apologize to the class for today's pop quiz that everyone flunked. "What I'm emphasizing is the need for balance." Even in his seat, Jackson seemed to have assumed a lectern, his hands rising to pin some talking points just above the attentive heads.

"Folks, after talking with leaders of the Chamber of Commerce this weekend, I think we need to reconsider the implementation timeline for some Lung Association items."

Jane grabbed the seat of her chair and squeezed. The snaps on her composure popped. Some items? Reconsider? The candidate was not looking at her. He was looking for someone to tell him to backtrack completely on tobacco. He was looking for someone to tell him he'd gone too far, tobacco such a nineties thing, a publicity sleeper. The once brooding Alice sat dangerously reanimated, the campaign manager poised for the launch of a glorious flight. The threat was real. So Jane stood, took a deep breath as Jackson went mute and all eyes rotated to her.

"On Friday, a man died in my arms." Every sound in the room disappeared. Thunder didn't growl nor lightning crack the ceiling as the amused Jackson leaned back in his chair, as he worked hard to appraise her from a greater distance. "Tobacco killed Alex Havelchej," she said. "Emphysema, asthma, heart disease—Alex was smoking less than an hour before he died." Lily was entranced, Alice perplexed.

"My husband and I—by a miracle and quick CPR—we were able to bring that man back. So Alex is now in the hospital, recovering." She paused, collecting herself and absorbing the awe on the faces that stayed with her. She enjoyed the attention. Time had once more stopped for her, fear and fury drawn a truce. This was her moment now. She commanded it to listen.

"And if we asked Alex this morning, I have no doubt he would tell us that tobacco matters just as much today as it did four years ago. For people like Alex Havelchej—and Georgia is full of them—reconsidering the Lung Association plan is a slap in the face. I say we do just the opposite. In this debate something up front must always be said."

"Amen," Lily shouted.

Loraine clapped, her hands in an energetic but isolated clap. Yet the isolation was quickly muffled as more claps arrived. The applause was pressured but polite, and once Jackson acknowledged the politeness with a skeptical eye and a tight-lipped affirmation to the now-seated Jane, all hands stopped. Jackson stood, resting his attention on Jane.

"And on even deeper thought," he told her, stopping his voice to reach into his shirt pocket and pull out a stick of gum. He removed the wrapper from the gum, gaping at Jane the entire time. "On second thought, Doctor Jane, you're probably right." He unwrapped the stick of gum, popped it in his mouth and started chewing. "A good Beekman man sure needs to keep his promises. He does, doesn't he?"

The question was barbed. It was aimed at her. It shot straight to the place within her where her husband stood like a target. Price was indeed a good Beekman man, so the answer to Jackson's question was *yes*—a good Beekman man keeps his promises. Yet that answer was being forced from her, demanded. So to Jackson's question and a room full of staffers, Jane simply nodded and tried to look pleased as she returned to her seat. Once more, her body's default mode was taking over.

"I agree," Jackson said. "Some mention of the tobacco settlement seems essential, given the tax situation."

"Some," Alice quipped, slashing a mark across her notepad.

To be patronized and to remain quiet in the process was to lessen yourself—this Jane had learned at CellSure, so she sharpened her posture in her chair, hoisting her shoulders and gripping her elbows as her voice rose. "In opening remarks?"

"Of course, in the opening remarks."

She was emboldened. "Including a promise to raise the tax on cigarettes to at least a dollar-a-pack? That is the goal. Correct?"

A couple of staffers bolted up in their seats. Roland slapped his forehead. "Oh my God."

Jackson ignored Roland and the squirmy team, centering his attention on Jane. "Of course, we have to remember the opening statement is a work-in-progress." He raised his right hand to Alice, opening his palm to her as if daring her to fill it with dirty verbal graffiti. "And that work-in-progress belongs to this young lady." An almost demonic glow arose on Alice's face, and stayed there as Jackson turned the meeting over to her. Alice, the living duck she was, wasted no time in assuming her navigating position.

"Okay, people. We need to get to these debate questions."

"Finally, the good stuff," Lily said, coughing to clear her throat of the fermenting anxiety. "A few strong one-liners in this debate and we're set."

An impromptu mock debate began, Jackson standing at a make-believe podium on one side of the room, Alice at another one directly across from him. The campaign manager spouted out tough questions for her boss, pointing and ranting. She got so hot with her question about a state senator's promise to draft a Medicaid expansion bill, she took off her vest. She slung the knotty cotton weave to the floor, where it lay like the slung tread from a sixteen-wheeler. "So, Mister Beekman, can you promise to support Senator Bryan's proposal?"

Jackson stood majestic before the hot question and the theatrics of Alice's flung vest. "What this comes down to," he said, "are the technical details within the senator's bill." His voice was velvet, the texture regal. "But while those details are nebulous at best, what I can say is this—when Jackson Beekman makes a promise, he keeps it." He turned to the crowd, gliding his eyes to a single stopping point.

"Right, Doctor Jane?"

Good Man

THE TINY LADY IN THE JUSTICE building lobby had large, alarmingly gonadal eyes, which seemed to roll in pleasurable pain when she couldn't find the name Price Beekman on the AG's calendar. He wasn't surprised. "Probably too late to make the list," Price told her. "Mister Beekman and I were talking late last night. He's my brother." Price handed over his driver's license. He peered over the high counter and watched the lady scrutinize the card, front and back, each side prompting looks of proud uncertainty.

"Price Beekman," the lady said. She pushed her glasses higher, planting them tightly on the bridge of her nose before comparing the face on the card to the man before her. "Guess I *can* see some resemblance. How come I haven't seen you around here before?" She raised a frail hand, waved and smiled to two people who breezed by her station.

"Too busy," Price answered. On the lobby's pink marble walls, an enormous gold-filigreed clock indicated five minutes before nine, the time Jackson said would be great for Price to drop by. He'd called it an opening. "Do you mind buzzing his office?"

The lady laid the driver's license on the open pages of a tall ruled-line ledger, bowing over it as she hawked forward. "What you mean too busy? Tell me. Just what do you do?"

"I'm a doctor."

The lady pointed the writing tip of a pen at him. "So, it's *Doctor* Beek-man?" She glared at him before diverting her eyes and lifting a palm to sweetly wave a throng of card-toting cheery-faced people past her position.

"I'm a pathologist." Price gripped her counter with both hands, made sure she saw him examine the clock. "I'm trying to catch my brother before he goes into his next meeting." A hand touched his shoulder and when he turned, a lawyer who once reviewed a contract for CellSure greeted him loudly. Darrel. Darrel of the impossible last name. They shook hands and Darrel, who must have known the tiny lady, inclined his face over her counter and called Price a good man.

"Of course he is," she responded, offering a coquettish up-sweep of her dry narrow lips to both men. "Give me just a second." She returned the driver's license and reached for the telephone. In a honeyed voice, she told the person who answered that Doctor Beekman was here. "He says he has an appointment, says he's too busy to wait." Her eyes never left Price. She was nodding in cautious approval of him and kept nodding as Price's lawyer friend Darrel and more people headed for the elevators. The little lady clutched the receiver and listened. She was still listening when she raised her free hand and waved Price into the streaming crowd. "Mister Beekman's busy," she announced in an official tone. "But he wants to see you." She lowered the receiver to her chest, stood and pointed hard to make sure he took the correct elevator. As the door started to close, she waved, sweetly.

The way Price was thinking this morning, Jackson was right. The gift of a money clip and a hundred bucks from a father you've only known as a scoundrel was the kind of family baggage a politician most definitely didn't need. And here Price had been expecting Jackson to lug those bags all across the state. And not for himself or the campaign but for his self-absorbed, retrogressive older brother. No wonder Jackson went so snotty. What Price was expecting was a selfish thing. Price was trying to be a good boy when a smart one would have known better. Jackson had nothing at all to apologize for.

The top-floor security guard pointed Price to another secretary's high counter. This time he was met with a smile and a pointing finger, at the end of which the door to the attorney general's office stood open. Voices were coming from inside it, so Price stood in the hall and listened. It was the top of the hour, another meeting no doubt started.

"Okay, I'll meet you at noon, back parking lot." It was Jackson, his tone rushed. A shuffling followed, steps on the carpet.

"Daddy's gonna join us at the restaurant, and I want you to be nice to him. Okay?" It was Daisy, her voice whinier than Price recalled it, almost nagging. "He's worried," she said.

Jackson was coming closer. "Is there ever a time when Daddy's *not* worried?" He was walking Daisy to the door.

"Jesus-lovers," said Daisy. "Daddy calls it the rising tide." Price stepped back, shook out his shoulders, circled about and approached the office door in a way that indicated the hall secretary had just waved him on in.

"Price, my man!" Jackson's tone was ebullient, no doubt pumped up for the top-of-the-hour meeting. In the doorway with Jackson was Daisy, her face going firecracker happy at the sight of Price. She offered him a hand and he accepted it, her thin chilly fingers dropping politely into the cup of his hands, proving that she viewed herself as special.

"Doctor Beekman, it's so good to see you." She jerked her hand back and smiled. "And will I have the pleasure of seeing you in Savannah?"

"No." Price dragged the single syllable, swinging it low and wide to emphasize his deep regret. "Afraid Jane and I have to do our cheering before a television at home." He was watching for a reaction from Jackson, a favorable one. After all, Jackson hadn't offered an invitation. Little doubt he was anxious and sensitive to the pressure, so sensitive he wanted them to stay at home, out of sight and mind. At heart, Jackson was a very private man. Price said, "Between work and fractious nerves, don't think we'd be of much use in the debate hall." He heard the unintentional drawl within his last word, its lengthy tail drooping all the way to the floor, positioning itself to be stepped on. For some reason he tended to drawl his words when he was around Daisy. Something about her air of anti-Southernism—how she went out of her way to make other people's Southernism so obvious and hers so remote. Price always played along with her, almost by instinct, and now he realized why: a hormone imbalance. He sensed a hormone imbalance within Daisy—not too little but too much, probably an overcorrection with supplemental estrogen. He also just now convinced himself that Jackson could do better.

"If practice matters," Daisy said, pointing to Jackson with her head, "then we're in for a star performance." She reached over and grabbed Price's wrist as if she needed to imprint her prediction on a tender part of his body, to stamp him as just another stay-at-home drawling sideliner. "You and Jane take care now and keep up the hometown spirit!"

Daisy could have been a great high school cheerleader, probably the girl on the top of the pyramid, the one whose high vision forever ensured her success. Price started to say something to her in response, something that proved Jackson's family would definitely be cheering even when he didn't want them physically present, but Daisy didn't give him the space or time. "See ya," she told Jackson, twiddling one hand's smallest fingers in a goodbye signal. She turned, flitting her heels toward the ping that indicated her high position could easily give way to an open elevator door.

In the wake of Daisy's departure, Price and Jackson looked at each other. A stretch of curiously unavailable seconds passed with neither of the brothers saying anything, Price facing Jackson and Jackson facing Price, something like truth shared with their eyes until the sharing began to feel too one-sided. Neither Jackson nor Price seemed eager to know the winner in this exchange, yet it was Jackson who must have felt the greater weight of loss because he turned away. Maybe Jackson also knew he could do better than Daisy Hoots.

"Finally got my big brother up to the big house," the candidate boasted, his attention directed to the top-floor environment, his head nodding in pleasure at the results of his survey. "Really something else, isn't it?" He slipped an arm around Price's shoulders, steering him into the office like a tour guide with a teetering guest. "No excuses or bellyaching up here," Jackson said, pointing with his gaze to the big desk in the center of the office. "No, sir. The buck stops right here."

Price enjoyed Jackson's welcoming tone, this conviviality of a man in control not only of himself and this building but also his world. Win or lose this next election, Jackson had defined himself as a freethinking man. No apology would ever be needed. If Plyer Hoots was worried about Jackson, it was because he knew a freethinking man could never be bought like a Jumbotron.

"Listen," Price said, slipping loose from Jackson's arm. He pulled the check from his shirt pocket. "It's like Jane probably told you—simply a gift from Momma's estate, what she would have done to help." Jackson took the check, smiled, and examined the writing on it. He stood amused, tall and patient before Price, looking down at him just as he had the night the attorney general election was called in his favor.

"Kind," Jackson said. "Just like her." He placed the check on his desk and began a tour of the office, pointing out the historical furniture that once sat in the old capitol building. He talked quickly, telling Price he regretted the time crunch before the next meeting.

Here, in the center of the massive blue rug, Price was looking up to his brother, looking at him more as a leader and less as a brother. It was the triumph of a once-babied brother who'd established his place in a world that allowed apologies but no excuses. "And I wanted to apologize for the other day," Price said. "I never should have brought—"

"No," Jackson blurted. "It was me." He was shaking his head in that gosh-darn style he would also probably use on the debate stage. Price admired it. Little doubt most everyone would. Jackson said, "When you brought up all those old things, Price, there was something about it, something that just seemed so out of place now—all that sickness."

Price winced. They were talking about their father, not a sickness.

"But hey, Big Brother, if anyone's apologizing, it's going to be me—"

"Oh no," Price demanded. "You read me like a picture book from the Cracker Barrel gift shop, and I was wrong. I know—"

"No, no. I've never done very well with something I just can't relate to. Guess it's the lawyer in me."

Price sank away, his attention roaming as he reexamined this grand office filled with relics from the state's history, including some very bad years. All now so revered and orderly. He said, "And here, I thought you were out of control." Price laughed at his comment because he knew Jackson knew all too well what he was talking about. He placed a hand on his brother's shoulder and jigged the muscles he had once clamped down in a take-control maneuver. "That motorcycle," Price said, "I'm letting it go also."

Jackson brushed away Price's hand. "So soon? What is it—six weeks at the most?"

"Guy at the office," Price said. "Consolation prize after Jane and I worked him into a heart attack."

Jackson turned radiant, his interest ruffling the air. "Man, did you ever? Heard all about it." He clasped his brother's shoulders, hugging him hard as though he needed to share an insider's secret on management. He was mumbling something amusing when a woman's head appeared in the doorway.

"Mister Beekman, the police chiefs are waiting."

"Yes, ma'am. On the way." Jackson okayed her with a dismissive finger, walking Price briskly to the door. "Big Brother, the lesson in this is for you to simply take care of your needs, not mine. I hate to run, but like the little lady said, got the law waiting on me." He jabbed a fist against Price's upper arm. "Yep. Gotta keep the charisma juices flowing through Saturday night. Tell me. Any last-minute advice?"

Price thought and kept thinking as they walked to the elevators. The button was pushed, numbers coming.

"Smile," Price said. "Smile like a man who knows there are some things money just can't buy, things Plyer Hoots can never stake a claim on."

Jackson hardened. And just when Price thought his brother might respond with a sneer or punishing look, Jackson scoffed. It was a cocky gesture, a signal of brotherly amusement that meant he knew what Price was talking about and how that concern made no sense at all. Yet Price felt smart for his advice, stupid for not saying more. After all, their father was a good man, far more a man than any sickness.

Morality Matters

STAYING IN ATLANTA GAVE JANE TIME to help Price with the Cell-Sure contract proposal, time to double-check the appendix. And much to his surprise (but not hers), she found a problem with the genetic profiling aspect of the project, which one quick telephone call confirmed was a government mistake. The acknowledgment made her feel proud, made her feel that her mother was in heaven and helping the Lord take care of her and Price and CellSure and Lily and especially Jackson, who any minute now would be headed for the stage, his opening statement whittled down to the essentials. Gone was the talk of enhanced enterprise zones; severed completely was any reference to expansion of the Atlanta airport. And even if some priorities had to be chopped, the key line—her line—was still intact—*Cigarettes taxed at a dollar-a-pack.* That line was such a priority, Alice and any more of her last-minute chops didn't worry Jane now. Not at all. Her mother had her eyes on that line, just as her mother had her eyes on Alex, the contractor doing better, maybe going home soon. Jane could still taste the tobacco on her breath. The wine helped. Indeed, another gift from her mother.

So, go ahead, a part of her brain said. *No way could a mad, last-minute Alice chop that line. Go ahead, now. Sip.*

Jane complied, first adjusting the sofa cushion that separated her from Price before swallowing enough of the Bordeaux for the taste on her breath to transition from tobacco to a mature velvety tannin.

Live from Savannah State University—Democratic Primary Debate 2004

The banner streamed red at the bottom of the screen, the television camera scanning the arriving audience, the steps of the old auditorium, the bush palmettos. Bugs swooped low before the camera lens, and when one attached its tiny black legs to the screen, Price redirected his focus to Jane.

"I have an announcement."

His voice had weight, an ominous sincerity. She didn't need an announcement. She steadied her wineglass using both hands, braced herself and listened.

"Unless you feel otherwise," he said, "the motorcycle goes to Alex."

Jane's elbows jerked. The bottom beneath her worries collapsed.

"He deserves it. Don't you think?"

Yes!—she shouted inside herself. But the internal celebration was cut short by the rising hum of a new worry. "Yes," she said. "Alex deserves it. So, does that mean you're buying a snazzier one?"

"No more motorcycles for me. When I stop, I tilt."

At the confirmation, Jane wanted to thank God for both her husband's decision and his unequal leg lengths. She wanted to consider the loss of the motorcycle an omen, a sign that verified God and her mother were now buddy-buddy. *Sip,* her brain said. So again she sipped her wine, allowing the smooth taste to fully ripen in her mouth before calling the motorcycle a perfect homecoming present for Alex. Glasses clinked in agreement and together, she and Price turned back to the announcements coming live from Savannah State.

The television camera shifted to the stage, to two empty podiums, maybe eight feet apart. Ceiling lights lay harsh on the stage. The shiny wooden floor glowed pink in the red reflection of a giant Georgia state flag that covered the back of the stage. The cloth rippled in the wake of an off-screen fan. The setting looked hot, volatile in fact, the coned lights unrelenting. People had to be sweating.

The debate moderator stepped to the center of the stage, where he grinned like a television lawyer with a special offer. The camera panned the audience as people waved and made faces. Some looked lost and some looked found, some happy, and a great many looked as though they couldn't figure out if they should sit or stand. Hands fanned many faces.

The candidates moved into position as the offstage music swelled and the camera caught the front rows of lookers settling into seats. The moderator began with game-show zing, hyping up the importance of the debate and outlining the rules with a pointed, professorial voice. Soon, the coin was tossed, the decision declared. "Mister Beekman first." The moderator stepped away and from a hidden place raised his voice. "Mister Beekman, please begin."

Jane and Price placed their wineglasses on the coffee table, leaned backed and watched, Price with arms folded over his chest, Jane with hands resting on the sofa, her tapping finger ready in case God needed a nudge.

"My fellow Georgians, this evening I'm privileged to be speaking to you from the campus of one of our great institutions, Savannah State University. This setting is not only ideal, but also emblematic . . . "

Price raised his chin, sealing his lips as though behind them lurked all the odd words that Jackson shouldn't say. On the screen, his brother kept going, almost all education, a finger pointing to the camera just as he had done with artistic skill in so many practice sessions.

"Folks, I say 'yes' to financial incentives for our teachers, 'yes' to compulsory school attendance through high school, 'yes' to . . . "

The camera panned wide to catch McGee making notes, the focus soon narrowing on the audience where some heads bobbed in agreement, most faces engaged, a few eyes shut as if to better see the future or maybe doze right through it.

Jackson moved to taxes. "My opponent has called for a draconian, across-the-board cut in income taxes. Ladies and Gentlemen, do we really want to give a pay raise to our state's millionaires? Do we?" Jackson swept a hand through the air, scanning the audience for an answer that he must have heard was against the rules. "No," boomed a voice in the crowd, and at it, Jackson smiled. The smile looked clever, and the longer Jackson held it, the smarter he looked.

The candidate continued. "Listen. When our state's revenue stream dries up—as we all know it will with the torch-the-earth program of my opponent—do we really want higher education turned into a luxury commodity, pre-school a virtual dinosaur, school lunches nothing but a memory?"

Again, a loud croaking "no" came from some guy in the audience. Roland, Jane imagined.

"No, of course not. Ladies and gentlemen, we can do better. I know we can. I know it because I was raised by a single mother, a woman who lived every day of her life trying to make a better world for her kids and community. First off, in the Beekman plan, we propose . . . "

Jackson dominated the camera view, jaw invincible and demeanor confidant. His entire bearing was gallant and to the proposals that accompanied it, Jane heard Price murmur a whole series of "yeses," the brisk affirmations continuing until Jackson was well into the wind-down phase. Yet of tobacco, nothing had been said. Not a word. But the words were coming; this Jane knew. They had to be, just as he'd practiced them so often with the team. To be sure, she tapped the leather sofa cushion. Did it discreetly, three times to be sure.

"Furthermore," Jackson implored, "I'm proud to report that my work in making the tobacco companies pay up has resulted in our state receiving over a billion dollars—let me repeat that—more than a billion dollars to help fund tobacco abstinence education and to improve the health of every Georgian. Even now, I have a team of experts working . . . "

Jane was ecstatic. She raised a fist to her mouth. But Jackson didn't—and he wasn't—saying a word about cigarette taxes, the goal of a dollar-a-pack. Her last-minute email reminders were proving pointless.

"And with healthy, well-educated citizens, our beloved Georgia will be poised to bring in jobs from around the globe, which is why I think it essential that we prepare a new terminal at our great Atlanta airport, one dedicated to international flights. Essential too, are enhanced enterprise zones, warehouse and manufacturing site renovations throughout our state's key transportation hubs . . . "

Jane's blood ceased its flow, her pumping heart stilled. A new airport terminal? She balled her hands together, coupling fingers, tightly. Every fiber of faith and disbelief within her, every worry, she held it all tight. The airport business was supposed to have been chopped, as had that chatter about enterprise zones. Lily had laid down the law. Everyone heard her. And Jackson had agreed. How could he do that to her? Jane stroked her wedding band with a thumb and tried to imagine how she and Lily should confront Jackson once they were back in his office. And how he would respond. Gnashing of teeth and teary, knee-bent apologies crossed her mind, the possibility of corrective follow-up statements. With those possibilities and the tight-fingered prayer she packaged them in, the locks on her heart gave. The blood began to rush through her most critical capillaries while on the screen, Jackson went on and Lily's voice rang in her ears. *Baby, it's all in the Lord's hands now.*

"And before I close . . . "

The candidate paused, grasping the podium and surveying the audience, those before him as well as the people in the balcony. He fixed on the camera, looked all Georgia in the eye.

"Ladies and gentlemen, in this new century, this new Georgia, I must speak of our great heritage and the moral imperative that now threatens it. Yes, folks. In this new Georgia I speak of morality. A morality that matters when we step up to cast our votes."

The sight before Jane's eyes was off, what she was hearing all wrong, totally unscripted. A moral imperative—where did this come from? Another last-minute add-on? Taxing cigarettes at a dollar-a-pack was the only moral imperative Jackson had yet to mention. That and nothing more. Price groaned. It was a low pleading groan, a supplication.

"Folks, let me tell you why morality matters. As you may know, my opponent has endorsed a candidate with questionable morals."

The camera caught an evangelical passion in Jackson's eyes. And to that close-up image, Jane pulled her feet from the coffee table. She lurched forward to better see. Those eyes, they were testifying eyes. "Lost it," Price said. "Absolutely lost it."

"Ladies and gentlemen, what my opponent has told us is that behavior doesn't matter, that choices lack consequences. To my opponent, a homosexual agenda is simply a question to ponder. Ladies and gentlemen, in a Beekman administration, what's right and what's wrong won't be topics to deliberate. My fellow Georgians, let there be no question about it—morality matters."

"Hell yeah!" came a whoop from the audience, which was followed by a barrage of clapping and stomping that seemed to keep tumbling from the balcony even as the moderator took to the stage waving his hands and yelling for order. Jackson stepped back from the podium, making hand gestures that, in concert with the moderator's call, quieted the crowd. The audience was unquestionably his.

"So in closing, I want to leave you with a vision, an image of a Georgia that leads this nation into the twenty-first century—education, solid tax reform, job opportunities, health, and security. In this future, we know what matters, don't we? In the great state of Georgia, we will always live our faith. We will always live a morality that matters."

An arcing applause, catcalls and yells came as Jackson tried to speak once more.

"Thank you . . . thank you all for your attention. And now, God bless the great state of Georgia."

Price and Jane sat immobile on the sofa. On the screen, most all in the audience were on their feet, fists in the air, the clapping frantic. The moderator stepped again to the stage, waved the clatter down and, after restating the rules on audience participation, the crowd hushed. The next camera shot showed McGee, his chest heaving as he worked to contain his laughter.

"Price, I had no idea, no notion . . . " Jane's thoughts were splintering, the words—her words—were not right. They were too quick, too raw. She said, "A moral imperative?" She said it with so much revulsion, she could hear the accusation in her tone. She wanted it said that way. She wanted Jackson to know how sickening it was to watch this, how his moral imperative smelled. She said, "How can he preach a morality sermon when he's essentially lied to the staff—that airport terminal talk, the enterprise zone gibberish?"

Just listing those travesties, reciting the lies, made Jane's sense of accomplishment seem false if not exploited. Jackson had given not the slightest hint of dollar-a-pack cigarette taxes. Her prayers had helped nothing. Had her mother looked away? Had God winked at the last minute to Plyer Hoots? Little doubt Plyer was this moment puffing a stinky cigar. But a morality imperative? "Price, what in God's name got into him?"

"I did." Her husband was fixed on the television screen. He said, "Me and my father." Price seemed virtually inanimate as he spoke, his lips barely parting. "Jackson chewed up me and my father, then spit us both out before the entire state of Georgia." His face was rigid. Jane could tell that sheath of composure was painful, keeping him from shouting or crying, from doing anything more than simply watching. And talking. At least he was talking. He said, "Jackson knows exactly what he's doing." Not a crease on Price's face suggested a worry, no color any anger. Every emotion inside him was tamped down and even if he didn't want that censorship, Jane could tell something within him was insisting on it. He said, "Jackson is totally out of control."

Her husband's voice was coming from a world that belonged to Egypt, Georgia. Price was now deep inside that world and she—well, all she could do was what Lily had first wanted her to do. She could only watch Jackson break promises he'd made before the full team. But to do it so boldly? She said, "I'll bet Plyer Hoots twisted his arm. Had to. That crowd—Price, just look at the crowd."

Her husband's face softened none. The rigidity was chilling. He said, "No. It's me. Jackson's not about to let me find any peace with what I remember."

Jane didn't buy it. Politics most likely and nothing more. Politics according to Plyer Hoots. What a man might do to up his poll numbers—that's where the moral imperative was coming from, that amoral Hoots method. Jane's mother would have been fuming, literally puffing away with anger. Yet Jane said nothing of politics or Plyer Hoots, for she could almost smell the smoke, the carcinogens that were far more toxic than any moral imperatives. The smoke was unbearable, its risk maybe outweighing any anger at Jackson's performance. Maybe. So she said nothing as McGee claimed the camera's center, his belly jiggling with laughter. The laughter didn't look like a political stunt. Nothing staged at all. McGee looked way too real, his confidence threatening.

"Well, well . . . ladies and gentlemen of Georgia, we know a performance when we see one, don't we?"

Moans came from the audience. An isolated clap quickly dissipated as McGee rose big above the podium and supplied a grandfatherly retort that, with a couple of eye darts to Jackson, soon had the audience giggling. McGee tried to suppress the laughter by motioning with his hands even as his eyes coaxed up greater jest at the Beekman performance.

"Folks, I come before you tonight as just a simple Georgian. No fancy law degree, no string of fraternity affiliations. Folks, I have no record of multimillion-dollar liability settlements, no billion-dollar deals with the tobacco conglomerates. I simply come to you tonight as a Georgian who has learned tough lessons from the red-dirt fields of Clay County. I come to you as a man who knows what it means to be down and out, a man who knows the dangers of name-calling, a man who knows how to recognize the immorality within the easy way out."

McGee swabbed his brow with a handkerchief as though to emphasize what he was talking about, the sweat and dedication. He glimpsed Jackson, a double take causing the glimpse to suggest pity. But McGee didn't simply look at his opponent, he pinned him down with his eyes, his teeth flashing white before Jackson the entire time. When a side camera measured the audience, a conversion process appeared to be working its way through the crowd, the faces now rethinking Jackson, now enraptured with McGee.

"Ladies and gentlemen, the heart of a McGee administration is simple. Opportunity. I know a great many folks are watching me and wondering how they can pay the rent or mortgage, buy groceries and still pay the doctor bills. And I know what those folks are asking—Where's the opportunity when the jobs simply aren't there?"

McGee hesitated, lifting a hand and instead of pointing, marking the air to scratch a solid objection to each of Jackson's proposals.

"Folks, over the past few years, our state lost three hundred thousand manufacturing jobs. To Mexico, to China, to Thailand, and on and on. And here my opponent comes talking about an airport with a new international terminal. You see it, don't you? Thanks to my opponent our hometown jobs will be flying out faster than ever. Folks, a bunch of high-tech ideas just won't cut it when our factories are shut down and our towns sit on the brink of extinction. We need to put our people to work immediately, to make sure everyone—and folks, I mean everyone—has the opportunity to improve their lives right now, to get to work this very moment in Georgia."

McGee made small motions over the podium with his fingers, delicate ones that appeared skilled and deliberate. He was a coarse man talking with elegance—hair silver, face lined with experience.

"Taxes?" McGee shook his head. "Folks, taxes are job killers. If you have any doubt, just drive up to Dalton, to Purvis, Mendenhall. More regulation?"

Once again, McGee answered his question with a turn of his shiny skull first toward and, in an act of freighted opinion, away from Jackson. Laughs came. McGee took an exuberant breath and hurled out a voice that seemed to grow louder and more important with every word.

"He's impressive," Jane said, and when she looked up, she found her husband's face cloaked in soft natural skin once more, relaxed even. Enjoying McGee.

The competition was making Jackson seem petty, those comments on Turner and morality now so small. Jane's heart felt stronger, the pumping more solid. McGee was making sense and her heart was following it. The logic was also coming clearer. Within her, the only possible answer was beginning to flow. No doubt about it. Plyer Hoots had been doing his best to buy himself a governor. It was just as obvious as the good sense McGee was so clearly making.

"Good Georgians, life is too short for name-calling, too tenuous to rely on a wing-and-prayer promise of things turning better someday. Folks, I'm no puffed up, white-shoe lawyer. I'm a simple man with simple answers. So, on Election Day, you just vote your conscience. After all, what and whom you believe in is your choice, isn't it? And come Election Day, I'm sure we'll all vote for a better way. Thank you all and God bless our great state."

The applause cascaded over McGee. His smile was broad and his eyes magical as the audience hollered and many people whistled. At least half the crowd was standing. The time it took to quiet the hullabaloo rivaled the length of the crowd-quieting efforts following Jackson's remarks.

Jane began rubbing her jaws, Price scratching his head. "Out . . . of . . . control," Price said, dragging the words off his tongue. A deep sadness lay in his laugh lines; dejection ringed his eyes. He was making no attempt to hide it from her.

Jane said, "This morality thing stinks."

"Ready to hold your nose?"

"Plyer Hoots, Price. Had to be."

Her husband jarred as though he just now realized what she had been saying. He moved his face close to her, quizzing her with his eyes.

"I hear things down there, Price. And what I know . . . " She wavered. She was a team player, not a tattler. She turned back to the television screen. She said, "I think I heard Jackson talking about this morality plan with Daisy."

"You think?"

"Oh, when Jackson lowers his voice on the telephone, I can't catch it all. But it had to be her. He thunders to everyone else." As the words left her mouth, they felt syrupy, tattler-sticky. "The airport terminal he was talking about—Plyer needs it, that I know. And polls—they're all worried."

Price huffed out his nose, the derision loud. "Well, even if Plyer Hoots does play him like a puppet, tonight that morality tirade was aimed at me."

"But Plyer, he doesn't bother you?"

Price paused, biting his lips as some of the wrinkles on his face settled. A resolution appeared to follow, some singular thought driving him to tap the rim of his wineglass with a purposeful finger. "No," he said. "Jackson can handle Plyer. And he also thinks he can handle me."

Price examined the small amount of wine remaining in his glass, holding quiet in a way Jane knew too well, complex thoughts reappearing, churning within the deepest part of his brain. It was an uncommon but distinctive pattern. When anger truly cut into Price, he often just shut down, going mute in a way that suggested the anger was his personal possession, a valuable but dangerous thing not to be shared with anyone. It irritated Jane at times, but now she welcomed his silence, his self-possession. He was probably correct. Jackson probably could handle Plyer. But she wanted to hear no more of these squabbling boys. What mattered now was the fact that Jackson had said nothing of the dollar-a-pack cigarette tax. He'd simply lied. It was a lie that probably weighed no more on him than the ones he'd made to Lily. Together, those lies had consequences. Jane would confront him, she and Lily, the two of them on Monday morning. Redemption for a Beekman is never easy, but failure to try is unbearable. This was what Jane was thinking as her husband contemplated the remnant of wine in his glass, his eyes not rising at all when the crowd cheered Jackson's answer to a question about Massachusetts and the threat to traditional marriage.

Greenland

LILY'S OFFICE DOOR WAS AJAR. the inside space was dark, shadows hulking about the glow from the desk lamplight, that bilious glow. Jane could not keep spying, but she could sense Lily's presence behind the door, her temperament, that force, so she stood transfixed in the hall, listening as Lily made the kind of tempestuous noises that meant the worst was here, noises Jane had feared from the moment she hung up the telephone last night, a profound sadness that should not have been coming from a winning campaign's chief financial officer.

Paper crackled, a drawer squealed shut, something—a book, her laptop?—fell to the floor with a thud. Maybe Jane was wrong. Maybe Lily was cleaning house, making room for a new computer, a slim, more modern desk. Maybe she was taking a higher campaign position, maybe moving to a field office. The thoughts were silly, foolish to even consider. Jane knew what Lily was doing, and the overpowering question in her mind was a selfish one—should she also leave, should she leave with Lily? Jane had failed her mother—that fact was unavoidable. Sticking with Jackson would never erase it. But leaving with Lily might at least make her mother's best friend feel better. Redemption, after all, had everything to do with feeling better.

Jane peered about the door to see Lily standing before her desk, her back to the doorway, her shoulders curved over a stack of books. She lifted the top one, looked inside the front cover and, seeing right away what she must have suspected, tossed it into a large cardboard box marked *TRASH*. Like that, no second thought at all. Clunk. Lily's fat black pocket calculator was missing from her desk. Gone were the framed pictures that once adorned the console, her plump old dictionary, the stuffed monkey with cymbals in its hands. Jane held her stomach. The light beneath the globe was a narrowing one.

She considered coughing. She considered tiptoeing away, pretending she'd been called back to CellSure on an urgent matter. She could later telephone Lily, blame Price or Alex for some CellSure emergency, or blame herself, her own absent-mindedness. She could give Lily time to calm down, time to reconsider. She could leave the campaign now and never return. Never mind the guilt—the drippy Beekman never-surrender guilt that would drape the rest of her life because she walked away just when things became smelly and tough—a half-hearted commitment, a redemption bailout plan. The thought was too much. Jane couldn't walk away from Lily's door. But she did have a decision to make, a feeling to repair.

Elevator bells sounded behind Jane's back. Voices from the front room bounced closer. A whistling staffer breezed down the hallway past her back, touching her shoulder in a tease. Jane could not escape. She had to face Lily and that sick green light. She had to face her feelings, so she tapped on the door, announced herself, and decided to take a stand with Lily. She would make a decision with Lily and never look back.

"Oh, Baby, thought you might be coming in a bit later this morning." The smile on Lily's face was tight, the same over-pressured smile she wore when Jane looked up from signing over the beauty shop, lips tense with regret, determination securing the corners. Only this morning, lipstick was missing. "Goodness," Lily said, "isn't this the biggest mess you've ever seen?" She hurried her eyes from Jane to the jumble of papers on her desk, the empty space where her laptop used to sit.

"Moving?" Jane asked.

"Done all I can, Baby."

"With what? This antique of a desk?"

Jane felt ridiculous asking such questions, but she wanted Lily to fully explain what happened this weekend, to repeat every word she and Jackson exchanged, the details. The more you talk through things—break them down to the critical components—the more likely things can be fixed. It was a lesson in management she'd learned time and again at CellSure, a lesson taught first by her mother. Her mother was always talking through problems with the beauticians and customers, helping people with their feelings, helping people accomplish things thanks to their feelings, the passion in rightness. Her mother would want Lily to stay. She would insist on it, wouldn't she?

"Time for this old gal to move along." Lily spoke in a rushed breath, straining to contain her emotions. "Replacement's on the way. You'll like him."

Jane dropped her satchel to the floor, hurried across the room to embrace the quaking Lily, holding her until the heaving stopped and her sobs slowed. "Cheap shots," Lily moaned, her voice unpracticed and slobbery. "They're not for me. Not now, not at my age."

Jane had been girding her mind for this moment, her thoughts testing explanations of how seesaws work in politics, that give and take Jackson always demonstrated with his hands. She was prepared to say the image one must endure in politics is always a distorted one—the world stretched flat as a map, so the truth blurs at the edges to create the distortion we accept as Greenland. This lesson was what the student of politics in Jane's mind had finally learned, this lesson Lily probably learned a long time ago. *You remember Greenland, don't you, Lily? It's just the nature of politics, the map still workable despite the flaws, everyone eventually winding up in the places where they needed to go. The birth of a virtuous effort must sometimes smell awful. But odors dissipate, Lily. Results endure.* This was the explanation her mother would have made, the directive she would have offered with unquestionable authority. *Keep doing what you can. Hold your nose. Rock your hands. The problem was simply Greenland—remember?*

Jane coaxed Lily to one of the chairs pushed against the wall, the accountant's steps small and wobbly. She seemed frail, and Jane recalled her mother making these same steps as she moved to the chemotherapy chair in those last months, that path growing longer with every trip to the doctor's office. Still, in those many weeks Jane had led her mother where she needed to go, both of them following a distorted map, the only map they had. They had done what they had to do, what their feelings demanded—that truth was not blurred at all.

Lily was dressed in a pink cotton outfit, blouse and pedal pushers appropriate for a moving day. On her feet were fluorescent yellow-and-green running shoes, red reflecting bands strapped about the heels—shoes made for serious runners, shoes to be contemplated once Jane and Lily were sitting in chairs that faced each other. And so the inspection began, Jane and Lily stooped over and together scrutinizing those fancy running shoes.

"I sure didn't want to cry," Lily said, her breath staggered but powered just enough to expel her voice. "Crying's not me. It's not." From the hallway, someone yelled, "Morning!" The exclamation seemed to lift the pall in the darkened office, for Lily shouted back at the empty doorway. "Morning!" An abruptly reinvigorated Lily turned to address Jane. "Like my new shoes? Want folks to see me when I come a-running." She crossed her legs and jiggled a foot in the air.

"So they can take cover?" Jane asked.

"So they can haul ass." Lily gave Jane's knee a girlish squeeze. "There's no stopping this old gal now!" She repeated the words, even louder. "No stopping this gal now that she's got a beauty shop to redo!"

"Lily, what happened?"

The accountant dodged Jane's eyes.

"It was Plyer, wasn't it?"

Lily raised a hand to her brow, running her fingers over the skin as if feeling for a bump. "No, Baby. Plyer's shameful but it's a legal shame. That I've made sure of. No, ma'am. For me, what Jackson said was personal."

Jane inspected the disheveled office, the void that had already moved in—dust outlining the spots on a shelf where family photographs once sat, emptiness replacing the slapdash sticky notes Lily always tacked along the edge of her desk. Jane said, "It was the airport, wasn't it?"

The chief accountant signaled "no" with her head, her eyes searching the office. She squirmed in her chair, finally fixing on Jane. "Baby, Brad Turner didn't deserve those comments from Jackson." Her voice was imploring, the comment all plea.

"That was also Plyer," Jane said. "Must have been."

The wells within Lily's black pupils were full, the deep-water calling. Her lips trembled. "I once had a brother," Lily said. "I did." Her eyes shut as her chin went up. "Oh, we always knew Carl was different. But something he did or maybe said—I don't know—something came up during that summer right before he was to leave for college, something that set my daddy to preaching. And my daddy didn't stop preaching. He stayed after Carl, warning him about the boy he was running around with, warning him about some sickness inside his soul." Lily's hand shook as she lowered her head. "My brother, Baby . . . after daddy ran him off, we never heard a word from him."

Jane drew her chair closer to Lily. She held the finance chief just as her mother once held her on a bad-news day decades ago in Baltimore. In this closeness, there was nothing more to surrender, nothing more to be said, endured, or explained. Jane could only hold Lily tight and rock with her as the kick-ass shoes clung to her feet.

Out front, a ruckus was building. The cheerleaders had turned on their boom box, the music coming from a pop music radio station, the announcer interrupting at times with a loud cowbell and orders. "Okay, ladies. Time to roll over!" People were rustling about the coffee and donut table. Another quick shout of "Morning!" from the doorway caused Lily to wipe her tears and return to sorting the books on the desk as Jane sat watching and wondering about Carl's age and where he might now be living.

"No," Lily said in a composed voice. "When Jackson was attacking Brad Turner, he was going after my Carl. That's the way I saw it, and always will."

"And you told him that?"

Lily lifted a paperback manual to show Jane the title—*Guide to Georgia's Election Laws*. She tossed it in the trash box. "Baby, I made damn sure Jackson knew why I was quitting, why he'll be losing more people if he didn't come off that morality high horse of his."

"And did he . . . apologize?"

"Jackson? That boy's not about to apologize. He's a politician; he rationalizes. Called it preemptive politics, said McGee was gonna go after him for staying quiet on Turner." Lily's shoulders went higher. She thrust out her head and wiggled her behind in her seat to pantomime an all-too-obvious chicken that had to be Alice. "Said he and Alice needed to make a last-minute decision—defense or offense." Lily jiggled her head in mock clucking gesticulations and slapped her hands together in a hearty dismissal of Alice. She motioned her eyes to the doorway, to the crowd of jabbering voices in the great front room. "Listen to 'em out there."

What Jane heard was the exultation of a mob intoxicated with publicity and the high prospect of winning. This was the frenzy Jane was thinking of leaving, for this kind of politics was just too dirty for her, the odor too strong. This kind of redemption wasn't worth a hurt Lily. "You know," she said, "I need to leave, too."

Lily, who had returned to sorting the books on her desk, raised her voice as she kept at her task. "Baby, let me tell you something that took me years to understand. Way back when your momma started doing my hair after that Magnolia Room incident, I was still into demonstrating some. So, of course I asked your momma to join in. Nothing big—just a bake sale and rally we were having one night at Spelman." Lily lifted her daddy's bible, opened the cover and examined the pages. "But your momma said it just wasn't her. That hurt me. Back then, it sure did. But after that, your momma—" Lily fixed her eyes on something pleasant she appeared to recognize inside the bible. "Your momma slipped me a hundred-dollar bill. She did it, slipped me that big money and told me not to tell a soul."

A soul—Lily had voiced it, had brought it alive. Jane could picture her mother's soul, her mother's soul within her body, her mother's back turned from the shop girls, her hands going through the leather pouch where she kept the shop's folding money. Jane could see her mother watching for other people's eyes, hiding the hundred-dollar bill as she slipped it into Lily's palm.

"Took me a long time to realize your momma was doing all she could back then."

Jane followed it—she thought. You do what your soul insists you do, what your body allows. You do it within the world that's watching. You hold your nose until you can't. And then you breathe a stinking world that relies on *Caesar's Woman* to keep the place livable. For the sake of your soul, you douse yourself in cologne and play along. You gamble with your feelings. "So why don't you stay?" she asked Lily.

"Like I said. It's personal. I just can't put up with that kind of preaching from somebody who never even met Carl." Lily put aside her daddy's bible, tossing the last of her books in the trash box before moving to a heap of disarrayed papers. She said, "Come that final day, there'll be ample room in the great rapture wagon for folks like my brother. Hell, Carl just might be sitting up front."

Jane followed this thinking also, she thought. She smelled Lily's cologne and she would smell the cologne and this putrid world as she helped Lily pack. She would help Lily leave and once a replacement was sitting at Lily's desk, she would spend a few more weeks developing talking points for Jackson's general election campaign and educating him on the surgeon general's new tobacco report. She would do what it took to make Jackson proclaim that a dollar-a-pack was the Beekman goal on cigarette taxes. Something noble had to come from all this make-do and suffering. She would seal a public health victory for Alex and her mother, for herself and all those other people whose diagnoses might otherwise come too late. She would wear cologne and people would smell it and think of Lily. She would remember Greenland, how it's not near as big as the map must make it look.

Mirage

THE RAIN HAD STOPPED AND the air was thick with its passing. The day had been long and hot, the sun relentless in its crawl, an early evening thunderstorm ungodly torrential but brief. The light that was left in the sky lay low and clingy. It was clinging to Jane and everything she saw, the business ledger in her lap, the icy gin and tonic in her hand, the porch where she sat in a rocking chair. In this light, the sun-scarred backyard was trying to come back, the parched grass and crinkle-leafed plants. The process was wet and heavy, so thick in the air it stunk, this aroma of awakening worms and hatching mushrooms, wet roots stirring manure into dirt. No. Nothing good in this world was forever beat down, nothing noble fully destroyed. Changed maybe, but not eliminated. She sipped.

The time for deep thinking was here, the time for evidence assessment and contemplation of a reworked strategy. When Lily left today, Jane couldn't stay in that basement—the contrast between the jubilation in the great room and the sick green shadows in Lily's office was simply too sharp. So she drove to CellSure, parked in her spot, killed the engine and watched the midday sun lay hard atop the hot car hood, the air above it vibrating. Energy was before her once more, a shifting plasmatic that, on any other day, she would have dismissed as inconsequential. But today the enigma of a soul-filled entity had set her brain to heavy thinking, to conceiving of the impossible as essential. Science, she knew, would call the air's agitation a trick of sunlight and variant densities, a deception in visual signals, a mirage. But today, the science mattered little. The quivering spectacle had taken her back to the bedside where her mother's soul troubled the air before it transitioned, that soul struggling to stay when it knew it couldn't. Today's sight above the hot car hood was a sign, a signal that Jane had so much more to do in this campaign's stinking world. Today's rippling air was a blessing, so Jane took a generous sip of her gin and tonic and returned the glass to a side table. She opened her mother's business ledger to examine the photographs and keepsakes, to find a better sign.

She flipped the pages until she found what she was looking for—a snapshot of her mother and Lily standing before the grille of Lily's bright yellow Cadillac, a Sedan DeVille. Here they were happy, two women in swanky pantsuits framing the inner engine, Lily dangling the car keys before the camera, Jane's mother holding the answer to the question that would appear in her daughter's mind more than thirty years later—that sign. The sign was a cigarette in her mother's hand. In 1972, Jane's mother and Lily were ready to hit the gas and not look back. And if that escape meant running over a politician and his wealthy manipulators decades later they might hesitate, but they'd go on, the sacrifice worth it. Probably laugh at the bump. Such facts were more than a blessing. The photograph was reassurance, the only science that mattered when it came to Jane's decision.

Today, she shouldn't have been looking to the Internet for other signs, but she had. Plug the name Plyer Hoots into a search box and up comes the homepage for StarSat Electronics, which is trailed by links to all the good deeds the chief executive has done. Scholarships, endowed professorships, a Jumbotron—Plyer Hoots was simply buying his way through this world, one governor at a time. The fact was indisputable. Replace Plyer's name with the words *mirage* and *soul,* hit *enter* and up pops connections to crack-pot psychology. Jump a few links ahead and the screen becomes a playfield of herbal remedies and essays on the diagnostic implications of hallucina-tions. Today, most searches kept Jane returning to the Internet's wacko land. At one point, she felt as if she belonged there. It was still an open question, which was a fear that prompted her to place her mother's picture back in the spine of the ledger where it belonged. She closed the covers on any new questions and took another sip of her gin and tonic. She rocked.

The gin was making her brain less anxious, memories more vivid, evolving images better and far more accurate. In this overheated day's last light, she let another world's breeze sweep away her thoughts as she held the ledger in her lap and prepared a strategy that included an ultimatum—*Cigarettes taxed at a dollar-a-pack, Jackson, or I'm out of here.*

The world Jane watched was a safe place now and became even safer once Price came home and joined her on the back porch. He was tired and didn't care for a gin and tonic. Wine maybe, but later. He rocked.

"I have something to show you," he said, pulling a folded piece of paper from his shirt pocket and passing it to her.

Light from the kitchen window fell on the unfolded paper and revealed the format of a letter. Jane went closer to the blackened type, the bold font that lay below the CellSure logo.

Dear Editor, I am writing in response to my brother's opening statement . . .

In the earth's tropical silence, Jane read an apology to Brad Turner and his family. She read a statement on Beekman family traditions, compassion for the down-and-out, consideration for the different and disadvantaged.

Nerves at the base of Jane's brain chilled as the letter's typewritten information went tingling to the tips of her fingers and bounced back like the buzz of a busy signal. Her spine was a metal stick. The furrows on Price's brow lay lank and determined. He stilled. Jane stopped her rocker and began to recite the closing paragraph out loud.

Morality matters most when you must choose between right and wrong, and what my brother chose in that moment was wrong. Still, I support him. His true policies are sound and good for Georgia.

"Price, what is this?"

"Maybe I should let it sit a while. See any typos?"

"Humiliating, Price. You're humiliating him. The newspaper can't publish this letter. It can't print—"

"I think the newspaper will be filled with letters like this."

"But Price, a letter from his own brother? You've got—"

"I've got to let people know that what Jackson said was an embarrassment to his family." His voice was resolute, convinced. The deep thinking time for him was over. Something real had come of it and to that triumph, he resumed rocking, turning from Jane to the backyard and the deepening dark.

She refolded the letter, let it rest atop the ledger in her lap. This letter was too much, impulsive, the product of brotherly bickering that had left Price's brain with an irritation in the motor cortex. She thought it wise to let the letter sit for a while, give the inflammation time to heal. She thought it even wiser for her to say nothing more of the letter tonight, to merely rock and listen.

The light from the kitchen window was too harsh for any hope of a noiseless evening with an irritated husband. So Jane offered him a sip of her gin and tonic. "The heat's convinced me," he said, drawing close to take the glass from her hand. He sipped a couple of times before returning the last of the disappearing drink to her.

"Price, will you show it to him first?"

"Hadn't planned on it."

Jane finished the liquid and returned the emptied glass to the side table. She made loathsome talk about Lily leaving and Alice's explanation for the last-minute change in Jackson's speech. She talked of the surgeon general's pending update to the original report on the connection between smoking and cancer. She did all the talking. "Forty years ago next week, the surgeon general issued the first report. Forty years now, and the facts are stronger than ever. Got to brief Jackson on the update." She reached over and placed a hand on the arm of her husband's rocker. "Maybe you can join us. Thursday at lunch."

"Why?"

"To talk." She handed him the letter, waving it first before his face. "Think about it, Price. You could cost us the election."

"I know."

Price wasn't looking at her when he spoke. His attention lay only on the letter, which he refolded and slipped into his shirt pocket before resuming his rocking. Beyond them, the earth lay unnaturally dark.

Ultimatum

To people with important opinions, the courtyard café was a haggle-free oasis in the midst of downtown's heat and hustle. A breeze wafted constantly among the diners thanks to two gigantic fans that spun on back corner poles. Walls of potted hibiscus and a black-suited host kept panhandlers and smokers at a safe distance. Jackson liked Clyde's for lunch, he said, because it was convenient, the waitstaff efficient. He didn't say it was a good place to be seen, but Jane knew it was. She'd been there twice, both times with a vendor who was courting her and Price for a CellSure business contract. Vendors always treated them like the imperial people *Atlanta Today* featured in photographs taken over tables at Clyde's. The magazine cameras once caught Plyer Hoots at Clyde's Café— Plyer with a cigar in his mouth, his right arm tight about his daughter, his left tugging Jackson closer. Plyer's cigar, rigid as an erection, seemed to dominate the picture. When Jackson suggested Clyde's, that pornographic image of Plyer was the first thing to enter Jane's mind, the dirtiness between his teeth.

Jane and Price were on time, but Jackson was late, so they claimed a table that allowed a good view of the front gate. They sipped iced tea and small-talked like tourists who didn't know Clyde's belonged to A-listers. They watched as the courtyard crowd grew larger and louder with the usual business types in dress-down summer wear and a need to be seen.

Jane's worried brain triggered her eyes to fix on every arriving guest. Overhead, a massive red canvas held back what it could of the sun, the orange under-glow painting a flush on every face, on some older men—the vendors, she guessed—the sense of pressure. In Jane's hand was a printout of the PowerPoint slides she'd made for Jackson, four decades of tobacco control efforts condensed into fifteen slides. Four slides to a page: from Surgeon General Terry's 1964 treatise to the updated report the Feds were to publish next week. She was proud of the slide distillation, thought of it as the Disneyland version. Thought of it as the basics with a twist—the twist being the last slide, which outlined a campaign commitment to raise cigarette taxes to at least a dollar-a-pack. *Cigarettes taxed at a dollar-a-pack, Jackson, or I'm out of here.*

Jane was set. She had the ultimatum in black and white, the slides ready to be projected or contemplated in private. The last slide, that ultimatum, was a must. The only question was the timing within the new tax legislation—a phased-in approach or all at once. Jane pondered this critical timing matter as Price kept talking of his simplified, newsprint-ready letter.

"Here, want to see it?" He patted the protuberance in his shirt pocket.

She pointed with her eyes to the front of the café, where Jackson stood. "Too late."

Jackson maneuvered his face over the host's welcoming podium, straining to search the crowd, delighting in the challenge of placing names on photogenic guests. Shortly, he stood tall and business-like, striking a confident pose as if to show anyone watching him what shoulders and stance he had. Shadowy stubble on his cheeks, blue seersucker trousers and amazingly white shirt. Eyes had indeed turned to him and he knew it. His right arm was strapped across his chest, the raised hand clutching his seersucker suit jacket, which hung over his left shoulder like the baby blue carcass of some cartoon animal he'd just killed. His smile went all white when he spied Jane, but at the sight of Price, his lips lowered. Still, it was a smile, so Jane and Price stood, watched and waved as the candidate worked the hands of an adoring crowd on the path to their table.

"Price, man. What you doing here?"

"Moral support." Price tilted his head to indicate Jane. His voice was snappish, but the answer prompted the brothers to grin and hug like men must do when they know they're being watched, spines stiff so the hearts inside their chests kept a healthy distance.

Jackson said, "Mighty important public health event coming up." He winked to Jane, pausing none as he slipped his suit jacket over the back of his chair. Like all the other lucky people at Clyde's, all three Beekmans were soon seated.

Price spread his napkin over his lap, examining the unfolded cloth for crumbs and grit that couldn't possibly be there. Jane imagined he looked for the debris because even a remote possibility seemed a fine reason for him to avoid any deep eye contact with his brother. Price continued to keep his eyes low, but his voice was clearly loud enough to be heard by Jackson when he said, "Moral support helps when morality's on the line."

"Indeed, it does." Jackson reached over the table, drummed his forefinger directly in front of Price as if to demand his attention. "Morality matters—sorta catchy, don't you think?" Price started to snort and probably frown, but the unsettled gestures were interrupted when the menus came and all heads sank for a merciful meditation.

More stilted banter followed once the orders were taken, Price boasting of the upcoming federal contract and Jackson bragging of Jane's contribution to the campaign. "Quite the serendipity," the candidate said. "Surgeon general issuing a new report here in the middle of our election year." Jackson lifted Jane's printout, pointed at the first slide to show his brother. "Might say preordained, don't you think?"

"Might say it," Price answered. "Yes, I might say it."

"Good enough, my man. Good enough."

Jackson, who had been peeking at the other diners in the courtyard, turned about in his chair to salute a couple of guys who had just appeared at the front gate. All the while he was telling Jane that he would review the slides tonight, telling her the timing was ideal because a reporter for *Time* magazine was interviewing him tomorrow. "Said she wants to profile—get this—the South's Leading Healthcare Hero." He reached over to thump a finger this time before Jane. "Can you believe it? Me—a healthcare hero?"

Jackson's voice was loud and bouncing between Jane and Price, the baritone drawing inquisitive looks from their neighbors, some covering their whispers with a hand as they tried not to stare. Jane felt her head nodding, the sweat of performance seeping beneath her arms. She was thankful for the electric fans. She was also thankful Price was here. She would have a witness to her ultimatum. She would persevere and probably even smile if someone showed up to snap a picture. She said, "Jackson, two things—"

"Name it."

"What we talked about my first day." She reached across the table and flipped her slide printout to the last page. She pointed. "I know Alice is planning a press release for Tuesday. So here I try to make it clear—cigarettes taxed at a dollar-a-pack. Good for the press statement, don't you think?"

Jackson squinted. As the words on the slide seemed to come all too clear to him, the orange on his cheeks yellowed. "Dollar-a-pack," he said under his breath. "That's what we talked about." He raised his eyes, fixing them not on Jane but on Price. "Big brother, how does dollar-a-pack strike you?"

Price sent a hand over the table, tapping at a spot directly before Jackson as if in a dare. "Overdue," he said. "Way overdue."

Jackson reached up to grab Price's hand, giving it a hearty squeeze. "Amen, Chief. That's what I wanted to hear." The brothers' strained hands slipped back to their proper places beneath the table, where they remained in a kind of polite ceasefire while the waiter served the meal.

"A toast," Jackson said, lifting his glass of iced tea. "To the real healthcare mover and shaker in our midst." He pointed to Jane with his glass, glancing about to make sure everyone watching him knew who the true mover and shaker at this table really was. Jane was reluctant to join in the toast—that typical tired ritual of notables caught in the pictures snapped at Clyde's, this cliché executed over impromptu deals that probably dissolved even before the grins and martinis wore off. But she could do it if that's what it took to up the tax on cigarettes to a dollar-a-pack. So she joined Price in toasting Jackson's raised glass. The clinking sounds entered her ears and rattled her brain with the hollow timbre of a make-believe deal.

Jackson's fork moved quickly to his salmon, the candidate eating and talking between bites. "You know, timing can prove a deal breaker in politics, especially when it comes to new legislation. You have to catch people when they're receptive, when they have to ask themselves why such a law was not already in place."

"Overdue," Price said, "that's what I meant when I said it's overdue."

Jackson was nodding. "And right you are from *our* perspective, but we also have to remember all those people who might disagree with us." He raised his glass of tea, sweeping it high to indicate all those potentially disagreeable people in the courtyard. He sipped and focused on Jane. "Alice has already drafted a series of proposals for the general election and this—the buck-a-pack tax—is near the top of the list."

A delay, Jane thought—the general election was four months away. Jackson was procrastinating. She pressed him. "Why not next week? Say, with the press release?"

Jackson pondered her question and seemed ready to respond when a woman came over and patted his shoulder. When he turned, the woman reached out to shake his hand. Several people at the other tables were watching, a trail of them promptly lining up to hobnob with the leading candidate for governor. And once a great many hands were shaken and the admirers gone, the candidate said the momentum was too high now for talk of taxes. "Just look," he emphasized, pointing to the remaining diners. "The vibe's all about deals. Can't you feel it?" He explained how talk of cigarette taxes must come right before the next publicity surge, which would flow just a few days before the general election. "The crew's already drafting a proposal to cut personal income taxes. Plan to roll the cigarette tax in with it, give the whole deal a star-spangled rollout. End run-around, they call it. One last touchdown before the game's called." Jackson kept his voice going to Jane, but his eyes were making for others in the café, especially two dark-skinned men holding cigars between their lips.

Jane was determined to hear something better. "But the press release is all about the connection between the tobacco settlement and the CDC update. Shouldn't we at least *mention* the cigarette tax?"

Jackson was picking at his salmon with a fork and when he spoke, he sounded as if he was consoling the pink flesh. "Yes, next week's focus is the federal situation. But the state specifics—like the cigarette tax—I'm reserving for the general election." He took a bite, chewed thoughtfully as if reassessing his opinion, some internal debate culminating in a brisk answer. "After all, we've got to have something important, truly important to talk about in November, don't we?"

Price swooped his face low to catch Jackson's attention. "Can you make that a commitment? Right after the primary, a statement on upping the cigarette tax to a dollar-a-pack?"

"And not phased in," Jane added. "What we need is a solid dollar-a-pack tax proposal in the first bill."

Price's face was heated, his jaw more jutting. The courtyard fans were working hard to keep the air circulating. "So, straight up. Will you speak out on the tax?"

Jackson dropped his hands to the table, clamping his fingers about its linen-draped edge as he pushed back to appraise the only family he had in this world. He gave a sly smile, one end of it far higher than the other end as he matched eyes with Price. "Of course. It's my promise to you." At the sounds of the words and the insider smirk that came with them, Price retreated. Still, Jackson tracked him. "And when I make a promise, Big Brother, I keep it."

Price dismissed the comment, repositioning his fork and appraising the glass of tea before taking a sip. A stillness settled over the table, a quiet so fierce the big electric fans could not remove it until Jane reassured herself of the success of her ultimatum. After all, nothing could change until Jackson actually took office. Too, the results were more important than the process. She said, "I think a promise is something we can all work with."

Jackson dipped his head in agreement. "So what's that second thing we need to talk about?"

"Price," Jane said, motioning to her husband. "He has something we need to share with you."

A fat man suddenly appeared at Jackson's back, his plump hands encircling the candidate's neck. "Good God," the man said, "look who's here!" Jackson twisted about and called the big man Dale, this stranger who proceeded to make sure everyone in the café could hear him. "Well, I sure couldn't leave without saying hello to our next governor!" Jackson started to stand, but Dale stayed him with a mighty hand. "Don't get up, Governor. Don't want to interrupt something really important."

With Jackson's attention diverted, Jane reached over and pulled the folded letter from her husband's shirt pocket. She placed it on the table, pressing it flat in a firm but light-hearted manner, which she was hoping Price would appreciate. She wanted to think the hard part of this conversation was over, that Jackson's promise to up cigarette taxes would not weaken one bit once he saw a letter with some tough words coming from his brother.

Jackson sent Dale away with a knuckle bump, and just as the slaphappy candidate was turning back to the table, Price grabbed the prepped letter, so all the repositioned Jackson saw before him was the picked-over salmon.

"Price—Man, you had something for me?"

More people were leaving, the departing crowd so noisy the big fans on the poles couldn't keep up with the perfumed banter. Jane imagined her husband explaining his opinion, qualifying it first, preparing his words because he might be reconsidering the letter altogether.

Price made a stern face. "What I wanted to talk about was the check. It hasn't cleared the bank yet. You still have it, don't you?"

Jackson hardened. He pulled his napkin from his lap, placing it to the side of his plate. He jostled his head in the savvy affectation he usually offered reporters with gotcha questions. "Dang," he said. "Slipped my mind. Been so busy, just haven't had a chance to deposit it." He gave a sigh, working not so hard to conceal a grin. "That debate, it just about did me in."

"Dang," Price answered. "Me, too." He smiled.

Shells

THE HOUSE WAS FILLED WITH the austere silence of things having been touched by other people, the coffeepot and toaster repositioned, a cup put away. It was the sensibility Jackson had grown to expect on cleaning days, but tonight the silence seemed deeper, cleaner. It was the silence of drawers opened and the contents examined, cabinets explored. Everything cleaned from the inside out. The sheen of tung oil on the dining room table had yet to dry, and the odor was strong. The hallway was dark but not darker than usual, not really. He stepped to the foyer.

The light from a front yard lamp fell through the windows and lay oblique on the wood floor as it always did this time of the night, sharpness aligned, the usual geometry. Beyond the glass, nothing was out of place, the brick pathway bare. Clipped limb, green pinecone. Brass padlocks held all the doors. Security sensors blinked red near the knobs. Jackson was simply too tired to be concerned about the silence of a too-clean house. He returned to the dining room table, to the stack of waiting mail, and there lifted a curiously wrapped little box.

After the 2001 attacks, capitol security alerted all elected state officials to not open any unsolicited mail, including that sent to a private address. Suspicious items were to be inspected, scanned for metal and sniffed by dogs. Concerns went to Clay Highsmith, the security chief who died of cancer last year. Jackson went to the funeral, shook hands with Clay's replacement, a man with a simple name, something like Bob. Maybe Bob sent an introductory email, but if he did, Jackson deleted it. Joe, it could have been. Never had Jackson sent his private mail for inspection by a bureaucratic replacement with a plan. Never had a reason to. He stood at the table, shook the box and wondered about Bob or Joe.

The box fit the size of checkbooks, a fresh set from the bank, the address maybe hand lettered by a teller with special needs. Black magic marker on brown grocery bag paper, ragged letters. Duct tape sealed the corners. This box was not from a bank. A bank teller, even with special needs, would never use duct tape. The bottom was stained by tung oil. Candelina did it. A good job that girl did, tabletop as well as the legs. Let the oil soak into the grain before starting the rub, just as she was supposed to. But she'd gathered the mail and left it on the table before the top was dry. Probably rushed—another job. Someday he would make her legal, a Candelina Law signed, say, in the third year, an immigration precedent for the nation. Ambassadors would visit, presidents call. Maybe the second year would be better.

Jackson shook the box, listening as something rattled inside it. Candelina was a good girl, and he was a good governor or would be, a great one in fact. He was too tired, the house too sleepy. The disabled hand had jittered as it moved across the wrapper—his name, the home address. A childish tiny heart claimed a corner. The postmark said Maryland.

Loopy Ellen, one of the division lawyers, was from Maryland. Momma's girl, an old maid, she flew home every couple of months. Would be just like Ellen to pop him tickets to the Orioles or, knowing her Baltimore tastes, knockoffs of the vintage postcards she kept on her office walls, or, given the size of the box, hokey salt and pepper shakers, one labeled *Luv Ya,* the other, *Hon*—a set exactly like hers. He couldn't recall whether old Ellen was one in the cubicle bunch with a crush on the boss. That he should have known, but he just couldn't recall, not tonight. He was that tired. He should call capitol security, look up Bob or Joe, or just toss the box, do some push-ups, suck down a few good puffs of Sinaloa Gold then soak in the tub and let his mind roam to Arizona and once there raise the border wires for a few more girls.

He opened it. The tape split clean when he took a steak knife to it, the grocery bag paper falling free to reveal a checkbook box from the Maryland Security Bank. He'd never heard of the Maryland Security Bank. He shook the box. Things rattled on this side and when flipped to the other side, everything inside it sounded loose. Something had broken. He ran the knife through the Scotch tape that bound the top to the bottom. He lifted the lid and out came shells.

Tiny white shells, actually little claws that in pieces powdered out on the table. Inside the box were chunkier parts. He stepped back. He squinted and sniffed before he remembered Bob or Joe said to never inhale, to hold your breath and run to another room, call 911. The shells had no odor. Ellen Hollingsworth was crazier than he thought. He picked about the chalky contents of the box with the knife until he could tell it contained nothing more than shells. Actually, pieces of shells and a few claws, most shattered. He lifted the box, holding it at arms length as he carried it to the kitchen sink. He opened the bottom cabinet, pulled out a trashcan, and upended the box. The shells tinkled like Cracker Jack toys as they tumbled one after the other into the trash. A folded, tightly pressed white piece of paper spilled last from the box. He'd missed it with the knife.

Jackson pulled the white paper from the trashcan and unfolded it to find a full-sized sheet of typing paper, a photograph laser printed at the top. The reprint was grainy, black and white, amateurish, faces gray. He held the sheet at a distance, moving it to the light from the stovetop hood. He looked closer. Two faces, two men face beside face in a hug. At the sight, his hands locked and his eyes sank closer to the paper. It was his face in the picture, him and Tommy Carpenter.

The night was too quiet, Jackson's nerves too dazed. Loopy Ellen was sick, Bob or Joe dozing like a bureaucrat with an outdated plan. Jackson placed the letter on the kitchen counter, positioning the knife so it held the page flat. He wrung his hands to warm his fingers. He examined the sheet of paper, all of it. And when he turned away, the house awakened. The refrigerator started to drone. The icemaker cycled through a spurt and hiss until a valve slapped back and the jet quit. Above the kitchen sink, the darkness beyond the window stretched all the way to Maryland, to the restaurant where the picture should never have been taken. Tommy couldn't have survived these years, not the way he was living. This was a joke. Tommy Carpenter, if not dead, was sick as Ellen. The security system was engaged, the house clean as a Mexican girl could make it. So perfect in fact, she deserved to be legal. He read the message below the picture, the squiggly print.

Hi Governor, Remember me? Remember us? Call me, Sweetie. We need to talk.
PS—I kept the claws.

The picture was back, the moment unlocked with a key that wasn't his. Jane had taken the snapshot, Price watching. It was taken in Baltimore, a place on Fell's Point Pier. That leather, that black leather in a corner booth—if only he couldn't place it there. But he could. It was the Iron Gate. Jackson was sure of it. The Iron Gate Restaurant. He and Tommy, they'd driven up in his silver Jetta on a damp chilly night that turned foggy and cold as Jackson drove alone back to Washington. The Iron Gate. The name made his stomach twist just as it had twisted after the meal that night, although this time his belly was empty. Jackson was twenty-four back then, a tenderfoot clerk at the Supreme Court. He was proud, adventuresome, smart. Reagan was in the White House, Tommy Carpenter a librarian on the Hill. Tommy had been in Washington for years, knew Edward Kennedy, had a pass to the congressional gym. In the picture, Tommy's hand was tugging Jackson closer. Tommy was tugging and shoving his cheek, his slap-ass silly cheek close to Jackson's ear. Tonight, some laser printer had Tommy Carpenter in Jackson's ear again, Tommy Carpenter still drunk and making a mess of his life.

Jackson folded his arms about his chest. He was safe here. Here any touched nerves could recover in complete silence.

At the bottom of the page, tucked beneath a deformed smiley face, was a telephone number. Jackson lifted the paper from the kitchen counter and looked up. The room had changed none since he'd opened the box. The hallway was no darker than he'd first found it. But inside his brain, all the working places were shrinking, the walls too close, too pinched by a scar of his memory spelling the name Iron Gate. The scar throbbed as the tissue swelled. He felt the compression, smelled the crab claw odor of Tommy's mouth.

The shucked shell odors were coming fast that evening when he and Tommy Carpenter joined Jane and Price at the celebration, the going-away dinner his mother's treat. She had mailed a gift certificate and, of course, she wanted pictures, good ones. Price and Jane were finally leaving Hopkins, what they called an ordeal done. Already the truck was loaded. It was September. The leaves had turned. Jackson wanted no pictures, but Jane insisted. After all, his mother was paying. Tonight, the Iron Gate was back, the cast-iron curlicues and damp alley shadows, the odor of claws and white meat sizzling.

"Picture time," says Jane, and Tommy Carpenter tosses his arm about Jackson and tugs. "Smile, boys. Say cheese." Tommy Carpenter presses way too close and as the flash goes, Tommy licks and whispers, loud. Price and Jane hear him whisper, they hear Tommy Carpenter say he'd been wanting to taste his boyfriend's ear. Jane coughs. Price tries not to look. Push Tommy Carpenter away and the drunken mouth laughs. Everyone in the restaurant laughs, all the perverts in Dundalk zip up and cackle. This does not happen. It never did, not these people laughing, this whispering that should have disappeared when Reagan left office. It did. It died. It needs to know that it died, that all the night's whispers were buried with it. The happy face on the envelope had a smudged grin.

Jackson leaned on the counter. He was at home here, secure, the paper nothing but a sicko's nasty obsession, what everyone in the public eye must expect from time to time. Jackson ripped it up, dropped the pieces in the trashcan. He replaced the can beneath the sink, poured a glass inch deep with Scotch and sipped the liquor while looking out the kitchen window. He flipped on the backyard lights and, seeing nothing out of place, he finished the Scotch and went to bed.

He couldn't sleep. He should have puffed some weed before going to bed, but the bag was empty. Too busy, just too damn busy. Rain dripped from the gutter outside the window, from the leaf-clogged gutter. He wanted to hear thunder, wanted to snuggle his head beneath a pillow and stretch out in a cave on a high cliff, assume a body-size indentation in the rock, a singular unreachable bed far above the thundering valley. He wanted to sleep, but the people of the valley wouldn't behave. They were too loud. They whispered and pointed. At their fears, God cried. His tears spilled over the dirty edges of Earth. The Lord God was trembling as he watched the people below. Jackson could hear it, he could hear God seethe and quake. The people were so stupid, their choices so lame. Yet they were pointing to Jackson as their best choice, Jackson still accessible here in the rain. So, no—he was not beyond the crowd, not entrenched in a hidden dry spot on a high cliff. He was within the deluge, the rain from a disgusted God. Yet the water that met his face was mixed with tung oil. Mexicans washed their fingers in it like dirty saints. They kept pointing to him, targeting him alone. He simply couldn't sleep, so he climbed from bed and returned to the kitchen.

The only light was from the nightlights, but that was enough. He could see just fine. He felt his way through the hall shadows and into the small haloes waiting below. He stepped down the stairs without making a single sound. No one would ever see what he was doing here in the dark, no one would ever know this secret cave that he could enter in his bare feet once the people hushed their talking. This would not happen and even if it did, the people in the valley couldn't care less. He would call it a dream tainted by tung oil, a Mexican hallucination. He would let the night sleep until the oil dried on its face, any odors evaporate. There was no end to what Candelina might keep clean.

He moved to the darkened kitchen and pulled pieces of the ripped letter from the trash. His cellphone was still on the countertop. He claimed it and returned to the hallway, dropping to the floor of his nylon-carpeted cave. Holding the pieces of the letter within the nightlight's corona, he eyed the telephone number. The paper was in pieces that he could put back together. That's what he could do. He could put it all back together and prove loopy Ellen was seriously psycho.

If loopy Ellen ever hooked up with Tommy Carpenter, she could engineer a clever gag. Tommy was up to it, but he was also dead. This, my dear Ellen, was not a clever gag; this was a pervert's joke. Loopy Ellen probably knew Tommy Carpenter was dead. The homesick Baltimore lawyer needed to update her joke book, and Jackson would tell her that, so he pressed the numbers on his cellphone as he sat on the fine-carpeted floor of his high hallway cave. Here he was safe. He would not press any more numbers. He might whisper, but he would never talk. If there was a record, it would be clean. The phone signal chimed and, as the chain of rings lengthened, he prepared himself for the recorded voice of foolish Ellen, the loopy twist of her Chesapeake twang.

"Hello."

The voice was no machine. The voice was the noisy breath of a devil. Jackson pulled the telephone from his ear and looked at it, this little black talker. He switched it to the ear that Tommy Carpenter never licked. He whispered to the voice only he would ever hear.

"I got the box."

"I'm glad you called."

"Why?"

"As you said, Governor—morality matters. I've been following you on the Internet, Sweetie. And all you said up until the debate made you sound so good, I sometimes wondered if it was really you. Actually, it did sound a little over the top, but I could follow it. After all, it's Georgia. Then there you were—up on that debate stage, you in your fancy suit and tie, you looking oh so good. And next thing I know, you start going all nasty on me. Whew-wee, Governor. For a nasty talker, you still look good enough to lick clean."

"You're drunk."

"My, my, Governor. I'm not drunk, but I'll bet you remember when the drinking was free. *Shirtless Men Drink Free.* Remember that night, Governor? You and me at the Lantern, late July best I recall. Everyone dancing all sweaty-chested and close, the whole world free. Remember, Governor? Remember when you and I were free?"

"You're sick."

"As are you, Governor. Bet you didn't know that, did you? Yep, I even thought you were a little sick back when you walked out on me. Sweetie, are you still impaired?"

"No."

"Good answer. Sounds like you're just as impaired as me. But we were looking oh so good back then. Remember how much better we could have looked if the pictures had only been close-ups? Almost made a magazine, remember? Or has your impairment erased those memories too?"

"Why do this? Tell me. Why?"

"Sweetie, those abs. You still have those swimmer abs?"

Jackson was stuck. The cellphone wouldn't leave his ear. The devil's voice was in it, the evil mouth too close, so parasitic his blood was thinning. Jackson deserved better. The people deserved better. These thoughts didn't help, so he swallowed them whole and once the weight hit his stomach, his trigger muscles responded. He fingered the carpet with his free hand. Beneath him, the people of Georgia were asleep. They were dreaming and this was entirely their dream, so any devils they heard were their own. This conversation, for what it was worth, had changed nothing.

The dreaming people needed their sleep, so Jackson whispered into the hole. "What do you want?"

"Governor, the Internet is such a moral thing. Keeps me fully updated on old lovers and their moralities. And what the Internet convinced me of is that I have a morality, and this morality of mine also matters. Only the doctors tell me mine will matter for less than a year. Funny, ain't it—how quick a morality can go once your liver dies of hepatitis C?"

Jackson could hang up. The hallway wouldn't care. It could see and say nothing. The telephone could play dead, could bend and shut off with one flip in his hand. Its breath was rancid, its tongue clawed. But the claws could be shattered, the pieces bleached and dropped in a can. He could clean it all up, hide the stink with tung oil. He could point with the crowd.

"Governor, you still there? Want to know how I will get some of your moral help?"

Jackson hesitated, but the crowd was asleep. Still, he kept his voice small. "How?"

"An apology, Governor. Need you to tell the good Georgians what you really know—that there is no homosexual agenda, that you *erred* when you said there was one, that you *erred* when you walked out on your boyfriend back in Baltimore. *Erred.* To hear it from your sweet moral lips is as good as a final kiss to little Tommy Carpenter. Like the sound of that goodness, Governor?"

Jackson remained mute.

"Hear me, Governor? An apology, a clear statement that you *erred*. And maybe elaborate some. Yeah, say you always knew the homosexuals had no agenda, that you have no problem at all with our Massachusetts friends. Oh, Governor, how you used to elaborate so vividly with me. Say in a week, Governor? Yep, a week will do just fine. You can make your peace on our favorite radio show. Sure can. You know they're already hyping your encore. My, my—what a treat awaits the ole Dusty listeners. This Internet is truly a remarkable tool. Puts a person in touch with all sorts of reporter types who probably would be glad to talk with a golden boy. Hear me, Governor?"

"No," Jackson said. He was snarling. He wanted to snarl. "No apology."

"Oh Governor, how you jest! I've kept some of the finest pictures, some of the finest shots one might someday find on the Internet. Most magazine quality. Sure are. And the hits would be oh so many from Georgia—our dear governor and his version of a long-lost immorality. Trust me. I know the hits will be many. And know what? It's just like they say—once on the Internet, hide-and-seek's a pretty pitiful game. Sorta immoral to even try, ain't it, Governor?"

"You're crazy."

"Maybe I am, Governor. And crazy people like me do crazy things—like talking to the people who would consider what I know quite a break-through. With our impairments, we really do need a breakthrough. We do—don't we, Governor? Don't you think a breakthrough would make a mighty fine story?"

"You make me sick."

"Now you're getting it. Just hope you don't turn all golden on me. Governor, this liver business does a number on your dance moves. You still dance, Governor?"

"How much? Ten, twenty thousand?"

"Oh, Governor. Like I said, little Tommy's gone golden. What good is money to a golden man?"

Jackson lowered the telephone from his ear. The man on the line needed to choke on a crab claw. But first, the man needed to declare this all a mistake, a wrong number, to plead like a devil about to be flushed down a cellphone's speaking hole. Fact is, nothing has ever come from this little black talker tonight, no foul devil voice, no loopy Ellen doing her just-kid-ding-the-be-Jesus-out-of-me shout out. Ellen has said nothing and never will. No one will ever talk. All those Georgians at his feet, they've heard nothing at all. Absolutely nothing.

"Governor, you have a week before I start talking. Might even put my pictures in gold frames once they're posted for the good people of Georgia to see. That Internet is such a good thing. Almost a blessing. Right?"

"You stink."

"No, Governor. I'm not dead yet. Just remember—no apology, no morality."

"You are a fool."

Jackson dropped the cellphone from his ear and flipped it shut. He unfolded his body on the floor's fine clean carpet. He pressed a hand across the head of every knotted-up, sleeping Georgian. He soothed their woolen snores, ran a finger over their tufted heads. He told them to rest peacefully, to relax with their babies and memories of the dreamed-up dead, to go on and sleep. This night will pass, just as an anguished God might worry the air and come to them as nothing more than a common breeze. The hallway was dry and safe, a heaven of Candelina's Mexican making. A heaven he controlled, him alone. The cliff, it too was his to control, his cave high as the people wanted, high as they needed it. Up here, the thunder never happened, nor the dream.

Skoal

IT WASN'T RAIN. IT WASN'T A clogged gutter or some weepy god supping up his snot-soaked disappointments. Instead a sprinkler, a misplaced jet some guy failed to adjust, was shooting water directly over the hedge, a cycling splatter against the window determined to clock, drop by drop, the night. And like the rain that never happened, the entire night should have been nothing more than a series of misperceptions, a box of unconventional checks simply confused for shells, the voice on the telephone nothing more than the rant of a gnarly telemarketer. All in all, a night doused into delusion by the song from a wayward sprinkler.

Jackson should have concluded it was a prank, or maybe a by-product of his worn-out brain's making, a fatigue-based illusion, a stress-addled thought. Say nothing, and maybe it never happened. But instead he told Daisy. He told her why morality had become a sore on the butt of a man who should have died years ago of an immoral disease. He told her why she needed her daddy to take care of that diseased man's morality fixation. "If your old man had listened to me, this mess never would have happened." He told her he'd had a bad feeling. He mentioned pictures. Apologies, he told her, were for losers, and the only thing a Baltimore loser might value more than an apology was money.

So here comes Daisy talking so ho-hum and unbothered at the news of a Baltimore wacko, all hot to declare Hapeville a waste ground of residential blight. As if Tommy Carpenter was nothing more than another dude to be paid off in a drive-through cash-and-carry deal. "Relax, Jackson. Daddy's an expert at risk control. He'll talk it through with you in a safe place. Get some details and that's that. Crazy people just go with the business. Guess that's why Daddy's always liked you."

❧   ☯   ❧

SO THIS WAS THE SAFE PLACE. HERE, sitting at daybreak with old man Hoots in a canary-colored Rolls listening to his big-mouthed blather about a downturn in the future of the Georgia Tech Yellow Jackets and an uptick in the Mexican stock market. The jolliness was biting, all Plyer, the venom unforgiving. It continued right up until the moment Plyer dropped his hands from the steering wheel, swooned his head about and fixed his eyes point blank on the point of his performance. "Son, I hear you have some trouble with an old acquaintance."

The car was idling beneath a pecan tree in a spot two turns off a Piedmont Park service road. The end-of-the-road pea gravel bed fit the dimensions of a single car, a thicket of briers to the left of the driver, a red dirt gully falling ten feet deep directly beyond the passenger door.

"Tommy Carpenter," Jackson said. "Some Baltimore pervert who wants an apology for that morality tirade, the one *you* started."

It had been years since Jackson spoke Tommy Carpenter's name and the sound of it now, the strange textures it left inside his mouth, made Tommy seem more powerful than he was. With Daisy, the Baltimore pervert had no name. But with her father, the erasure process required the contorted thing to be spoken out loud.

Plyer expanded his focus, gaping at Jackson as if he had just identified the candidate's past as a serious problem. Jackson felt more opinion than suspicion in the inspection, so he twisted in his seat to directly face Plyer, to not only confront the opinion but to redirect it back to its source. He propped a hand on the dashboard to brace himself and from that secure spot he fired. "Years back, I never knew when the guy might show up next.

Only quit harassing me when I threatened to file a report with the Capitol Police. Should have gone ahead and done it, had the pansy fired back then."

Plyer sighed, stooping closer to directly confront the eyes of the state's top attorney. "Tell me, Counselor. Just how did you *know* this Carpenter?"

Jackson didn't blink. He was prepared for an interrogation, all-out war if need be.

"Egypt," he said. "Tommy Carpenter's also from Egypt. We worked together back when I clerked in Washington."

Jackson stared into the tar-pit pupils of one of Georgia's wealthiest men. He looked all inside Plyer's black depth and saw only a reflection of himself, his face absolutely clean, nothing surrounding him the least bit offensive. He was fully professional, so practiced he felt his lips devolve to the thin courtroom-ready smile that he knew would force old Plyer's face back to a respectable distance. And it must have worked because the great glob of Plyer Hoots soon returned to a driver's proper listening position. To this redirected lump of an interrogator, Jackson expounded on the pervert's propensity to exaggeration now that he was dying of an addict's disease.

Plyer swept his eyes over Jackson in a head-to-toe appraisal. Then, as if to conceal the results of that inspection, he turned to the brightest point in the lightening sky beyond the windshield. "Hell fire, Son! When the clock struck the firing time, sounds like you fucked up." His cheeks were bathed in sunlight, both puffy with self-satisfaction.

Jackson's jaw was set, the great bone a monumental thing. He welcomed its weight, the immutability of truth. "Yes," he said. "You could say that."

Plyer was stoked, his sneer steady, pompous. Jackson's take on the situation was undeniably meeting Plyer's expectations, was making the matter proceed in the steps of a predictable process just as Daisy had described it. Jackson wanted to remember to tell her she was right. Tommy Carpenter was merely a ho-hum thing.

"Odd," Plyer said. "If the fellow simply needed money, you'd think he would've named a price up front." Once again, Plyer was scrutinizing. "Counselor, don't you see this all as a little *odd* for a man of your caliber?"

Jackson couldn't argue the point. And, in a way, he wanted Plyer to see the misery weighing on him, to see what the old mogul's miserable implication was doing to the man whose political success just might determine the future of a new terminal at Hartsfield, let alone the livelihood of the big dog himself. Hell, the entire state. And so, he tensed his lips in that contemplative style of a challenged attorney. He said, "Now Mister Hoots, you tell me. Just what's this *odd* matter you're so worried about?"

Plyer dropped his head forward, impaling his brow on the steering wheel. Once more, the Hoots show had begun. "Son, Son." He was shaking his head and turning his eyes between the candidate and a speedometer needle aimed at zero. "All I'm saying is that you set yourself up on a mighty high moral stage, so it wouldn't take much for some fruit of the flesh from your past to be tossed right back at you."

Every nerve within Jackson burned. He didn't have to take this. He leaned his shoulders over the fancy double-R console separating him from this globular honcho who had far more to lose than he did. He insinuated his face directly between the steering wheel and Plyer's sanctimonious eyes. And as Jackson prepared to speak, he felt the muscles in his throat tighten to form that judicial station where every erupting word must satisfy certain dimensions before it was spoken. Then and only then. "Mister Hoots, with all due respect, seems you may have forgotten that the foundation of that moral stage was built entirely by a company called StarSat Enterprises. Mister Hoots, is something about this engineering feat unclear to you?"

Plyer's breath moved over Jackson's face and the candidate breathed it in, that eruption from cigar-stained membranes and whiskey-cleaned cavities. Nasal hairs poked out, tiny veins crawled in. Jackson didn't waver, but Plyer did. He withdrew, hesitantly pulling back from Jackson. "Mister Hoots, you follow me?"

Plyer swallowed, shifting his bulk from Jackson, inching it back in full retreat. He settled against the door grip, as if cornered within his own power but also steadied by its limits. His countenance began to grow, shoulders lifting, enlarging to the point where he was almost hulking over Jackson.

"Counselor," he said, whetting his voice, "I hear there may be *compromising* pictures."

Within Jackson, the spine of an invincible attorney crumbled. He felt his bones soften, his torso twist in a complex distancing from Plyer. Jackson needed more stability, a place to better frame his points, which were multifaceted because Tommy probably had drugstore duplicates, lots of them. Jackson needed time to explain this, so he slid back to a passenger-side position and let his eyes rest on the scrub plum bushes beyond the windshield.

"Damn it, Son! You mean to tell me there really *are* pictures of you with this pervert?"

"It was a long time ago."

"Good God, man! What were you thinking?"

Plyer was almost frothing, his face suffused in the pulse of a purplish wave. He leered at Jackson a moment before returning his blubbery butt to the sinkhole of his seat. He groaned and wiped his mouth with fat trembling fingers. He flipped the air conditioner fan to the four mark and returned his attention to the morning sky.

"Drinking," Jackson said. "They were made when we were out drinking."

Plyer slammed a fist against the steering wheel. He twisted his fat head about to give Jackson a look that transcended disgust, for his head was rocking all the while, rocking as if the old businessman realized he, too, was trapped. And as that realization seemed to condense into something workable within his belly, Plyer's head steadied, ragged swaths of purple fading from his face to leave him once again awash in a deep crimson shade.

"Listen, Mister Hoots. Nothing ever happened in the way you seem to think it did. Hell, most of the time Tommy was stoned."

Jackson felt a new success in his voice, an energy focused on cleaning things up, not wallowing in delusions. Plyer was stroking his jowls as if he also felt this energy, as if the time for making Tommy Carpenter a ho-hum matter had come.

"I've got the money," Jackson said. "All you need to do is make the delivery, make it stick. Magic, muscle—whatever it takes." Jackson's stamina had returned, his lawyerly fortitude rallied. *Muscle* was a favorite Plyer Hoots word. "Fifty thousand," Jackson said. "Enough cash to send the bastard on a long cruise . . . maybe burial at sea."

Plyer's colors stabilized, but the pressure remained substantial behind his eyes. "Listen. You better damn well make sure there's no more abhorrent behavior lurking in your past! You follow that, Counselor?"

Jackson felt the urge to roll his eyes, but cartoonish gestures were dangerous when arguing a serious case. And so he simply reminded himself to keep his voice calm, confident as a seasoned attorney's. "Mister Hoots, just because your life has been filled with indiscretions, you ought not assume other people have had similar experiences."

Plyer grabbed the candidate's arm. He squeezed. "Son, you look at me! That preaching's only digging your hole deeper." He clamped down on Jackson's arm until the candidate cringed, his breath catching as the pain deepened. "Boy, you tell me that nonsense didn't start with you!" Plyer gave a harsh squeeze then relaxed some, allowing Jackson's shoulder to return to a more natural position. The old man seemed to be fuming inside his soul, some limit calling his power. He clearly had more to lose than Jackson.

The victorious candidate stretched his neck, took a couple of breaths, and once a rattled gumption loosened enough to rally within his chest, he looked down mockingly to the grip on his arm. He worked his eyes up to Plyer, letting his voice go just as confidently as he'd once cast it on a skeptical jury. "Mister Hoots, the only thing you have to worry about, Sir, is the cargo limit on an Airbus 330."

Plyer's grip wilted, and as his hand withdrew, the flabbiness in his demeanor returned. He was soon retracting his lips to form that closing smart-ass smile of a typical Hoots transaction.

"Damn, Son. Always have thought you'd be a star performer." He pulled away from Jackson, realigning himself like a responsible driver. He studied the star performer from his original distance, his eyes alive in deal-making glory.

The air was frigid between the two men, the engine idling like a recovering nerve. Plyer pulled a can of Skoal tobacco from his shirt pocket, flipped the lid and slipped a wad into his mouth. He passed the open container to Jackson. "Want some?" The offer appeared serious.

Jackson dismissed the invitation with a shake of his head, careful to avoid any sight of the container's dried sludge. Since when did Plyer Hoots start chewing tobacco? For years, it had been cigars.

Plyer raised the open tobacco container to his nose and sniffed. "Nothing more addictive than nicotine," he said. "But Mister Healthcare Hero here, he already knew that, didn't he?" The question was soaked in sarcasm, its point solely derision. Jackson felt no obligation to answer. To the absence of a response, Plyer put his Skoal can away. The whole time he kept huffing out his nose with satisfaction, his jaw churning as he masticated a sizable plug.

Beyond the windshield, the needles in a far heap of stubby pines stirred when a deer poked its head through a tangle of blackberry bushes. The deer stilled, gazing at the car for an unnaturally long moment, cogging its head higher at the sight of the men. It froze and over a short parade of seconds ratcheted back methodically into the thicket. Plyer was watching the deer and at its disappearance, he turned to Jackson. "You need to marry Daisy."

"What if she doesn't want to marry me?"

Plyer raised a hand and was moving to grab Jackson's arm once more, but this time he was stopped by the candidate's open palm. The angry old groper blanched. "Son, are you telling me I don't know my own daughter?"

"Timing. Daisy seems pretty caught up in your Hapeville project."

Plyer laughed out his nose. He drew back, his lips twisting this way and that until they formed a nasty pucker, which he held while pulling a Styrofoam cup from beneath his seat. He spit into the cup and proceeded to study its nasty contents. "Counselor, I can handle this Carpenter mess. But marriage, any mess you make of that belongs entirely to *you*."

You—that demanding dirty word wafted about the air, and Plyer must have been pleased with its hovering power because his chewing took on greater heft, his lips a pickling smile. He said, "Son, I need you to announce those wedding plans soon."

Jackson turned to brace himself against the passenger-side armrest, the cold leather protuberance meeting him as a fist, the firmness holding. "Don't you think Daisy has a say in this?"

"Son, you've strung my little girl along way too long. What you're going to do, you're going to *expedite* this process."

Plyer spit more tobacco juice into his Styrofoam cup, tipping the lip of the cup to show the juicy load to Jackson. "Care for a sip?" The candidate scowled, and at the sight of another rejection Plyer agitated the cup, pivoting it for a sling of the spent juice at Jackson. "Just kidding." Plyer guffawed at his joke, his plump cheeks swelling even more, which made Jackson look to the far thicket in search of another deer, some sign of a cleaner life.

Plyer gave a grunt of amusement, fixing his countenance in a position that a guard watching from a tree limb might call respectable. "Son, time is cash money in my business. And, in case you've forgotten, my business is your business too."

"Well, let's make it a big affair." Jackson's tone was total scorn. "Say a wedding in the mansion, next year—up for it?"

"Son, you can't outrun my ticker."

"Listen—the cash's gotta be quick. Friday at the latest."

Plyer slapped the heel of his right palm on the steering wheel. "Son, I can handle Carpenter! But you—you've got to deliver. That announcement's not waiting."

"In the mansion, next spring," Jackson said. "Promise."

"Ole Dusty, Son. He's good for these things. You hear me?"

Jackson said nothing, ignoring Plyer's question in favor of the better world beyond his car door window. He could identify with the deer that had seen too much.

"The show's perfect for the announcement. Son, you hear me?"

"Yes, Mister Hoots. I hear you. You take Carpenter and I announce."

The gully's dirt slopes were parched and solid. Rain was needed, a long slow shower of relief. The whole state was dying for relief, and on that vast scale, Jackson registered himself as the savior. The race was his, four years ample time to start reshaping this suffering Georgia geography. Plyer Hoots wouldn't even live that long. To Jackson, this decrepit lump of a tycoon was the most monstrous of this world's bottom dwellers. But this kingfish had dominion reaching far beyond Georgia and to that grubbing face, he said, "And you—you better be damn sure that money achieves its objective."

Plyer chugged back in laughter, careful to keep the tobacco cud beneath his lower lip. The great joy sent him reaching over to grab Jackson in a sporting hug. Plyer's bottom-dwelling breath came closer than ever, the odor turning fetid as it mixed with the damp emissions from his sugary cologne. Jackson held his breath. He pushed back.

"You know," Plyer said while releasing the candidate. "Daisy tells me you never had a daddy."

"He died before I was born."

"Well, Governor, I'm your daddy now."

Call Dusty

S TOP THE PRESSES! HOLD THE WIRES! YES siree! It's time to set every liberty-loving Georgia brain in gear and cut all those pent-up opinions loose! Folks, we're coming to you live from the glass-enclosed thought-provoking studies of WROL, and tonight we have a show that will set you to calling the kinfolks. Yes, indeed-ee-do. We got us a doubleheader in the making. That's right! Ole Dusty's had a last-minute redo in the program. So folks, just loosen up and listen close be . . . cause . . . it's . . . time . . . tooo . . . *Caaall Dusty!*

First off, Good People, I have to confess. My heart is stricken. Folks, tonight Ole Dusty grieves along with you over the loss of the most monumental voice in contemporary politics, the voice that has shaped our generation and generations to come, the voice that literally toppled the Berlin wall! Yes. Ole Dusty is dedicating this special doubleheader of a show to President Ronald Reagan. As you all know, yesterday our Great Maker called The Gipper home and to honor his passing, tonight we'll spend most of our show talking with a fellow Southerner who was the right-hand pressman to the president for years. But first, my previously scheduled guest has agreed to spend a few minutes with us, and folks, what a catch he is! Folks, this guy is collecting accolades from Republicans as well as Democrats and, in the process, moving to the front of the pack in our great gubernatorial race here in Georgia. That's right—Attorney General Jackson Beekman. First off, General—you don't mind if I call you General, do ya?

Dusty, you can call me anything as long as it's clean enough for our good people to support.

Folks, hear that? Clean-to-the-core, he is. No filthy blah blah blah here tonight. So, General Beekman, share your thoughts on the passing of our national treasure.

Dusty, as you and the good listeners know, I am a Democrat, but I'm also a Democrat who knows integrity when he sees it, politics aside. So Dusty, I want to thank you for having me here at this time of momentous national grief. President Reagan—the man, the leader, the inspiration—words can't express the depth of influence he's had on all our lives. No doubt about it. God's called a true hero home.

Yes, indeed, Mister General. And speaking of heroes, at least one newspaper has called you a—let me get this right—a "Healthcare Hero." So, Mister Hero, some folks are saying your people are getting a little carried away with their secondhand smoke thing, what some are calling the Gestapo approach to controlling public smoking. Sir, you care to comment?

Dusty, I want everyone to know that a Beekman administration will see to it that, just as the great President Reagan wanted, our young people have a safe environment to grow up in, including safe, clean air to breath. So Dusty, lessening the burden of preventable illness—like from cigarette smoking—is still important in my healthcare agenda. That, I do not deny.

Well, Mister General, Ole Dusty's the last one to argue with a hero. But hey, we've got Andy from Springdale on the line. Andy my man, what's on your hot-to-trot Springdale noggin?

Dusty, speaking of health, I just want to send a great big shout-out to all our veterans. Here on the sixtieth anniversary of D-Day, I think we need to say a special prayer for the health of our precious veterans. Mister Beekman, you have any thoughts on veterans? This is Andy from Springdale.

Well Andy, you thrill my soul. The D-Day anniversary is indeed a time for reflection. I, like so many Georgians, had relatives who died in wars so we can exercise our God-given rights. And Andy, one of those rights is the right to an education. What I want to emphasize now is the value of the Beekman education plan for veterans. Under my plan, 100 percent of college tuition not covered under the GI bill will be fully deductible from state income tax. And—listen to this—this plan includes a thousand dollars a year in tax deductions for expenses indirectly related to education—commuting, computers, tutoring expenses. Dusty, never have our veterans had a better deal.

General, you're talking now! Glory be to the Great Generation! Just the sound of it sets Ole Dusty's heart to racing. Peggy from down in Claiborne, Sugar, the speaker hole is all yours.

Dusty, the Claiborne Ladies Card Club wants to know just why Mister Beekman waited so long to endorse a constitutional amendment to protect marriage. At the rate these Yankee homosexuals are marrying and adopting children, something has to be done to keep this social cancer from spreading. Dusty, I want you to ask Mister Beekman his opinion on this. Is he with or against us Claiborne ladies?

Whoa, Miss Peggy. Sugar, you've put the dart on the heart. Folks, I tell ya—if we don't watch out, we're gonna have some mighty radicalizing gender benders among us here in Georgia. Mister General, when it comes to homosexual hitch-ups, why's your horse so late out the stall?

Dusty, at the debate I made my point crystal clear, but I'll repeat it. Make no mistake about it, the homosexual agenda stops at the Georgia state line. Marriage is—as my fiancée and I were talking the other day—marriage is the holy union of a man and—

Whoa-wee! Again, I say—stop those presses! You preachers ring the church bells! Is Ole Dusty hearing our hero correctly? Is Mister General telling all Georgia he's about to join the congregation of men hooked to the old ball and chain?

Well, Dusty, you caught me. That's right. You've got a mighty fortunate man sitting before you tonight. My beautiful fiancée has finally said "yes." And to make it official we plan a wedding ceremony—probably within the year. What I want to address right now though is the—

Pardon me, Mister B, but we've got to grab our suspenders and stomp till we shake the chandeliers! Folks, Ole Dusty's just got that news-breaker alert I've often warned you all about. Ladies, sounds like our heroic health-care stallion from Egypt, Georgia, has just headed for the stall! Mister B, anything to add?

Dusty, getting back to Peggy's question, I want to comment on that timeline matter. As folks know, I have had to maintain a clear line between my state legal responsibilities and my campaign obligations. When my opponent rushed the issue though, when he crossed the line, I decided it was time to speak out. And tonight, I want to make it clear once more—in Jackson Beekman there is no greater champion of the traditional values—the Ronald Reagan values of our great state.

Well, Good Lord calm down that fancy pants Democrat jabberwocky to Republican lingo translator in my brain. Mister General, you sure swing a mighty heavy bat. Whoa horsey, folks, Ole Dusty's not going into a bat-sizing arena. So ladies, you can keep all those metaphorical appendages a-dangling in your mind. Where Ole Dusty is a-goin' tonight is to Roger from Pikeville. Roger, got any decent words to share with Mister Beekman? Remember, boys, when ya call in keep it clean now!

Dusty, this is Roger in Pikeville. My wife Ethel swears that all the Beekmans she knew in Egypt were Jews. Dusty, any truth to that? You can put that Jew question to Mister Beekman, too.

An Indolent Disease

JANE AWAKENED WITH THE FEELING that any sensible person would be oversleeping this Sunday morning, the fan peaceably turning above the bed, the air conditioner blowing a little arctic. But the daylight seemed even more sensible, so she arose to small talk with Price, first about the upcoming heat and possible thunderstorms, but soon the storm talk turned to the news that he had carried his letter to the downtown office of the *Journal-Constitution*. With this revelation, she wished Price had been oversleeping, for this letter belonged only in his dreams. Instead, reporters throughout the state were likely already reveling in a Beekman family schism. She lay quiet and weighed the consequences. It was so boyish, the letter simply an extension of her husband's arms, Jackson all the more squirming. Vindictive even. She wanted to call it juvenile, her own misjudgment. Yesterday Price had been vacillating, rewriting the letter and asking her opinion of the rewrite throughout the morning. By late in the day, he'd gone silent, which she took to mean he was still weighing the comments or, better yet, had decided to trash the letter all together. She hadn't bothered to ask about it. She'd assumed Price, like Lily, had accepted a better judgment, morality a private matter, personal—the speech what Jackson had to do to win—and surely Price wanted his brother to win. He had to—at least for her. He knew how important it was. Maybe she feared her husband's answer. Maybe this fear was the reason she had awakened early and started talking when she should have been oversleeping.

This morning, the well-rested people of Georgia might awaken to see a letter that said Jackson Beekman did not have his own brother's support on issues of morality. "Otherwise, I made it very clear that he has my full support." Price paused after he said it. "Unquestionably clear," he added. "I think." The letter, whatever the editor was to make of it ("They told me it might be edited"), was the reason Jane and Price were soon poring over the newspaper. They had yet to find the letter when the doorbell rang. "You keep looking," she told him. "Jackson will be furious."

A car was parked in the driveway, an old car, boxy and blue. Again, the doorbell. The peephole was cold. She pressed harder. Her eyebrow brushed the tiny metal ring. There was a man on the porch, his complexion weathered, maybe Mexican beneath a slick crew cut, youthful for such a tawny face. A manila folder was sandwiched beneath his right arm. The sweater was Augusta green, oversized and frumpy. Somewhere she'd seen him before. CellSure? The campaign office? A convention?

Air blew cold from the ceiling vent. The man at the door looked hot and nervous, maybe frustrated by some bad directions or the street numbering system. Odds and evens sometimes flipped sides. You had to know the street's history; no doubt he didn't. The high morning sun lay white on the front yard grass. People were bound to blister. "Who is it?" Price yelled from the kitchen table. She didn't answer. The man's face was familiar, but where? She flipped the deadbolt, twisted the knob and cracked the door.

"Doctor Jane?"

She didn't answer. She narrowed her eyes. The face was beyond her. Her hands, both of them, steadied the door as the outside heat bathed her face.

"Doctor Jane Beekman?"

"Yes. Can I help you?"

"Tommy . . . Tommy Carpenter . . . from Egypt." He smiled.

"Tommy Carpenter! I thought I knew you." Her grip on the door softened. Yes. She did know him, she thought. Tommy. Tommy Carpenter from Egypt—a friend of Price, or maybe Jackson. Probably both, some neighboring family.

"Who is it?" Price's voice was coming closer as he left the table.

"Tommy Carpenter . . . from Egypt." Her husband was stirring behind her, stepping forward to see for himself.

"Well, what a surprise." Price slung back the door, stepped into the stoop and was about to offer a hug when, instead of moving forward, Tommy took one step back.

"I hate to bother you folks, but I wanted to drop by and say hello before I had to travel on." Price reached to more formally shake the visitor's hand, but Tommy's clumped-up fingers were balled tightly before his belly. His wrists were spindly, the skin a pale pumpkin color. "I'll bet you all were getting ready for church. Right?"

"Just browsing the newspaper," Jane answered. She looked knowingly to Price, who had cleared the doorway for a guest whose gaze was moving fast to the hallway, to the mirrors and rug, to the ceiling lamp and doors. "Come on in," she told Tommy, but he balked. He kept eyeing the hallway. It occurred to her that he must want something. Jackson used to say there was a small contingent of people from Egypt who were always calling or writing for money, donations for this or that, for favors. Well-intentioned and good causes, of course, but always money. That was Tommy now, Tommy Carpenter, Price or Jackson's friend from Egypt. If Tommy wanted something, Jane could already tell she and Price would give in.

"Remember this?" Tommy asked. "You mailed it to me, back when I was living on the Hill." He pulled the manila folder from his arm, opened it to show a photograph to Jane.

The sight cut the fog in her memory, sliced it apart so cleanly she felt its embarrassingly sharp edges. "Of course," she said. "Tommy, I almost didn't recognize you. From Baltimore. So good to see you again." Jane fought back her surprise, but Tommy had aged so much. She lifted the picture and recalled the photograph as one she made with the camera she'd bought when they first moved to Baltimore. The color was faded, the original somewhere upstairs. She had the copies made at a pharmacy, sent one to Tommy and was going to send one to Mis'ess Beekman, but Price told her not to mail it, not this one.

Tommy pulled the photograph from Jane's hand. "I'll never forget how nice you and Doctor Price were that night, how you drove me home."

Price hummed at the thought. "Well, we did. We drove you back to Washington, didn't we?" His voice was lazy with an amazement that on a workday would never have sounded so amazed. Jane could already tell the day was going to be a lazy one, or at least a morning when Price spent a great deal of time talking. He said, "Now, I remember. Jackson wasn't feeling well that night. Come on in, Tommy. We need to visit awhile."

"Didn't we have the hair?" Tommy asked, his legs fixed in the doorway, finger pointing to the picture. In the photograph, Jackson looked stricken, more flustered than sick. Jane had wanted to redo it, a group shot, and she was calling the waiter to take the picture, but before the guy arrived, Jackson clammed up and walked out. Tommy had embarrassed him, tripped some nerves that apparently had already been irritated. Never again did they mention Tommy to Jackson and never did Jackson ask what happened to Tommy that night, at least not to her knowledge. Of course, she and Price didn't think all that much of the friction back then. Jackson was stressed from his work, some upcoming deadline, and here Tommy was drinking like he couldn't care less about tomorrow. That night, she and Price were also a mess—all their belongings packed aboard a truck. And so, when Jackson snapped at Tommy then walked out, she and Price just figured that was Jackson being Jackson, his pride and self-sufficiency wounded by a friend who had way too much to drink. Despite Jackson's huffiness, that night all they could think about was how they might make a better life in Atlanta, how they might recover. Nothing anyone did in that God-forsaken Baltimore surprised them. Not even Jackson's little fit or the painfully liquored-up Tommy. They were that eager to move on.

"Please, come on in," Jane insisted, shooing Tommy inside.

"Gosh, I do hate to interrupt." Tommy seemed eager as he stepped into the hallway. "But I had a fairly long layover before I headed out, and as my good luck had it, I remembered y'all lived in Buckhead. So in my free hour or so, thought I might check out the neighborhood." He stopped in the hallway and turned, placing a bony hand on Price's elbow. "Really," said Tommy in an apologetic burr, "I have a favor to ask."

Price made a face and Tommy looked pleased at the reaction, this response he appeared to have anticipated. "It's simple," Tommy said, shifting to Jane. "I was hoping to get you both to sign the photograph for me. At long last, I'm getting my life organized, my things together before I leave Baltimore." His voice was chummy but dry. "Reconnecting with the hometown folks," he added.

"Well, what a surprise indeed," Price said. "Come on back to the kitchen table." He started to clinch Tommy's shoulder, but the guest flinched at the first touch, so Price raised a hand to sweep a wide welcoming salute through the air. "Coming home to visit your folks?"

"Wasn't sure I had the address correct," Tommy answered, "but the Internet's got us all situated in one place or another."

"I'll say it does," Price said, using his head to motion Tommy on through the hallway. "Great timing. We were just checking to see what campaign news the *Constitution* was sharing with folks this morning." He cast a gleeful look to Jane. "Come on back here, now. Got a fairly fresh pot of coffee waiting on us all."

Price clomped in his sandals while Tommy seemed to waddle, balancing his belly as he walked. Maybe that big belly was why he wore the sweater, Jane guessed, the cloth masking his girth. Beyond that bulk, Tommy was a devastated man, his face haggard, his cheeks sallow, jaundiced. Cancer, she thought, or maybe cirrhosis. All of a sudden, she felt cruel for having Tommy linger in the doorway, for her hesitation. Tommy Carpenter was getting organized for something dutiful and sad, some process that would prove heartbreaking for so many people. She couldn't help but think Tommy was coming home one last time before he died.

She had to admire him. Tommy had stopped by to thank them for the night when they drove him home nearly twenty years ago. It was all coming back to her, including her second thoughts about mailing the photograph.

But now she was glad she did it. The picture had accomplished her goal, the photograph and the note she attached to it had remade that awkward night into something pleasant for Tommy—the way she hoped it would. Tommy had been so boozy-brained that evening, she suspected he might want to forget the episode, the foolishness of the liquor. And perhaps he did forget it for a while, even as his alcohol continued to be a problem, end-stage cirrhosis the reason Tommy was now coming home. Tommy Carpenter, she told herself, he just couldn't quit drinking.

"Here, have a seat," Price said.

"Really fine place you folks have down here." Tommy claimed a spot at the table, yet his eyes moved all about the room. "Are those sunflowers?" He gestured with his head to the bank of windows. "Sorta short, but sure look like sunflowers to me."

"Aztec dwarfs," Jane answered. "It's my annual experiment in heirloom gardening."

"My grandmother grew sunflowers," Tommy said. "But never any flowers like that, so orangey-red." He tapped the spine of the manila folder on the table. "You put blood in the dirt?"

"No," she answered. "My goodness, why do you ask?"

"Just a guess since blood's so rich in minerals, and I know you doctors are around loads of blood. You folks are quite the blood doctors, I hear."

Jane tried to smile. "Oh?"

"Yes, ma'am. Read all about you and Doctor Price on the Internet. Biotechnology is a good thing."

"Yes," she said. "Yes. It is."

The sunlight was no longer falling so generously through the windows, and in the off-light Tommy was golden, his conjunctivae brilliant yellow, irises sea deep and antique. The skin on his fingers was almost mummified, each thumbnail scary as the seed of an inbred peach. Jane caught herself sizing up Tommy as a case, and when he seemed to see what she was doing, she was embarrassed. She excused herself and left for the kitchen to get the coffeepot and a cup for Tommy.

"Did I hear you right?" Price said. "You now live in Baltimore?"

"Guess you could say that. All in all, I've had quite a career in Baltimore."

Jane returned to the table, placing a cup before Tommy and pouring his coffee. It felt an honor, Tommy's first stop a return to say thank you to the Beekmans. "Milk?" she asked.

"No, ma'am. Been drinking black coffee and growing old in Baltimore for years now."

"Now, Tommy," she admonished, "it's not been that long." She took a seat across from the guest, pulling up the folder he'd laid on the table. Again, she examined the photograph. At one time, Tommy Carpenter was a handsome man. "Have one," she said, scooting a plate of muffins toward him. "Morning glory, from a new bakery near work. Has a hint of orange."

"Not for me," he said, pushing away the plate. His fingers unfolded like the blighted blossom of a gourd vine. "I'm orange enough. Guess you noticed."

"Oh, not really."

Tommy slanted his head to Price. "Doctor Jane was so kind to mail me the picture. She's a mighty fine lady. You know that, don't you?"

"Sure is."

"Yes," Tommy sighed. "You doctors are mighty fine people."

Price gave a feeble nod, his eyebrows going lower before Tommy. "You coming from or heading out to Egypt?"

"Maybe." Tommy had an amused tone in his voice, a dreamy quality. He looked down to examine his fingernails. "Yes, indeed. Years back Doctor Jane put a mighty nice letter in an envelope, and I made damn sure I kept the picture, but crazy me, somehow I lost the letter. Probably in a move. Moved like the dickens at one time, but eventually settled down in Baltimore. And that's where I've stayed, the last of Tommy Carpenter growing sick and old in Baltimore."

Tommy sipped the coffee, his eyes moving to Jane and then to Price. He started talking about himself, as if he needed to tell his story in abundant detail. No doubt now; he was coming home one last time before he died. Jane knew the final look of disease, and Price must have recognized it also, for they both said nothing. They just watched as Tommy went on and on. The air conditioner whirred outside the house, the air blowing cooler across the heart of the table as Tommy talked.

Tommy reached beneath his sweater, pulled out a pen. "Doctor Price, will you do me the honor and scratch a John Henry on the back?" He slid the photograph across the table. "I'm sort of deathly sick, so I want my things in order."

"Of course." Price took the pen and started writing on the picture's backside.

"Date it," Tommy said, his tone gruff. The brusqueness drew Jane's eye. "Please," came a peevish plea from Tommy.

"Sure," Price answered. "I sure will."

"Doctor Jane, your turn now." Tommy pushed the photograph across the table to her, his focus still on Price. "Doctor Jane did her best to apologize for Jackson in the letter she sent me. Sure wish I'd kept it. As you all can tell, Baltimore was not so kind to Tommy Carpenter." He pushed back in his chair, walking it out on two legs from the table, repositioning himself in a spot with greater exposure. He shifted his buttocks and spread his knees, so his belly bulged toward Price. His sweater rose to reveal a bright red fanny pack clipped to his belt, tourist-style. Quaint, thought Jane. Tommy's worked hard to make this journey a trip to remember.

"Wow, these years," Price moaned. "Jane and I, we both lost our mothers. You may have seen the obituaries on the Internet."

"I did." Tommy widened his eyes. The response was odd, like fascination.

Price also inched away from the table, wrapping one knee over the other and wiggling a foot. A wiggling foot usually meant Price was bored, but this morning it seemed to signal his need to accommodate Tommy. Still, their guest appeared to sense some boredom because he brought his chair once again close to the table, preoccupying himself with the coffee. It was obvious Tommy was going to spend much time in thought on this trip. He swirled the coffee in his cup. He soon lifted the cup as if in a special communion that began with a prayerful thought and ended with a sip. "Good stuff," he told Jane. She was pleased. So she finished her signature and placed the photograph back in the folder, sliding it toward the breakfast guest.

Tommy opened the folder, stared at the picture once again. "Doctors, time is a tough old bandit, ain't it?"

"Quite the rough spots," Price said, his tone sympathetic but measured. "You sure you don't want a muffin?"

"Time's stolen a great deal from me." Tommy rested an inquisitive orange gawk on Jane. She wanted to look away, but Tommy interrupted her effort. He told her, "Time is what keeps us from really seeing each other, even as our bodies age out in . . . bloody sunflower colors." He fixed his eyes on the window and the palm-sized faces of the Aztec dwarfs beyond it. "Yes, Doctors, one way or another, we're all going to dry up in our own bloody colors." Tommy again surveyed the skin on his fingers. He said, "As you can tell, I no longer need a bronzer." He chuckled at his joke, his brash laugh far more typical of Baltimore than Egypt, Georgia. "Wanna know something?" he asked.

"Sure," Price said.

"Years back my Hopkins doctors told me hepatitis C was an indolent disease. Indolent, they said, like indolent was a good thing." He rocked his cup slowly on the saucer, watching as the dark liquid rose and fell from the sides of the cup. "But know what?" Tommy stilled his cup, again rotating to the windows as if he wanted no answer. Odds were, Jane thought, he hadn't told his folks of the disease.

"Good Doctors, let me tell you. When I plugged *indolent* into the Internet, guess what popped up?" Tommy swanned his neck from side to side in wide swooping motions. "Indole," he spouted in a happy flourish. "And indole, as you smart doctors probably know, is a by-product of putrefying flesh. Coincidence, huh? A naturally occurring chemical with the color of . . . " He halted his voice to be sure they were watching and listening. "Yellow fecal material," he said. "Sure enough. Indole is the color of yellow fecal matter. Quite a coincidence, don't you think?" He dropped his eyes as though his observation was essential to acknowledge. "Yellow fecal matter—guess that's all I am."

Price coughed to clear his throat. Jane tried not to stare. In the windows, the sunflower faces had reddened.

"You're probably in a hurry," Price said, placing both feet on the floor.

Tommy didn't answer. He kept swirling his coffee and looking about the room, the aperture in his black pupils growing wider as the air conditioner stopped and the stilled air congealed to almost form an encasing gel. The silence was magnifying, so intense Jane could tell any spoken word would quickly swell and spoil in the stillness. The process for Tommy was not going to be a peaceful one. That fact was becoming obvious. It was also becoming obvious that Tommy needed some time alone. "Church is at eleven," she told Price.

"Wise to invest in vintage Wedgwood," Tommy said. He tapped the uncapped tip of his ballpoint pen against the saucer. "This, my dear doctors, is the real thing, isn't it? I used to crave real things. No more though." He recapped the pen and slipped it inside his shirt pocket, his attention deviating none from the saucer. "A real thing like hepatitis C can prove such a bitch."

Price moved to the edge of his chair. "Tommy, we need to get dressed for church." He pushed his coffee cup to the middle of the table. "And I'm sure you need to hit the road, also."

"You know, Doctor Price, time helps us prioritize, and that's why I'm really here."

"Why you're *really* here?" Price's brow was rutted, plump shelves rising hard above his eyes.

"See, dear doctors, I'm prioritizing my life. Yes, Tommy Carpenter is on his final tour, and his priority is to collect enough fine pictures to keep folks intrigued at the funeral." He raised his hands, angling them about to form frames for fake pictures that hung for only an instant in the air before their sizes changed and his hands adjusted. "Yep," continued Tommy. "I want my funeral to be a pictorial adventure. Like that approach to a funeral—pictorial?" He gaped at Jane. She didn't answer and to her silence, Tommy grinned.

"Doctor Jane, I just hate it when folks have to stand around in a funeral parlor with nothing really good to look at—certainly not my dried up old body. Folks just looking so confused about what they should or shouldn't be doing. Though it's gonna be a whole different story for this indolent fellow. See, at the Tommy Carpenter funeral, a scrapbook will be front and center, my whole life illustrated on pages people can dwell on if they care to." He appeared to study the scene, endowing it with the dark intrigue in his eyes. "Smart, huh?"

"No, Tommy," Price answered. "It's not smart." He drew his head closer to the guest. "You really need to be going."

Tommy slurped the last of his coffee. He started laughing, cackling at his thoughts. He said, "A death tour—funny, ain't it? Cher has her Farewell tour, Madonna that Drowned World gig, and now Tommy Carpenter will have his greatest hits played out on a real live death tour. Funny, ain't it?"

"I'll wrap up a muffin for you," Jane said. She started to rise, but Tommy dismissed her with a rivet of his fingernails on the tabletop. Within him, a cantankerous energy had arisen. She could feel its triggering anxiety, the anger of a man who had yet to come to terms with his disease.

"Doctor, Doctor, priorities. Remember? At one time, the priority for me was the dear brother of our Doctor Price. And, guess what, Doctors? He still is. Think our next governor might autograph the picture for his former Egypt playmate? Say, this morning?"

Price frowned. "Jackson's tied up. I know he's speaking this morning."

"You sure?"

Price hardened his face. "Of course, he's tied up. He's always busy."

Tommy yelped in amusement. "Doctor Price, you can't fool me. I've followed those speeches and never are they on Sunday morning. Down here the pews are filled on Sunday mornings. Always are, aren't they?"

Jane, still in her chair, reached for the folder. She heard words taking shape inside her chest, words that were sharp because—she had to admit it—she wanted Tommy out of their house. She said, "Next week, I'm sure I can catch Jackson and once he signs the picture, I'll pop it in the mail, Tommy. Do it just like I did in Baltimore."

Tommy shook his head, his lips thinning as the tethers on his smile cracked and his obstinacy became even more obvious. This was the same frightening expression Jane had seen on the skulls of cirrhotic cadavers, the anguish and all-too-tense skin. Tommy yanked the photograph from her hand and placed it back in the center of the table. She cringed.

"You doctors are such good people. I'm sure you'll understand how important it is for me to have both of you witness our great governor-in-the-making explain his version of morality."

"Tommy, let's go," Price insisted. He stood, but Tommy was waving him down. Yet Price was quick, his CellSure management style taking over, the decisiveness. Already he was looming over the man who direly needed help from his folks back in Egypt. Certainly not the Beekman family.

"You know," Tommy said, "I never heard a word from Jackson after that night—no phone call. No note. No nothing." Tommy was nipping at the tails of his words, pitching up his chin as if to bite a piece off each sound in his message. He shook his head in revulsion, reached over and snared a wad from the top of a crusty muffin. He popped the chunk in his mouth and chewed, smacking his lips and opening his mouth to display the cud to Price before swallowing it. "Ain't it odd," he said, "for a putrefying man to taste the color of his own blood?"

Price spread his shoulders. "Let's go, Tommy. We've got plans."

Tommy kept his seat, his eyes unfocused, his affect darkening. "Doctors, with autographed evidence and live witnesses, my funeral should be a killer. It should be. Don't you think?"

"That's enough," Price said. He reached over the table, gathering the remainder of Tommy's muffin in a napkin. "Okay," he commanded, "you need to go."

"Doctor, you're too uptight. Keep your seat." Tommy pointed to the vacated chair with his head, dropping his eyes as if to study a tough thought. He slipped both hands into his pants pockets and hunched his shoulders over the table, anchoring his body in a place he seemed determined to stay. Almost childish, the way he did it. Sad, if not for the abrasiveness of the conversation.

The photograph, Jane thought, if it had ever helped Tommy think better of the episode, that healing was over. It now was the centerpiece of what appeared to be deranged thinking. Tommy needed professional help and what they should be doing was calling for it, emergently. She wondered about a psychiatric hotline, a walk-in clinic, but watching Tommy, 911 wasn't out of the question. She would do it while Price kept him company.

Jane started to excuse herself, but before she did, Price moved closer to the sick man. He crouched on his knees, fixed himself face to face with Tommy. "Listen, Son. You've got to go." His voice was firm but caring, the tone Jane was hoping for. And maybe he was right. Price knew the families in Egypt far better than she did.

Oh, well—was the expression on Tommy's face, his shoulders rising as his right hand pushed down and withdrew a small pistol from his pants pocket. He raised the barrel to Price's face. "Doctor, why don't you just have a seat?"

More Important than Tobacco

THE EVIL WAS REAL, THE GUN'S SILVER barrel fixed on Price, his face as Jane had never seen it before, fury bloodless but bulging beneath his skin. Unlike him, she was empty, her thoughts reduced to remnants, the hard bones of disbelief. Not here, not now. Not with Tommy's hand in motion, not with his eyes flaring dandelion wild. "That's good, Doctor Price. Just have a seat. We need to talk this out."

Price followed the order, returning to sit beside Jane, his attention never leaving the gun.

"It's a fine thing," Tommy said. "Best little firearm I could buy on my Baltimore budget. Not quite as precious as Wedgwood, but still timeless, don't you think?"

Jane was locked in the impossible, her every nerve clinging to a reality that said such a thing does not happen here, not with the sun shining and the sunflowers still growing. *Security,* she wanted to scream—*Security to the kitchen table.* But it was too late for Security, too risky for a scream. She and Price, they must cooperate. Tommy was sick, probably encephalopathic, his brain inflaming itself. They could get him out of here. They must. She prayed and tried to keep praying as Tommy placed both hands on the gun.

Price sat seething. Jane felt the heat, the rage that Tommy, even sitting across the table, surely sensed. Her husband was ready to explode, to dive for Tommy, to make this reality all bullets and blood revealed. Money, thought Jane. They could give Tommy cash from their wallets and then he'd leave. Bankcards might help, his and hers, each with the PIN numbers. They would cooperate. They would cooperate even if Price must rage beneath his skin.

"Doctors, at this point, as our dear Jackson has told us so eloquently, only morality matters. So, this morning you good doctors will witness our future governor's morality in action—yes, the kind of morality that left me with nothing more than this photograph you both so nicely autographed."

Price was too full. Any moment now, he would pivot, flip the table over the deranged Tommy. "Listen, Tommy. Tell me! Just tell me what you want!"

"Time, Doctor P. I want a little of your time. See, preparing an entertaining funeral will be good for us all. And to do that, we need Mister Jackson to explain what he was trying to tell us back when he left me stranded in a restaurant that, as luck would have it, we would always remember as the Iron Gate. You remember the Iron Gate, don't you? There was never any morality in the Iron Gate, was there? No morality at all, don't you agree?"

Price remained stock-still, almost grating his teeth when he spoke. "Jane and I are going to lunch with a group. People will be expecting—"

Tommy jerked his head in objection. "*Were*, Doctor P, you *were* going to lunch." He secured the gun in his right hand, poking holes in the air with the barrel as he moved it before Price. "You doctors should not make me nervous. I start talking fast when I get nervous, and on a hot day like this one, we all best avoid a meltdown. See, I have a few things to say to our dear Jackson. And he has loads to tell us in return, a whole lot to explain." Tommy tossed his pen across the table. "Doctor Price, write this down. There, on a slip of the newspaper, make us a little list."

Price looked away, his brow immersed in red.

"Do it!" Tommy rammed the butt of the gun to the table.

Price broke. He ripped an edge from the newspaper. "That's right," Tommy said, "just think of it as a little shopping we all need to do. Morality, that's what we're shopping for this morning, a gubernatorial chunk of morality." Tommy laughed wet and hard, his cackle turning to a cough, a wild one that seemed to bring a glob of enchantment into his mouth, where he tongued it about in clownish pleasure before swallowing it whole. He turned to Jane, the flared dandelions she once saw in his eyes now waning, the wildness a little quenched.

"The muffin," Tommy said, "too much orange."

Jane tried not to watch the gun, to look only at Tommy, the sick Tommy Carpenter. To this sick man, she roused. "Coffee—how about more coffee?" The words felt alien but they were hers, and they belonged here because she knew she could talk to Tommy. She could pour him more coffee. She could talk Tommy down.

"No, ma'am. I'm good." The tone was chipper, almost manic. Tommy directed his face about the table, moving meticulously as he seemed to inventory his surroundings but lurching repeatedly back to Price. "First, Doctor Jane is to call Jackson on her cellphone. I'm sure our good governor will recognize the number. Right?"

Jane nodded, but Price held his pen to the table. Obsession entered Jane's mind. Tommy was psychotically obsessed with Jackson.

"Doctor P, you make me nervous when you don't cooperate. People in Baltimore learned to cooperate with Tommy Carpenter, so I suggest you do also. I may not be a doctor, but I know how to operate." He chortled at his joke, the gun jostling in his hand but the barrel's aim never leaving Price. "Write it down!" Tommy shouted. Price glared but began to move his pen.

"First," Tommy said, "Doctor Jane calls Jackson. She is to tell him to prepare the guards down at the Justice Building. He is to let them know that he has an important meeting, a private get-together up in his office, one that involves his brother's family and a special guest for a special occasion. Oh . . . say, a reunion. That's it, a surprise reunion." Tommy twisted in his chair, dropping his head to better catch the expression on Price's face. And when he caught sight of the few words Price had written, he pounced. "You're not writing fast enough, Doctor P."

Price halted his pen. "You're talking too fast."

Tommy's head teetered in befuddlement, dipping his brow as his eyes shifted directions. "Doctor Jane, am I talking too fast? Or is our Doctor P getting a little slow in his old age?" Within Tommy's glare, the pupils were pulsing.

"We can help you, Tommy. We can."

The puzzled man went tight, his face speckled with sweat as he turned back to Price. "Doc," he said, his hand now trembling, "you're making me nervous." He stretched his neck and drew a quick noisy breath. "Doctor Price, you are not to make me nervous. You hear that?"

Price looked down to the list he'd made. "I hear it."

"Repeat it to me."

Price fixed on his notes, his response to Tommy arising with projectile force. "Jane is to call Jackson. She is to tell him to prepare the guards, to let them know there will be a meeting in his office, a reunion." Never had Jane heard such deep revulsion in her husband's voice. Determination, action, impetuous action—it was all there and what she had to do, what she could only do, was pray.

Dear God, please make everyone cooperate.

"My, my, Doctor P. You are talented." Tommy's voice was a cutesy whine. "Now our dear Jackson is to instruct those guards to wave his brother's family on in, to give the family ample time to get situated up in his office before our true guest of honor arrives. Got that?"

Price nodded, moving his hand down the paper.

"Doctor Jane, you follow?"

She rocked her head in agreement. The psychosis had consumed Tommy. He wouldn't hesitate to use the gun. He would shoot Price, maybe both of them, and laugh as he did it.

Tommy looked pleased, ennobled. He resumed his directions to Price.

"Doctor Jane is to tell Jackson that this meeting has been called for a special reunion. She is to tell Jackson that the reunion is critical, that it must be held in his office at the Justice Building and he can't be late. She is to tell him whatever it takes to get him up there." Tommy clowned his eyebrows up and down, turning to share the festive expression with Jane. The photograph on the table, this was what she would watch, not Tommy. Price had been right. She shouldn't have mailed the picture. That night, maybe they should have joined Jackson in walking out on Tommy; maybe leaving Tommy to dry out in a Baltimore gutter would have helped him far more than a drive back to Washington.

"Now Doctor Price, you catch all those points?"

The rage within Price had subdued none, the contempt even louder as he spoke from his notes. "A reunion in his office, a special occasion, waving the family on in, whatever it takes."

"Correct-o! Doctor Jane is to tell Jackson to arrive at eleven-thirty, to be alone because this is private, a private family matter. Clear?"

"Clear."

"Now, hand it to Doctor Jane." Price obeyed, sliding the note across the table. "Recite it to me," Tommy told her, "and once we're all clear on the process, we'll start. Yes, folks. If we have complete cooperation, our little morality play will follow its proper timeline."

"And then what?" Price said, his demeanor oddly more tolerant even as his fingers were curling into fists. Jane tried not to watch Price so closely, her task only to pray and to keep praying.

"Well," Tommy drawled, "once we have Jackson's explanation of why he walked out on me and once he's autographed the picture, we all return to our regular lives. Only we'll be a whole lot smarter. We'll have the knowledge of justice having finally been done in the Justice Building. Clever, huh? That's assuming we all cooperate. See, if we don't cooperate, then we've got us a whole different story."

"Why?" Price insisted. "Why us?"

"Oh, Doctor Price, if only life were simpler. Alas, this little process accomplishes so many goals. Not only is justice finally served, but you good folks will have some important news to share with the people of Georgia. And me, well, I'll also have the final picture for my funeral album. Yes, a truly historical picture will be featured, the backside autographed by witnesses to justice fulfilled, including the signature of the dead man's most loyal lover."

Jane shuddered—his lover? The Iron Gate's black leather booth was back. Once more, she saw what that night was supposed to have been, what they had agreed it was—slurred Baltimore nonsense. Drunken babble and nothing more. That's all they'd said it was, what they most definitely heard. But this morning Tommy was not slurring his words. This morning Tommy was talking clearly. *Lover,* he'd said. The delusional man had come back to kill his lover.

Tommy's grin covered half his face. "It'll look good, don't you think, Doctor Jane? Two simple words—*Love, Jackson*—written by morality's main man. And with written documentation, the signature of witnesses!"

Jane nodded her head in agreement, forcing all possible compassion into her gaze at Tommy. She was prepared to plead. She was prepared to believe anything, to agree until she couldn't.

"This is sick," Price said.

Tommy smooched the air, his jaundiced eyes dancing as he launched the kiss to Price. "An indolent disease, Doctor. Remember what the experts in Baltimore said? And we've all got to cooperate with the Hopkins experts, haven't we? Now, Doctor Jane, please recite our little menu, so we're all clear on our assignments. Oh, you can add anything about tobacco, if you think it will help." He snickered at his cleverness, rolling his eyes to the ceiling and back, the act all comedy, all dismissal. "Tobacco," Tommy said. "Who would have thought we'd be talking about tobacco?"

Tommy agitated his head to Jane in outlandish pleasure, telling her he'd found her name on the campaign's Internet website. "Mighty noble effort with tobacco, Doctor Jane." He relayed a greater electricity to Price. "Fine woman you married, mighty fine."

Jane cooperated, the items spoken as Tommy had first uttered them, the cellphone located as he directed. Soon, as if completely on script, Jackson answered on the third ring. His voice was accommodating, so Jane completed her message, her answer to Jackson's questions a repetition of: "It's important" and "I'll explain latter." The tension in her voice stung her ears, the tone so dire Jackson had to follow through. "It's more important than tobacco," she implored. "At eleven-thirty, please. It's more than important. It's critical. Price has written a letter to the newspaper. It's about you, something you need to hear. This morning, at eleven-thirty, okay?"

The speech ripped Jane's soul and kept ripping until only fragments remained, but she had to believe those fragments would form a message Jackson could grasp, the passion in her voice way too obvious, too alarming. Jackson had to detect the hidden message. The emphatic speech unquestionably touched Tommy. He practically hummed as they moved to the kitchen, the trio marching to Tommy's orders, his voice atwitter and his gun waving like a pointer. He ordered Jane to pour more coffee, which she did so he could sip and outline the final directions—how Price was to drive the big car, all three of them seated up front like a tight-knit family.

"Can we change clothes?" Jane asked, her chaotic and ever-louder thoughts still telling her that cooperation was essential, that they needed to draw no suspicion at all, to complete all these horrible steps so everyone could awaken in a safer place, including Tommy. That's what it takes to talk a person down. You keep your head. You stay calm. You cooperate. "In these old clothes," she explained, "don't you think the guards will be suspicious, think something's off?"

"Doctor, in my eyes, you folks are in your comfort zones, and that's where we all need to be this morning, in our comfort zones. So, no. We get the keys and Doctor Price here will make sure we all arrive in a nice comfortable manner. Clear?"

Price tried not to scowl, but he couldn't hide his wrath, his chin rigid and his temples a ruddy granite. "Clear," he said.

"Of course, it is, Doc." Tommy pointed his gun to the hall. "Now, Doctors, after you. Oh, the cellphone stays here."

Price led the way, hobbling in his sandals and moving like a much older man. Tommy told him to pick up his feet, to walk like a soldier on an assignment. Tommy laughed as he talked of the upcoming mission, the fantastic funeral maybe only a few months from now. Price grunted under his breath and, at the back-door stoop, he stumbled on the first step. He reached for Tommy, who promptly captured the arm flung at his head.

Tommy twisted the arm of her husband with such a deft hand the interruption barely slowed their pace.

Fallujah

T HE SPEED LIMIT WAS THIRTY-FIVE and Price was driving well under it, the sedan surely appearing inconsequential if a police officer in an idling cruiser did a double take. *Another old couple,* the officer would conclude. *Good folks headed off for church, slow boy there in the middle.* The officer would yawn, his eyes returning to the boulevard's depopulated sidewalks, his observation of a curiously slow sedan perhaps recalled only once guards at the Justice Building intercepted Tommy, HQ having issued an all-city alert.

But that officer's idling car was nowhere to be seen, the route and timing part of the strategy Tommy must have mapped out from Baltimore. Thoroughly psychotic, Jane told herself—Tommy sitting before a computer screen for weeks, making notes and growing giddy as his liver died and his mental status worsened. No question about it. Tommy's hepatic encephalopathy had degraded to a manic psychosis. She felt confident of her diagnosis, almost certain of what her mother would have said—*No hill for a stepper, Jane. Tommy is sick. You made the correct diagnosis. Now, step.*

And she wanted to. She wanted to step into a therapeutic mode for the sake of them all, but the psychotic man was mumbling and breathing hard at her side, his right shoulder sometimes twitching as he strained to keep the gun between Price's ribs. Dead fish was the odor on Tommy's breath, the pungency coming and going with his darting face, his attention bouncing from one side of the windshield to the other. Jane was calm. She would breathe the stench in Tommy's breath and be patient with his impulses, reassuring with his doubts. She would step when the opportunity arrived. She would talk Tommy down by gaining his confidence and explaining in therapeutic words how there's really nothing to fear. The diagnosis was solid, the treatment only steps away.

Tommy arched his head forward, twitching his nose to the dashboard radio. "I knew you folks were the NPR type." He twisted hard to his right, dog-facing Jane. "Doc, how 'bout tuning out that chatterbox? We already know Iraq's a mess. Right, Doc?"

Jane held her breath. Tommy's mouth was too close, the aroma too toxic. "Fallujah," said the reporter and "Fallujah," Tommy echoed, the syllables putrid in the air, one sour wave after another.

"Fal . . . loo . . . jah."

Tommy thrust forth his lower jaw and puckered his lips like a chimp, the snout of his mouth rising. "Fal . . . loo . . . jah. Doc, you good Democrats don't need to hear anymore of Fal . . . loo . . . jah, do you?"

Jane reached for the dial, carefully avoiding Tommy as she silenced the radio.

"Fal . . . loo . . . jah," Tommy repeated, settling into his seat. "Sorta' sounds like a sneeze." He yawned and the empty side streets kept coming.

The sky lightened and dimmed and lightened again and behind those shifting clouds there had to be a God, a sleepy God who would keep watching over them even if it was all he could do to keep his weighty eyes open. *Step, Jane. Just step.* Yet Tommy's breath was going faster, his head once more dashing back and forth across her lap. He hummed in wonder at the sights. "You docs would be amazed at the things I've learned on the Internet."

"Sure," Price grunted. Jane flinched at the mockery, thumping her leather seat with a finger three times to try to keep a woozy God awake.

"Such details on the Internet," Tommy said. "Pretty crazy, don't you think?" He pointed to an upcoming street sign. "And if I recall correctly, we turn right up here on East Capitol. Doctor P, you catch that?"

To Jane, the Internet was the unfixable problem, what it could do to a psychotic man a cruel thing. She wanted to believe the only life at risk was Tommy's, the only danger to the Beekman family the memory of what it had to witness. She wanted to believe that Jackson would have Security poised for Tommy's take-down, that the guards would have him fully restrained, maybe gagged before he started calling Jackson other names. But Tommy had nothing to lose. A shootout was unavoidable. Prayer, she thought, for the sake of them all, unceasing prayers.

Price rocked his head as though acknowledging the route and nothing more. He turned the car onto a one-lane side street as Tommy hawked the passing bus stops and empty benches. "Looking good. Yes . . . Now, I think the garage is . . . that's it, right up there!"

Price slowed the car, hanging a sharp right turn down a steep driveway that led to an underground garage. He braked to a soft stop well before the guardhouse, which sat like a ticket taker's station at the bottom of the incline.

"Doc, you're a natural for this chauffeur gig." Tommy searched the driveway's wide concrete canyon with his eyes. "Now, we just ease on down to the booth and chat up our good man from Allied Security." He lifted a hand, snapping his fingers. "Amazing, simply amazing—all these revelations from the Internet."

"You know this won't work." Price was fixed on the guardhouse as he spoke, his foot firm on the brake. "It's crazy. You know Jackson has the police waiting. Probably tracking us now."

Tommy sniggered. "Doc, what you mean? You honestly think our sweet Jackson would call the police on his own family reunion? No way. You good docs need to know that our fine candidate had a suitcase full of money hand delivered to my apartment last week. Sure did. So don't you think he'd be the last guy to call the cops?"

Price sat dumbfounded, whiter than ever.

"Sure caught me by surprise," Tommy said, redirecting his voice to Jane. "Yeah, there I was sleeping like a baby when this guy shows up in the middle of the night with one hundred thousand in cash money and—get this—a plan to deliver four times that much on Inauguration Day." Tommy rotated his chattering head back to Price, his voice rising with elation. "Sure 'nuff—quite the deal, Doctor P. All assuming this *moi* kept his mouth closed. Bet you folks didn't know our nice clean candidate could make such a dirty deal, now did you?"

Inside Jane, Tommy's words—*deal* and *delivery, cash money*—those were a psychotic's words, his paranoia too much for her brain. Thoughts fell out of orbits, deranged insights so detailed she feared Tommy belonged to a vile reality, a world where he just might be telling the truth. Would Jackson actually do such a thing? Where would he get the money? She considered the possibility of it, the impossibilities. There was the check, the one-hundred-thousand-dollar gift Price hand-delivered, the irresponsibility of a bank actually dispensing so much cash. But the numbers were too perfect, Tommy's logic too plausible. *Lover,* Tommy had said. *My lover.* The possibilities and impossibilities had merged in Tommy's world. And that world was now their world also. The future was obvious. Tommy's justice on Jackson would be served with a gun.

"Jackson sure did," Tommy said. "And thanks to the generous funds, Delta Airlines let me enthrone my golden behind in a first-class seat. You folks fly first class?"

Jane gave a negative response, and then a positive one, her head motions small and equivocal. Tommy had zoned her out. The guard box was waiting. "Well, maybe y'all don't appreciate it but I sure do. Those hot little towels they pass out really are something. Guess our good Delta knows rich folks have a thing about staying clean."

Tommy hummed, basking in his observations. Jane felt the consequences of his words moving through her blood, the stench of gunfire pervasive, the taste repugnant. Something within her was already dead. Was the sick Tommy actually sane? Too many details were accumulating about a picture she never should have taken. Too many details were missing. In Baltimore, had Tommy already been showing signs of a delusional psychosis? The alcohol simply medication? The foul breath must be breathed, every diagnosis reconsidered. From the corner of her eye, she watched her husband harden his stare on the entrance to the underground garage. She turned to it also, this dark mouth wide open before them all.

"Yep," Tommy clowned, "guess you folks can tell that monetary deal didn't fit my personal needs. So to make sure our sweet Jackson has a better idea of the needs of an indolent man, we best head on down there and get this show started. Ah, what a heaven it will be to meet up with our dear governor-in-the-making." Tommy's head wobbled like the oversized cranium of a bobblehead doll. "Role of a lifetime, Doctor J—yours truly, live on the top floor, a solid gold star. Think I'll get an Academy Award?"

Jane felt her head nod. And to it, Tommy's eyebrows perched higher on his face, where they stayed briefly, before sinking. "Damn," he said. "Forgot the picture." Tommy switched the gun to his left hand and rammed it into Price's side, adjusting his shoulder once more to brace it there. "Fal . . . loo . . . jah," he droned. A long, lustful sigh filled the air as Price eased the car forward.

At the guardhouse, the man behind the glass was so elderly and stooped it seemed he might not be able to look up. His head, which appeared irreparably bowed, deviated none, even as the car came to a full stop beside his booth. Price lowered the car window, reached out and tapped the glass. The guard twisted on his lofty stool and slid back the window. Thanks to a God who finally was paying attention, the old man looked up.

"You folks lost?'

"We're here to meet with my brother up in his office. Jackson Beekman—he's expecting us."

"And who are you?"

"Price Beekman. Jackson's my brother."

"Who?"

"Price Beekman. My brother is the attorney general. He's expecting us."

The guard recoiled then came closer, curving down to inspect all three faces. "ID?"

Price twisted in his seat, reaching for the wallet in his back pocket, but before he could retrieve it, Tommy arched across his lap to occupy the window. "Fine morning, ain't it officer?"

Surely the guard could tell something was wrong, for one of Tommy's arms was impaled in her husband's side. And Price was grimacing way too hard as he grappled for his wallet. Surely the guard noticed it. But the guard was not looking. He was fussing with some papers and mumbling to himself. He was waiting. Price was jerky and subdued. And as he handed over his driver's license, the guard merely groaned at the task before him.

"So Mister Beekman's expecting you?"

"Yes, sir. He should have called."

"He should have called," repeated the guard, his gaze drifting out again to survey the people in the front seat. "Who's that?" The guard drew a bead on the gawking Tommy, who was still lumped across Price.

"Sir, I'm his cousin." Tommy plunged his free hand out the window. "Just got out of the service, sir. Lucky man I am, left Iraq just in time." The guard reached to shake hands with Tommy, but as the uniformed wrist advanced, the guard abruptly stopped, catching himself. The official hand began to withdraw, the guard's face reddening as though he just remembered a regulation against shaking hands with suspicious people. He craned lower, watching as Tommy motioned his head to Jane. "This here's Doctor Jane Beekman. Aunt Jane to me." Tommy batted pleasant looks between the guard and the woman at his side. "Aunt Jane, say good morning to this good fellow."

Inside Jane no rational thoughts were surviving. Any sense she could make of this morning was too contorted, too deformed for this world. Why had God sent Tommy to their door? Why hadn't her mother stopped it? Was God even watching? No answers were coming, only the silence of the entrance to the garage, the cavernous hole that was inhaling hard. She saw the guard but she couldn't speak. Instead, her fingers teetered to him. At the joints, her fingers teetered in a wave. She couldn't believe what her hand was doing.

"My wife," Price said, his voice pained.

Tommy filled the window with his face. "Got a big homecoming surprise for Cousin Jackson. He's expecting kinfolk, but he doesn't really know why. Chief, didn't they tell you?'

"No, Mister. They didn't tell me."

"Well, glory be!" Tommy turned, fluttering his eyelids to Jane.

"My brother," Price said. "My brother promised to call."

"Well, he didn't call the guard house."

"Can you double check?" Tommy asked. "We only have a few minutes to get our decorations up. Ain't that the truth, Uncle Price?"

"Yes. The decorations . . . they need to go up."

The guard retreated to his box, sealing himself away with a slide of his window. He propped the driver license next to the base of an old-fashioned, acorn-colored telephone and lifted the receiver. Someone must have answered immediately because the guard's lips started moving and soon he was making faces, the treads on his brow deepening as he listened. The seconds grew long and official, the guard's lips thinning with frustration. He said nothing more, but gave the receiver a disgusted look before returning it to its cradle. He twisted about, slid the glass back and parked a begrudged expression in the window.

"They say you're cleared." The guard returned the driver's license to Price, passing a thick gray plastic card with it. "You'll need this," he warned. "They should have called me."

Tommy, who was still plopped atop Price's lap, rousted up once more to the guard. "Thank you, Officer. Mighty kind." He yanked the security card from Price's hand and waved it at the guard like a winning ticket.

"Thank you for your service," the guard said, gliding his eyes from the three cleared visitors to the high street-level driveway that remained empty behind them.

"Well, you did just fine," Tommy told Price as the car inched ahead. "Now let's see if we can park next to the elevator down there." He nodded to the garage entrance. "Should have ample empty spots on the first level. Believe it or not, Docs—they gave us parking directions on the Internet."

Tommy's head slithered around to Jane, the voice at her side a purr. "Fal . . . loo . . . jah."

"Leave her alone," Price quipped.

"Just a joke," said Tommy, patting Price's knee. "Uncle, don't be so sensitive. You good doctors will have a ringside seat!"

Jane looked at her hands, the entwined fingers in her lap. They were useless as the hands of a dozing God.

The car walloped across the drain grate and entered the underground garage, an empty parking spot appearing, as Tommy had clearly anticipated, only a few feet from the elevator. The vacancy claimed, they exited the car and lumbered as a tight threesome to the glass door of the elevator foyer. From there on up, once the plastic card satisfied one dainty red eye after another, boxes clicked and doorways gave. A disjointed but euphoric Tommy steered the trio to the doors of the penthouse suite, where the final lock wasted no time at all before caving to a single swipe of the special card.

Trophy

LIKE MAGIC!" TOMMY SHOUTED AS the lock clicked and the bolt retracted. "Our time has come." He did a double take, eyeballing the brass plate etchings on the massive door—*Attorney General Jackson Beekman*. A two-tone hum of delectable pleasure followed. "Uh . . . um. Now docs, that's as sweet as it gets!"

Tommy shoved the door open, swooping a hand low to swish Jane ahead. "As always, the pretty lady first." She hesitated, but soon found herself being pushed ahead by the sight of Tommy's cadaveric eyes. Price followed, Tommy driving him with the gun.

"Whew-wee!" Tommy yelled, pausing only a moment to kick the door closed. He used his gun as a prod, steering Price and Jane to the center of the room's immense blue rug. "Even fancier than I was expecting!" Tommy seemed childish in his awe, far too charged to continue like this. Jane tried not to picture Tommy lying bloody on the floor, yet the bad image was there, the end of this sickness. The guards and state troopers, they had to be coming.

"The pictures on the Internet sure don't do it justice. Hey, that's kinda funny. Don't you docs think that's funny? So little justice for the Justice Building!"

The office suite was elegant, so refined there was a sanctity about it, the ambiance of a regal place that knew they did not belong here. The office knew this was an invasion, and from where Jane stood the grand furniture held motionless even as she felt every piece of it quake, this sanctum too stunned to shake. A sweep of windows stood full body-size behind Jackson's desk. Beyond the glass, the clouds had overtaken the sun, yet the energy was still obvious, the sky veiled in the full, bulging color of infected fluid. Jackson's desk sat like an altar, the flags behind it flaccid on their poles. A regal black leather chair was centered behind the desk while, before it, two generous Victorian-style sofas winged off an angle like opposing pews. An immense grandfather clock hugged a back wall, its ancient face gawking. Ticking was the only sound.

◆　●　◆

"AH, THOSE FLAGS!" TOMMY EXCLAIMED. "CAN'T THINK of a finer setting for our ceremony. Docs, can you believe it?" Tommy was rotating about in amazement, squinting to adjust to the dim grandeur. At the end of a full circling, he stomped both feet on the rug. "And look'a here." He pointed with the gun. "The great Georgia seal beneath our feet. Docs, we're gonna have that fine word *Justice* right beneath our feet! Whew-wee, what we have done this morning!"

Price raised a snarky jaw. "*We?*"

"Yes, *we*. Docs, you need to realize that we're here to finally witness justice, not only for me but also for the fine people of Georgia. Good God, the whole state might someday celebrate me. Yes, indeedee-do. Our dear Jackson just might wind up being the great state of Georgia's sa . . . cro . . . fi . . . cial lamb." He stepped before Jane, dipping his head but reengaging his mouth like a snout. "Baaah! Baaah!" And before Tommy's bleating left the air, he told her to take a seat on the sofa. "That one, Doctor J. Like mother of the bride—there." She obeyed, and once seated, Tommy and his gun soon had Price seated one wide cushion down from her.

The numbness in Jane's fingers had yet to reach her brain, for a rank pool of disbelief was swishing within her mind, the doubts and worries proliferating in their motion. Tommy, who had staked a spot before Jackson's desk, looked as if he could see the misery within her and the harder he looked, the more his smile rose.

Jane inched over the sofa toward Price, grabbing his hand. She needed her husband's touch, this tangible reminder of what Tommy could never destroy. And Price reciprocated, clutching her hand for at least ten seconds before releasing it once the bouncy Tommy noticed the connection. "Ah," he cooed. "Ain't this sweet!"

The gun barrel shifted deliberately, pivoting between Jane and Price. "This ceremony is going to be a paradox," Tommy said, rushing his voice. "Paradox, get it? Pair . . . of . . . docs! During the official ceremony, you folks will be sitting with Jackson, our great apologizer situated directly between you guys. You docs follow me, now?" Tommy's mouth was foaming, slobber bubbling out the corner of his lips.

Jane wrapped her arms about her chest. She nodded and maybe Price also motioned his head, but she couldn't tell because her eyes were stuck on Tommy. The gun's barrel was not deviating from her husband, Tommy's ardor fixed directly on Price.

The intensity was raw, Tommy's glare insistent, its core need exposed, more threatening than the gun. He stepped back and sat on Jackson's desk, hoisting his hips, one buttock after the other. Seated on the edge of the desk, Tommy faced them, his feet bobbing about the gilded state seal that adorned the desk's central panel. With one hand, Tommy unbuttoned his sweater and pulled it from his shoulders. The bright green cardigan fell about his waist to reveal a sleeveless sport shirt, Scotch tape sealing the front instead of buttons. He ripped away the shirt, tossing it and the sweater to the floor. Naked now from the waist up, the red fanny pack pooched below his belly like a horrific hernia.

"In five minutes," Tommy said, glancing to the grandfather clock, "Doctor Price is going to come stand beside me, so when our guest arrives, he will first be greeted by a familiar face. Follow me, doctors?"

Jane inclined her head, but Price did not reciprocate. She could see him from the corner of her eye, Price poised for a sprint from the sofa, his mind no doubt contemplating a rush for the gun. She again reached for his hand, but this time he didn't accept it. Her husband would pounce any moment now.

Tommy's eyes flitted between Price and the gun as if he knew Price's intentions, as if he enjoyed taunting his target. Arid amber skin shrouded Tommy's chest, his ribs protruding as his lungs churned. "Docs, time to get this party started!" He unzipped the fanny pack with one hand, loosening the pouch to pull out a boxy blue gadget. At the revelation, he gave a flamboyant look of discovery, both eyes at maximal size. "iPod," Tommy proclaimed, "battery powered, speaker attached." He jiggled his head in ecstasy. "They're all the rage in Dundalk. You doctors remember Dundalk, don't you?"

Jane nodded in a move that didn't feel of her making. Her body was once more taking over, and this time she was thankful for its insistence. Her body was preparing for whatever Price might do, her husband engaged for his chance at Tommy. If she could stop Price, she wasn't sure she would. Her body, she feared, would only cheer him on.

Tommy coughed to clear his throat, the gun again his pointer. "You docs remember what I said? When I give the order, Doctor Price is to step to my side. So, when I say, 'step,' he steps. Follow that?"

Jane looked away, allowed a "yes" to fall under her breath. Price sat silent. He gripped the ribbed seam of the sofa cushion, his arms ready to shoot his body forward at any moment. Tommy smiled as if he enjoyed the sight of the nervous repositioning. Yet when Price steadied his feet on the floor, the orange in Tommy's face went red.

"Doctor Price, you follow me?"

Jane tried once more to procure her husband's hand, but he brushed her back.

"Quit your squabbling!" Tommy yelled. "Doctor Price, you *will* step when I say 'step,' correct?"

Price tensed his jaw.

"Doctor Price, you with me?"

The air was swelling, the ticking metallic, unyielding.

Tommy stiffened. "Doctor Price, you hear me?"

No answer came, only the sound of the clock's untiring seconds. The ambient swelling wouldn't stop and within that expanding pressure, Price finally doddered his head. "Yes," he said.

"Good man," said Tommy, his lips coiling about the makings of a kissy smile. "Once we make our introductions, Doctor Price returns to the sofa, leaving a spot for Jackson to sit between you good doctors. And so, we'll all be back in our positions. Right? So much better than we were at the Iron Gate. And this time we will *complete* our conversation. Follow me, doctors?"

"You win," Price snapped, sinking into the sofa.

"Unfortunately," Tommy said, "this morning the only real winner will be morality. But morality is enough, don't you doctors think?" A hush followed his voice, the quiet entombing all life here in this majestic suite as if the office itself had given up and a symbiosis set in, the three of them no longer strangers to this high place. As if the infestation had been inevitable, as if the high propriety had long been waiting for an outsider to take control. *Lover*, Tommy had said, Jackson was his *lover*.

Tommy sat entranced before Price and Jane, his eyes large and foreign, the worlds within his two pupils filled with untamed creatures, all maimed and hunched down, each animal one kill away from starvation. And so, the slow hunt began, minutes stepping up to bow one by one before the altar where Tommy sat with his sick animals. The ticking only got louder, the grandfather clock continuing as though it knew it also must follow Tommy's orders. Within the clock's wooden walls, a lever tripped on time and a spring offloaded one long metal stroke. The hour had reached its halfway mark, so Tommy dropped his feet to the floor, leaned his buttocks against the desk and tipped his head in a cheerful salute. "Doctor Price, please come stand beside me." He tilted his head to Price like a meek but demanding puppy. "Yes, Doctor, the time has come. Now, step."

Price followed the order, moving just as he'd promised Tommy. And once in place, he turned and, following Tommy's instructions, shifted his back to accommodate the gun. He and Tommy were positioned before the desk, the two of them bizarrely solemn, a doublet of faces fixed on the door.

Tommy grinned. "Perfect."

Beyond the door, the elevator chimed. Steps came or maybe they didn't, maybe only the ache of knowing, of feeling the sounds. Jane was sure of it—the impalements within her heart, the unremitting progression, the steps. And when the brass lock clicked and the latch hammer gave, the sounds resounded throughout her chest. Tommy placed his chin on Price's shoulder, his lips fixed in a strained half-smile, his gaze lowered as if out of respect for the arriving guest.

The door eased forward and the sense of a single person, an entering person, appeared. Jane couldn't look back, but as the steps advanced and the door closed in a singular whine, the last of the emptiness inside her chest gave way to a rising sorrow. There were no trailing guards with guns, no advance men from a SWAT team. She knew the subtle odor and muted presence could only belong to Jackson, the one man stepping forward. Now she could see him, hands at his sides, his face—what she could see of it—stricken. Before him, Tommy's head wobbled on Price's shoulder.

"Morning, Governor." Tommy blinked. "Guess what? The election is over. You've won, and the prize is me."

Jackson stammered an indecipherable series of sounds, his head rotating in short jagged motions, his eyes moving all about the office. He stepped to the center of the room, fixing on Jane, scanning her face as if in search of anything within her that might explain this sight or settle his confusion. Yet she could signal nothing more than her fear, which sent his head turning back to Tommy. Holding the sight, Tommy pushed his tongue between his lips, the tip curling up in an obscene tickle of the high vermilion.

"You, you . . . " Jackson stuttered. "Why? Didn't you get the—"

"Yes, Governor. You've won all you never wanted and, guess what? That's simply me! Oh well, that's how morality works these days. Bummer, ain't it?" Tommy nodded to Jane. He rubbed his chin along Price's shoulder and lifted his head. "Right, Doctor P?" Price tensed his jaw, defying any other response. "Right, Doctor Price?"

"Jackson, he has a gun."

Tommy nodded again. "I am such a lucky man."

Jackson returned his attention to Jane. "Important," he told her, his voice splintering. "You said . . . You called . . . but . . . ?" Hands searching, shoulders weaving. He was dressed for a Sunday gathering, immaculate white shirt and the same blue seersucker pants he'd worn on the day when he'd met them at the sidewalk café. In the lunchtime attire Jackson now looked cornered, the clothes simply another part of the trap.

"Jackson, he made me call. He made me."

Jackson jerked his head about, moving one step closer to Tommy. "I don't . . . what? What happened to—"

"Doc, can you explain for our future governor?"

Price grimaced, his attention falling to Jackson's feet. "He came by the house. Pulled the gun and he . . . he made us call."

"Yes, Governor," Tommy said. "After we talked last week, I tuned into our favorite radio commentator and much to my disappointment, as well as surprise, I heard only chatter about the special guest's marriage plans. My, my, Governor. What a cruel way to reveal your decisions. Then, a few days later, guess what showed up at my front door?" Tommy pumped his eyebrows. "Yep. Had a not-so-handsome young man offer me the deal of a lifetime. Came with more money than I could imagine and also this little souvenir."

Tommy reached into his pants pocket, pulled out a leathery shoehorn of an object and threw it to Jackson's feet. "Governor, seems some Mexican's missing his tongue." He scoffed at the sight. "Yep. Got some dude's tongue and a sermon letting me know that silence was golden." He raised a proud jaw to Jackson. "Well guess what, Governor? As you can tell, I'm already pretty golden. Funny, huh?"

"You're crazy," Jackson said.

"Aren't we all? Hey—it's Georgia." Tommy's hand flew up, displaying the pistol like a trophy. "And guess what? My crazy brain used some of that miraculous cash to bring me home to you, Governor."

Price muffled a groan as Tommy shoved the gun deeper into his back. "So Sweetie, come on in and join the party. Doctor Jane here has saved you a seat."

Jackson raised his hands as though reaching for his head, but his movements stopped. His arms locked in the air, his body frozen in place as though all the power within his thoughts had ceased, every neuron stunned.

"Governor, the sofa. Please."

At the sound of Tommy's voice, Jackson's head began to ratchet, turning so he could leer at the man who was giving the orders. He gripped his head, his stance sturdier, as if all his disbelief had disappeared and in its place was unbearable disappointment.

"Over there," Tommy prompted, the barrel of the gun going to the reserved spot on the sofa. Jackson dropped his hands, cogging his head about to Jane. "Do it!" Tommy yelled. Jackson covered his mouth with a hand, wiping away any hint of disobedience before stepping to claim a seat beside Jane.

"And now, Doctor Price makes three!" Tommy rammed the gun to shove Price forward. "Step," he commanded, the order sending Price to the sofa, where he sank beside his brother. Triumphant at the sight of the seated trio, Tommy brandished the barrel of the gun between Jackson and Price, both men holding motionless as the black hole came and went.

"Just a week or so back," explained Tommy, his voice directed first to Jane then Price, "I was the one who offered up a correction plan for our governor-to-be. He was to make up for that night he walked out on me in Baltimore. He was to apologize in public and put his morality sermon in a proper perspective. Once that noble announcement was done, I was going to call my own campaign a success and . . . " Tommy slowed his voice, expelling his words as if he now smelled their odor. "Yes. I was going to let my in . . . do . . . lent disease take its course. Such peace of mind I would have had knowing the good people of Georgia were fully aware of our great governor's in . . . do . . . lent morality." Tommy plowed his face forward, fixing on Jackson, whose head was lowered. "But nooo," Tommy joked, "the good governor-to-be stood me up again." He grunted, mocking disgust. "Enough of that governor-to-be business. Sweetie, in my book you've always been a winner." Tommy smiled in churlish enchantment, his face virtually seraphic.

"You can't get away with this," Jackson mumbled, lifting his chin and growing his voice. "You can't." The sound was bitter, a truth within it that made Jane gag at the thought of all she'd overlooked, this truth too rancid to swallow.

Tommy's shoulders rose rag-doll wild. "Of course, I can't get away from this old body. After all, I'm in . . . do . . . lent and so, rather than go all gossipy to reporters, thought I'd let this pitiful flesh make some solid news while it still can. Oh, I can see the headlines now: 'Golden Boy Brings Justice to the Justice Building.' Like it, Governor?"

Jackson lifted his shoulders, the motion seeming to instill some authority. "No way. No way can you get away with this."

"Oh, tell me," Tommy hissed. "You tell me all about getting away. Say, care to talk about why *you* walked away that night, Governor?"

"They'll be up here any minute now. The police, the guards."

"Oh Governor, before they arrive, let's just talk about the men we were back in our dancing days. We were once such clever young men. Clever and good-looking ones at that. Weren't we the good-looking ones, Governor?"

Jackson balled his fists, rocked as he spoke. "Tell me . . . tell me what . . . what you really want."

"Oh, Governor. *Shirtless Men Drink Free*—remember?"

Jackson's breath halted, all signs of viable life frozen. Jane could feel the chill, the utter revulsion.

Tommy kicked his heels against the state's great seal. "Governor, the shirt. Off!"

Jackson fixed on Tommy. He stared a long moment, then, as if having reached a truce within himself, he raised his arms. His movements were serrated, halting as he unbuttoned and removed his dress shirt. Next came his white T-shirt. The robotic arms. The intimate scent of prickly cologne. Naked now from the beltline up, he dropped his hands to his sides. He seemed to sigh, but he held his head resolute, his full attention on Tommy's eyes and those starved animals watching there.

Free

TOMMY HIT THE BIG WHITE BUTTON on his iPod and the box erupted, the sound rude but billowing, the rhythm propulsive, unstoppable. The music sent Tommy's arms above his head, the gun wobbling in his right hand like a toy. He swayed to the beat, his buttery colors melting in unadulterated joy—bruised orange and tarnished yellow—the splotchy variegations glowing as the singer swirled ever higher in her amplified solo.

How will I know if he really loves me? Ohhh ... How will I know?

"Dance, Governor! Let's dance all over again!"

Jackson wrapped his arms about his chest and dropped his head. Jane couldn't tell for sure, but he appeared to close his eyes. His shoulders visibly shook as the singer's voice dipped and rose, her lyric plaintive, her words grasping and to the insistence itself, holding.

With every heartbeat I say a prayer ... Just how will I know?

"Governor, look at me! Look at me like you did in Baltimore. It's time to dance, Governor. Time to dance free all over again. Now's your chance, Sweetie. Let's dance!"

Tommy was exhilarant in his upper body contortions, mouthing the singer's words and dancing his arms in the air even as his eyes never left Jackson nor his grip the gun. He mouthed a long syllable with the singer, his head jostling to the cadence. To the euphoric Tommy, Jackson lunged, but the effort fractured in an instant, leaving the candidate on his knees, broken. Tommy held the gun directly before his face.

"Governor, your invitation to dance is gone."

Tommy was calm, his words so steady they seemed preprogrammed, like his iPod. It all came as methodical to Jane, so deranged and quick, this instant and why they were here, what they—no, Jackson—what Jackson had done to bring Tommy to this madness. Something was very wrong about that night in Baltimore; she always knew it, something corrosive between Jackson and Tommy, something she and Price never should have driven away from.

"Governor, your moves are not as smooth as they used to be. Such a shame. You were such a gifted dancer." Tommy held the gun in a fierce grip while, with his free hand, he lowered the music. His smile was gone.

The tamped song came metallic and impolite, in high parts a screech. The two men were poised within breathing distance of each other, Jackson's elbows extended, his arms bracing his shoulders up, his bent body like a beggar before Tommy's pendulous abdomen. Tommy's left arm hung limp at his side while his right arm swung wide, the gun now aimed for Price. "Feel it," Tommy instructed, placing his free hand on Jackson's head and pulling it forward. "Feel it, Governor. Feel this immorality that you swore would never reach Georgia."

Jackson's face was raised, his eyes on Tommy's belly, the bulging umbilicus.

"Yes, Governor. I said feel it—the immorality that needs the blessing of your lips."

Jackson's crouched lower half remained immobile, but his hands were rising, fingers outstretched in the air.

"Feel it!" Tommy shouted.

Jackson inched his hands higher, his reach fitful, fingers spreading before the bulk of Tommy's belly. Tommy tracked the progression of the fingertips toward his skin, his focus undulating as the distance narrowed. And once the connection was sealed, Tommy's pupils dilated beyond all normal size.

The touch now complete, Tommy swallowed, and what could have been the whole dirty world of devious creatures went down inside his eyes. He blinked. "Now, apologize, Sweetie. Apologize and kiss it good night." Tommy was breathing hard, the air accumulating within his chest to the point his voice seemed far deeper when the vast mass of breath broke free. And instead of demanding, the tone was wrong, almost motherly, consoling. "Apologize, Sweetie. Then kiss it good night."

Jackson's head began to pitch and jag, movements small but sharp as the belly loomed before his eyes. "You can do it, Governor. An apology and kiss—that's all it takes."

Jackson yanked his head about to fix on Price, to reach out to his brother with his eyes, to reach out from a horrible place. Within his hands, Tommy's belly fluctuated in and out as his lungs plunged up and down in the little chest above it. "Plyer," Jackson sobbed. "Plyer . . . he just wouldn't stop . . . and I couldn't stop him either. He promised . . . he promised to help me."

Price scooted forward on the sofa, craned to better see his brother's face. Jane leaned toward her husband, placing a hand on his knee and squeezing. Jackson trembled, his tears bitter and small, flowing. "And Daisy . . . she promised, she . . . they . . . would make it right...keep it . . . all of us, safe."

"Oh Sweetie," Tommy yelled, dropping his free hand to redirect Jackson's face to his belly. "Just keep yourself with me, me and the music. See, the goodbye is near and with its arrival, you've got the finest possible opportunity to come clean, to correct the record before the good doctors' eyes." Jackson's brow ratcheted forward then, at a resting point, fell to the skin of the golden swelling. At the touch Tommy shivered in bliss.

"Apologize, Sweetie. That's all you have to do. Just apologize and kiss all these things inside me good night." Jackson lifted his face to Tommy and as their eyes aligned, Tommy almost swooned. "Sweetie, we were so free, so very free. And . . . and you loved it didn't you?" Jackson was quaking, face engorged, sweating. "Just say you're sorry, Governor. Then kiss all you left good night." Jackson moved his lips closer to Tommy's belly. His hands shook and his chin rose, his mouth parting as if to address the skin. Jackson's lips were moving and sounds, stuttering sounds—what had to be an apology—came throaty and deep. He kissed Tommy's belly, resting his lips there, his face pressed fully against the skin.

Tommy sat triumphant on the desk, his face radiant, one hand resting atop Jackson's bowed head, the other still fielding the gun. "Doctors, now that our dear Jackson has corrected his mistake with the world he walked out on, it's time for him to correct his error with the fine people of Georgia. See, when our great debater preached his morality sermon, he was really only preaching to me. And the people need to know that. Right, Governor? The good people need to know this was a personal thing. They need to know, don't they?"

Jackson was mute, his hands clasping Tommy's belly as his head hung between his outstretched arms. He was nodding. He was weeping. The singer's lamentations continued, the music bringing a rough peace to the moment as Tommy kept talking. His voice was elegiac and composed, as if every beast inside him had been waiting years for some relief that, now that it was here, no longer mattered.

"As you fine doctors have witnessed, our Jackson has repented for his mistakes, including that night when he walked out at the Iron Gate. Right, Governor?"

"Plyer," Jackson wailed. "Plyer made me say it. He and his people— they made me."

Tommy curved low over Jackson's head. "Sweetie, if Plyer is your new boyfriend then maybe he needs an apology also."

Jackson moaned. He rocked his head violently, his face still directed to the floor. "He deals . . . he sells." Jackson sobbed, his voice growing louder as it broke. "Plyer has been . . . importing . . . shipping marijuana out of Mexico for years. And . . . to keep it going, he needed . . . me. He needed me to say it. He did." The words were wet and loud, in slurps.

Tommy raised an enchanted face to Jane and Price. "Weed," he said, a clownish smile growing outlandishly large as he spoke. "Now that's an immorality in need of no apology. A whole lot more than we bargained for. Right, docs?" Tommy snickered. "That's right, Doctors. Guess our dear Jackson has also been blessed by some kind of weed immorality. Maybe something else to mention when the guys in uniforms show up." Tommy lowered his eyes to the anguished man at his belly. "Sweetie, sounds like we could have made such a fine life together."

Jackson lifted his eyes to Tommy, who accepted the gaze as if no sacrifice could be greater, Jackson's face a complete surrender. And within that gathering, Tommy's bearing assumed a tranquility, as if all holiness had been delivered unto him, so composed it was, so total. No longer was Jackson trembling, his head now steady before Tommy as though some insight had come to him also, some peace. Tommy claimed the moment, stroking Jackson's hair with his free hand. "You're not alone, Baby. You'll always have me."

A curious stillness had settled in the air, a sense of resolution, which Jane took as the beginning of closure for this awful morning. Within this small mercy, she took a breath and as the air left her lungs, she stood. At the sight, Tommy went walleyed, jerking the barrel of his gun to her. "We are here to help you," Jane said. "And we can. We can help you, Tommy. Help you and Jackson also." She took one step forward.

Price sprung from the sofa. "Don't!" He froze, fixed in a stoop.

Jane stopped, lifting a hand, offering it up. "You're safe here, Tommy. We're only here to help. That's why you brought us, isn't it? You simply wanted help. And we can do it. We can help you." She had to believe it, still. She had made the diagnosis, confirmed it with her mother. The animals were back, the creatures even sicker.

"Doctors, Doctors!" Tommy yelled as he slung his head about, his grip on the gun hardening as he extended his arm, the barrel coming closer to

Jane. Price pitched forward, tackling his wife in a sweep of his arms that drew both of them back to the sofa, back once more to the witness positions Tommy had designed. Yet inside Jane, all her thoughts were still stepping toward Tommy, galloping in fact, and suddenly they were not—they were scrunched down and cowering in her head, this vocal commotion of disjointed prayers and demanding plans. Her thoughts of help and healing, all of them, had surrendered to Tommy's gun, to the arms that wouldn't let her go. She coiled her hands in her lap and watched as the beasts circled within Tommy's black pupils, the growls soundless, every tooth visibly bared.

"He's right, Doctor Jane. There's not much left in this show." Tommy seemed to fix his aim on her heart. "Doctors, you both just keep your seats because Jackson's work is not quite done. Governor, you're ready to complete this great moral task now before us, aren't you? You are, aren't you, Governor?"

Jackson offered no response and Tommy accepted the silence, telling Jane and Price, "All I need is for my dear Jackson to pull the trigger. That's how I'll know he really loves me, when he pulls the trigger for me."

Tommy lowered the gun, pressing it into Jackson's hands. And the kneeling Jackson claimed it, moving his fingers as Tommy directed, the barrel readjusted and shoved tight until Tommy's umbilicus puffed out like a disfigured nipple. His hands freed, Tommy turned up the music, raised his arms and swayed with the tempo. The singer's unanswered question soared unimaginably loud and in its plea, Tommy closed his eyes, cantering his shoulders to the beat.

Jackson's attention remained on Tommy's belly, the gun gripped with both hands to increase the pressure indenting the skin, which only seemed to enhance the thrill on Tommy's face. Price stood and inched toward his brother. Jane followed her husband, circling out in small soft steps to reach the telephone on the corner of the desk. "Thank God," Price said, his voice timid, as though to conceal a very private bargain with the God who had delivered them to this moment. "Lower the gun, Jackson and we'll get help up here. We'll get good help right away."

The color on Jackson's face deepened, the furrows on his brow ripening. Jane paused as she neared the desk. She could see Jackson's full expression now, the tempest beneath his skin, the pain. "Emory has great therapists," she said, working to keep her voice supple, her tone caring. "And we'll have them up here in no time."

Price kept moving toward his brother, his motion cautious but more assured, as if emboldened by the sound of Jane's voice. He said, "It'll work out just fine, Jackson. I know it will." Once Price arrived to the point where he towered over his brother, he bent toward him, locking his hands only inches above Jackson's naked shoulders. "We're safe now. We all are." Jane wanted to believe that they were safe now, that her husband was correct, that help would come. She and Price, they accomplish great things. They would help Jackson and Tommy, they could fix this thing, do better this time. She and Price, they accomplish great things.

Tommy opened his eyes. "Baby, you can do it. Just pull the trigger. Just do it, Baby, and we will dance so free, so very free. I know you loved it, loved it just as I did. I do."

Jackson plunged the gun deeper into Tommy's abdomen, one hand bracing the barrel, the other testing the trigger. Jane moved to the telephone and lifted the receiver, pulling it up in a slow-motion creep that ceased when Jackson glanced in her direction. "Put it down," he yelled. "You hear me? Put it down!"

Price jolted, steeled in place as he hunched over his brother. He was ashen, his lips stuck apart yet also moving, the force of his desire, it alone seeming to command his words. "It's okay," he murmured. "We can handle this, Jackson. You and me, we can." Except for the small quaver of his lips, no other motion was coming from Price. Before him, Jackson's finger crooked firm on the trigger. Jane had accomplished nothing. She could change nothing now, move nothing more. The facts were changing.

Tommy studied Jackson's face, his fix deviating only the moment it took to max out the music. The gaudier volume sent Tommy's arms again to the air, his limbs weaving in smooth, almost religious motions. Below him, Jackson moaned, the guttural sound dissolving in a sequence of sobs. A horrific hum. Price was sobbing also, his hand once again approaching his brother's back. "Please, Jackson. Just lower the gun."

"Get back! Both of you, get back *now!*"

"The gun helps nothing." Price was begging, his voice low but the clarity, the resolve growing. "Let's talk, Jackson. We can help. I'm sure of it." He touched Jackson's shoulder—two fingertips, two fingers only. "Give me the gun," he whispered. "The gun. Just lower it and we'll fix this. You and me. We'll be out of here in no time."

Sweat dripped from Jackson's brow. He turned, cast a helpless look to Price, the quick signal indicating that he'd heard everything his older brother had said and all of it was wrong, completely wrong.

"Price, I keep my promises. I do."

"Dear God," Tommy shouted. "Let this monster go!"

Jackson fired the gun and Tommy's belly exploded. Blood and bile flew through the air as Tommy collapsed backward over the desk. Price leaped forward to tackle his brother, but Jackson sprung up. He slammed an elbow into Price's face and flung him to the floor. Jackson jerked about, redirecting the pistol, shifting the aim directly to his brother's head.

Price lay sprawled across the rug, face up, blood erupting from a lip. Jane was locked in the instant, the scene before her moving far faster than she could process. Yet she felt her body move, her whole being rushing about the desk. She dropped to the floor beside her husband. She felt him there and she cradled him, slipping one hand under his shoulder and the other beneath his head.

Jackson patrolled the gun above Price, slurping back tears as he wept and redirected his aim, repeatedly. "It wasn't me, Price. But it was . . . so sick. And you . . . " Jackson shook his head, repetitively, squinting in the cry. "When Momma made us promise, I knew I would keep mine. I knew it then. Always would. Don't you see? And Plyer, he was helping. Like Momma did. Don't you see?" Jackson batted the gun before his brother's face. His sobs brutal, incessant. "He showed me, Price. He showed me it wasn't me. Plyer . . . it was always Plyer. Hangar thirty-one at Hartsfield. Price, you tell them . . . that world wasn't me."

Within Jane's arms, her husband lay limp and bleeding, his lip ripped. She dropped her shoulders to the floor, pressing her hand over his bleeding spot and fixing her head against his, her nose to his temple. If Jackson fired the gun, the bullet must take both of them, together. Every muscle inside her was prepared, this reality about her wet and dim but coming clear. The air was red, all the animals once inside Tommy now scattered dead across the floor, their bodies in pieces mixed among the bile and blood on the rug, the pools spreading before her eyes. She could feel Jackson moving above her; she could hear his sounds. But no longer did those sounds matter. What mattered now was her husband, the sacrifice she would share with him, the blood.

Price lifted a hand to his jaw and moaned. At the rousting, Jane turned to see Jackson backing away. She watched as he fired his gun to the windows, as he rushed to the windows behind the desk, his gun firing.

The sounds were quick, holes flaring into fractures across the glass panes, cracks streaking. Jackson rammed his shoulder against a splintered window and one massive sheet gave way, chunks falling from the top of the frame. He turned to Price, his face flushed, pressurized. "Price, you . . . you've got to let me . . . and your daddy . . . you've got to let us go." Jackson closed his eyes, reeling into the window's shattered space. He lifted his face to the sky, to the rush of in-coming wind. He lifted both hands. He leaped. The wind stopped nothing, the instant gone before her eyes, the sky simply pushing him down. The light was unrelenting, the void loud, the air that claimed him real.

Jane screamed, dragging her hands across the floor, her fingertips sinking into the rug's wet pile. The dampness was pulling her down. She was small and getting smaller. The wind, and only the wind, was getting larger, death itself invading. Shards of glass kept falling. The wind coursed mad over her face even as a quietness was rising about her body, a hush, and all of it coming closer. The blood there clotted beneath her knees, the golden wool and words sopping up the juices from Tommy's belly, his blood. Jackson's fine white shirt lay soaked on the floor, the red stain spreading. Jane anchored a hand on the rug and pushed up.

Price was stirring, levering his shoulders free from the floor, one hand reaching for his jaw, blood mixing among his fingers. At the sight of Jane, he batted his eyelids a great many times, focused and refocused as if he wasn't sure who she was. But his eyes soon settled and shifted, first to Tommy's body then to the window. Price was sitting, as Jane was, the two of them helpless on the floor, the massive window above them empty, the wind beyond all mercy. She scooted closer to her husband, holding him as he shivered and the air kept coming.

Jackson Beekman, 2004

W HEN YOU'RE FALLING FROM THE TOP floor of a majestic world, you flap your arms and legs in the air because your body is used to the struggle, this impulse to hold on even as your soul knows such reaching is pointless. Still, you do this nonsensical flapping, your body flailing in a kind of last campaign before the great stop comes. As perhaps you always knew it must, the struggle and release, the hush.

It's an inglorious benediction that greets your being, a sidewalk the only reasonable refuge now that your mortal performance has ended, your soul free to objectify this lump of flesh that, thank God, landed with its face turned up. It's a victory of sorts, the fresh spectacle of you deviating none from the eyes of God or any creature that happens by. You can't say such an exhibit is what you wanted your life to come to, but what you can say is that your vision has improved now that your soul chanced the transition, this transcendence to a street-level terminal where—as you can already see—the intangibles include a great many regrets. Truth be known, you were expecting even more.

But truth is known more for its impulses than insights, which may explain this desire to dawdle about the mess you've made of your body. Regret, even for a soul, is a sticky thing. It can explain this essence of you that now seems so much more than this carcass the reporters will call the late Jackson Beekman. Little surprise. Your nature was never a controllable

thing, nor a traditional exhibit. Ultimately, you just gave up. Which is probably the reason your curiosity is rewarded when you realize your soul is no
longer immobilized by bodily boundaries. It's the reward you were least
expecting, the hand that's no longer a hand, the twiddle of a finger that simply isn't there. It's the sight of an unpopulated sidewalk, the bedraggled
cadaver that—God bless it—you no longer can call only yours. To the people and their popular world, you have surrendered. No memorial could be
truer. So, from this lumpy smear of blood and bones, you arise and sit beside
it. You will keep this relic company until the process claims it, which hopefully won't take long or too many efforts. You cross your legs and sit like a
Buddha beside a messy *memento mori,* this offering that's already staining
the cement red. If you could apologize, you would. Instead, you shake.

No mortal who might help is out. No tourists on the capitol grounds,
not a cop in sight. But your perception must still be distorted because only
now you realize there's a voice coming from the front steps of the Justice
Building. You turn just as the guy starts pounding the glass doors. He's a
street dude. You can tell it, the rat-tail hair and dusty beard, the unraveling
camo vest. "Hey-oh! Hey-oh!" The man pummels the glass and glances
back at what he's already seen of you. Your form has not moved, but the
puddling blood has reached your shoulders. "Lord God a-mighty! There's a
bleeding man out here! A man with a pistol!"

The guard in the foyer unlocks the door and pokes out his head. His
stick is drawn. "Hey Mister—there's a man on the sidewalk out here! A
shootout and I heard it. Heard it all!" Together, they run.

"At Justice," the guard shouts to his gadget's speaker hole. "Near the
front door." This security professional now stands above your body, his
breath short and his eyes turning across the street to the capitol building
basement station. Confidence has taken him over, a certainty that knows
the other cops will come here pronto. He's about to flip the switch on the
process, and he knows the honor in that privilege. It's not much, but maybe
your demise has given this fine guard a day to always remember.

The street dude's crouched on his knees, leaning over your body and
inspecting its full dimensions. Dog tags dangle over your face. You had a

hunch the dude was familiar with war. The sight is humbling. Tommy would have been pleased to know the only witness was a vet, the alarm sounded first by a burned-out survivor.

The cops are here, sirens sounding, van doors opening so the medics can jump. One cop grabs the street dude by the back of his vest. He yanks the guy up, passing him along to a strong-armed confederate. "Lord God a-mighty," yells the dog-tagged dude. "That man needs help." It's the very words that always hung in your thoughts of Tommy, him and the others. And now you are one of the others, these truths hanging over you, the truth spouted from the mouth of a tattered old vet, no less. Probably did time in Vietnam, the last pointless battles. Tommy would have called the dude a true hero. As are the others.

The crowd is only beginning. A couple of well-pressed officers surround the fallen gun and point to the high broken windows. Before you, two medics drop to their knees. One consults the other as they check for any signs of life in your body, which, of course, they can't find. As you feared, your death leaves only questions. "Good God, think we can bag the body before the coroner gets here? This guy, the only shooter?" The duo slips on gloves before any responses come, their collection business proceeding in its stepwise method even as a honcho in a suit arrives to wave his arms like a late-to-the-service preacher.

The system is engaged, battalions deployed. It's a spectacle of service, a sure sign the voices are up there calling. So you race with a contingent of officers to the lobby of the Justice Building. What a battle these good cops think this is! What a job to be done!

It is a grand experience, the soul you steered through so many corridors now grounded among officers mustering in the lobby. A small squadron races for the stairs as a strongman trio enters the elevator, which you also claim. After all, this once was your territory. You stand beside three men in boots and black helmets as the elevator clicks its way to the elevated place you actually did once experience as a sort of heaven, you the god-eyed lawyer doing his best to defend the boundaries between right and wrong, the meaning within a promise. It wasn't all about your gift of perspective, though. It was your job. People expected no less. You had a role people looked up to, an assigned duty. At least, that's the way you tried to see it, the way you tried to see it given the ongoing war over feelings. Which had nothing to do with your job, which no soldier could do if he'd not won most battles.

Maybe these better-eyed men are not so disappointed when the top floor of the world opens, and everyone steps out to see there's no heaven up here at all. Still, you're honored to have your name scratched on a plaque. My version of a dog tag, you might indicate to the God of This Trouble if he ever asks why you passed in such a spectacle of blood.

"Police! Drop your weapons!" All the destructive instruments are drawn before the beautiful door, triggers poised.

You think of telling these uneasy officers things that might lighten their fears. You'd try not to make it a sermon. You might say—

Men, no need to worry. Inside, it's just Price and Jane and the body of Tommy Carpenter as he wanted it to be found. You guys will all be glad to know that Tommy had finally given up on his men, given up on every one of them except, of course, for me. Guys, it's safe in there and for that peace, I think Tommy would be proud.

You want to tell of Tommy's sacrifice to these antsy soldiers, but only nerves and guns go with the job of these fine officers, so you keep your thoughts to yourself and attribute all understanding to the God who, as the soul of any ditched body knows best, works in mysterious ways.

"Help us! Help us, please. It's okay now. Please. Just us!" The voice belongs to your brother Price. He is shouting behind the door. "Just us . . . please!"

You won't bother to tell the cops, but Price has always been unarmed. He's carried no visible weapon even as he's been a ferocious hunter, which makes him one of the most successful kinds. Indeed, your brother has always wanted to corner something he would never kill. That is a normal feeling, of course, the power in applause, the craving for completion. These fleshed-out troopers might call such an obsession simply a natural lust, this quest for something that must be caged before it destroys more than itself. Oh, what you and so many others could never understand, let alone explain. And Price, God bless him, sometimes it seemed he was only following orders.

One cop rams his foot against the door. It swings back and the trio storms inside, pistols sweeping the air.

"It's okay," Price sobs, wrenching his shoulders as he climbs up his legs. Jane is quick to follow the pattern. "Just us," Price says. "My brother, he jumped."

You don't like to hear Price say such pitiful things or see him in this terrible way, not that tone and overwrought face. Facts are all the good cops need—no drama in the explanation, no pain. Pain, they can surely tell, is all over this place.

The cops move fast through the room, yanking open the doors to a closet and, finding that place empty, the bathroom. "Tommy Carpenter," Jane says as she grips Price's shoulders. She points to the body splayed across the desk. "He drew a gun at the house, brought us down here and—"

"Jackson," Price says. "My brother is Jackson Beekman, the attorney general." Price looks at the blood on his hands, repeating your name, your final position. "Jackson Beekman is my brother." Price holds his head, telling the officers that there may be other problems, but his brother was a good man. In a crowd, you could always count on Price. He brings a hand to his lips, holding the bleeding spot as he drops his head on Jane's shoulder. Such a panorama of ache—even to the soul of an unclean lawyer, it is a bad sight to see.

"At the airport," Jane says. "At hangar thirty-one. Jackson said Plyer Hoots was behind it all. Marijuana. He talked of Plyer and marijuana." She watches Price as she speaks, watches as though looking for some signal to stop speaking or maybe to go on. You're glad she's talking even if she can't say the word *weed*. Never did you have any doubts about Doctor Jane. But you did the weed. Some things could make you feel better just because they were wrong, wrong and yet the only help that first didn't hurt.

Plyer Hoots was that kind of help, a deferred hurt. Something like a promise. As smart as Daisy was, you'd think she wouldn't have trusted her father so much. Then again, you wanted to trust him also. What can you say? Fathers have always been wanted men. In a way, pity is inevitable. Maybe pity was what attracted you to Plyer, this deal you could make with another sickness, the potential for a better weakness. The questions were so confusing. At least in your final minutes, you gave the correct answers. You gave Price what he needed to hear, Tommy what he always wanted.

The men start jabbering into the gadgets strapped about their shoulders, their words clicking back and forth as the room fills with more officers and the filling takes over.

You want to explain how weed is not such a bad thing, how its properties actually seem to heal the body if that body's been diving deep for others. You have to admit it. You want to defend Plyer and that deep world he and you had to operate in, but you can't take your eyes off Tommy and what deep diving did to him. It's a blessing to know he finally got what he wanted, his body like yours, its promise delivered.

"Oh God," Jane moans, pointing to Tommy's disarticulated liver. "Hepatitis," she says to the workers approaching his body. "Please be careful. Please." She covers her nose with an unsteady hand.

Tommy's body is indeed a dreadful sight, one not appropriate for viewing outside a war zone. Yet this location is a fitting finale, given that Tommy always wanted to die like a soldier, to die among his men. No wonder a vet was the first to pronounce your body.

Price and Jane clutch each other until they're pulled aside by a man in a dark official suit. Investigator Name-Be-Quick tells them he would like to make a video recording. "Yes," says Price, whose mouth seems incapable of many more words. "Yes. Jackson Beekman is my brother."

Jane steers Price away from the desk and closer to the unbroken windows. They stand a distance from the shattered glass, the wind racing past them as a video camera sweeps the room. "Jackson shot him," Jane tells the officers. "He had the gun. Fired it . . . like Tommy told him to." Her breath is only strong enough to surrender the key facts. Price knows her limits, so he wraps his arms about her in a clasp you have to admire, for it's a normal holding, a containment of nothing not meant to be held. Together, they turn to look out the window as the guy with the camera zeroes in on the bombed-out torso of Tommy Carpenter.

Outside, the sky is overcast, the entering wind hot and damp. Had the sun been out, it would have been a scorcher. Like Saigon, Tommy would have said. Only hotter.

Valuables

J ANE WAS COMING TO HERSELF in the back of a police car. In here, the safe world was close, yet she wanted to draw it even closer. The weave within her shirt, the buttons and seam moving with her chest and its breath, the splotch of age on Price's temple—when had the brown grown so much larger? The sharp white edge of the bandage on his jaw, the silvery stumps of his whiskers, his thinned fingers. Her fingers also, their wrinkles and ring, the diamond that had so thrilled her mother, the still tense hand of her husband, the grip that fit so well when her eyes closed she couldn't tell his fingers from hers—this was the world in which her heart beat. Encased, it seemed. In this world, she could do nothing more. In this world, her heart was an uncontrollable thing. She felt it in her chest, that thing still kicking.

This was the backseat world she shared with her husband and a listening silence. Price had been examined, his jaw x-rayed, his torn lip sutured, the wound bandaged. Even in the hospital, some danger always seemed near, police huddled or lining the corridors, men and women in blue, the gold-stitched decals, heroic voices and yells that belonged to the jungle, television cameras and their apish alien eyes, heels on the floor and guns in their holsters. Next, the police station downtown, they said. A debriefing they called it, a few questions. They said tapes from security cameras would help. They said the airport had been secured, an investigation ramped up.

They said counselors were waiting. A few questions, they said. They apologized at every turn, sympathized often. The word *dead* was used by no one. Price had tried time and again, this Jane could tell, but the man inside him had yet to scream.

The two officers sitting in the front seat were quiet, stiff and attentive to life outside the car, the colors flashing back in white and blue. Jane tightened the grip on her husband's hand, sorting through her thoughts, the upcoming questions: In the Justice Building, who said what and why? Where were you? But none of those questions could be harder than the ones tensing the ridges on Price's face. He was staring straight ahead like the officers, his gaze more procedural than engaged with the blue discolorations. Together or apart, she and Price, they could answer the official questions. But those questions working through her husband, those were questions for God. And because God wasn't answering, her husband's hand quavered at the absence, the questions suddenly palpable and moving through her: What had he—no, they—done wrong? Given the sudden shift at the debate, should they have heightened their suspicions? Why not an intervention? Jane's mother, she had to have been intervening, probably begging for something better. Why had God overruled her? So many questions this diabolical God would someday have to answer for. Jane's thoughts were illogical, their colors too changing. The air conditioner was blowing high as it could go.

Price lifted her hand and kissed the knuckles. In the process, a more natural texture arose on his cheeks, this face that was doing its best to return to the man he was this morning, the husband who was eager to find his letter in the newspaper. The newspaper this morning, remember? This morning, they had been looking. She had forgotten they looked. She had forgotten how childish and naughty they felt in the looking, how young they were before the doorbell rang. They had been looking for something that shouldn't have been there, but in fact was, that disagreeable letter. And just as Price found the right section, the doorbell rang. The letter had been a mistake. It was culpable. Because of that letter, the doorbell rang.

"It would have been different," Price murmured, "if Jackson had wanted the money clip, if he'd simply taken it home and put it away." His tone belonged to a question, one meant only for her. And even though she had no answer, he seemed determined to find at least some agreement inside her eyes. "It could have been so different," he said.

"Price, if Jackson had taken the money clip, what difference would it have made?"

He withdrew his hand from hers, sat back and studied some sight that seemed to stretch an unreachable distance. "A sign," he said. "A sign that Jackson had adjusted, that he was over it." He was using his hands, interlocking his points. "It would have meant that he'd dealt with things, just as I had. That he'd quit . . . " He paused, swallowed hard. "That he'd quit blaming our father. Maybe . . . himself."

Jane wanted to agree, but she couldn't. Accepting the money clip would have signaled nothing about Plyer Hoots, answered no question about lovers. So many clues from the campaign were already returning to chide her, so many signs she had misinterpreted, had chosen not to question. The stunt at the debate, wedding plans out of the blue, bundling and worried looks from Lily. Politics, Jane had concluded time and again—it's just the way things worked in a tough campaign. It's what she had wanted to conclude. She had been thoughtless, naïve, a convert. She should have confronted Jackson more directly, complained more to Price, left the campaign when Lily did. But she didn't. She stayed on and stayed quiet for selfish reasons. She had wanted a cleansing, her own selfish stain lifted from the death of her mother. Such a want demands deliverance, a do-over. Yet the campaign was a selfish redemption. And within her selfishness, had she done it again? With Jackson, had she misdiagnosed something that should have been obvious?

"Sometimes," she said, "I heard Jackson say things that I knew were not true, but in the moment they always seemed the right things to say. Price, he could fake his thoughts so easily to please people. Taking the money clip, he could have faked that also. But you, Price. He wasn't going to fake you."

"Why not? Why wouldn't he?" Price was moving closer to her, palming his voice away from the officers. "Jane, he was going to kill me."

"He was frightened, Price. You saw him, that fear. He was so frightened."

"Of what? Me?"

"Questions," she said.

❧ ◉ ❧

THE CONVERSATION WAS BEING RECORDED BY A knotty little camera that hung high above the officer's shoulder, so the lens was directed to the person—the witness, perhaps the suspect—being interviewed. Jane was the witness, but she felt like a suspect. The lens was pointed to her alone. She tried to ignore the camera, but her eyes kept leaping up to it. At the end of each response to a question, she looked up. There was a sneer on her lips every time she did it, one she couldn't suppress. It seemed God was at it again. And if God actually was watching her through that camera, she was glad for it because the sneer was meant for him, this Almighty who was evading all her tough questions. The officer's inquiries had nothing to do with it at all.

Sometimes the officer's questions carried the implications of a suggestion, some prompt to a ready answer. He was clearly trying to help her. She appreciated that. She agreed with almost everything he suggested. The only thing she didn't agree with was his implication that Jackson was a "threatening man." Jackson was a politician, she insisted, no more threatening than any other politician. "Bluster," she said, "was part of the game." Her sneer to the camera was an unabashed one.

"Did you have any prior contact with Tommy Carpenter?"

"Yes, about twenty years ago. Price and I were living in Baltimore, had dinner with Tommy and Jackson. They drove up from Washington."

"They?"

"Sure. Jackson and Tommy were friends. They grew up together."

"And?"

"And they both happened to be living in Washington. Jackson was a law clerk and Tommy . . . I think he worked for the government. So, Jackson brought Tommy along for dinner. We'd just finished at Hopkins and were moving back to Atlanta. A celebration, of sorts."

"Were they lovers?"

The words were heavy. Their heft grew as she balanced them in her mind. *Lovers—were they lovers?* The question was sharp, too abrasive even for God. She felt her head nodding and she stopped it. Of course, Jackson was a lover. He was a good man. A good man is always a lover. But Tommy Carpenter—he was no lover. She buttressed herself up on the arm of her chair and inside herself cried out for a world where they could all start over.

"So, were they lovers?"

"At that time, we had no idea . . . not at that time." Jane couldn't bring herself to restating Tommy's words, to drawing conclusions. *Lovers*—the word was a one-way street and on it, Jackson and Tommy had gone different ways.

"But now," the officer said, "you know they were lovers?"

Jane brought her eyes directly to the wide black barrel of the high camera. "In the office, Tommy Carpenter told us . . . he told us that he and Jackson used to dance."

"They danced. You mean together?"

"Yes, I think he meant together. That's what Tommy Carpenter said. He said they danced. So, I guess it means they were together."

"So, they were lovers. Right?"

The question had the air of accusation, of judgment. It was too much for that glassy black eye, too much for Jane. She sealed her attention on the officer, whose pen rested on his lips. He too was uncomfortable. He didn't want to look at her. His uniform was a crisp day-duty blue, the decal on his shirt ablaze with golden threads, the perfectly stitched phoenix arising from a prodigious fire. Beating deep beneath those flames was his heart. The officer had to have a heart.

"I think they may have been," she said.

"Lovers?"

"Lovers."

He wrote down the word. She saw it and nothing else, the word resounding as a loud question in her head. Lovers? The question could have come from God, and to her answer that was now documented, she wouldn't look away. She wouldn't disfigure it with a sneer.

❖   ●   ❖

THE INTERVIEWS DONE, FIRST APART AND THEN together, she and Price sat in the room reserved for the waiting. They had given permission to have the house searched. The house had been searched. Jackson's house—no permission requested—had been searched also. There had been a confrontation at the airport; an interception they were calling it. "The facts," as the last officer told Price, "were coming clear." Price said the officer hugged him, patted him on the back and told him to not be surprised if he came by the house later this evening. Price didn't say the answers would be waiting.

They had been cleared to return home. The house would be protected. More interviews would come in the morning, they said. They said they would call first. No one said anything about the possibility of starting over.

They sat on the sofa. Their hands could hold no more of each other, so their fingers rested on their laps. They had been emptied and rebuilt, parts rearranged and forced into places that didn't fit. The opportunity to simply sit seemed the final step, the annealing phase when the day's terror would hold them officially together but also apart, their hands finally resting alone, like their hearts.

Officer John, the one with a cross on his nametag, moved to the small kitchen area in the corner of the room and made new coffee. Small talk followed, Jane and Price sipping coffee with the chaplain in a windowless room reserved for people who had been involved one way or another, as she could now almost accept it, with crime. Crime, as she had never imagined possible in their lives, had come and passed. She felt safe now, almost selfish for feeling so safe. Price too seemed less tense, the wrinkles on his face slack and hanging.

"Oh," said the chaplain, "let me run downstairs. The valuables may have been cleared for release. In suicides, they sometimes . . . " He stopped, blushing with embarrassment. "I'm sorry. I'll be back in a few minutes."

Price fingered his chin, moving his eyes to the darkened television parked across from the sofa. "Can we watch?"

"News reports can be very misleading," the chaplain warned. "Even harsh sometimes."

"I can handle it."

The chaplain smiled. "I guessed that." He stepped across the room to retrieve a remote controller, handed it to Price, telling him, "It really shouldn't take much longer." Jane watched the chaplain tap the doorframe as if to bless it before he left. She liked Officer John, the simplicity in his manner, the ritual he'd made of simply sitting in silence.

WATL had live coverage, helicopter close-ups of the Justice Building and the cordoned-off street out front, reporters at the airport, early reports of a drug bust—marijuana shipped in cellphone boxes, a warehouse packed, possibly more—an official briefing at nine this evening.

Plyer Hoots was thought to be in Mexico, the mountains maybe. Cameras caught a handcuffed Daisy Hoots being escorted from the airport to the open door of a police cruiser. Seeing it on the television screen gave it a distance. They needed the distance. "It's sick, really sick," Price said. "Daisy Hoots," he added. "She always seemed fake to me."

The door to the waiting room was open, but the returning chaplain tapped it anyway before he stepped through the doorway, a fat large yellow envelope in his hand. "The car is ready and so are the valuables." He pulled a chair before the sofa, turning his head to the television as Price pointed. The streaming banner on the screen called Daisy Hoots a suspected accomplice, her father a drug kingpin. *Drugs, accomplice, kingpin*—tabloid words, cheap tabloid words that Jane knew were true.

As Daisy scowled on the screen, Price pointed, directing his voice to the chaplain. "Is she here?"

"Special Operations has the airport. They're probably questioning her out there." The chaplain pulled a slip of paper from his shirt pocket, passing it and his pen to Price. "All the valuables are listed here. I just need a signature." Price signed on the fingered line.

The large envelope, its contents bulky at the bottom, was sealed with a string. Price unwound the seal and moved down the sofa from Jane to create a display space between them. He widened the neck of the envelope, peered inside, and paled. He turned the envelope's opening to Jane so she too could look. Inside it, Jackson's wristwatch, the expansible gold-linked band, was wrapped about his wallet. Jackson didn't do this, and they knew he didn't. The state had taken over. The state of Georgia had reworked his things.

Price gave the chaplain a suspicious eye, shifting his head to indicate the envelope. "You don't need to keep this? Evidence, maybe?"

"It's all been photographed," said the chaplain. "Also traced for DNA, every item fully logged in. And, considering the family . . . " He paused, slumping beneath the weight of the process. "The custody is yours."

"The custody," Price repeated. He pulled the wristwatch from the envelope and examined the crystal face, lifting it to show Jane how the time was correct, nothing broken, the second hand sweeping despite the fall. He placed it on the sofa, positioning the face and its still-moving hands upright much as a surgeon might relocate a vital organ before completing a life-saving procedure.

And then the dark leather wallet—Price handled it like another extraordinary survivor as he lifted it from the folder. He pulled the wallet to his nose and sniffed, lowering his eyelids, inhaling as he freed the leather sides. And before he opened his eyes, he swallowed, an almost imperceptible swallow that only Jane could recognize for what it carried to a place deep inside him—that aroma of Jackson, all Price could pull of his brother from the leather. He placed the wallet neatly beside the watch.

"Two hundred and thirty-one dollars inside it," said Officer John, looking at the inventory slip. "And there was also some cash in his pockets." Price pulled Jackson's fat, gold-colored fraternity ring from the envelope.

He nodded to it and situated it beside the other things. "Oh, and the ring." Officer John seemed to apologize, as if he'd overlooked it. "The pocket cash is probably at the bottom."

Price stilled. His breath halted, noticeably.

"Doctor, is something wrong?"

"No, nothing." His voice was jagged, breathy. "He had . . . he had a money clip?"

"Yes, one money clip. Twenty-dollar bills inside it." The chaplain was poring over the list, circling an item with his pen. "From his right pants pocket, it should have an emblem on it, the letters, *U* and *S*. See it?"

Price pulled the clip from the envelope, manipulating the silver prongs in the fluorescent light, first at some distance and then pulling the clip closer, his face straining as he ran a finger over the intricate purple emblem. Inside the clip, the twenty-dollar bills were folded, a single crease forming the spine, pale green edges perfectly aligned. Price tilted his head as if to hide his eyes as he studied it. But Jane saw, as probably did Officer John— those wet and congested eyes, his eyebrows forced low to help contain the tears. And once many seconds of examination passed, Price placed the clip on the sofa apart from the other items, as if to assign it a special frame.

"Price, I thought he tossed it."

"He did. Threw it across the room." Price stroked the silver prongs, tears going free. "It's his," he murmured.

"But how—?"

Price cut her off, his breath short. "Guess he . . . after I left . . . I guess . . ." Price tried to hide his face. "But he . . . kept it." His chin quaked. He lifted the money clip and its bills, running the metal against his cheek, nuzzling the paper bills against his lips. He closed his eyes, dropped his head and rocked on the sofa as he wept and the chaplain bent closer.

Cobbler

THE HOUSE WHERE PRICE AND JANE had shared so many good years now looked as if it were hurting. Roof rain soaked, shutters dripping, all windows dark. Jane was eager to help this house, to turn on the lights and dwell among the injuries, to do whatever it took to heal the afflictions of the house the police had renamed a crime scene. Price said nothing as he eased the car up the driveway, slowing none as they passed over the water that had pooled in the spot where Tommy parked. Price remained silent as he clicked the garage door button and the wide door rose, panel by panel. He tightened his lips when the garage light came on, watching for that first inside view of the home Tommy had entered. Only when he eased the car forward, braked and killed the engine, did the words come. "Yes. I did have questions for Jackson . . . I always did . . ." He was talking low, through his fingers, his eyes fixed on the steps where he'd tried to wrestle the gun from Tommy. "But I couldn't ask them. I . . ." He stopped, turning to share something he couldn't fully express to her. "Jackson was right. I couldn't let them go." He squeezed her hand, closed his eyes and inhaled a breath so thorough it seemed it might never be fully surrendered.

Inside the house, the only notable disarray was in the kitchen and breakfast room—the tabletop barren and chairs displaced, Tommy's photograph missing, the coffeepot half-full, everything cold. Jane pulled the breakfast room curtains wide to allow the last of the day's light to enter. Outside the windows, the sunflowers were soaked but seemed to be standing even stronger because of what had happened in this house. Jane wanted to believe it was true. She wanted to believe Tommy had been wrong about the blood, the expertise of doctors, the belief in what they could do.

Price slipped off his sweaty shirt and started to gather the dirty breakfast dishes, tossing each one in the trash. Jane was glad he did it without asking. Never again would these dishes be used. Nothing from this gruesome breakfast could be saved or remade, certainly nothing Tommy touched. Besides, the Wedgwood was fake. It was a minor thing, but it deepened her grief to think Tommy had mistaken the dishes for china. It saddened her to think of so many other fake things Tommy had probably assumed were real. Was Jackson among those things? The question couldn't be trashed with the dishes. It would forever loom before her, like the face of Tommy, his relief as Jackson fired the gun.

Price insisted she shower first, so she went upstairs, showered and changed into fresh clothes—luxuriating only briefly in the process because it came with a sense of futility, the thought of never again being fully clean.

When she returned to the kitchen, Price had removed every sign of how this horrible day began: chairs in proper places, countertops swabbed. He sat at the breakfast table, sipping Scotch and motioning to the glass he had prepared for her. She brushed away the liquor, which he poured into his glass and sipped while watching her pour a small glass of orange juice. "Now, my turn," he said before downing the liquor and heading upstairs. Alone once more, she couldn't keep from staring.

The shower and fresh clothes were helping her mind assess the damage. The day had been so sudden, its cut so quick her thoughts remained ill-formed and raw, some nerves surely severed. No doubt the numbness she felt now would turn to an ache over the next few days. She needed to be prepared for the pain, to be strong for a husband whose pain might prove unbearable.

The house helped. The breakfast table Price had already used, the straight back chairs waiting to be reoccupied and the clock on the wall that had paused none as the damage played out below—so many things her brain was beginning to process. The process would lead to understanding, the understanding to peace. She wanted to believe she was already beginning to adjust to the memory of Tommy in this house. Yet her mind had not relaxed enough to form even a half-coherent image of Jackson. For him, the house wasn't helping. Could anything? Ever?

The doorbell—the doorbell Tommy had pushed—was ringing. A knuckle on wood, a yell. This was not Tommy. No way could Tommy be back. His car was gone, the spot in the driveway empty. The doorbell. Jane grabbed her elbows and went to the door.

Outside the living room windows, sunlight poled the low clouds, grass arrayed in an amber light. The falling colors carried Jane's eyes to the driveway, where a silver Mercedes was parked. It looked like Lily's. Behind her, Price was bounding down the stairway. He rushed to the front door and claimed the peephole. Dressed only in his pants, he flipped the lock and swung back the door.

"Baby, I'm a mess!" Lily didn't bother to look up. She was frowning at her moist shirt, tenting it up from her skin. She seemed more stooped than Jane recalled, more elderly. Her face was blotchy, devoid of makeup, and when she finally looked at Jane, her lips went in as though all her prepared words had suddenly dissolved in her mouth. She tossed both arms forward, reaching up like a woman ready to be rescued. "Oh, dear God. Baby, it had to have been just awful."

Lily's breathing was rushed, her arms restless. Her agitation ripped through the parts of Jane that had begun to heal. Had Plyer's men threatened Lily? Had she always known? Jane's soul braced for even more injury as she held her mother's best friend. "So thankful. Baby, I am just so thankful y'all made it." Jane was doing her best to hold on, to bear even more.

"And you, Lily. Are you okay?"

Lily's hug grew tighter as she fought back sobs. Indistinct, soggy words were coming. She grabbed Jane's shoulders and pushed her up with a stern shake. "Baby, we need to talk."

The former finance chief whipped her head about and again raised her arms. "And Price, God help you—what you have been through." He stepped forward, also reaching low to scoop up Lily's outstretched arms. But instead of an all-encompassing hug, Lily snagged his bare shoulders, drawing him close to plant her mouth in his ear. "God bless, I've been praying all afternoon for you. Prayers, non-stop prayers. Good Lord, don't you need a shirt on?" He moaned in agreement, casting a reassuring look to Jane before Lily freed his shoulders.

Lily took a great breath and sighed. "What a misery," she said, "what a horrible misery you two have been through." She eyed the big wicker picnic basket at her feet. "But I brought help." She fanned her face for an instant before grabbing the picnic basket handle and barging through the doorway. She marched headlong through the hall, her voice trailing. "Dazed, I say, a complete daze. Yes, we are. Me and the old man, we can't begin to imagine what y'all went through this awful, awful day."

Lily stopped before the kitchen table, turning back to Jane and Price, the picnic basket raised in her hands. "But here is the help." She heaved the basket to the table, flipped up the wooden lid and tilted the entire basket to Jane so she could look inside. "Raisin cobbler," Lily said, her tone more optimistic than boastful. Inside the basket, a foil-covered casserole dish was positioned beside a silver thermos bottle, wads of clumped-up newspapers holding everything in place.

"Baby, have to say it's just as much for me as the two of you. Still . . . " Lily stepped about, lifting the cobbler from the basket and positioning it just so on the table. She gave Price an imploring look. "Baby, unless you get a shirt on, the walking pneumonia's gonna' stomp all over you. Now, you go get that shirt on—then get yourself back down here for some home-cooked relief."

"My momma," Lily declared once Price was gone and Jane seated. "My momma always said the family never would have survived the Depression without her raisin cobbler." Lily pulled the foil from the glass dish, placing it beside the cobbler. She sniffed. "Momma's recipe." She patted the rucked crust. "Poor people's food, what the old man and me always eat during a bad time." Lily tilted her head to Jane, knowingly. "And Baby, this is a very bad time." She took a seat, gathering Jane's hands into her own.

Jane said nothing. Within her mind, Lily's words resounded like a blessing, the ceremonial sounds intoning some closure on this very bad time, forcing it.

"Baby, I can't help but wonder what would have happened if I'd stayed on. Maybe I could have changed things."

Jane squeezed Lily's fingers firmly before releasing them. "No, Lily. I doubt any of us could have changed things. You knew Jackson. You knew how he thought." Hearing the words, feeling them leave her lips, Jane sensed the weight of a lie. Any answers she might offer were immature, her doubts full-grown and powerful. She covered half her mouth with a hand and spoke through the free part. "No, Lily. I just . . . I just don't know."

Jane felt the beginning of a confession within the choppiness of her voice, the few facts she did know overpowered by the questions that were still stalking them. Guilt also. What she'd seen and heard throughout the campaign, what she witnessed in a Baltimore restaurant and also heard from Tommy's own mouth, what she'd forgotten about Jackson and tried to ignore—all of it fractured like those faces Jane now could only watch in the crinkled tinfoil of Lily's cobbler, the eyes going this way and that. "But we shouldn't be second guessing," she told Lily. "We shouldn't be, should we?"

"That's your momma talking, Baby. And she's right." Lily's hands moved through the air as if consecrating it, repeatedly. She said, "Something was going on, that much I knew. And whatever it was, I also knew there was nothing I could do about it, absolutely nothing." She turned to the wall, her chin wrinkling.

"And what I would like to believe," Jane said, "what I'd like to be certain of is that Hoots was behind it all."

Lily stiffened. "Well, he was. Wasn't he? They're calling him a drug kingpin. It had to be Plyer." She braced her arms on the seat of her chair, shifted closer to Jane. "You think others were in on it? Maybe some campaign folks? Baby, that's an awful thought."

"No. It wasn't just Hoots." Jane felt the urge to sigh but resisted it. She felt the urge to tell Lily that Jackson and Tommy were lovers, but she resisted that also. She dropped her eyes to the cobbler, to the sugary crust prepared for a bad time. She said, "Lily, there was a part of Jackson that didn't fit into what we saw. It was a part that . . . well, didn't fit at all . . . " She reached down and fingered the tinfoil, glancing to Lily out of the corner of her eye. "Tell me. Did you know?"

The former finance chief was also pondering sights within the tinfoil. "Alice," Lily said. "Don't tell me it was Alice."

"No. It wasn't Alice. Nothing to do with the campaign staff. Nothing at all."

"Or Daisy. Had to be—some of that gal's New York crowd. Right?"

"Later," Jane said. "We'll talk about it later."

Lily was winking back tears, her eyes set on an image only she could see. "I wish I could wallop Jackson's behind," she sputtered. "If he were here now, I believe I could."

"I'm not sure what I believe any more," replied Jane.

"We are all such poor people." Lily pulled the silver thermos jug from the picnic basket, followed quickly by the bottle of Jack Daniels.

Jane touched an empty chair. "At one point, I was certain Tommy would shoot us, here at the table." She scoffed at the thought. "Miracle, he didn't."

"Enough," Lily said. "I'll get the cups and plates. You keep your seat." Lily moved to the kitchen and started rummaging in the cabinets, yelling back the entire time. "Spent nearly two hours with a DEA agent this afternoon and all I could say was 'no.' Sure wasted a mighty nice gal's time."

Lily returned to the table with the dishes, her breath rushed. "Raisin cobbler and decaf with the engine running." She patted the cobbler crust, letting her hand rest on the golden bed as if the home-cooked dish needed to be comforted before she dove in with a big spoon. "Poor, we are such poor people." She dished a syrupy spoonful of the cobbler onto two plates and smacked her lips. "Poor," she sang. She poured the coffee from the thermos, topping off the top third of the cups with whiskey. "Yes, ma'am.

The strong stuff sure deepens the taste, makes it last longer." She swabbed a finger about the bottom of the dish, raised a fingertip full of the runny part and licked it, humming in approval. "Go ahead, Baby. Give it a go."

Jane sipped as Lily watched. The coffee was warm, astringent at first and soon mellow as the liquor thinned her blood, the great pumping efforts of her heart lessening as the taste of a better time took over. With Lily watching, Jane again raised the warm strong liquid to her lips.

"Baby, I lied."

Jane halted her cup, holding it in the air.

"Yep, Baby. I did. I lied big."

Jane seemed to flinch, but she wasn't sure at all of what her body was doing or ought to be doing. She wasn't even sure of what she'd just heard. Lily lied? Jane secured her cup in its saucer. Had Lily, in fact, played along? Had she actually known more about Plyer?

"Tobacco . . . " Lily said, shaking her head. "Baby, tobacco was always my idea, never your mother's."

Jane felt her brow condense, muscles moving within the tissues in ways she couldn't stop. After all this, we're back to tobacco? Not once today had she given cigarettes a thought, no real thought. "Tobacco?" she asked.

"Yep, tobacco." Lily's voice was curt but also loose, humble. It was the looseness of thoughts lubricated by liquored-up coffee, which she kept sipping as she talked. "Baby, I never heard your momma say a word about tobacco." Lily rocked her cup back and forth, watching as the black liquid rose and fell off the white ceramic sides, as if drawing some comfort from the small surfaces that she controlled. "But your momma, she did make me promise to search you out if I needed help. So that part was no lie, no lie at all." Lily dipped her head. "And Baby, I needed help." Fresh tears were damned up behind Lily's eyes. She was full. "Now," she said. "Now, I guess we all know why."

On the table, the cobbler contained a gaping empty corner. Jane studied the rich tawny syrup, the soft and swollen raisins. "Listen," she said. "I wanted to work in the campaign, and it wasn't for my mother. It was for me." She toyed with the serving spoon, plying the bottom of the dish. "Back when my mother was coughing—Lily, I never suspected lung cancer. Never gave it a second thought."

"Well, why would you?"

"She smoked." Jane placed both hands on the table, enjoining her fingers. "All that coughing," she said. "And I completely missed it."

"Baby, you hush up. Hearing a diagnosis from you was the last thing your momma wanted." Lily served Jane another spoonful of the cobbler, tapping the big spoon hard on the glass sides of the dish to dislodge a clump. She rested the spoon on the tinfoil and looked about the room. "Whew, this coffee's got my bladder to twitching. Baby, you help yourself, now."

Jane watched as Lily pushed back from the table, her motions paced and deliberate, her shoulders stooped as she headed for the bathroom. She yelled from the hallway, asking Price if he was presentable, telling him a cobbler was waiting. Jane kept staring. She was sitting alone at the table where Tommy had drawn the gun. She was sitting beside Tommy's chair. She wanted to believe neither Tommy nor Jackson had done anything wrong. She wanted to believe only Plyer Hoots was to blame. She wanted to believe assigning blame would help, that—at least for now—simply wanting was a sufficient answer to guilt and its questions.

The day seemed to be growing longer instead of shorter, the rain returning. Jane turned her head to the window and watched the early night lay damp on the glass.

In the darkened windowpane, her mother stepped out, light shimmering about her face. Soon, a few patio lights flipped on and spun about her. That fantastic, hip-hugging swirl of a party dress, that hair puffed up in great brunette waves, a naughty smile. She lifted a hand, drew a cigarette to her mouth and sucked on it as her eyes expanded. There was nothing less than accomplishment in the taste of the cigarette, in the smell. The pleasure was unquestionable. She kept her eyes on Jane, pulling the cigarette from her lips with a lavish sweep of her hand. And when she exhaled, a smile arose, her face alive in the fine smoke of the sixties, life as she'd made it in those years, life as she'd inhaled it with utter joy.

Jane felt her soul reach out for her mother, she felt her soul stretch its hands beyond her skin. She felt her soul lift off and struggle in the air, the panic building as it reached for the soul of her mother. This was the struggle that she had seen above the bed, her own soul doing battle with the soul of her mother. It had been Jane who was trying to keep her mother alive within that failing body, this watching world. It had been a selfish request—Jane fighting to keep her mother as she was, not as she needed to be. Maybe it had also been her selfish soul that had insisted on snapping the picture of Tommy and Jackson, her soul struggling to keep Jackson as everyone wanted him to be. And Price, perhaps he was simply trying to hold Jackson in case time itself lost control. These were the thoughts that dissolved in the shadowy glitter of her mother, the glass going black but for the lights falling on a clump of river birch trees and the reflections that were growing watery there.

❖

Acknowledgments

Translation of the Beekman family voices would not have been possible without the attention and patience of my husband, Gregory Bolton. To him belongs the magic of the light on his back.

The world's best editor-musician-teacher must be Billy Fox, and this novel celebrates his symphonic expertise.

I'd like to especially thank Jeffrey Levine, Alan Berolzheimer, Marie Gauthier, and the team at Leapfolio/Tupelo Press for sharing their expertise in bookmaking and bringing poetry to our world.

A world of thanks to my teachers and mentors over the years, especially the incomparable Hopkins professors Margaret Meyers, David Everett, Cathy Alter, Heidi VornBrock Roosa, and Elly Williams.

Very special thanks also to Carol Logun and Gregory Parker, whose close readings and discerning eyes made the Beekman family vision even more real.

I also thank the editors of *Cowboy Jamboree* for publishing and nominating a short story excerpt from the novel for a Pushcart Prize.

I thank my family in Mississippi, the Talk Radio callers of Alabama, and especially the impassioned people of Georgia whose lessons in audacity helped make the Beekman family legacy one with the light that graces all our covers.